White Scar Across the Firmament

By A.N. Milne

Edited by H.S. Crow and Camielle Adams

Art by Kevin Liew

Cover Art by Sierra Ashevaili Rottman

A.N. Milne

White Scar Across the Firmament

ISBN-13: 978-1-960067-03-6 (pbk.)
ISBN-13: 978-1-960067-04-3 (ebook)

The Otherworlds Inc.
www.otherworldsinc.com

Author: A.N. Milne I Editor: H.S. Crow I Associate Editor: Camielle Adams I Illustrator: Kevin Liew I Cover Artist: Sierra Rottman

Publisher's Cataloging-in-Publication Data

Names: Milne, A.N., author. I Crow, H.S., editor. I Adams, Camielle, associate editor. I Liew, Kevin, illustrator. I Rottman, Sierra Ashevaili, cover artist.
Title: White Scar Across the Firmament / Author: A.N. Milne; Editor: H.S. Crow; Associate Editor: Camielle Adams; Illustrator: Kevin Liew; Cover Artist: Sierra Rottman.
Description: United Kingdom Version I Lauderhill, FL: The Otherworlds Inc., 2024
Summary: A gripping tale of cosmic encounters and interstellar conflict, blending elements of hard science, space opera, and first contact in a riveting narrative.
Identifiers: LCCN: 2024901250 I ISBN: 978-1-960067-03-6 (pbk.) I 978-1-960067-04-3 (ebook)

Subjects: LCSH Science fiction, Space opera. I Hard Science Fiction. I First Contact. I BISAC FICTION / Science Fiction / Space Opera
Classification: LCC PS3563.I4216 W47 2024 I DDC 813.62--dc23

Acknowledgements

From the Author:

When you're writing your first novel, you run into all manner of advice on how to make it publishable. I ignored all of it. Partly because, well, I'm just a mulish contrarian that way. But also because I like books that are shaggy and extravagant and personal, and if I couldn't make mine that way, then there wouldn't be much point to the exercise; not when I already have a full-time job that affords me a decent living. I honestly don't think I'd be capable of writing a more conventional, commercial novel; not because I lack facility with prose (you be the judge of that, reader!) but because I doubt I could stay excited about a project that kept me hemmed in by those requirements.

Nevertheless, if you're reading this, it means that 'White Scar Across the Firmament' was indeed published, and that would never have happened if not for a few key people who felt similarly passionate about it. So I'd like to give thanks to them in print.

First of all, to all the great team at Otherworlds Inc. To the proprietor and my line editor, Carlos "H.S. Crow" Aramburo, who took a punt on me and saw it all the way through to the end. To my content editor, Camielle Adams, who persevered through personal hardship to make the manuscript the best it could be. To illustrators Sierra "Ashevaili" Rottman, Kevin Liew, and Nika, for taking the prompts I mocked up in Microsoft Paint and transforming them into beautiful, vivid, images. And to May Encarnacion, whose skills as an administrator were indispensable in keeping all of us cats herded.

Furthermore, I'd like to thank my parents and my sister, whose love and support has kept me afloat throughout all of my hare-brained endeavours. Thanks also to those who offered feedback and encouragement on the manuscript during its developmental phase: Steven Whittaker; Dustie Spencer; Donald Carrick; Brett Windnagle; Pancit Canton, Kyiel Rotap, Pio Angelico Encarnacion, and Finny Wread.

Last but not least, my thanks to my writing buddies, Dr. Mandy Albert and Rioghnach Robinson (the latter of whom, who's a better author than me, provided an incredibly generous testimonial under her sobriquet Riley Redgate, which in my view legitimises this whole undertaking).

Special Message from Otherworlds Inc:

We, at Otherworlds Inc, are profoundly grateful for the pivotal roles played by our esteemed Gatekeepers - Finnic Renn, Kyiel Rotap, Mario, and Pio Encarnacion. Your keen insights and unwavering support were instrumental in discovering A.N. Milne's brilliant manuscript. Without your guidance, navigating the literary landscape to uncover this gem would have been a formidable challenge.

Special recognition is due to May Encarnacion, whose dedication and efficiency in communication and meeting deadlines have been nothing short of remarkable. Your commitment to our growth and success is deeply appreciated and has not gone unnoticed.

Finally, our heartfelt appreciation goes to A.N. Milne for entrusting us with your creation. As a budding studio dedicated to crafting immersive worlds, we are thrilled and honored to have your enchanting universe become an integral part of our Otherverse. Your belief in our vision as we grow and evolve is both inspiring and humbling.

Together, we embark on a journey of magical storytelling and imaginative exploration. Thank you for being an essential part of this adventure.

Table of Contents

White Scar Across the Firmament

All that I know

Of a certain star,

Is, it can throw

(Like the angled spar)

Now a dart of red,

Now a dart of blue,

Till my friends have said

They would fain see, too,

My star that dartles the red and the blue!

Then it stops like a bird; like a flower, hangs furled:

They must solace themselves with the Saturn above it.

What matter to me if their star is a world?

Mine has opened its soul to me; therefore I love it.

(Robert Browning – *My Star*, 1855)

A.N. Milne

Prologue

They found me!

The realisation cut through the Angel's idling mind like a razor.

No, not now! Not when I'm this close!

Her destination planet loomed below her, a tranquil blue-green sphere, filling a full quarter of her frontal field of vision. Silhouetted against the moon behind her, her rear vision had registered a black speck; when her passive sensors had detected the radio transmissions emanating from it, they had screeched an alarm into her primary consciousness. Adrenaline coursed through her neural pathways, the optimal dosage for combat, rousing her instantaneously from pseudo-sleep to near-painful lucidity.

There could be no doubt that they had seen her. Her silver wings were at their maximum extension, flaring out from her shoulder blades over a kilometre wide and only a few molecules thick, the best to catch the solar wind from the local star. If she had been able to spot the dark, compact Scarab transport visually, then she may as well be broadcasting her own presence on a 12-gigawatt radio array. The Angel cursed her complacency. She had felt sure that if she was to be caught, it would have been along the quantum relays between the stars. Using them had been a calculated risk, and she had breathed easily when she had thought she had got away with it. For the Scarabs to have engaged her here, within sight of the planet, they must have been following her for several days at least.

They were only five thousand klicks out, and closing fast. She withdrew her wings to their standard four-metre span, tuned her frame from quicksilver to vantablack, and switched over to her primary power source, the antimatter suspension unit in her chest, trying to gain some distance. She selectively warped the fabric of space around herself, compressing and expanding it to propel herself at interplanetary velocities, soaring through space with the avian elegance the original designers of the Archangel frame had envisioned.

A missile blew past her right flank, missing her by a good twenty kilometres. The momentary flare of light from the explosion forced her to briefly dim her frontal vision but otherwise caused no harm. The Angel recognised the Collective's diversionary tactics. They couldn't hope to score a direct hit on a target as small and agile as her with long-range missiles; their aim was to occupy her attention, drawing her concentration away from the approaching individual close-combat Scarab units. They would take her alive if they could.

She wouldn't let that happen under any circumstances. If it came to it, she could override all her frame's safety protocols and violate the integrity of her antimatter core. The detonation would be visible from the planet's surface, even during the day – her death might provide its inhabitants warning enough, the opportunity to scatter before the Collective reached them. She had seen enough of her friends and comrades be dragged away by Scarabs, silently screaming in the vacuum as their nervous systems were turned against them, to resolve that she wouldn't meet the same end.

The Scarab transport was a scout unit, meaning that it would contain the standard complement of six individual units. She could see them launching now, concealing themselves in the midst of another missile salvo. The signature of their particular warp drive gave them away – they weren't more than minutes out.

The sensory data being feverishly processed by the Angel's secondary consciousness alerted her to a cloud of orbital debris on the outer fringe of the planet's atmosphere. Granular chunks of rock and ice, some of them several metres across. She could hide in amongst the boulders, confusing the Scarabs' targeting, forcing them to manoeuvre more intricately, balancing the odds to compensate for their numbers. She would be subjecting herself to the pull of the planet's gravity well, but she would cross that bridge when she came to it.

The first beam passed her by mere metres before she could reach the debris field – her auditory processes simulated a crackling sound to match it out of the silence of the vacuum, as though she lacked the necessary context for what the Scarabs' weapons would do if they connected. Her rear vision registered the units behind her, now less than five klicks out, moving in a hexagonal formation. Their burnished black carapaces glinted with orange light, reflecting the local star half-hidden by the planet's western horizon; their six limbs aggressively splayed, searching for a target lock.

The Angel reflexively peeled away as more beams like the first burned past her, turned about, and returned fire in kind. The incandescent energy generated by her antimatter core surged along the filaments in her right arm, concentrated and directed by the optical lens in her palm. Previous dogfights had given her an instinctive feel for the Scarabs' evasive patterns, and she scored a hit on one, impaling it through its chest. It spasmed and then went limp as the circuitry in its torso melted and fused together.

The remaining five broke formation without missing a beat, their flight patterns changing from rigid, military coordination to the agitated insectoid movements that begat their name. Their energy beams came in staccato bursts, crossing each other at oblique angles, attempting to hem the Angel in, exploiting the arcing, swooping motions favoured by her winged form to direct her into the line of fire.

Hard-won experience worked in concert with her processing subroutines, creating a geometric overlay upon her vision that predicted the Scarabs' shots milliseconds ahead of time. She pitched each dive and timed each swerve accordingly, weaving her way through the latticework of buzzing energy. It was a chess game played out in three dimensions and at lightning speed, with gigawatts of lethal power contained in each move. She could see two turns ahead of her opponents, but their numerical advantage meant that the cognitive strain was grave, and it was only a matter of time before she made a mistake.

The fight was descending rapidly, the Angel realised – the planet had swelled below them, the curve of the darkening horizon now much less pronounced. She was increasingly conscious of the tug of gravity. All at once, the debris field was around them, and the Angel found herself dodging to avoid impact with a jagged rock five metres across. One of the Scarabs was less mindful of its vector and was blindsided by a meteor moving with the relative velocity of a cannonball, crushing its armour, and dragging it down to burn in the mesosphere.

Their numbers reduced to four, the Scarabs' potential attack formations were exponentially reduced, and they could no longer concentrate on an all-out assault in the midst of a meteor shower. They closed in more tightly, attempting to box her, trying to offset their new and unwelcome tactical disadvantage. The Angel now had the scope she needed to go on the offensive.

Her wings flared – the quantum fluctuations in space they projected to propel her in interstellar flight radiated outwards instead, disrupting the Scarabs' flight paths, buffeting them as though in hurricane winds. Two were able to compensate, pulling themselves away from the disruption's area of effect. The other two fell prey to her gambit and were blown into the path of oncoming projectiles. One was shattered to pieces instantly; the other was beaten into the planet's gravity well on an irrecoverably steep descent. In the absence of available evidence, the Angel imagined it screamed with impotent rage and frustration all the way down.

Of the two survivors, one peeled away beneath her, firing energy blasts wildly from all six of its limbs. Most of them never even came close to their mark, requiring only the most token of spatial manoeuvres to avoid. The drain on the Scarab's power supply must have been enormous, impossible to sustain for any length of time. The reason for its mad gesture of defiance became clear when the Angel saw its remaining partner circling around toward her through the particulate clouds, six limbs outstretched as though to form a grasping fist. It was a last ditch effort to capture her in the way they had Petersen, Velasquez, and Hoyt; the Scarabs had clasped them in a vice-like grip and penetrated the Archangel frames' mercurial armour while they struggled, attaching themselves to the spinal columns and taking control of their bodies.

In a snap judgement, the Angel allowed her secondary consciousness temporary bilateral command of all her functions. Her body now hosted two minds on an equal footing, each capable of autonomously making and executing decisions. From her perspective, her right arm began to move of its own accord, her head independently turning to track the trigger-happy Scarab's vector and search for the perfect opportunity to strike. She remained focused on her rear vision, on the one now charging towards her on her left, its furious limbs open wide to embrace her.

The Angel's left arm reformed itself, the fingers melding together, the forearm and hand flattening out into the shape of a straight blade only molecules thick, micro-vibrations coursing along its length. She swept it down in a wide crescent arc that the Scarab desperately attempted to parry, its limbs wrapping about it to protect itself. Too little, too late; the blade cut through all six limbs and the squat, ovoid body they protruded from in a single motion.

A brief flash reflected against the ambient dust—her secondary consciousness confirmed that the right hand had found its mark, and reassumed subservient status. That made all six—she saw the last Scarab's melted husk drifting inert.

Inwardly, the Angel breathed a sigh of relief and began to take stock. Her victory would be short-lived. The scout transport that had followed her would have received final status updates from each of the Scarab units as they had died. The Collective knew her face and they knew her destination— reinforcements would be no more than days away, this time in numbers she couldn't hope to counter alone. If there was to be any hope for the planet's handful of residents, they needed to be alerted to the impending threat as soon as possible.

Her wings had been made to act in zero-gravity; the best they could do within the planet's gravity well was offer a controlled, safe descent, and she could feel that she was rapidly approaching the threshold beyond which she could not escape its pull. She realised that the dust and grit swirling around her was beginning to clog up the joints in her armour, slowing the internal functions of the Archangel frame. The debris field would wreak havoc with her ability to land; she plotted a vector north, away from the equatorial regions. It would potentially add hours to her attempts to contact the surface-dwellers, but it was a necessary risk.

Without warning, a large meteor behind her exploded, and through it burst a Scarab, its limbs splayed towards her.

Impossible!

She had never encountered a seventh Scarab in a squadron—the Collective had always fastidiously adhered to base six, never deviating from multiples of that number. This rogue unit had concealed itself from her sensors, cloaking itself in the debris field to wait in ambush. Their tactics had been more sophisticated than she had credited them for.

The Angel spun around, but before she had a chance to react, the black machine bound itself to her in a vice-like grip, its body crushed against hers, its appendages pinning her arms and wings to her side. Its faceless, stumpy head pressed up against her own, the two of them tumbling together infinitely downwards.

The thing's claws dug ravenously into her lower back, probing for her spinal column, gouging, tearing, drilling, and burning away at layers of her armour even as her autonomic repair functions worked to compensate. Her vision turned bright red; her auditory channels filled with harsh white noise; she could smell acrid, toxic smoke.

In a distantly remembered past life, when her body had been comprised of flesh and bone and sinew, the sensory stimuli she was receiving now would have registered as debilitating agony, white-hot pain beyond comprehension. But reborn in her present form, her own senses would not be turned against her so easily, and her resolve redoubled, crystallising itself as a clear, piercing hatred for the devices that hounded her across the stars.

This is not where I end.

The programmable molecular platelets that formed the outer layers of the Archangel frame reconfigured themselves once again, swarming up her torso towards her head. Her face contorted, her jaw bulging outwards. Her mouth stretched out over half a metre wide, enough to engulf the Scarab's whole head; her teeth elongated into wicked graphene daggers. She bit down, wrenching and tearing at the thing with all the strength her frame could muster, ripping through its faceplate and the mesh of wires and circuitry below.

The Scarab twitched and writhed, still alive but rendered blind, deaf, and dumb. Its grip on her loosened—the Angel kicked it free, sending it as far away from her as she could.

The damage to her back repaired itself easily, new platelets swarming in to replace the ones that had been stripped away. The more pressing issue at hand was that she had reached the edge of the atmosphere, spinning head over heels uncontrollably. Her descent had become irrecoverable. She was now falling in earnest, the darkening blue expanse below rising to greet her.

This is not where I end.

She reconfigured her whole body's molecules—adopting a foetal position, her platelets formed a spherical chrysalis of hyperdiamond around her crucial components. Her exterior sensors were smothered to insulate them from impact—the universe turned dark and silent. The Angel didn't see the wreath of flame that enveloped her as she entered the thermosphere.

This is not where I end. I'll see you soon, Starman.

PART ONE

WHERE ANGELS GO, DEMONS FOLLOW

Chapter 1

June 25th, 2326 C.E.

The meteor cut a white scar across the firmament, a flash thousands of kilometres long bisecting the cloudless night sky. Light poured across the plains of TransTerra as though the heavens had been slit with a knife and the day behind was gushing through.

Jonah Harrison adjusted his corneal implants; they had automatically corrected to filter out the sudden brightness. The pale glow of dusk reasserted itself and he saw the loose crowd dotted about the field before him, maybe a couple of hundred people. Certainly, a good quarter of the population of Pilgrim's Progress, TransTerra's only settlement.

They were mostly older folks, those past their first centennial. The ones for whom the monthly meteor showers held a particular nostalgic appeal. Once a month, they would gather beneath the closer of the planet's two moons, the one with the cracked face, and look reverently skyward, their worries and their daily labours forgotten. The spectacle of the shooting stars would draw their gaze, but their eyes were focused further afield than the meteors or the moon. They looked towards a star, fifty-nine degrees to the northwest along the galactic plane, 40.93 light-years distant. A nondescript, mid-cycle yellow star, unremarkable save for the third planet which orbited it, from where their parents and grandparents had departed two-hundred and thirty years before.

Mostly older folks; but not all. Jonah scanned the assembled figures, and found the three he was looking for. They were sitting together on a hummock in the grass, necks craned upward; they didn't notice him coming until he theatrically cleared his throat behind them. Jack Nguyen, the groundborn teenager sitting nearest the angle of his approach, flinched upon noticing him, coughed, and stubbed something out in the dry dirt where he sat, trying and failing to be surreptitious about it. The telltale scent of cannabis slowly faded.

'Hi, grandad,' said the figure in the middle, not looking down.

'Hi Alyssa,' Jonah replied. 'Do your parents know what you and your friends get up to out here of an evening, young lady?'

'No,' she said, unabashed. 'Are you going to tell them?'

'Probably not,' Jonah admitted. He never could find it in himself to admonish her.

'Did you see that?' Alyssa asked. Jonah noticed the characteristic glazed look that suggested she was consulting a recording from her corneal implants, circumventing her real-time vision.

'I was recording tonight for my journal, so I had my eyes on their max resolution. When that big airburst split the sky a moment ago I swear I saw a flare of something bright purple, just for a split second. It caught me off guard and I wasn't looking right at it, but it didn't seem natural. No one else caught that?'

'A flicker in your circuitry, maybe? Or was it just the flash leaving a trail on the back of your eyelid?' Riley O'Brien, Alyssa's oldest friend, was seated on her other side. She sounded concerned at Alyssa's intensity.

'Yeah. Or any number of other possible factors.' Jack was working very hard now to bury the remains of the joint in the soil while still appearing nonchalant.

Alyssa bit her lip. 'You're probably both right. Still, I guess this is always how I dreamed it might happen, if Earth ever came back for us. First, vague signs and portents in the sky, and then–' she made an expansive gesture with her arms '– everything changes.'

'You have a Romantic streak, girl. Mind if I join you three?'

Alyssa shrugged, and budged over to make room. 'The more the merrier, old man.' Jonah sat, and took a sip from a thermal flask of the single-malt whisky he saved for these nights when the meteor showers were especially brilliant. A Glenmorangie single-malt; he'd taken six bottles with him at the outset of their voyage in 2096, an indulgence in his private mass allocation. He'd eked them out, allowing himself only a few drops to commemorate the most special of special occasions; the last of the six bottles was still two-thirds full.

If a night like tonight didn't qualify, what did? Sitting together with his granddaughter, contemplating the brilliance and the mystery of an alien sky. In billions of years, only he and a few hundred others, settlers of the first extrasolar human colony, had had the privilege of seeing it. A Romantic, he'd called Alyssa, as though he didn't still have a Romantic streak of his own, even after all this time. Evenings like these made him feel, fleetingly, that perhaps their sacrifices had been worth it after all.

'It might have been a potassium deposit,' he mused, 'igniting in the upper atmosphere. That could have produced a purple flame.'

'Hmm. I hadn't thought of that.' Alyssa broke off her implants' playback and looked at him with interest. 'I wonder what sort of angle it would have to fall at to get −'

Her sentence was cut off by a blast from overhead. Multiple sonic booms resounded, and his cochlear implants contracted, reducing every other sound to white noise. Seconds later, a trail of fire was impressed across his vision from right to left, before a final, thunderous impact sounded nearby.

'Holy shit!' were the first words he heard when his implants admitted sound through again. Everyone in the crowd was staring in the same direction, and it quickly became apparent why. One of the shooting stars had landed at their doorstep; a crater half a meter deep had been blown into the soil of Mercanta Steppe, ringed by plumes of bright orange flame where the dry grass had been heated to ignition point.

Jonah sprang to his feet, long-held command instincts kicking in. 'Alyssa,' he barked, 'Jack, Riley, get back to your domiciles.'

'But −'

'Now, Lys. It's not safe.' On the community's general channel, he issued an order to the same effect; the massed settlers out in the field were to make their way back to their homes, with all haste. In another tab, he sent an emergency notice to Eoin O'Brien, the settlers' Chief Engineer, and informally appointed head firefighter. TransTerra's atmosphere was more oxygen-rich than Earth's, and after days without rain, the whole Steppe was potential kindling.

13

Eoin arrived less than five minutes later, in a tank-treaded Caterpillar mounted with a water cannon, and less than five minutes after that, the fire was out, smothered by water and monoammonium phosphate foam.

The bearded, intemperate Irishman, nearly two metres tall despite the stoop he'd developed in his old age, stood on the edge of the cooling crater, mopping his forehead with the sleeve of his overalls as he gazed down on its epicenter.

'Christ alive, Jonah,' he breathed. 'Have you ever seen anything like that?'

Captain Jonah Harrison, the man who had christened the starship *Prospice* and commanded its voyage across 40.93 light-years, had not. What had fallen from the sky, right at the perimeter of their settlement, wasn't an inert rock knocked loose from some local celestial body. It was metallic, burnished black; an ovoid two metres across, buckled and striated from the impact, but unmistakably artificial. Around it, fused to its steaming carapace by the heat of atmospheric entry, were wrapped six appendages, like the limbs of some impossible, mechanical insect.

***

Eoin volunteered to keep a vigil over the crater for the next few hours, in case any stray embers caught. A more thorough investigation of the fallen object would need to be instigated the next morning; the nights on TransTerra were pitch black, and probing it by torchlight would be unsafe.

The immediate crisis averted, Jonah made his way back on foot towards the lights of the *Prospice* a half-kilometer away. The hollowed-out hulk was the only structure on the plains taller than eye level, making it prominent in every direction from horizon to horizon. Most of the settlers rarely had cause to go so far afield as to place it out of sight.

The Mercanta Steppe where they now resided had been selected from orbit as an ideal landing point-slash-resting place for the *Prospice* after its two centuries of devoted and loyal service in deep space. Orbital reconnaissance nineteen Terran years ago had flagged up a temperate climate, nutritive soil, and none of the hazardous levels of ozone rendering the planet's poles inhospitable. The needle-toothed mountain range to the east provided a buffer against the destructive summer storms, and in the present autumn months, stillness covered the region like a thick blanket.

Out of the deepening gloom, the settlement resolved itself; a cluster of boxy structures built from cannibalised parts of the *Prospice*. The ship's husk still sat at the center, the makeshift village of Pilgrim's Progress having sprung up around it like a medieval abbey.

Jonah settled himself into his cabin, letting out an involuntary groan as he sat on his bed. The phrase 'feeling his age' came to mind, although in his case, he really had no frame of reference for what 'feeling his age' felt like. The telomerase supplements that he had begun taking at the beginning of their long journey had been a recent pharmacological development at the time, only a couple of years removed from human testing and not yet available to the general public. There was a lot of theory about how long they could preserve a person against the aging process, but obviously, the only definitive test was time itself.

The face that greeted him in the mirror in the morning, he would have identified as being in its mid-sixties by the standards of the Earth he had known when he left it, the skin worn and lined, hair that had once been light brown now a bright white. Thanks to the exercise regimen that had become a near-subconscious habit after centuries of preserving his body against the punishing environment of space, he still felt a degree of the vigor of a young man, able to work with the grandsons and granddaughters tending to the fields and the machines that made their settlement run. Nevertheless, he had felt a general, palpable weariness creeping in over the last decade, labours that had been routine for years leaving him increasingly tired and eager for sleep at the end of TransTerra's 22-hour day. The telomerase supplements were never 100% efficient, and it seemed they were finally nearing their limit. Jonah doubted that he would see the end of his third century.

His schedule for the following day had him inspecting the progress of the expansion to the botanical nursery and the solar farm in the morning, then meeting with Chief Science Officer Ilsa Mendeleev to discuss the requirements for her proposed eastward expedition next spring. He cancelled the appointments, and set his alarm for half an hour before first light. Sleep was slow to come; he couldn't stop dwelling on the sight of the strange machine. If he didn't know better, he'd have guessed that it was a remnant of a satellite whose orbit had decayed. But the *Prospice* had left no such satellites behind when it had made its descent, and anyway, that insectile shape resembled no spacefaring object of human origin Jonah had ever seen.

What conclusions did that leave him? He could already hear Ilsa scoffing at any suggestion that it might be the handiwork of little green men – in all their time on TransTerra, they'd found no trace of animal life, let alone sapient life.

And yet, there was the ubiquitous grass that blanketed the Steppe. They'd isolated microbes in the water and the air. Photographs taken by trans-Neptunian telescope arrays in the 2070s had flagged TransTerra as the first identified exoplanet that might support carbon-based life. The Merantau Program, the costliest scientific expedition in history, had been launched to confirm the findings of those photographs. Over two centuries later, the hypothesis had been proven more thoroughly correct than the scientists of the 21st century could have dreamed. Multicellular, carbon-based life was indeed a general phenomenon in the Milky Way. And having made this discovery, they had no one to report it to.

It had been nineteen years since they'd landed; long enough that the oldest of the groundborn generation, like Alyssa and Jack, were on the cusp of adulthood, never having known any world other than this one, outside of stories and TSI sims. Ten times as long, 190 years, since contact with Earth had been lost. And still they knew so little about their new home, or what had become of the old one. It would be as foolhardy to dismiss any possibility out of hand as to assume any conclusion, sight-unseen.

Rumination wouldn't help, he knew that. He made himself sleep.

What was it Alyssa had said? *Signs and portents?*

***

He was jolted awake what felt like seconds later, an insistent, repeating tone sounding in his cochlear implants that was *not* the alarm he'd set. He rubbed the sleep out of his eyes and drew up his HUD – his clock read 3.12am, still hours before dawn. The tone was a private connection request from Marcus Lawson, one of the younger shipborn crewmen. For him to be calling the captain directly at this hour was unusual.

'Dammit.' Jonah rubbed the sleep out of his eyes and slowly pivoted out from under the sheets. His joints creaked and a shiver ran up his body when his feet came into contact with the smooth metal floor. He granted the connection request. 'Engineer Lawson. What's going on? Did something happen at the crash site?'

'No sir. I mean – I don't know sir, I'm calling about something else. I'm sorry, I know it's the middle of the night, and there are protocols for this sort of thing, but I think you really need to hear this ASAP.'

Lawson was babbling. That was another ill omen – he usually wasn't one to get easily flustered.

'Slow down, son. Tell it to me in ten words or less.'

'There's a signal.'

That phrase properly woke Jonah up.

'There's a *what*?'

'Just – it's better if I show you. I'm at the Lighthouse.'

'OK. I'll be with you in fifteen.'

'Please hurry, sir.'

He dressed quickly, throwing on yesterday's shirt and jeans covered by a thermal jacket to counter the chill of the autumn predawn, and trudged out into the empty settlement, dew from the coarse grass underfoot clinging to his boots.

The Lighthouse was on the southern outskirts of Pilgrim's Progress, a squat structure perched atop a two-storey scaffold. When contact with Earth had dropped out in 2145, Jonah had ordered that the communication array should be maintained indefinitely. Much as some of the younger generations resented the task, if the home planet ever did see fit to get back in contact, he was determined that they shouldn't miss the message due to neglect. The order had remained in force after landing, and the array had been transplanted to the surface intact, but it had proven useful for the secondary task of meteorology.

The exceedingly sensitive instruments, primed to detect and compute the infinitesimal variations in physical phenomena needed to send messages across light-years, could sense changes in temperature and air pressure subtle enough to predict weather patterns with pinpoint accuracy. Marcus Lawson was charged with its upkeep ('the Lighthouse Keeper,' he had been nicknamed to his chagrin) as part weather station, part observatory.

Jonah noticed Lawson waving to him manically from the tower's balcony, beckoning him up.

He made the ascent up the ladder in record time and was greeted by the Lighthouse's cramped, low-ceilinged chamber, most of the floor space occupied by its multitude of displays, both analogue and holographic. The nature of the displays varied widely, from line and bar charts to atmospheric dioramas of the surrounding region.

'I was looking over the records for the last day at the start of my shift,' Lawson explained. 'At first glance, nothing out of the ordinary. I mean, the spectrographs are always a bit spicier during a meteor shower than on other nights, but that's not what grabbed me. Around six o'clock yesterday evening, there's a cluster of high-energy light pulses in some unusual spectra in high-orbit, localised within a tight quadrant of sky over the equator.' He showed Jonah a series of blurry digital photographs as he spoke; visual approximations of the spectrographic data he described. They appeared to Jonah like threads of silvery filigree against the dark of space. 'That lasted about forty minutes, then stopped,' Marcus went on. 'But then at seven-oh-four pm, I found this.' He presented Jonah with another chart, and the anomaly this one displayed didn't need to be pointed out to him; there was a spike in the vicinity of the 100-nanometre wavelength that rose past the top of the Y-axis. He thought back to the events of the previous night. 7.04 pm would have been right around the moment of the massive airburster they'd seen streaking east to west. The one Alyssa had thought she'd seen a purple flash emanating from.

'A hundred nanometre ultraviolet laser,' Jonah said, slowly. He was unsure whether to feel elation or dread. 'That's the wavelength Earth's communication array used, before.'

Marcus nodded. 'As you say, sir. The signal's weak; it seems it was broadcast by something small, and passing by us at great velocity. I cleaned it up as best I could, but there's less than a kilobyte of usable information, only a few seconds of audio.'

'And?' Jonah prompted, growing impatient with the preamble.

Lawson looked pale. 'And, well sir, that's why I figured you should hear this before anyone else does. Listen.'

He sent Jonah the file. Beneath the fizz and crackle of compression, he heard through his cochlear implants a toneless, androgynous voice speak nine words: '...repeat: Abandon your homes. They are coming for you.'

Chapter 2

December 3rd, 2135 C.E.

Jean Harrison strode through the corridors of the Mong Kok arcology's 255th storey. Its hallways were wide enough for five people to walk abreast, but apart from her, this floor of the complex at the centre of this major global financial hub was silent.

The world had changed dramatically in the weeks since The Engagement, and not for the better. The global economy was in freefall, with multinationals and leaseholders liquidating their assets as quickly as they could. Given the uncertainty the world faced right now, both private citizens and corporations were keeping their heads low. Especially in Hong Kong.

She arrived at her designated rendezvous in the southeast-facing corner apartment at 5:30 pm, ahead of schedule. She let herself in without any password, secretive knock, or any other archaic notion of spycraft—her contacts would have locked onto her biometric signature when she got within half a kilometre of the meeting and followed her remotely to the door. It took some of the romance out of the procedure, but such was the price they all paid.

The five men waiting inside were all dressed in loose-fitting linen shirts and trousers. Even in December, the heat in Hong Kong could become oppressive, and the air conditioning was currently *verboten* along with the lights and any other tell-tale infrared signifiers. Jean squinted in the failing light, meeting the inquisitive eyes that had converged upon her.

'Jean.' The voice that greeted her in a curt English accent belonged to David Manderly, upon whose invitation she was here. 'Bloody good to see you.' He clasped her hand, and the two of them briefly embraced. He looked gaunter than the last time she had seen him in the flesh, when they had served together in the Orbital Reconnaissance Corps; he had always cut a skeletal figure, but his eyes seemed darker, his cheeks more sunken, his hairline further receded. He evidently wasn't a believer in telomerase supplements, but she could attribute his appearance in part to the stress of the last couple of months.

One of the sources of that stress could be seen from the window of the apartment's spacious living area. Across Kowloon Bay on Hong Kong Island proper, a segment of the famous city skyline was becoming increasingly distinct in the encroaching dusk. As lights flicked on in the windows of apartments and office blocks around it, an area spanning three kilometres of the waterfront encompassing North Point and Quarry Bay was gradually outlined, from which there emerged no man-made light whatsoever. The area within was a labyrinth of tightly packed streets and alleyways, some scarcely wide enough for two people to walk abreast, winding between kilometre-high skyscrapers jostling for space. For the purposes of the current operation, it had been dubbed "The Enclave."

"Glad to be of service again, Dave," she said. She exchanged formal introductions in rusty but serviceable Cantonese with the four Chinese men in turn, Agents Zhou, Kwok, Liu, and Chan. Their interactions with her were brief, terse, and reluctant. They were tense enough this evening, dealing with as many unknown factors as they were. Her presence was an unwelcome additional wrinkle.

Agent Kwok directed her attention to a handheld recording device that he held at her eye-level; she began recording on her corneal implants, so the records from this evening could be verified against each other and authenticated later. She cleared her throat and spoke into Kwok's recorder in English: 'My name is Jean Harrison, an independent British citizen. On behalf of the Pan-National Coalition, I swear that this account of Operation: Closing Noose on December 3rd, starting from five-thirty-seven pm, is authentic.'

***

'How's London bearing up?' David asked. They were filling time away from the Chinese agents while they calibrated their surveillance equipment on the other side of the room, waiting for nightfall so the operation could begin in earnest.

'Better than here,' Jean replied, truthfully. 'Martial law was in place for the first few days, but after people realised there weren't going to be any "aftershocks," they started to calm down again.'

What she had seen of Hong Kong since arriving by vacuum-pod four hours earlier had been disheartening, police clashing with crowds in a classical vision of urban unrest not often seen in the 22nd century. Southeast Asia seemed to have been hit harder than the rest of the world by what the virtunet was now euphemistically calling 'The Engagement.'

'I might pay a visit once this is all over, for old time's sake. I owe you one for this Jean, I mean it.'

He leaned out over the low balcony, gazing toward The Enclave, the dead metropolitan district illuminated from behind by a blood-red winter sunset. She joined him at the railing and extended a hand to him. Her former lover accepted it, his fingers intertwining with hers. Peering across Kowloon Bay, they drew comfort from one another.

She noticed a drone gliding on the air currents high overhead. There were dozens like it, at least one for all the major news networks, arrayed in helical patterns around The Enclave's airspace; all probing for clues from a distance, all searching for some answer to what phenomenon had gripped these few square kilometres of this one city.

**

The Enclave lay at an intersection of historic forces. On October 18th, a telescope belonging to Caltech in geosynchronous orbit had detected a celestial body on a collision course with Earth. Its mass and its velocity pointed to an impact on the order of the K-T extinction; nothing on the surface would have survived.

The reaction of the world's superpowers had been swift and panicked. The orbital weapon platforms they had trained on each other for decades were turned outwards toward space.

Salvoes of kinetic harpoons tipped with nuclear warheads were launched to intercept the encroaching body from American, European, Chinese, Indian, and Japanese satellites.

At 2.20am Greenwich Meridian Time, on October 21st, the world had held its breath at the moment of impact, the salvo impacting the comet in a burst that could be seen with the naked eye in parts of the Northern Hemisphere. Every available telescope in orbit and on the surface had been oriented on that one fast-moving dot in the night sky; hundreds of billions of tons of rock and ice.

Like everyone else on the planet that night, Jean had been cloistered at home, in her London apartment, watching the live feed in the knowledge that if the best weapons humanity could bring to bear couldn't turn it aside, her life would end. As would her mother's, and her son's and daughter's, and the vast majority of the human race. Some might cling to life on the sparsely populated colonies on Mars, and the moons of Jupiter and Saturn, but theirs would be a hard, borderline existence.

And then there was her father. Jonah Harrison; The Starman himself. He was light-years away by now, contactable only by the communication relay operated by the Merantau Program. If the world's governments' best and only gambit didn't work, if the apocalypse was to come and nothing could stop it, there might still be time to send a last, farewell message to him in the hours that remained. She'd considered that as she'd watched the live feed: what the content of such a message might be. The exercise had been something very much like prayer.

At 2.21am, a silent plume of light had filled her vision, a release of energy equivalent to gigatons of TNT. When the glare died back, the comet was nowhere to be seen.

A breath had passed; a heartbeat. And then Jean experienced a nauseating burst of sensory information. The primary, overwhelming impression had been of pain; sickening, burning pain that she might have pitched herself out of the nearest window to escape if she had been able to co-ordinate herself.

Almost as disquieting, though, were the alien sensations that had accompanied it; a sense of dilated time; alternating rushes of euphoria and despair; hallucinations flashing across her vision faster than she could parse.

It came to light afterwards that her experience had been shared by almost every person on the planet and in orbit. Even with most of the world huddled indoors, the ensuing chaos had been extraordinary – vehicles careening off roads, fires erupting, people breaking their necks from the physical contortions, or choking on their own saliva and vomit.

The initial death toll worldwide had been in the hundreds of thousands, and more continued to be found even now, whether accidents or suicides by those who had sought to escape the blinding pain. Nor, it seemed, had the phenomenon been limited to humans – stories rolled in of dogs attacking owners with frothing mouths; of schools of dolphins beaching themselves; of flocks of birds dropping out of the sky.

***

She was grateful for the interruption when Chan summoned them both over. He was mopping at the back of his neck with a handkerchief, already sodden. Out of the five men in the room, he was the frontrunner for the most ill-at-ease. Jean had clocked that he reported to the HKPD. Under normal circumstances, they would be taking the lead in an operation like this within the SAR. Presented with a phenomenon as thoroughly abnormal as the Enclave, Mainland intelligence had swept in and taken charge without regard for such bureaucratic niceties. Chan was here as a representative of the local government the way Jean was of the international community, and broadly powerless to affect the operational decisions Zhou, Kwok, and Liu were making in his city.

The four Chinese agents had finished configuring a jury-rigged mainframe in the corner of the room, a black obelisk enmeshed in a tangle of exposed wiring. 'With your permission, Ms Harrison, Agent Liu will presently upload a program to your corneal implants. In the interests of security, we must forgo external displays.'

'Very well,' she replied. Liu was splayed on his front, tinkering with the mainframe's finer inner workings. He seemed to be the tech-head of the group, while the others were responsible for operation and supervision. An electronic invitation popped up in the centre of her view, its designation a cryptic combination of alphanumeric and Chinese characters. She accepted, and after a couple of moments of buffering, a live feed appeared in the lower-right corner of her field of view. It was a view of the Enclave from the outside, from an elevated position to the southwest, judging by the light.

There were multiple feeds available to her – she could tab through them with minute twitches of her eyes. There were two other views of the Enclave: one from the air, another from across Kowloon Bay at sea level. A fourth showed almost perfect darkness, with only slight variation in the dark's texture suggesting that the feed wasn't broken.

'Can you detail what we're seeing, please?'

Zhou responded without looking at her, his glassy eyes suggesting his vision was entirely occupied outside of the apartment. 'Four teams, each of four commandoes, preparing to move in on the Enclave at six-twenty pm.' It was now 6:13. 'Team Alpha will approach on foot from the streets to the southwest. Bravo, from due south by VTOL, Charlie from the northeast by speedboat. Team Delta will be following the course of a disused subway line under North Point.'

'All cloaked, I hope?'

'Of course. All teams are outfitted with the latest model armor from Yang-Mitsubishi, as is the VTOL. They're undetectable across the visible spectrum and infrared by practically any current equipment, as well as resistant to cyberwarfare or neurohacking.'

'You think that's what affected the civilians in the Enclave—an outbreak of neurohacking?'

'I'm sure I couldn't say, Ms. Harrison; that's what we're here today to find out. In any event, the teams are also equipped with flechette rifles and maser cannons, heavy enough to dispatch any civilian resistance they might encounter.'

Jean raised her eyebrows. 'I thought this was strictly a reconnaissance mission, not a declaration of war.'

Zhou snapped his view away from whichever feed was occupying him and shot her a resentful look.

'For all we know, we may already be at war and we're just the last to learn of it. I don't know what things are like in England, Ms. Harrison, but you don't seem to appreciate the depth of the fear afflicting this part of the world. It was difficult enough to find sixteen volunteers willing to take on this job, even with the assurances afforded by this equipment. Impossibilities appear left and right, and no-one knows the cause. It feels as though certainty has abandoned the world. If we can't trust in the sanctity of our own minds, or of our own homes, or of the movements of the stars in the sky, how can we take for granted the good intentions of our neighbors? Or of other nations, for that matter?'

Jean had no good answer to that last remark, nor was she ignorant of its implications toward her. She decided not to rock the boat any further for the time being.

***

The Enclave had first appeared on November 23rd—an area of Hong Kong Island encompassing a few square kilometers had gone dark without warning. No physical or computational barriers surrounded it. Nothing was disrupting the provision of power or communications. And yet, all the use of utilities inside had ceased—no lights shone, no vehicles moved, and no people could be seen from outside, like one of the world's most densely populated areas had declared itself a ghost town for no discernible reason. Any communications addressed to devices inside its perimeter were met with stony silence, and any individuals who crossed the invisible dividing line surrounding it had vanished within. Hong Kong resounded with the cries of parents, spouses, and children whose relatives had become unreachable.

As spooky as all this was, it had initially been considered a domestic issue; something for China to figure out while the rest of the world collected itself in the wake of the last month. Then a series of virtunet pundits had observed that the area of Hong Kong which would become the Enclave had been precisely aligned with the original vector of the Body prior to the Engagement. Once this had been confirmed by reputable institutions, it quickly graduated from paranoid virtunet fantasy to a fact with global import.

On the afternoon of December 2nd, Jean had received an urgent transmission from David, who was employed as a liaison between the British and Chinese governments. The Chinese were planning an incursion into the Enclave to figure out, in technical terms, what the hell was going on. A consortium of frenzied diplomats had worked out an ad-hoc agreement whereby an independent, neutral observer would be granted access to the operation's inner workings in real time to ensure that everything was above board, and that any revelations about the nature of the Body would be open to the world beyond China.

David had vouched for Jean as a candidate, based on her competence and impartiality as a former member of the transnational ORC and currently self-employed security contractor with no partisan affiliations beyond her British citizenship. And so, she had found herself here, sharing a 255th floor apartment with a group of standoffish Chinese intelligence officers.

***

'That's six-twenty. All teams, report in,' Zhou barked. Jean's cochlear implant buzzed, opening an audial feed to accompany the visual.

'Team Alpha, acknowledged.'

'Team Bravo, acknowledged.' And so forth.

The Yang-Mitsubishi camouflage worked as well as advertised—the view through the feeds corresponded to the perspective of each team leader, but both their own bodies and those of their teammates were entirely invisible. Liu had programmed in a HUD displaying their silhouettes so the agents could observe their movements.

Jean tabbed across to Team Alpha, who were presently descending a steep, winding road down Mount Parker, twisting around sleek, upmarket bungalows secluded by the woods but with a view of Quarry Bay through the trees. The HUD was displaying a curious fuzz emanating from the team members' outlines.

'Surveillance mites,' Liu explained. 'A Chinese innovation. Too small to be seen by the naked eye, but the commandos' armour is coated with millions of them. Every one is equipped with a camera—individually low-res, but we can collate the info we receive from them and construct a 3-D simulation of the environment they cover.' A trace of geeky enthusiasm could be heard in his voice.

Kwok loudly swore in Cantonese. 'Team Charlie's feed was just disconnected. Liu, I don't know what you cocked up, but fix it!' Jean tabbed over and saw that, sure enough, the feed coming from Team Charlie showed nothing but a panel of dead blue, the signifier of a lost uplink. Their boat had been on the approach to The Enclave seemingly without incident.

Liu's eyes went wide, and he dove across to the mainframe, hastily double-checking every switch and socket. 'Everything looks fine on this end. Whatever disrupted the connection, it could only have come from their side.'

'Goddammit. Team Bravo, do you have a visual on Team Charlie?'

Jean's cochlear implant buzzed with the Bravo leader's response. 'I can see the boat, sir, but it's idling in the water. No trace of the team members on the visual spectrum, and there's no sign of their signatures on the HUD.'

The voice of the Alpha leader cut in: 'We have now arrived at Quarry Bay. Preparing to cross the periphery of the Enclave.' The Alpha feed showed the lightless shapes of the Tai Koo skyscraper complex looming overhead, the narrow streets passing between buildings retreating into opaque gloom. The theoretical periphery of the Enclave was rendered on the HUD as a pale wall of translucent yellow stretching into the sky. Jean, together with the rest of the apartment, held her breath as the team cautiously crossed the boundary one by one, at every point checking potential angles of approach for an ambush. The crossing seemed to go without incident—the feed remained uninterrupted.

A bright flare of orange light suddenly burst through the apartment window, momentarily casting long shadows against the walls. An explosion had erupted high above the Tai Koo complex; out of it fell the burning husk of the VTOL carrying Team Bravo. The Bravo feed showed a panel of blue.

'Christ!' someone yelled in English.

'Team Alpha, report,' demanded Chan, audibly straining to keep his voice level. 'What in God's name is happening in there? What shot down Team Bravo?'

'Sir, the explosion appeared to be completely spontaneous! There's no sign of any projectile or beam weapons having been fired. It could only have been a cyberwarfare attack, but the VTOL's systems were supposed to have been ironclad against intrusion. I – I...'

There was a moment's pause during which time seemed to sit on the edge of a knife; and then, the Alpha feed crashed to blue.

'Liu, do something!' Zhou shouted. 'What about the surveillance mites? They're being carried by currents in the air, correct? They should be all over Quarry Bay by now!'

'I'm trying to reach them, but the signal from the mites is routed through Team Alpha's suits, which have all been cut off. We're completely blind inside the Enclave.'

'Team Delta,' Chan intoned, his voice beginning to crack. 'The mission is a failure. Pull back and rendezvous with us in Mong Kok.'

'No!' Zhou interjected. 'Team Delta, under no circumstances are you to retreat. Any resources we concede to the Enclave at this point have the potential to jeopardise the security of China and of the human race. If you withdraw now, you will be charged with treason and collusion with hostile forces. Is that understood?' Jean saw a crazed glint in Zhou's eyes.

'Acknowledged, sir,' responded the Delta leader, after a moment of deeply uneasy hesitation. 'We're currently in the tunnels between North Point and Tai Koo. Will update as we progress towards the centre of the Enclave.'

Minutes passed. Jean's fingernails bit into her palms. The feed from Team Delta showed little but darkness, but Liu had rigged up a two-dimensional overhead map that tracked the squad's progress. They were now well within the periphery of the Enclave – none of the other teams had lasted nearly so long – why?

A shaft of light abruptly pierced the subway tunnel from overhead. Someone had opened an old service hatch in the storey above. Team Delta immediately trained their weapons on the new aperture.

The outline of a figure appeared on the HUD, climbing unhurriedly down the ladder to meet with Team Delta. The HUD tagged the figure with a name – Li Xiaosheng, one of the members of Team Alpha.

'Xiaosheng!' the Delta leader called, his voice infectious with relief. Xiaosheng didn't respond, but advanced wordlessly towards the Delta leader, his silhouette's right hand outstretched.

The feed paused, and then turned blue.

Chapter 3

June 26th, 2326 C.E.

There were tens of thousands of Total Sensory Immersion sims in *Prospice's* meticulously indexed data banks, included at the voyage's outset for the education and edification of the crew during their downtime. Most of them referred to periods on Earth in the latter half of the 21st century, before the starship had departed, but after sensory implants had become widespread. However, a fair number of period pieces were mixed in, as well as adaptations of works from the early 21st century and before—classic films and video games that Earth's cultural consortia had deemed should not be lost on a generation accustomed to full-body escapism.

Alyssa had dug through a significant portion of these by now, sometimes whiling away hours of the evening reliving the more dramatic periods of human history, much to her parents' consternation. War settings, both fictional and documentary, particularly fascinated her. A couple of times, when she had the domicile to herself and was sure no one would come running if they heard, she had even activated the pain simulation component of the sensorium, first having to override a series of concerned warnings from the system's interface. Experiencing the Battle of Khe Sanh, recreated through the eyes of an enlisted Marine, had been overwhelming enough with the noise, violence, and the vortex of crazed motion. But when she was gut-shot... that was truly a new frontier. She had ripped out the uplink, canceling the pain simulation immediately, yet its phantom lingered. She had lain in her cot clutching at her belly for fifteen minutes, biting her lip until it bled to stifle her cries. Yet she went back for more the following night.

After they'd been evacuated by her grandfather, she, Riley, and Jack had bid each other goodnight, and retreated to their own domiciles. At a loss for anything else to do and unable to sleep, Alyssa sat in her cot with the uplink clamped to the back of her neck, browsing the archives for something she hadn't already experienced. She found one that piqued her interest: a documentary series on the life and work of Galileo Galilei.

She became so absorbed in the story of the 16th-century astronomer that she didn't notice the hours passing. The warmth, smells, and sounds of Pisa in the 1590s as she walked in the long-dead man's shoes; the excitement of his experiments with falling weights disproving Aristotle; the sheer weirdness of his conflict with the Catholic Church over the theory of heliocentrism, an argument so divorced from her own perspective as to be surreal.

Planet Earth—the crucible of human history. Billions of years of evolution; billions of people over millennia of struggle, progress, and discovery. Her entire ancestry, all the processes that had made her what she was, all confined to a place she would never visit for herself, could never see, touch, or know. The TSI recordings were never enough, no matter how many she devoured.

It was only when she was approaching the end of the scientist's life, in the 1630s, that she realized with a start that she'd forgotten to sleep. She cancelled the uplink and was transported instantly from Italy to her darkened bedroom, once more in the cool, overcast autumn of the Mercanta Steppe.

She groaned when she saw the time her implants listed: 4.21 am. *Damn*. In less than three hours, her shift at the botanical nursery would be due to start. She curled up in her cot, fully clothed, and wondered if she had any favours she could call in with Jack for off-the-record stimulants to get her through the coming day.

She squeezed her eyes shut, hoping for at least a couple of hours, but through her eyelids, there intruded light from a source she wasn't accustomed to. She had slept in this same bed, oriented the same way, for nineteen years; as per the fable of the princess and the pea, she knew when something was off.

The invading light came through her window, which looked towards the dead hulk of the *Prospice*. From its topmost deck—the deck reserved for officers during its long tenure in deep space—she saw a dim glow emerge, the glow of a fluorescent bulb. The topmost deck was where her grandfather went when he wanted to confer in private with the other senior figures in Pilgrim's Progress. For them to be meeting at this hour was very strange; something clandestine was afoot.

Too curious now to sleep, she rose and dressed. She neglected to wash—it was that time of year when it was still too warm to justify burning their fuel to heat water in the domiciles, but too cold to endure an early morning sponge bath unless there was no other option. With time to kill until her shift, she kept watching that glow from the *Prospice*, idly hoping she might catch something she wasn't supposed to.

Around 5 am, the light shut off abruptly. Minutes later, a procession of figures made their way out from the base of the structure into the encroaching predawn. She sat forward, and raised her corneal implants' light sensitivity. There were Jonah and Eoin, as expected; the Captain, and the Chief Engineer, generally understood to be his second in command. There was Rahman, Chief of Security, and Mendeleev, Chief Science Officer. All of the Big Four. And bringing up the rear... was none other than Marcus Lawson.

The Lighthouse Keeper himself. Well, well, well; now that was very interesting indeed.

***

Alyssa knew the route Marcus would take to return to his domicile. He was rounding the corner of the briquette warehouse when she ambushed him. She milked the moment for all it was worth, jumping out at him with a hiss like a killer in one of the late-20th century horror-sims she enjoyed. His reaction was worth it; he yelped and staggered backward, one hand clutched to his chest.

'*Jesus fucking*—Lys?'

She laughed, despite herself. Marcus wasn't usually this quick to startle; if he was so on edge, that told her something all by itself. 'Hey Marc,' she said. 'Big meeting, huh? Jonah just messaged me to tell me all about it. This changes *everything.*'

'What... but...' Marcus sputtered, 'he swore the rest of us to secrecy! Why would he have let you in on it right after...' He spotted the broadening grin on Alyssa's face, and realised he'd been played.

'So something big really was going on, then,' she said. 'C'mon Marc, tell me. You know me, I promise to be discreet.'

He shoved past her, refusing to make eye contact. 'No. Uh-uh. Nope. I'm not saying anything else.'

'Oh, come on!' She rushed to keep up with him. Marcus was shipborn, reared in false gravity; like most of the men of his generation, he was over two metres tall. With her hundred and sixty centimetres, she had to pump her legs to match him at a brisk walk. 'Marcus, people are already talking about the meteor that landed next to the settlement last night. Did it have something to do with that? Blink once for "yes", twice for "no."' She got in front of him, and fixed her gaze on his, not giving him the opportunity to avoid eye contact. 'You don't want rumours to spread, right?'

Marcus met her gaze for a moment, then sighed and contemplated his boots. 'When did you get to be so headstrong, Lys?'

'I've had a lot of practice.'

'OK. Jonah and Rahman are mounting an expedition west today, in the Hummingbird. They reckon something fell a thousand kilometres to the west that needs to be studied, urgently. That's all they told me, I promise.'

He turned his back on her, clearly uncomfortable with having been compromised the way he had. Alyssa, for her part, considered what he'd told her – something fell to the west, a thousand kilometres away. She consulted her corneal implants' records, computed the trajectory of the airburst she'd seen the night before, the one which had emanated the purple flash.

That was *her* meteor that Jonah and Rahman were going after.

***

She spent the first part of her shift in the botanical nursery distracted and ill at ease. Twice, she fumbled a rudimentary cell-pruning; Riley chastised her in full foreman mode, taking on Eoin's vocal cadences and his knack for profanity. The minutes crawled by like hours.

They broke at noon for half an hour as usual. Rather than eat lunch, Alyssa marched out into the settlement and searched for her grandfather. He'd ignored all the private messages she'd sent him over the course of the morning, but he couldn't avoid her so easily if she confronted him in person. Pilgrim's Progress, home to 800 people, was all she'd ever known, but it barely qualified as a small village by Earth standards, and there were only so many places in it a person could be.

Jonah wasn't in his quarters or his office. He'd not been seen at the solar farm, nor was he at the impact site where the shooting star had landed last night. That was still surrounded by AR cordons. Eoin sat atop his caterpillar, parked at the edge of the crater, marshalling a team of his underlings as they combed through the furrow searching for who-knew-what.

Finally, as she drew to the end of her break, she came to a clearing on the western edge of the settlement, surrounded by head-height fronds of grass. It was the kind of spot where she and Jack might come if they wanted to be inconspicuous of an evening.

There, she saw Rahman and Jonah together, painstakingly assembling the Hummingbird by hand.

Marcus had been serious. Most of the components that made up the structures of Pilgrim's Progress were modular, able to be broken down and reassembled into new configurations as the need arose. But the fuel cost of sending a helicopter on a thousand-klick expedition at a moment's notice, and this close to winter, suggested something genuinely urgent was going on.

Jonah spotted her, heaved a sigh with exasperation she could feel all the way across the clearing, and climbed down from the Hummingbird's half-finished rotor to meet her.

'You've been ignoring me, grandad,' she accused, before he could get the first word in.

'Not ignoring you, Lys. I've just had a lot on my plate.'

'I bet. I saw you talking with Marcus this morning.'

'You don't know what you're talking about, Ms Cavendish,' Rahman interjected. The Chief of Security fixed her with a hard look. Of all the *Prospice's* senior staff, she'd always found him the most imposing. Eoin could be loud and imperious; Rahman never raised his voice, but the small, wiry Javanese man had an unblinking intensity that spoke louder than words.

'It's OK, Rahman,' her grandfather said placatingly. He had the same look of strained patience her mother had inherited, that she saw in her whenever she got argumentative. 'Yes, we're taking off this evening on an expedition to the west. What else did Marcus let slip?'

'Oh please,' she scoffed, 'I can read between the lines. A secret meeting with the Lighthouse Keeper, just after a weird meteor storm? There was a signal, wasn't there?'

Jonah considered her for a long time. She met his eyes, and refused to blink first. Eventually, he relented. 'Fine,' he said. 'There was a signal.'

Her heart skipped a beat. *Earth really came for us. They really are back!*

'But,' he continued, 'here's what the signal was.' He sent her a file via private message to her implants. A few seconds of audio – she accessed it and heard: '*...repeat: Abandon your settlement. They are coming for you.*'

'Wait... what?' she said, confused. '"Coming for us?" What's that supposed to mean?'

'I wish I knew,' Jonah replied, expression grave. 'It sounds like a warning, but from whom, or against what? Now you know as much as we do. We agreed we need more information before we decide what to do about it, so we're going to investigate the source before making the recording public and causing undue panic.'

'The meteor. My meteor.'

Jonah nodded slowly. 'Yes, Lys. Your meteor.'

'OK. Great. Good. I'll be going with you then.'

Jonah and Rahman exchanged a disbelieving look so well-timed they might have choreographed it before she arrived.

'No. No, you bloody well are not,' Jonah replied. 'We have no idea what could be waiting for us out there. I'm not exposing anyone unnecessarily to danger, and that's final.'

'I'm coming,' she repeated, obstinate. 'I'm the one who saw the flare from the meteor first. If I can't go, I'll share that recording with the whole settlement.'

Jonah looked shocked. Rahman's expression darkened. 'Ms Cavendish,' he said, 'do you understand there are consequences for trying to blackmail a senior officer?'

'Arrest me after we return,' she shot back. 'Fine by me. When do we leave?'

She didn't allow herself to waver, didn't let her face betray how nervous she was even as her grandfather looked on with incredulity. How to make him understand? That if first contact with Earth was made, and she wasn't allowed to be there when it happened, he would be robbing her of the most important moment of her nineteen years of life?

'I know you have your reasons, Jonah, to want to know what happened on Earth since contact dropped. I can't pretend I understand what you must have felt back then. But you have to understand – that hunger to know? I feel it too.'

She could see, the moment she said it, that it had worked. Jonah didn't like to talk about the family he'd left behind on Earth. She'd pieced the story together over the years from her parents, and gossip from the older crewmembers. The wife he'd divorced when he'd been selected for his dream mission. The daughter, Jean, who had been six years old when he'd blasted off in the *Prospice*; Jean's own children, Victoria and James, who'd been just on the cusp of adolescence when contact with Earth had been broken. The long, guilty nights he'd spent alone in his cabin in those years, wondering what had become of them.

He'd borne other children during the *Prospice's* long voyage; it had been mandatory. With or without telomerase supplements, the settlers had to procreate to ensure the continuity of the mission. Jonah had done his duty – Alyssa's mother had been one of those born from *in vitro* fertilisation.

Even if he wasn't exactly close, Alyssa had long been aware of the way her grandfather treated her with leniency, even indulgence sometimes. Sometimes when he looked at her, she could feel those two centuries of regrets in his eyes – she was a living reminder of the home he'd abandoned.

Jonah pinched the bridge of his nose, and exhaled softly. 'You're going to be the death of me, girl. We're leaving at sunset. Six o'clock sharp. If you're not here on time, we go without you, understood?'

Alyssa nodded, fighting not to break out into a broad grin.

'Good. Please, Lys, don't make me regret this.'

***

They had the Hummingbird fully assembled and fuelled just before dark fully set in. Alyssa strapped herself into one of the two cramped rear-facing passenger seats, beside Marc Lawson, who kept shooting her reproachful looks. He had argued with her grandfather about the wisdom of setting out at night, shooting meaningful glances at her all the while. However, the night was clear and cloudless, with the tower indicating low atmospheric pressure for thousands of kilometres all around. Jonah sat in the co-pilot's chair while Rahman piloted, restricting conversation to instructions and technical updates.

Before they departed, Rahman had slung a flamethrower over her shoulder, and with a sour expression, provided her with a short, curt tutorial in its use. Weapons were hard to come by on TransTerra. Setting out on *Prospice*, no-one had seriously considered guns to be a requirement; on the few occasions that order had to be enforced, Rahman's security team had got by with riot shields and batons. What they had needed upon landing, however, was a means of quickly clearing broad swathes of grass in preparation for cultivation, and for de-icing frozen pipes in winter. The components O'Brien had jury-rigged to spray ignited methane were less than ideal as a defence solution, but they were the best option available to them.

'I hope you know what you're doing, Lys,' said Marc after a few minutes of uneasy quiet, opening a private channel to Alyssa's cochlear implants to be heard over the Hummingbird's twin engines.

'No more than anyone else does. But come on Marc, how could anyone not want to be where we are, right now? You're not desperate to find out what Earth looks like now? What if they've developed faster-than-light travel in the time since departure? Or true digital immortality, not just archived UI constructs? Or hell, I don't know, other things we probably can't even imagine yet. Basic stuff we've always assumed about how life and death and time and space work could all be changed, and it could all be waiting for us a few times over the horizon. That's got to be worth sticking our necks out for.' She heard her voice growing more manic as she spoke, her words compounding her own excitement when voiced aloud. She realised that she was actually trembling with anticipation. What she had fantasised about for so long was within reach – a bigger, fuller world, one that encompassed something, *anything* more than stultifying expanses of grass.

'I've accessed sci-fi sims as well, Lys, and there's more than one kind. It could be the answers you think you want, you really don't. And "abandon your settlement" doesn't exactly set my mind at ease. I'd hold off on the celebrations for the time being.' Marc frowned, uncomfortable talking to her like this. He was among the younger shipborn at 34, and he had often lent Alyssa a sympathetic ear when she was growing up, filling the role of an older brother when called upon to do so. All the same, he had always seemed a little wary: protective, but unsure of how to approach her. 'I understand that it seems like everyone wants to keep you down, it can get that way when you're young. But I don't want to see you get hurt, none of us do. We care about you.'

'Thanks, Marc. I appreciate it. I mean it, but I've made my decision. I'll be OK out there.'

***

The flight passed slowly, hours drifting by without any meaningful sense of progress. The moons and the stars shone brilliantly on such a clear night, but the landscape they illuminated remained frustratingly devoid of landmarks. Alyssa passed the time ruminating on the signal, and what could possibly have compelled Earth to contact them this way after almost two centuries of silence. If indeed it was Earth at all.

Eventually, they came upon the point Marcus had estimated the meteor to have landed. Her grandfather whistled softly. 'I'll give them this much, they don't believe in making a quiet entrance.'

Alyssa squirmed around in her seat to get a better view, and through the window saw a dim red glow flickering out of the darkness. As the Hummingbird descended, she could see a broad swathe of the grass was burning, the flames spreading outward from a long furrow of ash and embers. It hadn't rained out here in days; the fires must have been burning continuously since the meteor shower the previous night. At the western end of the furrow, they illuminated a rounded object maybe a metre in diameter, emitting irregular violet pulses.

It was unnaturally spherical, appearing not at all as though it had just made a crash-landing from orbit. Rahman put down at what he judged to be a safe distance in the clearing the object had left in its wake; the four of them hopped out and advanced toward it, flamethrowers slung low across their chests. The purple flashes were bright enough that Alyssa applied a dimming filter to her vision. They seemed to sparkle, refracting in ways that formed crystalline, kaleidoscopic patterns on her eyes.

'What the hell?' Her grandfather moved up to the sphere as if he had suddenly recognised something. He extended a hand and felt its surface with the lightest of touches. 'It's diamond,' he marvelled. 'The whole exterior is one great, flawless diamond.' Something stirred in the sphere's translucent depths, as though reacting to his touch. The flashes suddenly shut off.

A few perplexed moments passed. Underneath the crackling of the flames all around them, Alyssa became aware of a faint rustling sound somewhere in the tall grass. She looked around, trying to find its source; the others still focused intently on the sphere. Through the foliage, hard to discern through the smoke, a dark shape lumbered into the clearing. It was the size of a small horse, and yet its silhouette didn't correspond to any animal or machine she had ever heard of. It lopsidedly staggered along on six splayed legs. Two of these on its right-hand side looked to be inert, the other four compensating to drag along its central, oblong mass. It was moving in their direction.

Alyssa raised her flamethrower and levelled it at the thing. 'Identify yourself!' she cried, feeling absurd even as she said it. Marcus, Rahman, and her grandfather turned sharply to follow her gaze, and promptly raised their own weapons when they saw what she saw. The thing paused and turned towards Alyssa. It pointed one of its spindly limbs at her; a dim light radiated from its point.

'No!' came Marc's voice from behind her, and an impact sent her sprawling to the ground just as the world became much brighter. A beam of furious charged particles pierced the space she had occupied a split second before, cracking and fizzing in the air it transmuted to plasma. A human figure, which had been Marcus Lawson, stood in its path for a heartbeat and then vanished, disintegrated into molecules of hot gas.

Jonah and Rahman charged at the monster, bellowing in defiance and terror. The jets from their flamethrowers burned at 1,500°C, more than a match for grass or ice, but they could scarcely do more damage to whatever black metal made up its exoskeleton than cause it to shine red in the heat. Yet it recoiled, jerking away from the hot gas. It had already been damaged; there were dents and pockmarks on its right flank, gaps in its carapace where its innards were exposed. She picked herself up and threw herself into the fray, probing for weaknesses in the thing's armour with her own jet of flame.

The monster pivoted with surprising agility, swiping at her with one of its limbs. The blow caught her in the abdomen, pulverising what felt like every one of her ribs and throwing her through the air like a ragdoll to land in a soft bed of grass. She raised her eyes to see the thing advancing on Rahman and her grandfather, the two of them backing away, their flamethrowers failing to discourage it.

Another beam, brighter and louder than the first, lanced across the clearing. The monster stopped dead: a hole had been burned lengthwise clean through its torso. Alyssa, slowly and with great effort, turned her head to see where it had originated. It had come from the diamond sphere; except, strangely, through her blurring vision the sphere seemed to have vanished, and in its place crouched a silver figure holding out its palm. Its shape was that of a slender woman, save for a pair of angelic wings extruding from the shoulder blades. The Angel's body glinted metallic in the firelight.

This should have piqued her curiosity, she realised distantly, but she was having trouble concentrating on anything other than her own breathing, which seemed to be getting more and more difficult. She touched her hand to her stomach, and it came away wet with blood.

Just like Khe Sanh. The thought came to her unbidden, just before unconsciousness rose up to greet her.

Chapter 4

December 5th, 2135 C.E.

'And so, you are certain that none of the commandos emerged from the Enclave alive?'

Jean fought not to let her exasperation show. According to her implants' clock, the formal debriefing had gone on for an hour and 45 minutes, but it had begun to feel like days.

The question was addressed to her by a severe PNC bureaucrat representing the USA, peering down at her from an elevated bench. To her side were a stoic David and a glowering Agent Zhou. Also present in the chamber was a deeply pissed-off senior figure in China's intelligence service.

'I am certain that none of the commandos emerged from the Enclave, whether or not alive, during the time I spent in the Mong Kok arcology,' she answered slowly, choosing her words carefully. The committee had dragged out details like this to a tortuous extent. Every specification they had made had been pored over by the cluster of diplomats in the room, from the apartment number the operation had been supervised from, to the make of speedboat which had carried Team Charlie, to the date the tunnel had been decommissioned where Team Delta had vanished. Every fact and figure had first been extracted from Zhou, and thereafter corroborated in Jean and David's own words. The unspoken hope among the diplomats, it seemed, was that if they interrogated the events of the evening in Hong Kong closely enough, they might salvage some face-saving nugget of meaningful information from this colossal botch of an intelligence-gathering exercise.

'And are you satisfied that Agent Zhou and his subordinates did everything in their power to ensure transparency to you and Mr. Manderly?'

'I object to this line of questioning,' cut in the Chinese official. 'We have been over this already. My agency has complied with every request for co-operation thus far, and we believe we have sufficiently demonstrated proof of our sincerity in this matter.'

'Patience, Mr. Koo. I'm sure you appreciate the gravity of the situation facing the world, and it is important that our selected intermediary be allowed to speak freely. Answer the question, Ms. Harrison, if you please.'

'I believe that China and its intelligence officers acted in good faith,' responded Jean. Both Zhou and Koo visibly exhaled; she had just averted a potential international incident. She didn't feel so reassured. The recordings from her corneal and cochlear implants had been independently verified by experts, and there was no doubt that the light levels and weather conditions they conveyed aligned with those that had been observed by other recordings in Hong Kong on December 3rd. What she had witnessed hadn't been faked, which meant that either China had sacrificed several heavily armed commandos to the Enclave in service of some elaborate bluff whose purpose she couldn't guess at, or that they were being honest with her. Occam's Razor led her to the latter conclusion, which, in turn, forced her to acknowledge that there was some force controlling The Enclave that was as mysterious to the world's governments as it was to a private citizen like her.

'Thank you for your contributions, Ms. Harrison. Do you have anything else to share with the chamber, any insight that might illuminate the events of December 3rd?' The American representative peered at her, eyebrows arched expectantly.

Jean paused. She had not, thus far, been asked to editorialise. 'Only this, Madam Representative. Team Delta managed to penetrate deep into the Enclave before communication with them ceased, in stark contrast to the other three. Team Delta was several metres underground at all times; my guess is that whatever phenomenon affected Teams Alpha, Bravo, and Charlie, it was propagated by some form of exotic radiation. Something our sensors weren't primed to detect, but which would be impeded by barriers such as rock and metal.'

Jean noticed a prompt increase in scribbling on notepads and tablets at her words. 'Very good, Ms. Harrison,' said the American representative. 'If no one has anything further to add, I will declare this meeting adjourned.'

Koo rose from his seat. 'I will need to be getting back to Beijing,' he pronounced. 'On behalf of the Democratic People's Republic of China, I would like to extend my formal apologies to Ms. Harrison for taking up her time. I hope that this farce–' (he fixed Zhou with a freezing glare) '--of an operation does not colour her opinion of Chinese intelligence. Good day.'

Zhou stood, ashen-faced, turned sharply about, and marched out of the room.

***

'So, that went well,' said David, mock-pleasantly. Together, they exited the headquarters of the Pan-National Coalition via the skybridge on the 112th floor. Ahead of them, to the north, loomed the Bay Area arcology, a three-kilometre-high pyramid with one foot in the Pacific Ocean and its peak wreathed by clouds, dominating the coastline of northern California. 'Want to get a drink before you head home? Christ knows I could use one.'

'Sure. At Frisco prices, you're buying, though.'

'Fine. Twist the arm of a man on a civil servant's salary, why don't you?'

He said it as a joke, but there was an edge of real tension beneath the words.

The USA had yesterday taken the unprecedented emergency step of closing their end of the undersea vacuum tunnel stretching from Tokyo to San Francisco, only hours after Jean and David had returned from Hong Kong. The civil unrest in Southeast Asia in the wake of the Engagement, rather than tapering off, had instead begun to compound itself. Protests in Vietnam, Cambodia, and the Philippines, which had begun as populations demanding to know what their leaders were doing in the wake of the Engagement and the psychic trauma that had followed, had, in turn, dredged up old sectarian and socio-economic grievances. Businesses were open in affluent regions of the world like the Bay Area, doing their best to project a sense of normality, but between the worsening refugee crisis and supply chains creaking under the pressure, the price of keeping up that illusion was being reflected in shopfronts and bar menus.

'That's only going to get worse before it gets better,' she remarked, nodding westward towards the ocean. From the skybridge, they could see a line of boats spread out thinly from horizon to horizon, being held at bay by the coastguard.

'Don't remind me,' David grumbled. 'I'm expected back in Beijing first thing tomorrow, and at this rate, I'm probably going to have to snag a seat on a spaceplane at twelve times the cost of a vacuum pod. I'll be buggered if they let me claim that back as an expense.'

Many of the city's historic districts had been demolished after the San Andreas Fault had finally ruptured in 2043, following which city planners had reinvented it as a complex network of enclosed, pedestrianised pathways high in the air, held aloft by the tensile strength of newly cheap carbon nanotubes. It had been a futuristic architectural fad at the time, one that had been mirrored in other wealthy, technophilic hubs like Dubai and Singapore, but now seemed quaint in the era of arcologies.

The paths became more crowded as they wandered closer to the Bay Area pyramid, with other levels stretching high up above and down below them, weaving in and out of the upper storeys of well-appointed skyscrapers. Inside these were galleries of up-market clothiers, restaurants, and TSI boutiques, the forces of commerce soldiering on as though nothing had changed, as though all humanity hadn't recently been made aware of how tenuous was its continuance.

David settled on a cocktail place that advertised itself as the best on the west coast – she scoped out a table, and he followed minutes later carrying two citrusy gin concoctions that she recognised as the bar's most expensive item. She raised her eyebrows at Dave, who shrugged as though by way of explanation.

'Fuck it, right?' he said. 'What's a little indulgence these days?'

'That's a reassuring sentiment,' she said, archly sarcastic, 'coming from a man with his ear to the ground.'

'You saw the same things in Mong Kok I did, Jean.' His voice carried a hint of hurt, just enough to make her regret the tone she had used. She'd been having dark thoughts about the future; why wouldn't he have felt the same?

'I know, I didn't mean it that way. It's just, I felt so helpless watching that incursion, and I feel even more helpless now. I hate that feeling. At least you're involved at the top level. Me? After I handed my name badge in at the front desk this afternoon, I became just another civilian again. One more anonymous member of the human race, waiting to find out how we'll be judged.'

'I understand,' he said, and she believed him. She extended a hand across the table, and he took it. For a moment, they sat that way, saying nothing.

'Do you miss it?' David asked, eventually. 'The ORC, I mean? After high orbit, it's hard coming back to—' he gestured vaguely around '—*this*, isn't it?'

Jean probed her feelings. 'I miss it,' she said, 'but I don't regret leaving. Vic needed me, after the accident.'

'Well, that's something to cling to if you're ever feeling helpless, I suppose. Someone you know you helped.' David raised his glass in a toast. 'It was good to see you again, Jean.'

She raised her glass in a sympathetic salute. 'You too, Dave.' She took a sip. It was good, whatever it was; not a-hundred-and-twenty-dollars good, but good.

The tranquillity of the moment was disrupted by a commotion from the rear of the bar. She turned to look and saw Agent Zhou, apoplectic, shouting in Cantonese at another suited man. The other party in the conversation had his back to her, and her real-time translation software couldn't discern their words from the background noise, but it sounded like the phrase "*puk gai*" comprised much of what Zhou had to say. The shouting reached a crescendo and then Zhou abruptly stormed away, barging past other discomfited patrons in the bar as he went.

David ducked his head, trying to conceal from the operative's view, but his stature gave him away. Zhou caught his colleague's eye, and jerked his head towards the exit, a wordless demand for a word in private. If he noticed Jean at all, he didn't deign to make eye contact with her.

'Shit,' David groaned. 'Duty calls. When Zhou looks like that, it's usually because someone's about to get it in the neck.' He finished the rest of the cocktail in a single joyless swallow and stood. 'Catch you in London sometime, okay?'

'Er... yeah, sure.'

His fingers, intertwined with Jean's, lingered a moment longer, then withdrew. David hurried after Zhou.

The man Zhou had been ranting at composed himself, straightened his ruffled suit, and turned back to his drink. Jean caught sight of his face in profile – it was Liu, the technical specialist from Mong Kok. He glanced around, caught sight of Jean where she sat, smiled at her affably, and beckoned her over.

'Rough day?' she asked in English, taking up a stool next to him. Age was hard to judge nowadays, but she would have placed him in his early thirties to look at him, and he had the animated, expressive demeanour she associated with younger men. He was tall and slim, with a sharp-featured face and thick black hair slicked back with oil.

He smirked. 'More for Agent Zhou than me, perhaps. I was celebrating, actually. I just got word that I've been promoted to a new position. He was upset because the position had been his until very recently.' He sipped at what she took to be a gin martini. 'Hell with that idiot. We lost good soldiers, and it was no one's fault but his. He deserves everything that's coming to him.'

'No one in that room knew what we were up against. He made the call he thought was appropriate under the circumstances.'

'He thought wrong,' Liu said bluntly. 'Incidentally, I feel I didn't properly introduce myself the other night. Tony Liu.' He held out a hand, which she shook.

'Jean Harrison.'

'So I gathered. I thought I recognised the name when I heard it, but it wasn't until later that I put it together; you were one of the orphans of the Merantau Program.'

She frowned at him; she had always resented that term. Sensing he had committed a *faux pas*, Tony held up his hands in a conciliatory gesture. 'Apologies, I didn't mean to offend. In fact, I'm glad I ran into you, I'd planned on getting in touch, anyway. I hear the debriefing at Third-Time-Lucky didn't do much to clarify the issue at hand?'

Third-Time-Lucky was a term for the PNC much beloved by right-wing politicians back in Britain, poking fun at its efforts at international solidarity by calling attention to the failure of the League of Nations in the 20th century and the United Nations in the 21st.

46

Jean pursed her lips, reluctant to respond in any way. She had been required to sign a non-disclosure agreement at the outset of the meeting, which had exhaustively detailed the many circumstances in which she could be prosecuted by an international tribunal. Tony chuckled at her silence.

'It's OK, you know,' he said. 'I'm privy to everything that was said in that chamber. "Exotic radiation," eh? Very perceptive; our own scientists came to the same conclusion. It just makes sense if you think about it. The antipode of Hong Kong on the globe is the border between Bolivia and Argentina; if you listen to the testimony of people from that region of the world, many of them only felt the effects of the Engagement very faintly. Some of them, not at all. They had the full mass of the Earth between them and the Body. It follows that if the effects were projected from the Body at the moment of the Engagement, then they must be disrupted by physical barriers. If the Enclave is, as we suspect, related to the Body, then perhaps the power at work inside it functions according to similar rules, no?'

Jean considered her response carefully. 'Why are you telling me this?' she asked. 'My involvement with this matter is over. At this point, I'm just a civilian like any other.'

'Not quite like any other. Bear with me.' He fished out a tablet from his jacket pocket and scribbled. An icon flashed in Jean's vision, a file which she opened with a flick of her eyes. Contained inside it was a litany of images of the Enclave, apparently taken that morning. Physical cordons were being erected around it, soldiers and gun emplacements gathering around the perimeter. Drones flew around it, their flight paths treating the boundary as a cylinder reaching infinitely skyward.

'I found these on a Mong Kok resident's blog this morning,' Tony explained. 'China is working to prevent images like these from circulating on the virtunet too much, but there's only so much that can be done. Everyone for a hundred kilometres around the Enclave saw the VTOL explosion.

'Waste of time, anyway, if you ask me. Even if every square centimetre of the boundary is under 24-hour surveillance, people are forgetting that the boundary only represents the end-point of the effect at work inside it, and that effect appeared without explanation. At any moment, the boundary could expand a kilometre outwards, or two, or disappear entirely, and we'd have no way of stopping it. Above all, we need to understand what the effect is to have a shot at combatting it.'

'Well, if you think it is some form of radiation, then you should be talking to particle physics researchers, the ones with the equipment to detect and measure a phenomenon like that, if it exists. I read someplace that Tsinghua University's department is well-funded.'

'I've heard even better things about the facilities available to ORC.'

There it is, Jean thought. 'Want me to write you a letter of introduction?'

'I had hoped you might introduce me in person, honestly. You'll be well-compensated for your time: one-and-a-half times your firm's hourly rate, plus a generous expense account. Secretary Koo has authorised me to head up the investigation into the Enclave phenomenon and he's being liberal with the purse strings.'

'China is one of the ORC's signatory nations; why not just approach them with a subpoena instead of going through me?'

'Because, Ms. Harrison, you come highly recommended for your discretion, and both Secretary Koo and myself would like to keep this out of official channels, as far as it can be.' Tony sipped his drink, and when he continued, he had lowered his voice to a murmur. 'You and I both saw the same thing. Xiaosheng, the team Alpha member – at the end, he was acting under some sort of influence, whether it be neurohacking or "exotic radiation" or something else we haven't encountered before. The Enclave, or rather, whatever intelligence is *controlling* the Enclave, has to be regarded as hostile; and if it can cause people to do its bidding, then our society may already have been infiltrated before we had our guard up. We don't know that the effect is limited to the Enclave. Hence, I want to keep my investigation as quiet as possible.'

Jean didn't outwardly react, but a chill ran through her. She hadn't known what she had expected when she sat down, but it hadn't been an invitation to join in a covert war against the Enclave. Yet, there was something else underneath her trepidation that gave her pause. Anticipation, she supposed, of the same sort she had once felt flying orbital raids on the equatorial cartels.

'I may still have a couple of friends who could be persuaded to circumvent due process,' she said. 'Although, you probably already knew that. I'll give the matter some thought on my way home.'

'Here are my contact details,' Tony said, handing her a physical business card. It looked blank until Jean took it, upon which a holographic display flashed into view. *Already configured to my thumbprint.* He had clearly anticipated she would prove pliable. 'Please don't take too long to decide, Jean, not longer than a day if you're interested. We're working to an accelerated schedule.'

***

The vacuum-pod terminal was crowded, and by the time Jean cleared security and the uncommonly stringent passport control, it was mid-afternoon before she could get a pod to London *via* Montreal. The length of the journey combined with the time difference meant she didn't get back home (now having completed a circuit of the world in three days) until the small hours of the morning. She resolved to spike some stimulants and power through the rest of the day before she slept.

It was dark and bitterly cold when she arrived at her third-storey tenement in Camden, an old-fashioned, moderately well-appointed flat whose price had been driven down on account of it living in the shadow of the Thames arcology. Snow lay three inches deep on the pavement; the effects of the climate change that had caused such upheaval throughout the 21st century had begun to recede in the wake of large-scale carbon trapping projects, but winters in London were still far harsher than they had been when her home had been constructed, and when she had moved in she had needed to hire contractors to insulate it from the freezing gales that rattled the windows through to March.

After a few days retained by the PNC, she had accrued dozens of messages, most of them from anxious local business owners looking for help shoring up their stores and warehouses against rioters in the wake of the events of the last month. She disregarded them for the moment – she was still ruminating on Liu's far more interesting offer of employment.

Why would he entrust her with all this, she wondered, if he was, by his own admission, so paranoid about tipping off Enclave sleeper agents? He had seemed awfully casual about feeding her information on the state of China's intelligence.

Perhaps it was as he had claimed. She was an independent contractor whose discretion could be relied upon, but without official ties to any security forces, which would keep her off the radar of any hostile agency as an asset. Additionally, she was British, which meant she had been out of the firing line of the worst of the Engagement, making her statistically less likely to be one of the drones whose will he suspected was being co-opted by the psychic effect of the Body.

Or, as her more cynical instincts proposed, Liu was playing on multiple levels. She had been present during the failed operation, after all, the only person in the room with whom he had no prior familiarity. It could be that he had *her* in his sights as the one who had sabotaged their reconnaissance, and by attempting to recruit her like this, he was actually feeding the mole; waiting to see how she would react, whether she would confirm his suspicions about Enclave infiltrators.

As the flat began to warm up, Jean changed out of her business suit and showered, relishing the cleansing of the hot water after three straight days of international travel. Finishing, she caught sight of her reflection in the bathroom mirror. She was forty-five years old, but telomerase boosters meant that she could still pass for her mid-twenties. She had let her hair grow out after her time in the ORC had ended (long hair was a liability in zero-g), but she retained the hard, muscular physique that intense training and an epigenetically enhanced metabolism had conferred upon her during her service. Faint surgical scars crossed at orthogonal angles around her torso and limbs, reminders of the augmentations she'd received a quarter of a century ago.

The image in the mirror was of a woman at the apex of her physical and mental capabilities.

'Ada,' she announced to her flat's UI assistant, 'please clear my schedule for the next week.'

'Yes, Ms. Harrison,' buzzed a disembodied voice in her cochlear implant. There were no holographic projectors in the bathroom, as a concession to users' modesty.

Jean had no real need to work, and never had. Part of the Merantau Program's operating budget had been allocated to the families of the crew; given the gargantuan nature of the project, even a fraction of a percentage of the money its directors could throw around was enough for the crew's spouses and children to live comfortably for decades. Her security consultancy now was a nice stipend, but mostly just a way to keep herself occupied.

Even her time in ORC had been a way of proving herself, of wilfully avoiding turning into one of the ghastly self-absorbed socialites that the children of her mother's upper-class friends had all seemed to. 'Poor little rich girl' had been the go-to insult reserved for her in basic training. The other recruits had muttered amongst themselves that she was trying to live up to the legacy of her famous father, a charge that might have seemed to Jean to betray a note of chauvinism if it hadn't been completely true, and something she didn't consider a flaw in her personality.

In the last ten years, she had come to think of herself as residing in the twilight of her existence: a widow; a single mother; a reclusive, melancholy figure, like something out of Nathaniel Hawthorne. *Bullshit*, she impugned herself. The Engagement was her wake-up call. She was uniquely positioned now to make her life every bit as meaningful as that of the legendary Jonah Harrison, and if it meant playing Liu's games, so be it.

'Open a channel to this contact address, Ada,' she said, holding up Liu's card for the UI to read.

'Yes, Ms. Harrison.'

It took a few seconds to get a response, and when it came, it was in text rather than audio feed. **jean, glad u r calling so soon. Have u thought further about job?** He must have been manually typing.

'I'm interested,' she dictated to Ada. 'I'll have a contract for my services sent through to you first thing in the morning, Pacific Time.'

not necessary, came the response. **im in congo, at kisangani arcology. meet there asap. make up a story for why you're going.**

'You said time was of the essence, that I would understand why. What did you mean?'

check my card.

She did so; there was an image file that came unlocked as she watched. **taken from olympus mons observatory. took a few days before alignment was right. you won't see these pictures on the net.**

The Olympus Mons observatory was perched on top of Mars' highest mountain, three times higher than Everest, its peak piercing the veil of the thin atmosphere. It was the only one of its kind on the permanently, but sparsely, populated Red Planet; Jean dimly recalled having once read that it was funded by China's space program. The images showed a silver body hanging in space – Earth's moon, but observed from the back, the angle unavailable to those on Earth's surface or its sub-lunar orbit. The images zoomed progressively closer, the pockmarked surface filling Jean's vision in increasingly fine resolution. At a scale that corresponded to the view Jean would have had if she were hovering about fifty kilometres above the Moon's surface and looking down, she spotted something that clearly didn't belong among the desolate configurations of rock and dust. An organic-looking mass, vaguely cetacean, perhaps two kilometres long. Six appendages extended out from its body.

A creature; a vast, dead, *alien* animal.

the body didn't just disappear. something came out.

Chapter 5

June 27th, 2326 C.E.

The roar of the Hummingbird's engines was deafening, even with the sound being dampened by Jonah's cochlear implants. Rahman was flying with the safety limiters off. His manner was composed and professional in his ex-spec ops way, but Jonah had known him for a long time, and he could recognise the profound alarm in his security chief's face.

His own face probably looked much worse. Cold sweat beaded on his brow; the adrenaline high from the fight with the black beast was wearing off. Sitting uselessly in the co-pilot's chair now, he could feel the threat of genuine panic, like an amorphous mass of fear and guilt pressing on the back of his skull.

Alyssa lay motionless in the rear of the helicopter, the Hummingbird's only stretcher collapsed beneath her. A field dressing was stemming her loss of blood, and he had improvised a pneumothorax from the Hummingbird's first aid kit to reinflate one of her collapsed lungs. However, the deep dark patches now showing on her abdomen betokened massive internal bleeding that was being further aggravated by the motion of the aircraft, shattered bones being ground into soft tissue.

Strapped into the passenger seat behind him was the—*entity*—that had destroyed the black beast. Jonah grasped for an appropriate noun with which to refer to it – "machine-angel"? It had a human face, but it exhibited neither signs of life nor of death. It slumped against its harness, a lump of inert matter, wings unceremoniously crushed against the seat.

After it had fired the energy blast that destroyed the monster, it had frozen in place, sitting upright with its palm splayed. In his haste to tend to Alyssa, he had almost been tempted to leave it behind. Only when Rahman reminded him of the original purpose of their mission had he hurriedly carried it over his shoulder to the Hummingbird. It had offered no resistance, its limbs conforming rigidly to any position he arranged them. Whatever it was, it seemed broken or spent somehow.

A dim light was visible on the eastern horizon, the first inkling of dawn. An icon on the dashboard alerted Jonah that they were within hailing distance of the settlement.

'Pilgrim's Progress, this is Jonah,' he said into the radio transceiver. 'Acknowledge. We have a situation of extreme urgency, over.'

'I read you, Jonah,' came the immediate response. His blood ran cold – the voice belonged to Brandon Lawson, Marcus's younger brother. He must have been manning the tower in Marcus's absence. 'Awaiting your instructions, over.'

'Report to sickbay, Brandon, we have a settler here in critical condition. Tell Will Derrickson and his staff to expect Alyssa Cavendish, and that they should prep for emergency abdominal surgery, over.'

'Yes, sir. Is Marc with you sir? He said you needed him for something before he headed out.'

A long pause.

'Is he OK, sir?'

Jonah moved the transceiver away from his mouth, took a couple of deep breaths, and returned it. 'Marcus is dead, Brandon.'

'What? No, I mean… what happened?' The voice at the other end of the line suddenly sounded very choked and weak.

'Brandon, I promise you, when we get back I'll explain as best I can. But right now, I need you to report to sickbay. Can you do that for me? Please? Over.'

'…Yes, sir. Over and out.'

Jonah replaced the transponder and exhaled. As hard as that brief exchange had been, it paled in comparison to the conversation he was dreading with Robyn and Patrick Cavendish when they saw what was left of their daughter.

***

They arrived back at the settlement by 8.00 am. The moment they touched down, Alyssa was bundled out of the Hummingbird by a pair of medics and borne off towards the sickbay. They both shot confused glances at the silver figure sitting stock-still inside the aircraft, but thought better of prying any further when they saw the state of their patient. Robyn and Patrick came sprinting across the plain to meet them and followed the stretcher inside, holding each other for reassurance at the sight of their daughter. Before they disappeared amongst the structures of the settlement, Robyn fixed Jonah with a look that rooted him to the spot.

He warded off another young medic probing him for superficial injuries and turned to O'Brien, picking his deep red face out from the cluster of onlookers that had begun to gather around their landing site.

'What in God's name happened out there, Jonah?' he exclaimed, his baritone voice audible above the loudening crowd. 'Lawson's *dead*?'

'Eoin, we need to leave. All of us, as soon as we're able.'

'Come again?'

'The danger, the message, whatever *that*—' he gestured to the Angel '—was trying to warn us about, it's real. There was a machine waiting for us, like nothing I've ever seen or heard of before. It was equipped with some sort of maser cannon. Lawson was vaporised, and it would have done the same to us, except for our passenger here.'

'What the... is that a woman? No – a robot?'

'I've no idea. Whatever it is, it's what was broadcasting the signal, and it destroyed the thing that attacked us. After that, it shut down or something. I'd say it's time to make good on its original advice.'

Eoin nodded slowly, comprehension dawning on his face. 'I'll rally the troops, start getting essential equipment broken down and loaded onto the caterpillars. We can head east, towards the mountains. Should be somewhere we can hole up for winter, fortify in case of, ah, *trouble*.' He placed a lingering emphasis on that last word, as though tasting it, mulling over its implications. 'But, listen: they're going to need to hear it from you. Why we're running. What we're running from.'

He was right, Jonah realised. The settlement had developed in the last nineteen years to the point where they could comfortably weather TransTerra's winters. It was easy to forget how tenuous their survival on this planet was; if they were going to uproot themselves with autumn coming to an end, they would need to know damn well that what they were escaping was a foe worse than the elements. And right now, he had only one source to help clarify that dilemma.

'Is Riley in the lab just now?' he asked, deliberately avoiding Eoin's point. 'I might need her help. I'd like to learn everything we can about our visitor.'

***

They carried the Angel into the botanical nursery, Jonah holding its heels, Rahman hoisting it up under the arms. 'Clear a space!' Jonah called, registering shocked looks from the wide-eyed youngsters populating the bright white laboratory. To their loudly vocalised dismay, he swept several rows of crop samples luxuriating in petri dishes off a countertop in the centre of the lab, making room for them to lay down their subject for examination.

He would have identified the angel-thing's face as that of a woman in her mid-20s by pre-telomerase standards, high-cheekboned and statuesque, with short, jet-black hair. Its skin was pale; its eyes open but unfocused. As he placed its dead weight on the countertop, he had the dispiriting impression of a corpse being laid out on a mortician's slab.

'Fucking hell, Jonah!' Riley O'Brien marched towards them, a mother bear defending her cubs. 'What are you doing with my specimens? Who is she, and why is she on my workbench?'

'Riley, Alyssa was right. That meteor she saw the other night, remember? Earth came back, and they didn't come with good news.'

He shared the transmission Lawson had intercepted with her, and an abridged version of the night's events. As he spoke, Riley's expression slowly transmuted from incomprehension to horror.

'Kaori,' she barked at last, 'get me a scalpel and a fresh petri dish.'

Riley was one of Eoin's great-granddaughters, and she had inherited all of his commanding presence. At 25 Terran years of age, she held the title of being the youngest of the settlement's shipborn. When the *Prospice* had touched down, she had been six years old – having spent her infancy surrounded by white plastic and steel bulkheads, the grass that grew taller than she was had been an endless source of fascination and delight to her.

That fascination had blossomed with time into a love of botany, and she had been instated as the settlement's head agriculturalist, charged with finding ever more efficient ways to reconcile their seed banks with TransTerra's soil. She had taken aspirational groundborn under her wing and formed her own little coven of botanists dedicated to feeding the Mercanta Steppe (Alyssa had been counted among their number). The equipment they commanded for biochemical profiling and epigenetic editing was some of the most sophisticated to have been brought from Earth.

Kaori Mitsuda, one of Riley's underlings, dashed over with a molecular scalpel – once activated, the outline of the blade appeared to waver in the air, the micro-vibrations that allowed it to cut with beyond-surgical precision generating a whine pitched high above unmodified human hearing.

'Careful,' Rahman said, sharply. 'Last time she woke up, she burned through about two metres' worth of metal just by gesturing at it.'

'I'll have a white flag ready,' Riley responded, drily. 'Kaori, I need a sample cut from the tip of the index finger of the right hand, as thin as you can manage. Whenever you're ready – take your time.'

Kaori took a deep breath and moved in. She was esteemed among Riley's clan for her extraordinary sureness of hand and the delicacy with which she was able to manipulate cell cultures. She took hold of the Angel's hand and proceeded as though to slice off a sliver of what would be the uppermost epidermis of a human fingertip, only a few cells thick. She moved the scalpel so gradually that Jonah had to magnify his eyes to meaningfully follow its progress.

Several moments went by as the lab held its breath. A look of uncomfortable exertion came over Kaori's face.

'What's wrong?' Riley asked, frowning.

'I don't understand,' she replied. 'When I touched it, the exterior felt soft, like human skin. But I can't seem to cut it, not even when I – *aah*!' The scalpel slipped off the unyielding silver finger – the pressure Kaori had been applying was directed instead into her own left hand, the blade cutting deep into the webbing between her thumb and index finger. She let out a long, pained whimper when she saw how much blood was pouring from the wound.

'Goddammit,' Riley exhaled, sounding more exasperated than worried. It wasn't the first time she'd seen an accident like it, although usually, Jonah understood, they happened to novices rather than savants like Kaori. 'Blake, patch her up, would you, and then get her over to sickbay for stitches. Jonah, whatever you've brought us doesn't seem to like us sticking foreign bodies into it.'

'It's like she was fighting me,' Kaori said through gritted teeth. 'Like there's some force inside determined to keep her together, repel any outside intrusion. Whatever she is, there's something in her that's still alive.'

'I'm not sure if "alive" or "dead" are terms that apply here,' Jonah mused.

***

They had better luck with an industrial CO_2 laser that Riley purloined from her great-grandfather's garage. The beam successfully carved off a few dozen milligrams of material from the Angel's fingertip, which promptly disintegrated into a fine black powder. The Angel still did not wake up.

'It's not metal,' Riley pronounced, examining the sample under an optical microscope. 'It's almost all carbon, with traces of silver and copper distributed throughout.'

'When I found her, she was in some sort of cocoon of diamond,' Jonah said. 'Even so, there must be more to her composition. Carbon doesn't just autonomously turn itself into diamond or nanotubes at will.'

'You don't need to tell me, Jonah. My best guess would be that there's some force at play below the molecular scale, maybe some kind of femtech directly interfering with atomic bonds on a quantum level. But this is getting way beyond my pay grade.'

Jonah squeezed his eyes shut and pinched the bridge of his nose. The midday sun had begun to peer through the skylight in the nursery, glinting off the Angel's "feathers" – he was dimly aware that he had been awake for almost 30 hours, and he didn't foresee himself sleeping at any point in the near future.

Femtotechnology had still been considered an engineering pipedream when last the *Prospice* had been in contact with Earth – they were completely in the dark as to the functioning of this Angel that might have the knowledge and the power that would save them.

'OK,' he said levelly. 'What if there's some sort of deeper interior structure inside her that could tell us what makes her tick?'

'Could be there is; I couldn't tell you. X-ray radiography shows her up as completely opaque. Not even Superman could see what's going on below her skin.'

Jonah made an executive decision. 'Alright. Use the laser to cut out a bigger chunk, down to wherever the bone would be on a person, and let's hope she's well disposed towards us if we can wake her up.'

Jonah prepared himself to override Riley's objections, but he was silenced by a top-priority transmission in his implants from Eoin.

'Jonah. Sorry, I know this is important, but you need to hear this. The medics did everything they could, but they couldn't stem the internal bleeding. Alyssa's dead.'

***

Robyn and Patrick were huddled closely over Alyssa's bed; when Jonah arrived in sickbay, Patrick stood up with such force that his chair was knocked over, and advanced toward him with fists raised.

'You *son of a —*' His curse was muffled by a pair of orderlies who struggled to restrain him, but Jonah hardly registered it; his attention was occupied by the diminutive figure on the bed, swaddled in white fabric stained deep red. Alyssa's eyes had been closed in the traditional mark of respect for the dead, but the impression of peace the gesture was intended to convey was undermined by the fact that her torso was still spread wide open from the surgery, internal organs exposed to the world and drenched in blood that would soon start to coagulate now that her heart had stopped pumping.

'They tried to remove the fragments of bone,' Robyn said, numbly. 'The hemorrhaging was just… it was too much.'

Jonah was familiar enough with death to have relinquished any notions of dignity associated with it. He had lost his own father to heart disease in his teenage years, and his mother to senescence in his thirties. He had seen crewmen on the *Prospice* lost to micrometeoroid strikes on spacewalks, to cancer brought on by cosmic radiation, and to suicidal despair in the wake of Earth's loss. Yet, none of it prepared him for the crushing reality of this moment – the lifeless body of his granddaughter, and the baleful, truthful accusation in Robyn's eyes that it was all his fault. He slowly sat next to her, feeling numb.

'I should have been here at the end,' he said, his voice sounding flat.

'Don't you think you've done enough for her in the last day?' The depth of scorn in her voice, by contrast, was fathomless. 'Just tell me, Jonah. What possessed you to bring her out there? I'll go insane if I don't know.'

'I can't justify it, Robyn. I could tell you that a day ago, the notion that there really was danger out there hadn't sunk in for me. She pushed to come, tried to leverage her position; at the time, it seemed the right call to let her have her way.'

'"Let her have her way"?' Robyn repeated the phrase, disbelieving. 'You're supposed to be a *leader*, Dad.'

'I know. I know you'll never forgive me, Robyn, and I know it's no consolation for me to say I won't forgive myself either. All I can do now is work to ensure that no one else has to feel what we're feeling right now.'

He reached over to touch his daughter's shoulder. He and Robyn had never been close. She had been conceived through IVF using his genetic material; born from the *Prospice's* gestation chambers; raised in a communal effort by the crew. She had been reared from birth as a sailor in his crew, and a Captain couldn't be seen to have favorites. Now, though, he felt the tug of heredity; the need to make his daughter know she wasn't suffering alone.

She slapped his hand away.

'Why couldn't it have been you, instead of her?' she said quietly. Her eyes were rimmed with bright red, but she wasn't crying anymore – she had reached some lower, colder depth of grief.

He didn't have an answer. He'd asked himself the same question, many times. Yet another person he loved, gone forever beyond his reach. Yet another piece of himself they'd taken with them.

The silence was broken by a crash against the sickbay's outer wall.

The door flew open – filling its frame was the Angel, moving of her own accord, wings flared. Her eyes, which had been a dull black when they had found her, now glowed a bright, iridescent blue. She had pinned Eoin against the doorframe when he had tried to block her path.

Eoin, like many of the first generation, had entered the Merantau Program from the fledgling ORC. He had received epigenetic therapy to stimulate muscle growth; he had carbon nanotube fibers woven throughout his sinews, and his bones were reinforced with titanium. When a robotic plow had rolled over on a hummock their first year on TransTerra, Jonah had seen him raise it back to its upright position by himself, the entire ton-and-a-quarter mass.

And yet, the Angel was handling him as though he had the substance of a scarecrow. She dismissively pushed Eoin away and advanced into the room, her gaze fixed on Alyssa's body, her expression neutral.

'No. No, you get away from her, *you get away from my child*!' Robyn threw herself at the Angel as she crossed the room and was similarly shrugged off. Jonah rose and planted himself between the silver shape and the body of his granddaughter. Her brilliant eyes met his.

'Captain,' the Angel spoke, 'please stand aside. There isn't much time, but I can still save her.' There was a glassy quality to her voice that was hard to pin down – her enunciation was too precise to be spontaneous, and yet not robotic either. There was something like the subtlety of human emotion undergirding the words.

'Can I trust you?'

'You will always be able to trust me.'

Hell with it. What did they have to lose? Jonah stood aside. 'Do whatever you can.'

The Angel extended her right hand towards Alyssa. For a moment, nothing seemed to happen – then he observed movement under the silvery skin of the arm, like fluid shifting towards the appendage's end. A mass began to swell in her hand, reminiscent of a balloon filling with water.

When it reached the size of a small melon, the swelling reached a threshold of surface tension and detached itself from the end of the arm, akin to a droplet of water falling from a pine needle, splashing down into Alyssa's still-exposed abdomen. Initially, the blob resembling mercury just lay there – then, with increasing speed, it began to spread out, molding itself to the shape of the organs and bones beneath. It filled the perforations in the lungs and intestines like plaster, ejecting chunks of bone as it went. It formed spurs in the spaces where the ribs had previously been. Finally, it extended tendrils that pulled the parted skin together like a pair of double doors and knitted them back together, leaving behind a silver scar.

Long seconds passed while the material's progress was hidden from view; Jonah and Robyn looked on, dumbfounded. The Angel's eyes flicked back and forth.

Alyssa's body jerked, as though being defibrillated with a massive voltage – her back arched, her muscles contracted. Her eyes opened shockingly wide, the pupils narrowed to pinpricks, and she inhaled a gasping, rattling breath that seemed endless.

'Jesus God, what are you doing to her?' Robyn cried, her hands clutched to her mouth. She moved as though to intervene; Jonah held out an arm to prevent her. Another breath, shallower this time, and then another. The breaths turned to moans, which escalated to blood-curdling screams of pain.

'Shh.' The Angel leaned in. 'It's OK. Focus on my voice, the pain should subside in a moment. You were on the verge of brain death – your body needs time to reacclimatise. Can you tell me your name? Do you remember?'

Alyssa made a visible effort to stop screaming – she breathed her answer through gritted teeth, a barely audible whisper. 'Al-Alyssa. Alyssa Ca-Cavendish.' She began to shiver violently. The Angel drew a blanket over her.

'The blood in your veins is starting to circulate again,' she said. 'You'll feel freezing cold for a few minutes. Don't worry, you'll be fine.'

She turned towards the onlookers and was met with a gallery of dropped jaws. She inclined her head in a small bow, her face solemn. 'I apologise for the trouble I've caused you all. Please know that I have your people's best interests at heart. You are more precious than you know; I traveled light-years and risked the Collective's wrath because I believe there's still hope. My name is Victoria Harrison, and I am a lieutenant of the Insurgency.'

She met Jonah's gaze, and a small smile played at her pale lips as she saw the dawning comprehension in his eyes.

'I must look rather different from how you remember me in the messages from home, grandfather.'

Chapter 6

December 7th, 2135 C.E.

Thirty-five thousand kilometres above Earth's equator, Jean floated with practised ease through the reception area of the ORC's base atop the Congolese space elevator. Slowing and finding a handhold, she braced gently against the eastern bulkhead and swiped the single-use ID badge that had been printed for her upon arrival. The scanner flashed green, approving her to enter, and the transparent hatch parted to admit her.

Agent Liu followed close behind, attempting to mimic the way she handled herself in zero-g. He partly succeeded, managing to absorb his body's inertia upon collision with the bulkhead well enough that he didn't break anything. He fumbled a moment with his badge, struggling with the way every small motion subtly shifted his balance while weightless. No matter how poised he had seemed while he was on the ground, you could always recognise a person's first time in freefall.

There was a half-second when he scanned his badge that Jean forgot to breathe, feeling an adrenalising thrill at the chance of being caught. She was officially allowed to be here; being an ex-officer within the ORC and having a serving family member conferred upon her certain privileges, like being allowed to visit her daughter on-site and even bring along a guest, pending a routine background check.

Tony was another story—a member of a national intelligence service showing up unannounced would set all manner of interdepartmental and international alarm bells ringing. Jean had double- and triple-checked his spoofed identification, looking for cracks in his phony birth certificate, medical records, employment history, anything that might raise a red flag during algorithmic cross-referencing. She was as certain as could be that his legend was airtight – ninety percent of her day-to-day work consisted of optimising her clients' security protocols, running audits to identify weak points. If she wanted to bypass them for real, she was uncommonly well-equipped to do so.

But there was always the possibility that this time was the one she'd slipped, overlooked something crucial...

The light flashed green, and Tony swam in after her. He gave her the slightest of nods, signalling that, so far, she was earning her fee.

The station's corridors were broad by the standards of orbital structures, but they were bustling with grim-faced ORC personnel. All leave had been cancelled after the Engagement; the political tensions afflicting the surface were being felt in space as well. Every day brought fresh headlines: human traffickers trying to slip past international cordons in high orbit; ultra-wealthy moguls trying to shift their assets to Mars or Jupiter underneath the chaos as a tax dodge. The organisation's resources were being stretched in a way they hadn't since its inception.

They reached the station's inner torus, where the rotation generated centripetal force equivalent to about one-tenth terrestrial gravity. Jean moved with a loping, bouncing gait around its interior, but slowed when she looked back and saw Tony trailing behind, clutching a handrail, seemingly fighting the impulse to be sick.

'Here.' She tossed him a blister pack of anti-emetic pills. Impressively, he caught it on the first attempt, and gratefully swallowed a couple. 'The Coriolis getting to you?' she asked, gently.

He nodded. 'I can't decide what's worse,' he said, 'the nausea that comes from my internal organs not knowing which way is up, or this damn dizziness. How do you live like this?'

'Once upon a time, you'd have spent hours training in centrifuges and gyroscopes to accustom yourself beforehand. Now, spaceflight's common enough that no one thinks anything of it, until they get up here, and realise they're not as tough as they thought.'

She allowed him a moment to catch his breath. They'd stopped adjacent to a window looking downward at the planet, gradually rotating as the torus turned. The elevator they'd ridden up fell away below them and out of sight, an incomprehensibly long, fibrous umbilical cord that connected them to Central Africa. Two others like it extended above Borneo and Brazil.

Tony's gaze fixed upon the view, and his breathing levelled out. 'Strange,' he murmured. 'All the fighting, all the confusion, all the mistrust; it all seems so petty when you consider it's all contained to that thin skin of atmosphere.'

'Now that,' Jean said with a smirk, 'is the other side of the coin. The nice surprise when you get up here. It's called the Overview Effect; an appreciation for the fragility of life, for the commonality between all humans, and so on and so forth. Enjoy it, by all means, but we have an appointment to keep.'

Tony shook himself. 'Right you are, Ms. Harrison. Business before pleasure. Where were we?'

'We were going to meet with my daughter. And please: it's Jean.'

***

The cafeteria in module 8-A was jammed with personnel, like the rest of the station, but the two of them managed to secure a booth that would afford a modicum of privacy. Jean ordered food for them both; water and a small salad each. She wasn't hungry, and Tony certainly wouldn't be swallowing anything but more anti-emetic pills, but it was for the sake of show. She received a notification to her implants that Victoria had been informed of their presence, and permitted an hour's discretion to meet with her family.

Jean nudged Tony's leg gently with her foot under the table. 'Word of warning: don't stare.'

'Excuse me?'

'Just don't stare. She won't admit it, but she gets self-conscious when people stare.'

It was easy to pick her daughter out from the crowd when she arrived, even mixed in as she was with the other cadet uniforms. Full body prosthesis remained rare enough in the 22nd century that there was cause to look twice if you passed someone wearing one in the street. Her body was a composite of metallic alloy, hard plastic, and carbon-fibre mesh, all painted a Caucasian skin tone, but unmistakable for its artificial smoothness and the visible seams at the points of articulation. She gave the impression at first glance of a living mannequin; her face was a highly animate doll's face, a skilled sculptor's impression of Victoria Harrison using reference images of her as a young girl, extrapolated to how she might have looked if she'd been allowed to grow naturally past the age of twelve and through to adulthood. It was a face that served as a reminder of the body her daughter had lost, even as Jean had come to know it as the true face of her child.

On seeing her mother, Victoria grinned and hurried over to greet her. She and Jean embraced, savouring their first reunion since the Engagement.

'Long time, no see, Mum. Is the end of the world such a big thing that you can't make time for your favourite child?' She said it mock-chidingly, though Jean felt a twinge of real guilt.

'Oh, hush,' she countered. 'Things are manic groundside as well, you space-cadets don't get to have all the fun. It was all we could do to get away for thirty-six hours.'

'I bet. Who's the new boy-toy?'

Tony extended a hand for Victoria to shake, with persuasively strained formality. 'Good to meet you, Victoria. My name's Roy Sheh,' he said. 'I met your mum a few days ago when she had a job in Hong Kong, and we hit it off. I said I'd always wanted to visit one of the space elevators, and she got to telling me all about her prodigy daughter stationed here. We thought we could take a couple of days off and kill two birds with one stone, pay you a surprise visit and let me see the world from geosynchronous orbit while we're at it.'

Victoria slowly accepted his hand and shook it with a loose grip, letting the awkwardness of the moment percolate and ferment.

'Well, good to meet you too, boy-toy-Roy,' she said. Her glass eyes swivelled back and forth between her mother and this stranger she was introducing. 'I'm not about to find out I've got a new baby brother on the way, am I?'

'Victoria!' Jean reproached.

'Sorry, Mum. It's just unusual to take off on a holiday right now, with everything going on. And I heard that Asia got hit worse than we did.' She turned to face Tony. 'Aren't you worried about, I dunno, mad cultists breaking into your house while you're away? Not that I'm not pleased to meet you, of course,' she hastily appended.

'Don't remind me,' Tony said. 'If anything, a couple of days seeing the world from far above is just what I need right now. It seems a lot less chaotic from this vantage point.'

'I can't imagine what the Engagement must have felt like for you, if what they're saying about the effects in Asia are right.'

'It sucked pretty badly, yeah,' Tony said, absently massaging his temples as though to quiet the pain the memory caused him. 'Like someone put my brain in a blender. I thought I was dying. Took me two hours before I came to my senses, and I'm grateful that's all it took. Some people I know never came to their senses at all. That's why your mum was in Hong Kong to begin with, she was organising protection for a diplomatic procession from the PNC, keeping the crazies away from them. I'm a programmer for the PNC's offices in the city.'

'A programmer?' Victoria released his hand and gave an appreciative nod. 'I always told Mum, she needed to try getting together with an egghead. How did you end up meeting Mum, if she was beating off crazies all the time she was in Hong Kong?'

Some of the latent tension evaporated from Tony's face, and the conversation proceeded more smoothly from there. He and Jean took turns in regaling Victoria with the story of their meeting in a cocktail bar after hours and discovering an unlikely shared passion for 2060s direct-auditory music and one thing leading to another. Victoria sat and made all the right polite noises in all the right places.

The truth was, Jean had had a series of flings and semi-serious relationships since the accident. The hi-I'm-your-new-dad talk was familiar enough to mother and daughter both to have become routine. Of the three of them, Tony was the only one who appeared uncomfortable. If he was acting, then he was a capable performer.

'Roy, honey, I'm thirsty,' Jean said eventually. 'Could you get us some water from the dispenser over there, please?' Tony followed his cue and did as he was asked.

'He seems nice,' Victoria observed, when he was out of earshot.

'He is.'

'Care to tell me what's actually going on?'

'What makes you think there's something going on?'

'Come off it. Who spends a whole day riding up the elevator to enjoy the view of the Earth from a barracks canteen? And you know full well you could have introduced me to Roy in a message.'

Jean took a couple of seconds to contemplate her answer, then she leaned forward, lowering her voice.

'Did you see the Starman's last message?'

Victoria frowned. 'You mean the one from October 7th, right, before all this started? What about it?'

'I liked the segment of the message he addressed to you. That he knew you'd get an A in your biology test, so he'd already arranged for Ilsa to give you that little demonstration of the tubers germinating in zero g.'

It was a phenomenon that everyone in communication with the *Prospice* had to deal with, one way or another. The starship had left its dock above the Bornean elevator thirty-nine years ago, and was now moving at one-fifth of light speed from Earth. The message they'd received from Jean's father had taken roughly six-and-a-half years to arrive, and the Jonah Harrison in the message was, in turn, working from information that was five-and-a-half years old when he'd received it from Earth's communication array. As the *Prospice's* journey continued, that delay became more and more pronounced. Every reply they received was like unearthing a time capsule.

In the mind of the Jonah in the October 7th message, his granddaughter was still a sweet, precocious young girl, whose idyllic childhood was a source of comfort to him. The day was fast approaching – less than two years away, now – when his messages would begin to reflect Victoria's existence after the accident. Although Victoria would never admit it, Jean knew how to read her daughter. Whenever the subject was raised, she could tell that she dreaded that day.

'Yeah, it was sweet,' Victoria said. She leaned back in her seat and broke eye contact with Jean. 'I ask again: what about it?'

'Nothing, really. It set me to thinking, I suppose. Your unit leader, Albrecht, he owes me a favour. A word in his ear, and I could get you ground leave for a few weeks over Christmas.'

Victoria's eyelids flickered shut in a pained frown, and her speech programs generated a frustrated sigh. 'Jesus Christ, Mum, not this again.'

'The Enclave isn't going away, Vic. The post-Engagement situation, it's going to get worse before it gets better, and I'd rather have you away from the front lines until it does.'

'No-one offered you ground leave when you led the raid on the Silva cartel's base. Or when you spent thirty-six hours clearing out radioactive material from the Erikson station before its orbit decayed, as though you haven't told me that story enough times.' Victoria's tone was sullen.

'That's different,' Jean insisted. 'Those are things anyone who joins ORC knows they might be signing up to do. This, though... I just have a bad feeling.'

'Why? Do you know something I don't?'

Jean let the question hang longer than she ought to have done. 'No, of course not,' she said, hating herself. 'You'd find out any new intelligence on the Enclave long before I did, obviously. But we're talking about forces here that no-one understands, and I'd hate to see you be the first one in the firing line dealing with them, and damn any code of honour that would ask you to. I want to see you safe. I love you, Vic.' Her voice caught on the last words.

'I love you too, Mum,' Victoria replied hesitantly. She turned back towards her mother, and clasped her hand where it sat splayed on the cafeteria table. 'I know you have my best interests at heart. I know you worry, and I'm sorry about that. But I won't ask for special treatment. It's not fair to my comrades, and it's not fair to anyone on the ground who's scared and confused as well.'

'No,' Jean replied sadly. 'No, I suppose it isn't, at that.'

After some more small talk, Victoria was called back to her drills, and Jean and Tony were freed to pursue their real objective. They floated silently together through the corridors of the Congolese station, following the signs towards the R&D division.

'I hope you're happy,' Jean said, more to break the tension than anything, 'dragging my daughter into your web.'

'It's fine,' Tony reassured her. 'You did beautifully. Victoria's involvement with this affair is over, she didn't suspect a thing. She doesn't even know my real name – in a couple of weeks, you can tell her we split up, no harm, no foul.' He smirked. 'Tell her I had some sort of unseemly kink, whatever works.'

'I'll pencil it in.'

Ruefully, Jean had to concede that Tony was right. The best lies contain an element of truth, as the saying went, and it was true that Victoria hated people treating her as though she needed protecting. By the same token, the kind of treatment she dreaded receiving was the same kind of treatment she was most inclined to believe was genuine when she received it. The deception was helped by the fact that Jean genuinely wanted to see her protected. Hence, she and Tony had a pretext for being in an ORC facility that left no-one else the wiser to their true intentions.

'So,' Tony piped up as they made their slow way through the station to its less populated thoroughfares, 'what happened to her, exactly?'

'None of your business, Agent,' she replied, more sharply than she'd intended. 'As a pretext to explain our presence here, I was willing to let that little charade slide on the basis it seemed harmless. But from now on, your work and hers don't intersect. Understood?'

'I understand. She has no further bearing on my operation; on that you have my word. She just... I don't know. Idle curiosity. I've had teammates before who she reminds me of, who used bravado to cover for loneliness.'

Jean mulled that over. Tony was a curious specimen – altogether too blithe and conversational in his dealings with her, quite the opposite of the kind of stone-faced, monosyllabic spooks she was accustomed to in her career.

She equivocated. What harm could it do? Her family's past wasn't secret; there was nothing there that a national intelligence service couldn't uncover with a couple of man-hours spent digging. And it might be therapeutic to put that history into words.

'She used to play the violin,' she began, the words coming slowly. They kept their snail's pace along the corridor; Tony was keeping himself anchored

72

to the floor as best he was able, moving hand-over-hand along the handrail. He didn't say anything, or prompt her to follow up the thought, just waited for her to continue of her own accord.

'She started when she was six. Took to it like a *bona fide* prodigy; by the time she was eight, she could play any scale or arpeggio her tutors could name. By ten, she was reciting Bach, Paganini, Vivaldi. It was her life. She had posters of Baroque composers on her bedroom wall.

'When she was twelve, she had a recital in Oxfordshire in front of an audience. I was on duty at Scolt Head Island, watching by livestream. Her brother, James, he had no taste for music, so he'd stayed home. It was just Vic and her father in person at the concert.

'It was after nine o'clock when they finished; it would have been almost midnight by the time they arrived home. It was January. There was a blizzard blowing in from the north.'

She took a deep breath in through her nose, and out through her mouth.

'Their car… went off an overpass around High Wycombe. The insurance people, they told me afterwards that there had been a glitch in the car's self-driving guidance systems. That the image recognition software had misidentified a flurry of snow as a crowd of pedestrians, and swerved off the road to avoid a collision.

'You know what's funny? When we were buying cars, Stephen – Victoria's father – he was the one who insisted on getting a model with utilitarian protocols; one which, when forced to choose between the lives of its passengers and the lives of anyone it might hit, would make the decision that it computed would save the optimal number of lives, regardless of who was or wasn't in the car. It was the "ethical purchasing decision," he said.

'I got the call from the hospital at two in the morning; I arrived in London just before six. They'd told me I needed to identify my husband's body, for the death certificate. It was him; that much I could confirm. Laid out on that slab was Stephen Basinger-Harrison; one-time father, husband, and conscientious moral agent; now a cadaver with his skull fractured in a dozen places.

'The morticians had a silver lining, though. Stephen had been instantly killed, his brain damaged beyond repair. Victoria, though – she'd been "lucky." Her internal organs were scorched when the car's engine ignited, but by some miracle, her brain and spinal column came out unscathed. The paramedics had the presence of mind to remove them when the rest of her body couldn't be salvaged.

'That was how I found her. My daughter, now just a brain and spinal column, hanging suspended in a jar of preservative gel in the Royal London's tissue sample laboratory.

'The hell of it is, she was conscious. I like to think I could have coped with the horror of it better if she'd just been in suspended animation, waiting for a shock from an electrode to bring her back to the land of the living. But no: the doctors told me that it was imperative that she be awake, and subject to sensory stimulus. That was a part of keeping her alive. Her visual and auditory senses were hooked up to cameras and microphones in the lab.

'The moment she saw me, she started wailing. I'll remember her words until the day I die, from the moment I stepped into that lab, into her field of vision. "Mum! Where am I? What's going on? Why can't I move? Why can't I blink? Where's Dad?"'

The two of them were silent for a while, Jean letting the memory of the worst moment of her life stew. Eventually, Tony cleared his throat.

'Does she... does she still play the violin?'

'Not anymore,' Jean said. 'The new bodies the insurance paid for were top of the range, but she had to adjust to them. She had to relearn how to walk; how to talk; how to write. One time, she tried to play a few chords on the violin. It broke when she tried to brace it against her shoulder. She never spoke about playing again. She took up martial arts as extracurricular activities, and that was that.'

**

The construction of the space elevators had been a boon to humanity in most regards—with escape from Earth's gravity well now available at a fraction of the cost and effort it had once incurred, they had brought the bounties of asteroid mining and orbital solar farms, giving rise to an unprecedented global economic boom. One side-effect, however, was that the mass emigration of Earth's private industry to orbit created a new frontier for crime, piracy, and terrorism. This was catalysed by a pushback from the equatorial countries, where the elevators were rooted by physical necessity, at this newest avenue of colonialism and economic exploitation for the established global superpowers.

The occupation of an American, high-orbit helium-3 processing plant in 2072 by a rogue Bolivian gang and the slaughter of the staff therein had demanded the institution of a new organisation equipped to combat such threats, following the US military's dismal response time. The Orbital Reconnaissance Corps had been the result; the stick to the PNC's carrot.

The ORC, however, begat its own unexpected consequences in turn. The presence in orbit of an organisation backed by most of the world's national governments meant an injection of funding for extraterrestrial operations that dwarfed even NASA at the height of the space race. The glut of cash had led to a glut of proposals from scientists looking for grants to perform practical research in zero-g conditions that the world's universities were ill-equipped to provide. As a result, the ORC had established its Research & Development division—far from being merely space police, they became the equivalent of America's DARPA in the 20th century, a vanguard of scientific progress, particularly in the realm of particle physics. The quantum fluctuation drive that had gone on to propel the *Prospice* had been a product of ORC's facilities.

The man credited with its invention greeted Jean and "Roy" at the entrance to the R&D labs.

'Jeanie,' Carlos Alvarez pronounced, 'you must be better suited to the cushy civilian life, because you're even prettier now than when you left us.'

The Chilean doctor, now in his eighties, looked much the same as Jean remembered him, with his round, tan face that steadfastly refused to wrinkle. He sported a brilliant snow-white shock of hair and a beard to match, which she suspected had been epigenetically modified to give him a more distinguished, professorial air. He kissed her hand in an exaggeratedly chivalric gesture.

'Shush, you dirty old man,' she replied, grinning. 'You'll make me blush in front of my boyfriend.'

'Perish the thought! Please, introduce me to this fine young gentleman.'

'Roy Sheh, sir,' Tony said, shaking Alvarez's hand, or trying his best without the motion propelling him into the corridor walls. 'It's an honour to meet you. I have an amateur interest in physics myself, and I was so excited when Jean told me I could get a tour of the most advanced research facility in the solar system.'

'Well, now you're making *me* blush,' Alvarez beamed, as though he didn't take to praise like a fly to honey. 'Come inside, both of you. You've caught me at a loose end, I'm glad to say.'

Carlos Alvarez was an octogenarian genius in a middle-aged body, with the personal demeanour of a teenager, and he organised his laboratory accordingly. Every flat surface was covered with Velcro to accommodate the clutter of diagrams, models, and spare parts, and even then, a variety of widgets whose purpose Jean couldn't guess at were floating freely around the hexagonal room. In contrast to the rest of the station, the lab was deserted except for themselves.

The R&D division's funding committee were willing, up to a point, to allow Carlos to treat these labs as his personal man-cave, in light of the prestige he conferred upon ORC. After all, the reasoning went, the vast majority of the division's funding was tied up in the enormous particle accelerator hovering over South America, a vast construct engirdling the outermost torus of the Brazilian elevator station. If a fraction of a percent of that money was allocated to the passion projects and private hobbies of the man who had made interstellar travel a reality, it was basically harmless, and kept ORC in the good books of tech bloggers who revered Carlos Alvarez's name.

'What are those?' Tony was pointing across the room with an eagerness Jean suspected wasn't altogether fake. Following his finger, she saw harnessed to the wall a sculpture of a pair of metallic bird wings, like those of a falcon or an eagle or some other raptor, scaled up to several metres across. Their elegance stood out in the space dominated by amorphous clumps of lenses and exposed circuitry.

'Ah!' Carlos exclaimed, beaming with pride. 'My newest gizmo. I've been working on progressively downsizing the quantum fluctuation drive, as you may have read, and with a couple of decades' worth of tweaks, I think I've finally got it down to human scale. An individual wearing these in conjunction with the right equipment might, in time, be able to soar through the solar system, propelled by cosmic radiation. The avian design is purely aesthetic, you understand—my brother Joachim's notion, he's rather more artistically inclined than I. But it would be a fabulous elevation of the human form, wouldn't it? A poetic bit of self-directed evolution, to be able to move between the stars unaided and unimpeded? I call it the "Archangel Frame."'

'Tremendous,' Tony breathed. 'May I...?' He gestured towards the device, indicating he wanted to examine it more closely.

'Please do, but I must insist there be no touching. It's a prototype, you see, quite fragile. The console adjacent to it contains technical details you may find stimulating.' Tony floated over toward the Archangel Frame, gingerly bracing himself on work surfaces as he went, leaving Jean and Carlos alone in each other's company.

'I must say I was surprised, Jean, to get your message this morning,' Carlos said. 'It's been, what, four years since our last correspondence? I would have expected a little more warning that you were in the neighbourhood, particularly in the current climate.'

'Forgive me, Carlos. Something came up suddenly, and I came here on short notice.'

Three bemused furrows appeared in Carlos' otherwise smooth brow. 'I get the impression this isn't just a social call?'

Jean had been rehearsing her sales pitch for the whole of the 18-hour ride up the Congolese elevator's main shaft. 'Not just a social call, no,' she conceded. 'I've actually come to offer you a hot tip, I guess you might call it. You have all sorts of instruments hovering in vacuum primed to detect exotic particles, right? Tachyons, electron-positron pairs, that sort of thing? Manoeuvre them to observe the outline of the Moon, you might be surprised by what you pick up. You could have another big discovery to your name, another chapter to the legend of Carlos Alvarez.'

Carlos bit his lip. 'I sense there's some sort of *quid pro quo* coming.'

'Just a little one. Whatever it is you find out there, we need to be the first to hear about it. Give me a couple of days' head start before you send your findings out for peer-review, that's all I ask.'

'You say "we,"' Carlos said. 'This fellow Roy, where did you say you found him again? Some research institute, maybe? Caltech? Or perhaps Tsinghua?' He emphasised the last name, probing for a response. Jean could see the gears turning in his finely-tuned brain. 'Are you trying to recruit me to your ragtag band, Jean? I think there's a clause in my contract somewhere that prohibits against participation in ragtag bands.'

'Of course not, Carlos. I'm afraid that for the time being, you'll need to take my word that I have the interests of all the world at heart. I'm with the spooks, but they're the right kind of spooks, the ones you want on your side. Beyond that, all I can say is that I hope you know me well enough by now to know I wouldn't abuse your trust.'

Carlos absently rubbed his shoulder, the site of an old flechette wound that Jean knew still itched from time to time. He sighed. 'No, Jean, I suppose you wouldn't.'

Chapter 7

June 27th, 2326 C.E.

Alyssa jerked awake and immediately regretted it. The sudden motion sent a barb of pain through her midriff, which lying back alleviated a little. She squeezed her eyes shut against the sensation. She heard a voice call her name and felt a hand pressing something cool against her forehead.

'Alyssa. Good to have you back.' The voice was male, guardedly concerned. Alyssa's thoughts were sluggish; it was a couple of moments before she remembered where she was. She eased her eyes open, blinking feverishly against the light of sunset streaming in through the sickbay's window. Derrickson, the head physician of Pilgrim's Progress, was leaning in close, holding a straw to her lips. 'You've been under heavy sedation for the last few hours. Drink this, you'll be thirsty.'

She was, she realised. The back of her throat felt like a desert. She sucked greedily at the straw, savouring the taste of the dilute glucose solution even as her head throbbed from the motions she was making. When the dryness in her mouth had receded to tolerable levels, she lay back and just breathed for a minute.

There were other figures in the room, she noticed, though she had to work to bring them into focus. Her mother and her father on her left-hand side, peering down at her with expressions of worry more severe than she had ever seen on their faces; at the foot of her bed was her grandfather, whose eyes darted away when her gaze moved in his direction. And in the corner of the room, fixing her with an unblinking stare, was a dark-haired woman whose name she couldn't recall, but who she felt she knew from somewhere very recently.

'Hey, everybody,' she said, straining to raise her voice above a whisper. 'What'd I miss?'

An exhalation resounded in unison from the four figures gathered around her bed, somewhere between a sigh of relief and a groan reproaching her for that feeble attempt at levity.

'No more field trips for you, young lady,' her mother said weakly. She looked as exhausted as Alyssa felt. 'And for as long as I live, never scare me like that again.'

'How do you feel, hon?' her father asked.

It was a surprisingly complicated question, requiring her to take a mental inventory of her present condition. 'Sore,' she answered, truthfully. 'Groggy. Confused. How did I get here, exactly? Something feels strange around my stomach. Not painful, just sort of *off*.'

'You'll get used to it, in time,' spoke up the dark-haired woman. She had a long, heavy coat wrapped around her. 'There's programmable matter replacing your damaged bone and tissue. It's lighter and stronger than what was there before, but it'll take some time for your immune system to adjust to it. You'll feel fragile for a few days, like you've got the flu. Don't worry about it, but try not to exert yourself too much.'

Alyssa stared at her. The woman's voice swam across the surface of her memory, like something from a fever dream or a hallucination. There was something tremendously important about her. 'I feel like I know you,' she said.

The woman smiled. 'It's a pleasure to meet you, Lys. I'm Victoria, our grandfather has been telling me all about you. From what I hear, we're cousins, of a sort.'

'It was you who destroyed that thing. You were there when... when...'

Up until that point, the order of events that had led to her awakening in sickbay had seemed remote, like a half-remembered sequence of dry facts from a textbook she might have read years ago, subordinate to her immediate and disorienting surroundings. Abruptly, they became as real to her as the most polished TSI sim; the battle in the burning meadow; the crackle of the energy beam missing her by centimetres; the impact of Marcus shoving her out of its way.

Something darker and more frightening than pain rose in Alyssa's chest, wrapping its tentacles around her heart. Her vision narrowed; her pulse quickened; her breathing became quick and ragged. She tried to say something to the effect of, '*I can't believe Marcus is gone,*' but instead, she found herself sobbing, 'Marc. Oh no. Oh no. Oh shit.' Tears streamed down her cheeks unimpeded. A rational corner of her mind realised, with astonishment, that she was experiencing a full-blown panic attack.

'Lys, try to hold still,' Derrickson said levelly. 'I'm going to give you something to help you calm down.' Alyssa felt a pinprick in her right shoulder, and a different sort of drowsiness took hold of her. Her thought processes slowed dramatically, and with them, the physiological ravages they inflicted. The anguish and grief remained, but for the time being, they were indistinct and generalised, their piercing clarity stripped away.

Victoria walked over to her side. Under her dark coat, her armour glimmered in the orange light of the sunset. 'It wasn't your fault, Alyssa,' she said. Her strange, glassy voice was firm. She took Alyssa's hand in hers, her fingers hard and smooth as marble. 'It was mine; I should have been faster. I'm sorry about Marcus Lawson. I know what it's like to lose someone you cherish right in front of you. That pain, that grief; don't let them rule you. Use them. Harness them.'

***

Jonah left the sickbay with Victoria by his side, surveying the crew's progress as they walked together to the convoy gathering in the clearing where he had first seen her fall. He, Eoin, Ilsa, and Rahman had spent most of the day wrangling the other settlers, persuading them that, yes, the situation really was urgent enough to abandon the settlement, without being able to disclose exactly what the situation was. The paramilitary command structure that had been enforced aboard the *Prospice* had never been formally dissolved, but it had loosened after landing and transitioning to an agrarian lifestyle. The Big Four, as they were known, had nominal authority over the community but rarely had cause to enforce it in the day-to-day running of the settlement. In this time of crisis, Jonah's prerogative for unilateral command was being stress-tested; his implants were being flooded, second-by-second, with demands for an explanation, in tones that varied from courteous to worried to angry. His authority held for the moment; people were doing as they were asked. But an explanation would need to come soon.

By nightfall, Pilgrim's Progress had been stripped down to a phantom of what it had been that morning. All non-essential materials were being left behind to make room for food, fuel, seed banks, and the like on their eastward journey. It made for a peculiar tableau, like an extrasolar Joad family gearing up to leave the Dust Bowl. Victoria had insisted to Jonah and Eoin that their schedule for the evacuation had to be accelerated and that everyone be ready to move out by morning. She had declined to say exactly why, so far. 'Best to let everyone know at once,' she had said darkly. 'It would do more harm than good if rumours or misinformation were to spread.'

The settlers they passed were frantically busy, but they all paused in what they were doing when Victoria walked by to stare and mutter. Jonah himself couldn't resist shooting her furtive glances, trying to get a handle on this uncanny entity claiming to be his granddaughter.

She had convinced him, to his satisfaction, that she was, in fact, the same Victoria he had once seen play Vivaldi for him in recordings sent to his cabin on the *Prospice*. She had been able to repeat back to him, verbatim, messages from over a century ago that no one other than she, Jean, James, and possibly her grandmother, Astrid, would have seen. Even so, her sudden appearance was stranger than he could fathom, let alone in this form she had adopted, which seemed closer to divine than mechanical. She had donned the jacket he had lent her in an attempt to make her silver endoskeleton less conspicuous, her wings having retracted into her shoulder blades. She stuck out like a sore thumb all the same, and would have done even in a community where everyone didn't know everyone else.

There was something about the way she moved that unnerved him. She didn't have the staccato, stutter-stop quality to her movements that had characterised the prosthetic body he remembered; she seemed to possess a degree of articulation at least as fine as any human body or face. Her movements were, if anything, too perfect, lacking the subtle irregularities, the unconscious little twitches and shifts in bearing that characterise human motion. He'd noticed that she never blinked.

'Those wings aren't just for show, are they?' Jonah asked her quietly. 'You can actually fly?'

'Right now, I can fly about as well as the Prospice can,' she replied, nodding in the direction of the derelict starship. 'The Archangel frame was made to move around in space, in the absence of gravity or atmosphere. I couldn't generate nearly enough force to keep myself in flight here, let alone escape the gravity well of a planet the size of TransTerra.'

'In that case, how exactly were you planning to get back to Earth?'

She gave him a look he couldn't decipher.

'I didn't come here from Earth.'

'Wherever it is you did come from, then?'

'There might be nothing left for me where I came from. In any case, I'll cross that bridge if I come to it. One day at a time, Starman.'

***

Jonah accepted a deep bowl of lentil broth and a mug of water from Julie Nguyen. She and Jack, her younger brother, operated a hastily-assembled stand at the edge of the massing convoy, doling out food to the settlers, doing their part to help them work through the night. Jonah consumed the soup quickly, wiping his mouth with the back of his hand; he'd been famished, and in the short term, he anticipated taking meals whenever he could.

Eoin greeted them upon their arrival at the convoy. Jonah hoisted him up from where he lay underneath a caterpillar transport's treads. His hands were sticky with the viscous vegetable oil he had configured the settlement's motors to run on. He had spent the afternoon hooking up cannibalised components from the settlement to ensure they had as many vehicles available as possible.

'What do you think, Jonah?' he asked, gesturing across the meadow. 'Seven caterpillars ready, another two close to completion, and four dozen Humvees awaiting your command. Even with modular design on our side, it's a bloody engineering miracle to have done this in a day.'

Jonah pursed his lips, quickly calculating in his head. 'It's not enough.'

'I knew you'd say that, you prick.'

'We've got just about enough here to carry six hundred souls, Eoin, even before we consider supplies. And if just one person has to walk, it'll slow our progress eastward to a crawl.'

'Maybe they'd run if we told them what might be nipping at their heels. Speaking of which, might you get around to explaining what that is while we're still young, your Highness?' Eoin presented Victoria with a mock bow. He was still upset about how he had been manhandled earlier that afternoon.

Victoria surveyed the massed settlers in the meadow. 'Is everyone already here, Lieutenant?'

'Almost. A few stragglers are still disassembling their dormitories.'

'Would you summon them, please? You're right; it's high time you all knew what you're up against.' She nodded towards the crater where the machine – which he now understood to be a 'Scarab' – had fallen two nights earlier. 'Over there would be good.'

Jonah sent out an announcement to the general population. Their corneal implants flared up with a message whose subject line read **TOP PRIORITY – GATHER IMMEDIATELY ON EASTERN PLAIN.** 'Done,' he proclaimed. 'I'll arrange a stretcher so that Alyssa can join us as well.'

'Thank you,' she said. 'While we wait for everyone to arrive, tell me if I can help with the preparations in any way. I'm quite strong, you know.' She flashed them both a smirk. Eoin grumbled under his breath.

'You can help by disassembling some of the remaining modules and bringing them over for reassembly. We're going to have to start getting ruthless – taking apart the sickbay, the water reclaimers, the Lighthouse...'

'The Lighthouse?' Victoria repeated, quizzically.

'It's the name we have for the communications array,' Jonah said, gesturing southwards towards the structure that could be clearly seen over the heads of the other buildings in the twilight. 'Everything that we used to keep in contact with Earth before we were cut off. Nowadays, its main function is meteorology, but we maintain a passive signal at all times in the hope we might...'

Victoria's head snapped around, the glow of her blue eyes intensifying to a bright glare in the encroaching dark. She raised her left hand, palm splayed in the direction of the Lighthouse, and a beam lanced out towards it.

The effect was like seeing a house fire play out in fast-motion. The kilometres of wiring that occupied the tower, instantaneously superheated by whatever laser variant Victoria was emitting, burst into flames. In the enclosed space of that room where the only aperture was the doorway, oxygen was sucked in from the air outside, feeding an exponentially growing firestorm. In a matter of seconds, the walls of the tower could no longer contain the building heat and burst apart, the scaffold below collapsing and the entire structure tumbling to the ground. The plume of flame from the explosion illuminated the whole settlement and the surrounding fields. People shielded their eyes and covered their ears; many screamed.

'Jesus Christ, woman!' Eoin roared. 'What the hell are you thinking!?'

'That array was a liability to all of us, every second that it stood,' Victoria answered, disquietingly calm. 'Don't panic. I checked for infrared signatures first. There was no one in the immediate vicinity; no one was hurt. And besides, I think that's a better way of getting the stragglers' attention than a text message, wouldn't you say?'

***

Victoria stood atop one of the newly assembled caterpillar transports. Below her gathered 816 men, women, and children, everyone unerringly attentive to her words. Floodlights had been hurriedly erected to ensure everyone could see. She had discarded the jacket and spread her wings, the better to command the crowd's attention.

'The Earth you knew is gone,' she pronounced. The Archangel frame somehow amplified her voice so that it boomed out across the Mercanta Steppe. The silence she left in her wake was deafening.

'On 18th October 2135, something entered Earth's solar system. Some...' she seemed to grasp for words, '...some sort of interstellar leech. A parasite. The world's governments shot it down with nukes, but it survived, concealing itself on the dark side of the Moon. As it transpires, we are not alone in the universe.

'At first, nothing seemed to have happened, but then a kind of psychic plague began to take hold of the world's population. The parasite enslaved minds, turning people to its will. The ones under its control appeared to remain themselves, retaining every aspect of their personality while they moved amongst the population until they were able to mount their insurrection. We call them The Collective.

'For all intents and purposes, Earth is now occupied territory. It did not go without a struggle; during the fighting, the array broadcasting messages to the *Prospice* was destroyed, hence why you were cut off in 2145. We developed a means to resist psychic incursion, but too late – those who resisted the psychic influence of the Collective were simply culled. Some humans, a few thousand, escaped, most of them using early Archangel frames. I was one of them.

'A human insurgency was formed under the command of Captain Hermann Albrecht of the Orbital Reconnaissance Corps. We sought shelter on the Martian and Jovian outposts, but the Collective came and drove us out of those too, metre by metre. The inhabitants who did not join the Insurgency were either assimilated into the Collective or were shot down trying to escape.

'Most of our members transitioned to prosthetic bodies capable of harnessing solar radiation, so that we might survive in space indefinitely. The Collective pursued us, drove us further and further from Earth, from one moon and asteroid base to the next, out beyond the solar system into deep space. We fought back where we could, destroyed supply lines and scout transports, tried to slow the Collective's advance. We made upgrades to the Archangel frames, implemented femtech and programmable matter to make ourselves more effective guerrilla units. But it was three thousand of us against eleven billion of them, and that ratio has only grown more in the enemy's favour in the past one hundred and ninety years.'

Here she paused in her speech for a moment. Abruptly, she floated down into the crater. Seconds later, she emerged, holding the dead Scarab aloft before her in one hand. The crowd flinched back from her where she looked, but remained silent, listening with the utmost intensity.

'The Collective's control now extends beyond the solar system,' Victoria resumed. 'They have made technological strides at an incredible pace. One of these has been an extension of the principles involved in the quantum fluctuation drive. Rather than warping space as a means of propulsion, they employ twinned relays to allow for instantaneous movement between two points, even across light-years. A network of these relays has been constructed, expanding progressively outwards from the Earth.

'The Collective is determined to complete its subjugation of our species. This colony represents the final piece of its mission, the last outpost of free humanity in the universe. The Insurgency has worked to divert its attention from the *Prospice,* and later from TransTerra, for almost two centuries. We've sabotaged its operations, slowed its advance, but we have only ever managed to divert the tide, not stop it. Six months ago, we intercepted a communication indicating the Collective was finally ready to attack this settlement.

'Commander Albrecht dispatched me as the vanguard of a rescue effort. We've occasionally been able to hijack the use of the quantum relays. Acting swiftly, we managed to arrive ahead of the Collective by a few hours. I successfully destroyed their advance force two days ago – that was the dogfight you witnessed – but my frame was critically damaged in the fight and crash landing. My higher functions shut down to conserve power while my automatic repair processes did their work. I encoded the emergency signal to be broadcast in the event that I couldn't reach your colony directly.

'Although I destroyed the Collective's scout units, when news of their failure reaches their command post, they will undoubtedly return in greater numbers. We have a head start of days, perhaps only hours, to conceal your presence on this planet and wait for extraction by my comrades in the Insurgency.'

She tossed the dead Scarab to the ground and hooked her fingers into a groove in its melted armour, where there might once have been a faceplate. She exerted herself – Jonah thought he saw her biceps and shoulders bulge with effort – and ripped off the alien thing's blunt protuberance that loosely equated to a head. She held it before her like a trophy. The crowd murmured; the words were indistinguishable, but the cadence was one of horror and fear.

'They will kill you,' Victoria declared, 'or they will tear open your spinal column, turning you into one of them. An appendage of that parasitic hive-mind, with your consciousness trapped and wordlessly screaming while your body betrays your own kind. I've seen it happen. If you're faced with the choice: choose death.'

The settlers dispersed once Victoria had made her point clear. Eoin leaned in and whispered in Jonah's ear, 'That ought to light a fire under 'em.'

***

Her new ribs and abdomen still ached abysmally, but Alyssa was discharged by Dr Derrickson at 2.00 am. To his own incredulity, he didn't see any urgent need for her to be treated or that she shouldn't be walking around – and anyway, a stretcher was one more item of cargo the overladen convoy didn't have space for.

In the pale light of the predawn, the gutted settlement had an ethereal, haunted look to it. Alyssa had accessed video footage before of 20th and 21st-century cities that had been abandoned by inhabitants fleeing the advance of a war; skeletal brick-and-mortar structures with their empty insides exposed to the elements, serving as their own tombstones. She wondered how long it would take the foliage and the winds of the Mercanta Steppe to completely reclaim her birthplace.

Against her mother and father's protests, she had been helping to assemble their family's Humvee. Some of the parts used in the internal combustion engine were twins of equipment she had used in the botanical nursery, and she knew them like the back of her hand, but every few minutes she had to pause when the pain in her midriff became too severe. Even in the chill of the early morning, she was perspiring from the exertion. She didn't care – she needed something to occupy her attention, anything to distract her from the events of the last day.

She felt a presence coming from behind while she was installing the battery. She looked over her shoulder, grimacing at the twisting motion it entailed, and saw Victoria standing there, cloaked again in the coat she seemed to think made her inconspicuous. Her expression was as unreadable as ever, but she was noticeably hesitant in the way she approached her, stopping when Alyssa made eye contact.

'How are you feeling, Lys?' she asked, gently. She had immediately taken to the nickname Alyssa's close friends and family used for her.

'Better now, thanks. Relatively speaking, anyway. I'm still pretty freaked out.'

'Of all the ways we could have met, right?'

'Right. But, you know, I'm glad we did. You are, by far, the most interesting out of all of my cousins.'

Victoria snorted at that, which took Alyssa by surprise. It was the first time she had heard her exhibit a spontaneous response. There really was something human in her. 'Thank you, Victoria, for everything. For saving my life, what, three different ways? In a day?'

'Think nothing of it. What else could I have done?'

Alyssa thought how best to answer that when another spike of pain passed through her midsection. She gasped and slid to a sitting position, her back against the Humvee's bumper. Victoria started towards her.

'Are you alright?'

'Yeah, just give me a moment. It passes.'

'You shouldn't be pushing yourself. I told you, it will take a few days for you to acclimate.'

'All hands on deck just now, right? You said yourself, we don't have long to get out of here.'

'Let me help.' She moved in and peered under the vehicle's bonnet. 'My father used to like classic cars. He kept an old manual-drive Aston Martin that was his pride and joy. He used to let me help him tinker with the engine on weekends.' Her mechanical hands moved through the vehicle's interior like a concert pianist.

'Manual-drive? God, how old did you say you were?'

'That's a bit of a complicated question. In objective time, I suppose I would be two hundred and twelve years old. But by now, I've spent so much time travelling at relativistic speeds that, to me, it seems a lot less than that. I lost track of my subjective age a long time ago.'

Alyssa whistled and could think of nothing further to add. They sat in silence for a few moments.

'There's just one thing that bothers me,' she said eventually, voicing her thoughts aloud.

'Just one thing?' Victoria asked, with what Alyssa could swear was sarcasm.

'OK, a lot of things, but one thing in particular. Why did you never contact us before?' She turned her head to look inquisitively at her peculiar cousin, the Archangel. 'You said that the communications array was destroyed in the fighting a hundred and ninety years ago, but surely your Insurgency could have warned the *Prospice* about everything that happened to Earth at some point on its journey? Why wait until the Collective was about to attack us to get in touch?'

Victoria remained quiet for an uncomfortably long time, her attention seemingly fixed on the Humvee's engine. Finally, she replied, 'Commander Albrecht will be able to answer that better than I can. You'll meet him after we get to the rendezvous point to the east.' She turned to look at Alyssa, a genial smile animating her features. 'Until then, you can trust me to keep you safe, I promise. I won't let anything else happen to my family.'

Chapter 8

December 7th, 2135 C.E.

The ride from the top of the Congolese elevator back down to the surface lasted ten hours. Jean and Tony's transit pod was a little over halfway down when the next phase of the Enclave's expansion began.

Jean had spent most of the ride down reviewing the financial news feeds with increasing dismay. Her stock portfolio was tied to various interests in Southeast Asia; if these trends continued, she'd have to start taking her day job a little more seriously. Tony was being quiet, the vacant flickering of his eyes a telltale sign he was conferring with his superiors through his implants.

The pod was sparsely furnished, but it included a transparent floor and walls through which she could observe the brilliance of the sunset to the west. The Brazilian elevator cast a shadow that quickly lengthened from horizon to horizon. As the sunlight failed, a ripple of artificial light moved gradually eastward as the world's cities transitioned to night. To the east, she could identify Nairobi, Mombasa, and Mogadishu; to the west were Lagos and the offshore Liberian arcology with its roots in the Atlantic seabed. She imagined what it might be like to see them from an Archangel frame, soaring free in space, coasting on thermals of distended vacuum.

The first sign she noticed that something was wrong came when Tony's eyes stopped flickering. For three or four full seconds, he stared straight ahead, unseeing, then jumped to his feet.

'What's wrong?' she asked.

'The Enclave,' he answered. Sweat was beading at his temple. 'Something's happening inside it. A massive power surge lit the whole place up like a Christmas tree for just a few seconds.'

'I thought all of the power lines to the interior had been cut?'

'Well, I don't bloody know how it's happening, do I!'

Alerts started streaming into the peripheries of Jean's vision all at once from her news feeds. Visuals of the Enclave in Hong Kong from a hundred different angles. The dark mass squatting at the city's centre appeared to *pulse*, a dull glow building to a blinding intensity in a matter of seconds, then receding to blackness just as quickly. Not from the street and office lights; this was more like an ambient luminescence, permeating the air, throbbing outward in a dome like a nuclear explosion.

In her real sight, outside her implants, she noticed something out of the corner of her eye. Far below, in the Horn of Africa.

In the centre of Nairobi, looming steadily larger in their field of view as they descended, a perfectly circular region maybe ten kilometres in diameter was no longer emitting any light.

A new Enclave; far larger than the one in Hong Kong.

The news feed images continued to corroborate one another in real time. Another pulse followed like the first. Then another, and another. After the fifth, the world held its breath. Finally, no more.

Tony flicked his head in a way that indicated his attention had been caught by something in his cochlear implants. 'It's happening all over,' he said. 'More Enclaves appearing in Sydney... Athens... Vancouver...' He swallowed and looked Jean in the eye for the first time in hours. 'London,' he finished.

***

Upon arriving in Kisangani, security guards bundled Jean and Tony out of their pod with the bare minimum of procedure. The arrivals lounge buzzed with the voices of angry travellers. Within minutes of the appearance of the five new Enclaves, all departures by orbital elevator and vacuum pod had been cancelled globally – no doubt the PNC's edict. They had to be seen to do something to quarantine the Enclave Effect's spread.

'So, we're stranded then.'

'Maybe not.' Tony's retinas were flickering back and forth in an unnerving fashion. His new position clearly required him to be an adept multitasker. 'Give me some time. I'll lean on a few people and get us a transit concession through to Beijing.'

Her implants chimed with new updates on the international crisis practically every second. She applied a few notification filters to get a better idea of what had happened at her home. The Enclave that had appeared in London encompassed the area southeast of the Thames, stretching from Croydon to Dartford. The rest of the city had resumed martial law. Her own apartment lay just outside of the affected circumference.

The videos flooding the virtunet all told the same story, a reprise of the one that had been seen in Hong Kong weeks earlier. At 3.21 am, every man, woman, and child inside the area of effect had just... *stopped,* at the exact same moment, their features overtaken by the same glassy, absent expression. In the few seconds' worth of footage that were broadcast from the affected area before all communication ceased, they'd all turned and moved indoors, out of view of drones and spy satellites, their movements taking on an uncanny synchrony.

One clip that was achieving fast virality came from an adolescent girl, returning home from a night on the town with her friends, livestreaming the tail end of a drunken evening through her implants. 3.21 am hit right as she was on the boundary of the effect. Alcohol had dulled her faculties, so tens of seconds passed before she noticed that her friends were trailing behind her. She turned back, and saw her companions standing stock still, all sharing that same, vacant expression.

'Abby? Mandy? Th'fuck? What's wrong with you guys?'

The girl moved back toward her friends, stumbling in heels through the snow blanketing the pavement. She crossed the invisible barrier demarcating where the new Enclave began. The drunk mumbling ceased, and she halted in her tracks. She straightened, and the livestream ended without fanfare.

Jean shuddered.

She realised with an unpleasant jolt; her son James would have been within the area of effect if it had happened just three months earlier. He had moved to Birmingham in September from his old flat in Thornton Heath. She felt relief at the narrow escape, but her mission took on a new urgency in her mind.

Her cochlear implant buzzed – a call was coming in from Carlos Alvarez. She found a corner which, if not private, would at least prevent her from being jostled by slighted commuters making their frustrations loudly known.

Judging from the image he presented to the camera, Carlos hadn't moved from his lab since Jean and 'Roy' had left him – his normally sparkling eyes were dull and bloodshot. 'Are you alone?' was the first thing he asked, with none of the joviality he'd presented hours earlier.

'Relatively speaking, yes.'

'Relatively speaking, or yes?'

Jean sighed, and ducked into the bathrooms nearby, cloistering herself in a toilet stall. 'OK, happy?'

'It'll do. But I hope you understand, Jean, I'm only talking to you, not your companion. I wouldn't even be doing that if I didn't think I was in your debt.'

'Anything you can say to me, you can say to Roy.'

'Ah, yes, "Roy." I know you're not an idiot, Jean, so please don't take me for one. You must realise that he has ulterior motives for this technology.'

'Technology – what? What are you talking about?'

'I trained the lab's sensors on the moon, just like you said, and what I found was unlike anything that ought to be able to occur in nature. Stray photons, electrons, neutrinos, all radiating outward from the Dark Side, but their spin and polarisation were changing spontaneously! It was enough to call into question the Uncertainty Principle itself. Heisenberg, Schrödinger, Einstein – they all have to be re-evaluated, that's how massive this is.'

'Carlos. Please, I only have high-school-level physics to go on.'

'Didn't they teach you anything about how my inventions work in Basic?' he exclaimed. 'Anyway, the point is, whatever – let's call it what it is – *alien* phenomenon I was measuring, it spiked when these new Enclaves appeared groundside. And considering the source of your tip, that means the Chinese know more about the nature of this phenomenon than they're letting on to the rest of the world.'

'The Chinese are only playing their cards close to their chest because they're afraid other organisations might already have been infiltrated by the Enclave. That's why they came to me in the first place.'

'Jean, you can't afford to be this naïve, not in your line of work. Your Tony Liu – don't look so surprised, of course I know who he is – he's been flagged as a potential person-of-interest in ORC's database. He's only been with the Chinese intelligence services for eight months. Prior to that, he was a cyberwarfare specialist working for Yang-Mitsubishi, the head of a corporate counter-espionage unit. He left the company without notice or explanation and showed up in the ranks of China's spooks two weeks later. I'm told he's moved up the hierarchy quickly and that he has access to a very generous expense account.'

'So you're suggesting... what? That the Chinese intelligence services and Yang-Mitsubishi are in bed, and that they're somehow responsible for the appearance of the Enclave Effect? That their first impulse was to use it against their own populace? Why? To what end?'

'Surely you've heard of MK Ultra? If it can happen in America, why not China? You don't think that there were organisations – governments – who saw a political opportunity in the Engagement, a chance to get a toehold in a new theatre of war?'

'Paranoia doesn't suit you, Carlos.'

'Maybe not. But I've worked with scientists from Yang-Mitsubishi before, and I still keep in contact with some of them. Do you know what the hot topic has been there in the last few years? Using quantum entanglement to design a next-generation neural lace, one that enables genuine, mind-to-mind telepathy. All I'll say is that if the Engagement didn't change the course of their research, then they're fools beyond compare.'

Jean remained silent. She was naturally inclined to distrust conspiratorial thinking, but the information that Carlos brought to bear was hard to disregard. She didn't like to think that she had been used as a pawn in some grand political power-play – even though it was an outcome she should have been ready for when she got into bed with a foreign secret agent.

'I'll take it into account. Thanks for thinking of me, Carlos.'

'Don't thank me; just watch your back. If it helps, consider my obligation to you fulfilled.'

***

The virtunet's public fora were ablaze; the PNC was catching hell for shutting down the world's transportation network. The very kindest of the 'net's pundits called it a rash, poorly thought-through means of containing the Enclave Effect when the vector of its spread was a total mystery.

Then there were the ones who, Jean would, under normal circumstances, have dismissed as fringe wingnuts, but whose discourse was beginning to gain an alarming amount of traction with the mainstream. It was the oldest play in the conspiracy theorist's handbook – the PNC were accused of being the cause of the appearance of the Enclaves; that they were using them as a false flag operation, creating a pretext to steamroll over the governments of sovereign nations and institute their planned New World Order. Within hours, the world would see organised, populist violence an order of magnitude greater than that which had consumed Southeast Asia for the past weeks.

What worried Jean most was that she couldn't discount the possibility they were right; it wasn't any crazier than what Carlos was proposing about the Chinese. The world was going insane, and, for her sins, she'd been tasked with making sense of it.

She found a seat in the arrivals lounge and sat down heavily. She chewed her lip.

Another thing: which company was it that had supplied the equipment that night on December 3rd for the commando squadron's failed incursion in Hong Kong?

She tabbed away from the push and pull of acerbic political commentary and looked up Yang-Mitsubishi's publicly accessible site. She was greeted by a UI secretary – manifested as a slender Asian woman, of course – against a sensory backdrop of abstract, shifting patterns of white and teal, scored with impersonal etherpop.

The UI was primed to address enquiries in over 200 languages, and Jean quickly realised that answers in every one of them would be some variation on the same nebulous corporate-speak she loathed about the private sector – words like 'solution,' 'innovation' and 'integration' wielded like they were incantations, while declining to provide the listener with any information they could actually *use*. However she phrased her request for the locations of Yang-Mitsubishi's regional offices, she was politely and circumspectly directed to leave a message with the UI so that it could 'address her query to the party it would concern.' The entire site was a roundabout way of telling the public to piss off.

No matter. In the time it took her to order a coffee and a pastry from one of the arcology's overcrowded food stalls, Jean was able to manufacture a virtunet signature associated with one of Yang-Mitsubishi's clients, an independent vertical farming operation based out of Nigeria. No one big enough to warrant attention, but still worthy of access to their corporate portal, and with it, direct contact information for their worldwide offices.

Yang-Mitsubishi was a global conglomerate, one of the Earth's largest high-tech manufacturers, headquartered in Tokyo but with satellite offices on all seven continents and in virtually every major city in the world, to say nothing of orbit. That knowledge didn't get her anywhere; remembering what Carlos had said, she narrowed her search parameters to include only the offices primarily concerned with communications technology. The graphics in her corneal implants rearranged themselves, and just like that, she had her answer, complete with street addresses and bird's-eye-view images:

Yang-Mitsubishi plc.

Floors 186-195

Vancouver Arcology

Vancouver

British Columbia

Canada

Yang-Mitsubishi plc.

771 Indigo Bay

Sydney

New South Wales

Australia

Yang-Mitsubishi plc.

Muthurwa Business Centre

Nairobi

Nairobi County

Kenya

Yang-Mitsubishi plc.

Floors 88-92

Xenofontos Neocropolis

Athens

Attica

Greece

Yang-Mitsubishi plc.

Floors 14-36

Thames Arcology

London

United Kingdom

Yang-Mitsubishi plc.

Units 47-89

Tai Koo Complex

Hong Kong

People's Republic of China

'Hey!'

Jean was startled out of her TSI reverie – Tony had grabbed her shoulder. He peered at her, a curious look on his face. Back on the ground, the vulnerability he'd shown in orbit had evaporated. 'Thought I'd lost you for a moment there. Come on, I've managed to get us a vacuum pod through to Beijing *via* Dubai.'

Jean worked not to let her concern show.

'They're seriously opening up the tunnel just for you?'

'My higher-ups have the PNC's ear, and they know how important what we're doing is. Now, more so than ever.'

They squeezed their way through the arcology's vacuum terminus. Kisangani was bustling at its quietest, but it was only becoming more crowded as more and more travellers found themselves stranded in the arrivals lounge. The noise and the stink of the crowd jammed up against the souvenir stands and the fast-food outlets was overwhelming.

'So, who was that you were talking to just now?' There was something in Tony's manner that either hadn't been there before, or that she just hadn't noticed; an eagerness like hunger. She considered the possibility that he might have been watching her more closely than he let on; and if so, how much she could feasibly lie to him about.

'It was Carlos, as chance would have it.'

'And? He didn't mention anything about measuring the effects of the Body? It's only the whole point of everything we've been doing, Jean.'

'I asked him, but he's not got a terribly refined sense of urgency. He's only just now setting up the instruments to make the measurements we need. He called because he knows I live in London, and he was concerned that I might be caught up with everything going on groundside. Believe it or not, Tony, he called because he cares about me as a friend.'

Tony snorted. 'Well, then I wish he'd stop pissing about and get on with it. In case it isn't abundantly clear, the world's about to come crashing down around our ears, and the information he can provide us with could help to prevent that. OK, this is us.'

A pair of harassed security guards were ushering them into a private vacuum pod bound northeast. Jean paused with a dozen metres to go.

'What now?' Tony barked, making no effort to hide his irritation.

'You go on ahead. I have another call to make first.'

'It can wait, do it *en route*.'

'No, it can't wait. It's my mother, Tony. She's ill, and she's just outside the London Enclave. I need to know if she's ok.'

'Jean, for God's sake, the best thing you can do for your mother's welfare is to co-operate with me just now.'

'You can go to Beijing without me, be my guest. I'll happily terminate our contract here and now, if that's what you want. I can look after myself, believe me.'

Tony sighed, and glanced the guards. 'Two minutes. But no more, ok?' He stalked into the vacuum pod by himself.

Jean walked off, pantomiming that she was looking for privacy in the throng of pedestrians. When she was sure that she was out of Tony's direct line of sight, she began striding as fast as she could without breaking into a run. She ducked out of the crowd, and made for the seldom-used capillary walkways and staircases that would lead her away from the terminus, toward the arcology's ground floor. She couldn't leave by vacuum pod, but she would find a car by some means and drive north. Hell, she'd hike if she had to. For now, the most important thing was to put as much distance between herself and Tony Liu as possible.

Without slowing her pace, she sent out a communication to David Manderly. She waited thirty seconds for him to respond before her call was rejected. Not really surprising – it was midday in Beijing, and David would be buried under the stresses of the morning's events. His answering service prompted her for a message.

'Dave, it's Jean. I need to speak to you the minute you get this. I believe Yang-Mitsubishi is implicated in the appearance of the new Enclaves. Right now, I need someone I can trust. Last time we spoke, you said you'd owe me one. I have to call it in sooner than I thought.'

The sun was rising, its harsh equatorial glare making itself known through the arcology's glass exterior. Looking out at the city below her, she could see that many others had the same idea as her – the roads were already choked with the kind of traffic that hadn't been seen in decades. Their emissions shimmered in the heat haze; some of the bumper-to-bumper automobiles must have been antiques, with manual drive and fossil fuel-powered.

She knew a couple of ex-servicemen in Kisangani. Not more than distant acquaintances, but there was an off-chance they might give her a ride out of the city. She tried to raise communication with them, but she had trouble connecting to the local server. Distracted, she rounded a corner into a stairwell and collided with someone's chest coming the other way.

'Excuse me.'

'I beg your pardon, Ms Harrison.'

Jean glanced up, and staring back down at her was a lean-faced African man, fifteen centimetres taller than her. He wore a nondescript black shirt and cargo trousers, but his posture read as former military.

The unobtrusive graphics that lived at the fringes of her corneal implants during her waking hours stuttered briefly, and then shut off. Her connection to the 'net had been severed.

Another man as big as the first approached, arms folded, wearing the same carefully anonymous wardrobe as his friend. Together the two of them blocked the way down the stairs.

A throat was cleared behind her; she turned and saw two more men approaching from the way she'd come, hemming her in. Looking around, the corridors that had been swarming with other pedestrians moments ago now seemed curiously deserted.

She turned back to the man that had jostled her. 'Move aside, please. I'm in a hurry.'

'We'll need you to come with us, Ms. Harrison. You're needed elsewhere.'

'I'm an independent British citizen. Tell Mr. Liu he has neither any cause nor any right to detain me.'

He and his friends closed in, and he made to grab her by the shoulder.

Old instincts took over. Jean seized his wrist in a pincer-like grip with her right hand, pivoted counter-clockwise and drove her left elbow into his cheek. Her carbon nanofibre-enhanced muscles generated the force of a pneumatic piston, focused into a point of bone laced with titanium. His cheekbone and jaw shattered – his head was smashed into the adjacent concrete wall. He slumped to the floor. As she'd suspected, he'd received some enhancement himself – otherwise, she'd have left nothing but a red smear where she had struck.

His comrades, to their credit, reacted quickly. Jean saw a flicker of surprise in one man's eyes at his ally's incapacitation; it lasted for maybe an eighth of a second. Definitely ex-militatry; fight-or-flight reflexes wired to a hair trigger.

They weren't armed, what with their being inside the security checkpoint of a major transportation hub. One of them, a sinewy white man, attempted to bull-rush her. He hoped to use his greater weight to pin her to the ground and incapacitate her, but he hadn't had Jean's experience of time in space; he lacked her ingrained appreciation for the dynamics of mass and momentum.

Rather than try to meet him head-on, she sidestepped and caught his arm, jumped off her feet and brought them both crashing to the floor. After a moment of his ineffectual grappling, she wrapped her legs around his bicep, locked in an armbar, and wrenched. Every ligament in his shoulder tore like tissue paper, the bone popping out of its ball-and-socket housing like a champagne cork. Whatever combat instincts the man possessed, they didn't stop him from howling at nearly having his arm ripped off.

Jean sprang to her feet and vaulted over the railing of the stairwell before the two remaining mercenaries could react, dropping to the floor below – the impact rattled her teeth, but her augmented bones absorbed the shock unscathed. Without pausing for breath, she ran. Two thuds behind her told her that the same idea had occurred to the mercs, and they were giving chase.

She'd been relying on the guidance of her implants to lead her out of the arcology; without them, it was a rat's maze of crisscrossing tunnels and corridors. She ducked into a staff door at random, hoping that she could lose her pursuers by losing herself. She was out of the arcology's public areas; sanitation facilities, administrative offices and storerooms flashed by as she sprinted.

Just as she was convinced she'd lost her pursuers, a door to her right was flung open and an impact in her side knocked her to the ground. She fell hard on her front, air rushing out of her lungs. Before she could properly draw breath, a cold metallic vice closed around her throat from behind, dragging her to her feet.

She thrashed, but her new attacker had fully bionic arms, and his grip was unyielding. In the struggle, she almost didn't notice the stabbing sensation of a needle at the back of her neck, just above the top vertebra.

Her vision began to blur, and she tried the only thing that occurred to her; clenching her abdominal muscles, she raised her legs above her head so that her whole body was suspended. The corridor they were in was narrow – she found purchase with her feet against the wall facing her and kicked back as hard as she could. Her adversary overbalanced and fell in a heap with Jean on top of him.

His grip briefly loosened. She wrenched his arm free of her neck and turned to face him; the profile that greeted her was that of another crew-cut, private-security lackey type. Gunmetal grey limbs extended from his collarbones on down. She aimed carefully and punched him once, hard enough for his head to crack the linoleum floor where it snapped back. His nose crumpled in a bloody mess; teeth clattered down the hallway.

She rose to her feet, gasping for breath, and made to keep running.

One step.

Two.

And then the world exploded.

The burst of sensory stimuli was unlike anything Jean had ever experienced; she was untethered from reality, floating free in the midst of an infinite, eternally morphing, kaleidoscopic orgasm of light, colour, and sound. It was akin to the terrifying dissociation she had felt during the Engagement, but a hundred, a thousand times more acute, more lucid. Yet, it was different – it lacked the nauseating existential horror, the dreadful pain. In their place, she felt a sense of tremendous wonder, even joy. Or rather, all of the thousands of different emotional states she concurrently occupied were in some sense tuned towards joy.

There was no notion of time in this sensorium; she could have been suspended for seconds or a hundred years. Eventually, though, the deluge began to narrow in its focus. White noise resolved into a babble of voices. Shapes and abstract patterns coalesced into faces and bodies. There were other beings in here with her, Jean realised, other units of consciousness. The multitude flocked towards her, attracted by her confusion and disorientation, like a chattering school of dolphins greeting a human lost at sea.

They welcomed her, beckoned her to join them. They knew her as intimately as anyone had ever known her; they were privy to her every fear and regret, every hidden desire and guilty impulse. They knew of the buried resentment she had borne her father since he had left her behind at six years old. They knew of the irrational anger she had felt towards Victoria when she had suddenly found her floating in that awful hospital laboratory. They knew of her fleeting wish that it had been Stephen who survived, and of her profound shame at having felt those things.

They understood all, and they forgave all.

Their presence remained, but some sense of her own body and her physical surroundings began to return to her. She was surprised to find that she was on her knees. Tears were streaming freely down her face, and she was alternately sobbing and laughing maniacally.

Jean had never been inclined towards religion, never truly given the matter much serious consideration, but she had heard the accounts of men and women who spoke of the presence of a benevolent God as a necessity of the human condition, of the need for the forgiveness of a universal mind to mitigate the terrible isolation of being a person. Now, just such a universal mind had been made manifest to her, and she had been granted a salve for pains so deep and fundamental that she had pushed them out of her conscious mind. Fear of death, fear of pain, fear of bereavement, all evaporated, dissolved within the shared consciousness. And in their absence, a new feeling; an awful, unfathomable sorrow, directed outwards to the pitiable, lonely souls who could not share in what she felt. The billions of men, women, and children, all of them benighted the way she had been up until this moment. She wanted them to join her in this paradise she had discovered.

She racked her brain for a name for it, and her new companions piped up that the world had already provided one – *Enclave*.

She added her own, new voice to the collective, bolstering it, strengthening it. One of them was close by, she realised. Through tear-blurred eyes, she saw a man in physical space standing before her, holding out a hand to help her to her feet. She accepted and stood. She was face to face with Tony. He was beaming at her.

So, you understand now?

She drew a deep, shuddering breath. *Yes. I understand. What can I do to help?* She asked the Enclave, and the Enclave answered.

Chapter 9

June 29th, 2326 C.E.

The settlers of Pilgrim's Progress travelled east with all the speed they could muster. The treads of the convoy's caterpillars flattened the grasses of the Mercanta Steppe at a steady thirty kilometres per hour. Ahead, the foothills of the Prometheid mountains loomed, and the air carried with it a bite of frost.

The sun was sinking in the rear-view mirror; Jonah yawned in spite of himself. He had managed to catch a couple of hours' catnap the previous night. Otherwise, he was running on three times the recommended dose of stim tabs, which kept him awake but not necessarily lucid. Victoria looked at him.

'You know, I could drive for a while if you feel the need.'

'Drive' was a strong word for it. The caterpillar's course was pre-programmed; Jonah was responsible only for keeping his hand on the manual override in case of emergency. He shook his head. 'I'm fine. What about you? Do you ever sleep, or is that something else you left behind?'

'Not at all, I sleep. I'm sleeping right now, in fact. Dreaming, even.'

Jonah blinked, uncomprehending. 'So, who am I speaking to?'

'My secondary consciousness. Sort of a second "me" that comes out when I need her.'

'And all of your Archangel bunch have this?'

'Certainly. We need to be able to operate autonomously in space, sometimes for months at a time. You need another person there to bear part of the mental strain. You'd go crazy, otherwise.'

'I can't even begin to fathom that.'

'It's not all that outlandish, actually. It's a cognitive design trick based on flesh-and-blood human psychology – don't you ever phrase thoughts as a dialogue between yourself and another voice in your head?'

'I suppose so.'

'Same thing. The voice in my head is just a bit more proactive, that's all.'

Jonah opened his mouth to argue that no, that wasn't the same thing at all, but all that emerged was another yawn. Victoria smiled.

'Shift over,' she said. 'I'll take us through the night. We're making good time. We should be among the first ones at the rendezvous.'

At Victoria's insistence, the 'convoy' was in fact thirteen small convoys. In order to deter the Collective's pursuit, they had fanned out from their point of origin at the settlement, following a variety of different, arcing trajectories east. They would re-converge at Victoria's rendezvous point with the Insurgency at the foot of the Prometheid mountain range, 2,200 kilometres away as the crow flies. The course Jonah's group had plotted curved northward a fair distance – their entire journey would take them over 3,000 kilometres, all told.

The caterpillar he was sharing with Victoria and the lion's share of their food and fuel carved a furrow through the interminable grass. Behind followed four Humvees, each stuffed with as many passengers as they could carry – bales of maize and containers of purified water were lashed to their roofs with bungee cords. Among the passengers were Brandon Lawson and his extended family.

Before departure, Jonah had allocated a few minutes for a sparse service to the memory of Marcus Lawson. Brandon had shaken like a leaf throughout – groundborn, only sixteen, his brother had been like a parent to him. Jonah had made a point of checking in on him every few hours by walkie-talkie.

He reluctantly shifted over and conceded the manual override to Victoria. His body felt heavy, freighted with age and responsibilities. The moment he allowed himself an iota of relief, he sagged, feeling himself drift away from consciousness.

'Sleeping feels like a betrayal,' he muttered. 'Like it's only by staying alert that I can keep those monsters at bay.'

'That's a good instinct,' Victoria replied. 'But for a few hours at least, leave it to me. You're only human, Starman.'

The thought crossed Jonah's mind before he closed his eyes: *So, what does that make you?*

***

He dreamed of Earth as a blue pearl in the distance. He sat in the command deck of the *Prospice*, ordering Eoin to accelerate toward it, harder, ever harder, but it kept receding in the blackness. He turned to regard his crew, but where they ought to have sat, there were Scarabs. Dozens of them; but rather than the featureless oval faceplate, the part that Victoria had ripped off, each of them had Jean's face. Her organic skin and hair extruded from their smooth, oil-black metal bodies. Her eyes were closed, her features slack.

He was startled awake by the sound of thunder. Sleet rattled against the caterpillar's windscreen. The convoy was now climbing in earnest, switchbacking up the Prometheid foothills. The weather and the terrain would be rougher from here on out, and the going slower. Victoria faced forward, her hands on the override in the same position they'd been before he'd slept, her face the same unblinking, unreadable mask she defaulted to.

The walkie-talkie buzzed on the dashboard, Alyssa's voice coming through with a slight crackle.

'Welcome back to the land of the living, grandad,' she said. Jonah was relieved to hear a little of the girl's old bravado coming through in the staticky connection. A little shakier than it might once have been, but she'd rallied from her ordeal with remarkable strength. She was riding with her parents in the caravan Ilsa was leading, far to the south of them. 'Glad you're awake, I wanted your input on something.'

He rubbed his eyes and stretched, working a knot out of his lower back. 'What's the problem, Lys?'

'"Starman"? What's that all about?'

Jonah groaned. 'Oh. That old chestnut. Were you talking with your cousin about me while I was napping?'

'Yep. So, come on. Are you going to give me ammunition to tease you with or not?'

109

It was strange. It had been when Victoria had called him that old nickname, the one he'd only ever grudgingly accepted, that she'd convinced him that this strange being really was his granddaughter, returned from a previous life. 'It's a reference to David Bowie,' he admitted. 'Long story.'

'David-who?' Alyssa pressed.

'Bowie,' Victoria confirmed. 'He was a pop star in the late 20th century. Wrote a song called "Starman" in 1972, a fable about an alien bringing hope to Earth.'

'Bowie died on January 10th, 2016,' Jonah said, picking up the explanation from Victoria like a relay baton. 'By coincidence, it was January 10th, 2116 that the *Prospice* crossed the 4.24 light-year mark in its journey, making it further from Earth than Proxima Centauri, the moment we became truly interstellar. The media back on Earth loved that, apparently. They made a theme of it. Spun it into a narrative about humanity's ongoing aspirations towards the stars, or something.'

'They did,' Victoria confirmed. She turned to look at Jonah, and her smile had a warmth to it he hadn't previously supposed the Archangel frame was capable of. 'It's one of my earliest memories, seeing your face in those broadcasts, always accompanied by that one song. James and I, we took to calling you "Starman," and Mum ran with it, and it just sort of stuck.'

Alyssa laughed, the sound coming from the handset in bursts of white noise. 'Well, can I hear this song?' she asked.

'Your wish is my command,' Victoria replied. She opened her mouth wide, and the sound that came out wasn't a human vocalisation but a recording from 1972. For four-and-a-half minutes, the caterpillar's cabin was filled with strains of ragged acoustic guitar chords, overlaid with Bowie's caterwauling voice.

'Wow,' Alyssa breathed when it was finally over. 'That was *terrible*.'

'Wasn't it, though?' Jonah sighed. 'Now imagine being inexorably tied to it by your grandkids.'

Victoria shrugged. 'Aesthetic standards were strange in the 20th century,' she said. 'After electric instruments were invented, but before the direct neural interface, artists got drunk on power. They delighted in making sounds that were coarse and rough, and took them in all sorts of regrettable directions.'

'Still,' Alyssa said, 'it's at least *interesting*, isn't it? As a time capsule? And now...' Her voice quavered. 'We had so much saved in the *Prospice's* databases. Centuries of knowledge and experience, and now...'

'It's not all lost,' Victoria reassured her. 'The Insurgency isn't just a barracks full of fighting machines. We try to do our part to carry on humanity's legacy. We have to, otherwise the Collective wins. And anyway, how else are we supposed to pass the time between the stars?'

'You mean you have artists? Poets?'

'Sure. I still dabble in composing, myself.'

'Really? I'd love to hear sometime.'

Victoria was silent for a moment. Then she opened her mouth. What emerged sounded like an interplay between a cello and a harpsichord; mournful, arpeggiated figures from the two virtual instruments swirled around one another in slow, deceptively complex harmony and counterpoint. The concerto made Jonah think of mortality, of late autumns and late evenings, gentle decline towards silence and stillness. After a couple of minutes, it tapered off, no crescendo having been reached.

'It's a work in progress,' Victoria admitted. 'I haven't thought of a name.'

'It's beautiful,' Alyssa breathed. 'The walkie-talkie doesn't do it justice.'

'I'll let you hear it properly once we get to the rendezvous, I promise.'

'It's a date. Over and out.'

Victoria was quiet for a while after that. She gazed absently out of the window, though what she could see in the blackness of this stormy night, Jonah couldn't guess. It dawned on him that she was avoiding his gaze.

'You know,' he said, 'there's a question I've wanted to ask ever since you woke up, but I haven't been able to figure out how.'

'About Mum, right? And Gran, and James?'

Jonah nodded, ignoring the lump in his throat.

'I wish I knew,' she said. 'They're not with the Insurgency. Whether or not they're still "alive," is anyone's guess, but if they are, they aren't them. Their bodies might still be walking on Earth, as extensions of the Collective, and they might still look and sound like them, but they aren't them.'

'So that's it, then?' Jonah had spent decades wondering how he would react to this news; more than anything, he was angry. 'They're either dead, or they might as well be?'

'If I believed that, I would have given up fighting a long time ago.' Victoria faced him, defiance blazing in her blue eyes. 'However the Collective functions, whatever it does to its hosts, there is a way to reverse it. One day we'll find it. That's the hope that keeps us going.'

'If we get through this,' Jonah said, 'what kind of life is there waiting for us? Will we all have to become Archangels? Join in this war, even those of us who never knew Earth to begin with?'

'No one will force you. But you should, and for my part, I hope you will.'

The walkie-talkie buzzed again, this time with a higher pitch. The video screen bolted to the dashboard hummed to life. It displayed what was left of Pilgrim's Progress, dark hulks silhouetted against a starry sky. They had rigged up cameras in the long grass before they left, primed to alert them if their motion sensors were triggered. Sure enough, they could see monstrous figures moving within, shapes like the one that had vaporised Marcus Lawson. Unlike the limping, cumbersome figure Jonah had encountered at the crash site, these moved with a precise, predatory gait, their speed surprising for their bulk. They scuttled around his former home in sudden, explosive bursts of motion, seemingly probing for signs of life. His skin crawled.

'Scarabs,' Victoria hissed.

The Collective was moving as she had foreseen, a reconnaissance party converging on the largest and most obvious structures visible from orbit. Nodding in tacit agreement, Jonah withdrew his detonation switch and entered its five-digit key.

This had been Riley O'Brien's idea, which worried Jonah a little. For a girl whose job was to help life flourish, she possessed a surprising bloodthirsty streak. She had pointed out that TransTerra's atmosphere was slightly more oxygen-rich than Earth's, about 24% by volume, just enough to make fires burn a little brighter. Just enough to make incendiary weapons a little more efficacious.

The year's mild climate had provided the settlers with a bumper crop of maize, which, by this point in the autumn, was well on its way to being ground for the fine flour it produced. There was more than the convoy could hope to carry; dozens of tons had been left behind to spoil in the damp open air. Rather than waste it, Riley had contrived an ingenious method to conceal their tracks while also raising two defiant fingers to the Collective. A pump she had jury-rigged together with her acolytes in the botanical nursery compressed, and blew thousands of kilos of the finely ground meal into the dusk surrounding the settlement, mixed with just a touch of vaporous, highly volatile vegetable oil. After that, a spark was all it took. The Scarabs paused and turned in sync, alerted too late to the thermobaric cocktail now enveloping the settlement. Their faceless forms almost seemed to register surprise in the split second before being hurled into the air. The feed cut out in a flash of fire.

When he had been ten years old, Jonah had witnessed a silo explosion. Twelve kilometres distant from his parents' rural homestead, it had visibly brightened the horizon that cloudy afternoon. Firefighting drones had been deployed from four neighbouring counties to combat the spread of the resultant wildfires through the surrounding fields. The low-tech fuel-air explosive the settlers had improvised was an order of magnitude more potent. Although they were hundreds of kilometres away from the site of the detonation now, Jonah thought – imagined? – he saw a faint glow emitting from the western horizon.

Whoops of vicious joy resonated from the walkie-talkie. 'Got the bastards!' came Riley's voice, incandescent with fierce pride. Jonah joined in with the communal celebration through his handset, grateful for the spike of adrenaline waking him all the way up. Here, at last, was proof positive of a corporeal enemy who could be fought and defeated, something his military-trained imagination could contain more easily than the riddles and mysteries of the last few days. He stopped only when he noticed Victoria's solemn profile, with a single furrow in her smooth, pale brow.

'We've bought maybe a couple of hours,' she said. 'Be assured: they *will* keep coming.'

***

Wary tension permeated the following day and night. On Jonah's orders, radio silence was to be maintained except in the direst of emergencies. The Collective were monitoring for any slip-up on the settlers' part, and even Victoria couldn't vouch for how sensitive their instruments might be.

Progress for the 36 hours following the detonation was slow but steady. The landscape became steeper and more rugged as they entered the Prometheid mountains in earnest. Over six hours, their procession gained more than a thousand metres in elevation. The grass, which had been a constant in the settlers' lives for two decades, began to thin out as they ascended into biologically barren river valleys. Topographical maps, drawn up by the *Prospice's* sensors when they first arrived in the system, came in handy, finding passes through the forbidding slopes, some over 3,000 metres above the planet's sea level. Jonah privately offered thanks to whichever deities might be listening that the winter snows hadn't yet closed in – the caterpillar was having a hard enough time grinding a path through the silt and scree as it was.

When they were within 200 kilometres of the rendezvous point, Jonah called a halt for half an hour. His group was ahead of schedule, and his joints had stiffened enough that he could almost hear scraping sounds when he shifted in his seat; they could afford a brief break before meeting with Victoria's allies and God-knew-what challenges that might pose. The caterpillar and the Humvees in its wake drew to a stop on the shore of a mountain lake, disgorging their haggard passengers.

Half a hundred men, women, and children milled around the stony valley floor, absently working the knots out of their muscles. Under more auspicious circumstances, they might have looked like a tour group come to gaze at the surrounding scenery.

As it was, there was no mistaking them for anything but the refugees they were. The emotional and physical toll exacted by the last three days had begun to show in earnest; families huddled together, sheltering each other from the biting mountain winds. They exchanged few words; most took the opportunity to bolt down some cold bread and broth. Jonah stripped to the waist and quickly washed in the lake, welcoming the bracing cold of the near-freezing water with a shiver. Only a week ago, he realised, Ilsa would have flayed him alive for contaminating a virgin water source with his terrestrial sweat and

114

dead skin cells. Now, the sanctity of TransTerra's biosphere was so far down his list of concerns it didn't even register.

While drying himself off, Jonah overheard a conversation conducted in hushed, urgent tones. Behind one of the Humvees, he found Victoria being confronted by a red-faced Brandon Lawson. She stood impassively, three inches taller than the groundborn teenager, but he had planted his feet in defiance, his hands balled into fists.

'And *I'm* telling *you*,' the boy said, in what would have been a shout if he hadn't been whispering, 'that we have the upper hand. The bomb in the settlement proves it! I've accessed TSI sims about Afghanistan, back on old Earth. The Graveyard of Empires, they called it. We could be like the Mujahideen, learn to fight as guerrillas. Make the Collective hurt so badly that it won't be worth their resources to keep pursuing us, and then we'll be free!'

'You don't understand,' Victoria implored, a note of exasperation audible in her glassy voice. 'The Collective isn't like the USA. It isn't like the Soviet Union. It isn't even like the Crusaders. It's a hive intelligence, committed to one singular purpose: erasing other minds and replacing them with copies of itself. There is no threshold beyond which it wouldn't commit more resources. As long as it knows one human remains free, it will bend its entire will towards finding that human.'

'But—!'

'Brandon!' Jonah snapped. 'What is this?'

The pair turned to face him; Brandon looked considerably less humbled than Jonah would have liked. 'I'm saying that this planet is our home. My ancestors dedicated their lives so that we could live here. My brother... my *brother died* defending our right to live here. And now she snaps her fingers, and just like that, it's all over because she says so? Shouldn't we at least *try* to fight?'

'Brandon, I understand how you feel, but this is not open for discussion. We have to think of what's best for the settlement, and, like it or not, we're meeting up with Victoria's people. Now get back in the Humvee; we're heading out in five minutes.'

The boy glared back at him, his eyes moist.

'I should have known you'd take her side. You've been following her lead like a dog ever since she showed up. Jonah Harrison, the great starship captain. What happened to all the leadership you showed when it got my brother killed?'

Brandon turned and stalked away. Jonah had half a mind to call after him, to tell him that he was right, that it was his own fault, his stupid boldness that had cost Marcus everything. But the words stuck in his throat.

***

'He and his brother were close,' he said to Victoria, feeling sheepish. 'Brandon never had much of a relationship with his biological parents. Marcus was like a father to him.'

'It's OK,' Victoria reassured him. 'This war, no one knows how to process it. I've seen it in my own comrades, even people I've known for decades – emotions come out in odd ways, at odd times. If it's any consolation, I'm sure he'll be fine in time. He's reckless because he's brave. He has…'

She froze mid-sentence; her eyes bloomed with the same blue luminescence they had shown the moment before she had destroyed the Lighthouse days earlier. Her head snapped to face west, down the valley in the direction they had come.

'Wasps!' she cried; her voice amplified enough to make Jonah's ears ring standing next to her. 'Take cover! Behind the rocks, under the vehicles! HURRY!'

The other settlers appeared bemused at first, but upon hearing the panic in the Angel's tone, their questions died before reaching their lips. They scrambled to conceal themselves, glancing about for the source of Victoria's distress. Jonah huddled underneath the caterpillar with Nino and Giuliana Orsatti and their daughter, Olivia. The angle at which it had been parked meant they had to crane their necks while lying prone to see down the valley, the direction Victoria's attention was focused. The four of them held their breath.

Minutes passed. Jonah became increasingly aware of a shard of scree digging into his ribs. He was almost ready to ask aloud what 'Wasps' were when the answer made itself clear.

A dark cloud appeared in his view, moving up the valley unnaturally fast, swirling to and fro in patterns that gusts of air couldn't account for. It glittered with flashes of pale blue light. Magnifying his corneal implants, Jonah realised with a shudder what kind of particles the cloud was constituted from.

Tiny, robotic insects, each no more than a couple of centimetres long, clustered tightly together in a swarm of hundreds that coordinated itself as though with a single mind. Individually, they resembled miniaturised versions of the hulking Scarabs prowling around the settlement before the bomb: featureless, jet-black, ovoid bodies with six protruding limbs, grasping as though feeling the texture of the air, tasting it, smelling it. The glitter he had noticed came from a blinking light in the centre of the body. Just as the thought occurred to him, he was dazzled by one of the blinking lights turning to meet his gaze. Within a fraction of a second, a thousand others like it turned in unison, all pointing straight at him.

Before he could recoil, he felt a needle being forced through his eye and upward into the grey matter of his brain. It was a sensation he vividly remembered from when he was eight, and, over his mother's protestations, he had looked directly into the sun with an unfiltered telescope. Sensing the photonic overload, his corneal implants compensated by narrowing their aperture to a pinprick, and Jonah saw scores of the Wasps falling to the ground, melted, twitching, and smoking.

The beam emanating from Victoria's palm burned through their ranks. The survivors scattered, dispersing throughout the valley, their coordination abandoned.

Victoria hopped down from the rock on the northern slope where she had perched herself and beckoned the settlers out from their hiding places. As Jonah approached her, he was unnerved by what he saw. He was certain her face was constitutionally incapable of turning paler, but it appeared to have done so all the same.

'They saw us. They saw *you*,' she said, pointedly looking at her grandfather. 'The Collective knows our location. Worse, it knows our vector. Scarabs will already be descending from orbit, locked onto this convoy. More than I can fight off this time.'

A dismayed murmur rippled through the group. 'What do we do!?' The cry came from behind Jonah; turning, he saw it was from Brandon, all the bravado the boy had shown earlier having evaporated.

'We...' Victoria hesitated. 'We have eight, maybe ten hours at the most before they're on top of us. Our best option is for this group to disperse and make the best possible time to the rendezvous point. Give them multiple heat signatures to track, and hopefully thin their ranks. The Insurgency is our only chance at this point. Yes. Yes, if we can meet up with Commander Albrecht before they reach us, we win.'

***

The caterpillar's engine whined as the treads ploughed through the gravel and detritus of the Prometheid mountains' eastern slopes at sixty kilometres per hour; every gauge and digital readout in the cockpit glowed red. Jonah ignored them; he was preoccupied with raising each of the other convoys on the walkie-talkie. He had weighed the risks: on the one hand, by breaking radio silence, he potentially led the Collective to the other convoys' doors. On the other, if he or any of his group were captured by the Collective, to judge by what Victoria had told them, the others' locations were forfeit, regardless. Better that they should be forewarned.

The mountain valleys wrought havoc with radio signals, but as their elevation declined, he started to discern human voices responding to his hails through the fuzz of static. More and more of the other convoys became intelligible in their communication, beginning with the nearest one twenty klicks to the north led by Will Derrickson. Jonah laid out his warning to each of them in turn. None of the other group leaders reported having witnessed any sign of the Collective's pursuit like he described. This didn't particularly set Jonah's mind at ease – without Victoria present and cognizant of what to look for, something like the Wasp swarm could quite easily have passed the other travellers by unnoticed, particularly at night. Nevertheless, he was grateful that they realised the gravity of their situation in short order, and all duly began to redline their engines.

That was, until he tried to raise Ilsa's frequency. She had been leading the southernmost convoy, her plotted route skirting the edges of the marshes and swamps that characterised TransTerra's equatorial regions. At first, he thought he was just struggling to get a signal over the distance that separated them –

118

the walkie-talkies were reliable, but their range was limited, and they were next to useless across distances of much more than five hundred kilometres. But then he heard a series of violent concussions penetrate the static, and it became clear that something was terribly wrong.

'Ilsa!' He yelled into the handset that he held in a white-knuckle grip. 'Respond! What's going on?'

More concussions, followed by a faint, strained voice.

'Scarabs!' Jonah had never heard Ilsa sound panicked before the way she did now, not even during the communications failure on the Prospice all those years ago. 'Jonah, don't come here! Get as far away from our vector as you can. God, there are dozens of them! We'll try to lead them away, try to buy you some—'

A final concussion sounded, louder than the last, and then the connection was severed altogether. Jonah replaced the handset, dazed. He tried for a moment to process that this was how his relationship with one of his oldest and most trusted crewmates spanning two centuries had ended. As a result, he punched the caterpillar's dashboard hard enough to bloody two of his knuckles.

'I'm sorry,' came Victoria's voice from the seat next to him.

'Ilsa was... she was... goddammit!' Jonah cried. He could feel his composure failing him, and he suddenly felt so very old and weary.

'No, I don't mean that. It's... Jonah, I'm so sorry.'

He turned to look at his granddaughter, and she appeared nothing like the regal demigod who had inspired awe and fear throughout the settlement. He recognised the look on her face; it was the same expression Jean had worn when she was six years old. When she had learned that he was leaving on the Prospice forever, she had asked him tearfully if it was because of something she had done.

'It's my fault,' she said. 'I made a mistake.'

'What are you talking about?'

'When I fought the Collective in orbit, before you found me, one of the Scarabs got a hold of me. Dug its claws in. It was going for my central nervous system; that's how they take control, make you into one of them. I fought it off, but they've adopted a new tactic recently. If something stops them from getting through our armour, they leave behind a kind of tracer for their friends to find: a radioactive isotope that becomes commingled with the Archangel frame's matter. It's faint, almost undetectable if you don't know what you're looking for, but to the Collective, it's like a beacon. With everything that's happened, I just forgot to run the diagnostic for it. It's how they knew where to look for us, and how they…'

Jonah saw his own dawning realisation reflected in Victoria's eyes. She had donated some of her body's matter to Alyssa to save her cousin; the matter contaminated with this beacon isotope.

Alyssa, who had been riding with her parents in Ilsa's party.

***

Three of the other convoy groups had already arrived at the rendezvous point when they got there. They were led respectively by Rahman and two of his former sergeants from the *Prospice's* security team, Anahita Lajani and Eric Carmichael. The two hundred-odd settlers in their care milled around the plain Victoria had designated as the Insurgency's landing site. There was no sign of their supposed allies.

The mood that greeted them was grim. Even the unfailingly stolid Rahman looked close to exhaustion. Upon seeing Jonah and Victoria emerge from their caterpillar's cockpit, they converged on them, clamouring for directions about what to do next.

'Where the hell are your people?' Carmichael demanded of Victoria point-blank. 'According to the itinerary you gave us, they should have been here an hour and a half ago.'

Victoria looked impassive, no longer displaying any of the vulnerability or the pain she had revealed to Jonah hours earlier. 'Most likely, they're tied up evading the Collective in orbit. They probably had to plot a more elliptical course to evade detection after the enemy's reinforcements arrived. It's imperative that their presence remains concealed in this system for as long as possible; the escape plan hinges on it. Rest assured, Commander Albrecht is coming. He's led hundreds of operations, many of them more difficult than this one, and pulled through every time.'

The crowd grumbled at that, but didn't press the issue any further.

Two hours passed, and the eight remaining convoys rolled in one by one. Ilsa's group was all the more conspicuous for its absence. Jonah ensconced himself in his caterpillar's cockpit, trying repeatedly to raise them on the radio, while Victoria remained outside trying to placate the growing and increasingly agitated crowd. Again and again, his hails were met with silence, not even static on the other end; he kept trying anyway. There was still no sign of the Insurgency, and Scarabs could very well be dropping out of the night sky at any moment. His remaining life could potentially be measured in minutes; knowing this, he realized that all he wanted to do was talk to Alyssa again, however briefly, however remote the chance she had survived.

He had failed her in the battle in the crater; he had failed her when she fought for her life in sickbay. He had failed her, the way he had repeatedly failed his family all his life; providence had kept giving him chances to redeem himself, only to fail again. He had determined that if fate afforded him one last opportunity he didn't deserve before the end came, then that would be the one he didn't miss.

He was distracted by a rapping on the cockpit door. Rahman's face peered in through the window. 'We need to talk,' he mouthed through the plexiglass.

Jonah sighed, reluctantly replaced the handset, and stepped out. 'What?' It came out sounding more petulant than he had meant.

'It's about her.' Rahman jutted his jaw in Victoria's direction. 'Captain, I know you don't want to hear this right now, but her story doesn't sit right with me. I don't think she is who she says she is.'

'You don't think she's my granddaughter? Rahman, we've been over this – she knows things no one else could know.'

'Sir, if you truly believe that, then I believe you. But it's not her lineage that concerns me. The things she's told us don't add up. If she has allies coming to back her up, why didn't they all arrive at the same time? Why didn't they contact us at any point since 2145? And then there's the big picture – alien hive intelligences, deep-space resistance movements. Doesn't it all seem too fanciful to you?'

'You have a better explanation for why we lost contact with Earth? For everything we've seen these last few days?'

'No, I don't. But not having all the answers doesn't mean I have to accept the first story I hear. That's how religion happens.' Rahman was the only person Jonah had ever known who could be glib under these circumstances.

'OK, fine. It's a lot to swallow. What do you suggest we do about it?'

'Confront her, get the whole truth. I don't believe she means us harm, but whatever her motives, whatever her agenda, we have the best chance of making it through this if we know where we really stand.'

Jonah made to argue further, but his reply was cut off by the faint sound of multiple sonic booms overhead, followed by cries from the settlers. Looking up, he found the source of the sound at once. Trails of flame were tracing across the night sky, brighter than the stars, too fast and too low to be astral bodies. He counted thirty-six. Adjusting his corneal implants to their maximum resolution, he could discern within one of the streaks of hot gas a matte-black shape, six limbs swept back behind it. To judge from the screams erupting around him, everyone else had done the same.

Among the seven hundred-odd settlers, there were a total of fifty-six flamethrowers. Some of the engineers had taken the initiative to convert components of hydraulic construction equipment to fire bolts at subsonic velocities. Others had cobbled together homemade Molotov cocktails and nail bombs. Jonah helped distribute these in the minutes left before the Scarabs landed, his heart weighing heavy in his chest. Aside from Rahman and Victoria, none of the others had seen the enemy up close; they didn't have the sense he did of how entirely useless the resistance they could offer even one fully functional Scarab would be, let alone a squadron of them.

Victoria appeared at his side, peering up at him. 'Grandad,' she said in a small voice, and his breath caught. She didn't call him Jonah or Starman but 'grandad'; an appellation he hadn't heard since she was a small child. 'Promise me. Promise me you won't let them take you. I couldn't watch that. Promise me you'll die first. I heard you speaking to Rahman. I don't blame you for doubting me. Know that I would have told you everything, eventually, and that I would never, ever hurt you. I never stopped loving you, not once in all these years. So please, promise me this much.'

Jonah swallowed and, wordlessly, nodded.

Victoria gave him the smallest of smiles. Above them, only tens of metres overhead, the nearest of the Scarabs bore down on them with its appendages splayed, like the night itself had grown claws and grasped for them. Victoria raised her hand overhead to meet it. Her eyes glowed blue; filaments of energy coursed along her forearm.

The Scarab was impaled upon a spear of blinding light. Jonah closed his eyes against it, the sudden illumination leaving a lurid purple bruise on the inside of his eyelids. When he dared to squint again, the spectacle that greeted him left him at a loss for words.

Maser beams were raining from the heavens, scorching through Scarabs left and right. The machines flailed around, scanning for the unseen adversaries that had caught them unawares. Some managed to get off one or two retaliatory shots before they were run through in turn. Within a minute, all thirty-six were lying on the plain, twitching and crippled if not completely inert, white-hot exit wounds dripping like melted butter.

A soft thud, muffled by the thick grass, sounded behind Jonah. He turned, startled, and standing there was a young-looking, androgynous figure with blonde hair and pale skin. Its armour and wings changed colour as he watched, from pitch-black to burnished silver that glinted in the moonlight.

More Archangels like him dropped to the ground around the settlers; they seemed to snap into view, but despite their speed, their impacts scarcely disturbed the ground where they landed. Jonah counted fifteen of them.

Time seemed to stand still, neither the Angels nor the settlers moving. Then one of the Insurgency's number stepped forward. He was distinct in appearance from the rest – where they all looked like beautiful youths, he sported a shock of white hair tapering to a widow's peak, and a sharp jawline and cheekbones. Apart from the wings, he was like an illustrator's idea of a decorated career soldier in his late forties or early fifties. His expression was mirthless.

Victoria approached him and offered him a peculiar salute, which the man did not return. 'Lieutenant Harrison,' Albrecht pronounced, his voice clipped and void of inflection, 'as of this moment, you may consider yourself relieved of duty, pending court-martial on charges of desertion and insurrection.'

A.N. Milne

124

Chapter 10

July 2nd, 2326 C.E.

Albrecht's indictment of Victoria hung in the air. None of the settlers had known what to expect of their first contact with their would-be rescuers, but that hadn't been it.

Victoria offered no response or rebuttal to the accusations levied against her. Jonah cleared his throat and tried to catch Albrecht's eye. 'Commander,' he offered, 'on behalf of the *Prospice's* crew, thank you for the assist.'

Albrecht's head turned almost imperceptibly to regard him, but otherwise, he didn't move. His face was unreadable, but Jonah was beginning to get the feeling that he didn't warrant much of the Archangel leader's attention. 'Captain,' he replied finally, speaking with only the faintest trace of a German accent, 'I'm glad you and yours made it here mostly unscathed. I'm aware of your service record, and your granddaughter speaks very highly of you. I wish we could have met under more auspicious circumstances.'

'I feel the same way. So, what's the plan here?' He gestured expansively at the massed men and women around them. 'Victoria tells me that you have a strategy mapped out for extracting us off the planet.'

Albrecht frowned, and the expression rendered his artificial face even more severe than its default. 'She does, does she? As it happens, we have a transport cruiser parked in orbit, large enough to accommodate your people. Automated personnel shuttles were dispatched along our descent trajectory an hour behind us; they'll be here shortly to pick you up. After we've reconvened on the transport, we'll need to run interference against the Collective's pursuit. Once we've lost them, we'll return to our forward operating base 190 AU outside the system. Have your people rest up, Captain. If you'll pardon me, I need a word with the lieutenant in private.'

He turned on his heel and stalked away; Victoria made to follow him.

'Wait!' Jonah cried. Albrecht paused and turned back to face him. The other Archangels were all staring at him now; he had the disquieting sense that he was now the specimen in the petri dish. 'What's this business about insurrection? Aren't you going to tell us what's really going on here?'

'Respectfully, Captain,' Albrecht said in a tone that conveyed anything but respect, 'the lieutenant's infractions are of concern to she and I, not you. You had your part in this operation, and you played it well, but now it's over. I have business to attend to, so please let me do my job.' He continued on his way, Victoria close behind. Chastened, Jonah returned to the crowd; the other settlers parted to let him through.

A weather-beaten hand clapped him on his shoulder. '"Respectfully, Captain,"' muttered Eoin, his voice mocking Albrecht's. 'Who does this wanker think he is? Doesn't even outrank you.'

***

The Archangels didn't tend to communicate with one another verbally, Jonah noticed. With all the time they spent in hard vacuum, separated by millions of kilometres of distance, their customary method of communication must be through an electromagnetic medium. After a while, he supposed it must become second nature. They directed the settlers, organising them into orderly groups in advance of the shuttles' arrival and checking for any medical conditions that spaceflight might disagree with. They did so mostly with monosyllabic grunts and gestures; their interactions with each other seemed to consist entirely of meaningful looks and pregnant pauses.

Commander Albrecht must have accused Victoria out loud for the settlers' benefit, as a way of publicly shaming her. He found himself liking the man less and less.

Albrecht's subordinates made no move to stop Jonah from approaching their Commander – what threat could an unarmed flesh-and-blood human offer, after all? – where he was perched with Victoria, away from the convoy's headlights. The two of them crouched, facing each other, their wings making them look like roosting silver eagles. They were silent, naturally, but stared at each other with unblinking intensity.

Albrecht glanced up at him. 'Should I have made it clearer that I wasn't to be disturbed, Harrison?' The veneer of politeness he had afforded Jonah earlier was nowhere to be found now. That suited him just fine.

'Perhaps I should make a few things clear to you,' Jonah shot back. 'Over the course of a Terran week, I have had maybe a cumulative twelve hours of sleep. I've been shot at by machines like something out of a nightmare. I've learned that the Earth I left behind may have been conquered by an alien hive mind. I've seen my home of two decades levelled by a fifty-tonne fuel-air explosive that I set off. And I've witnessed friends and family die while I was powerless to stop it, most recently my eighteen-year-old granddaughter. So, with all due respect, Commander, I'm in no mood to be treated like something you found on the sole of your boot. If you want my co-operation from this point forward, you will address me with the regard that my position and my official rank warrant. Beginning by explaining to me what your problem is with Victoria.'

Albrecht glared at him, then made the motion of heaving a sigh; another nuance of human communication Jonah presumed was for his benefit. 'I'm disappointed that you couldn't piece it together yourself, Captain. I thought you, of all people, would know what it means to play a long game.'

'Lieutenant Harrison told you the truth about Earth. She told you the truth when she said that six months ago, we learned of the Collective's plans to take the settlement inhabited by the former crew of the starship *Prospice* and their descendants. What she neglected to mention—' (Victoria averted her eyes) '—was that upon gaining this information, I deemed that it was not a worthwhile use of the Insurgency's time and resources to prevent that attack.'

Jonah said nothing, but his anger must have shown on his face, because Albrecht continued.

'Put yourself in my position, Captain Harrison. Do the arithmetic. I'm fighting a war to liberate eleven billion humans from Collective control. We number in the thousands. And your colony – of what, eight hundred? – doesn't represent any kind of meaningful tactical advantage in either direction. Certainly not one that I planned to risk good soldiers to protect. The lieutenant here, though? She had other ideas. Would you care to hear the communication she sent us, after she went AWOL?'

Albrecht opened his mouth; what came out wasn't his own voice, but a recording of Victoria's, compressed and tinny sounding.

'Commander,' it said, 'by the time you receive this, I will already be one hundred AU away. I'm going to TransTerra, and you can't stop me. Here's what's going to happen: you will follow me with a full squadron of Archangels and the means to extract to deep space at least four times the *Prospice's* original crew complement. Fail to meet my demands, and I will surrender myself and my frame to the Collective. They will know everything I know. Maybe *now* a rescue mission is worth your time. This is not a bluff. Do not test me.'

Jonah stared at Victoria in astonishment, hoping she would defend herself, protest that the recording was a fabrication. Instead, she kept her gaze fixed on the ground and remained silent.

'Don't misunderstand me,' Albrecht continued, again in his own voice. 'Truthfully, I think it's quite inspiring, the devotion the lieutenant has shown you, Captain. But as a military man yourself, I'm sure you realise that this doesn't remotely excuse the way she jeopardised the Insurgency she swore allegiance to. That is why, after this crisis is past, your granddaughter will be dishonourably discharged and her Archangel frame requisitioned, to be conferred instead upon a candidate I deem better suited to its use.'

'What?' The Commander's implication hit Jonah like a body blow. 'You're talking about a death sentence! She's been using artificial bodies since she was twelve; you can't—'

The Commander rose to his feet, glaring down at him. Jonah couldn't swear that he had reorganised his frame's programmable matter to add centimetres to his height, but Albrecht suddenly seemed very, very tall. 'Captain Harrison, it is on account of Victoria's blackmail attempt that I am here at all. Since I am here, I will see this rescue operation through to its conclusion. But be under no illusions – you and your people represent nothing other than a strategic liability to me. If you want to be afforded the respect you feel you deserve, I advise you to shut up and behave like the cargo you effectively are.'

***

Jonah found himself back in the caterpillar's cockpit, despondently trying yet again to raise Ilsa's frequency, with no more success than before. At this point, it was less an earnest attempt at finding Alyssa than it was an unthinking reflex, like scratching a rash.

Victoria had gone off to join the other Archangels in the strange, wordless communion they shared. He couldn't reconcile the figure who had sat and accepted Albrecht's diatribe without complaint with the invincible, fiery apparition who had appeared before him days before, slaying monsters and shaking worlds to protect him. He realised, now, everything Victoria had sacrificed coming here. Her fire had been a finite resource; she had pushed herself to the limits of her frame's physical capabilities and her own resolve to save them from the Collective. And now, having done so, she was spent.

A tentative knock sounded on the caterpillar's passenger-side door. Welcoming any distraction at this point, Jonah opened it and found himself faced with the blonde-haired Archangel, the first of the squadron he had seen land. Even by the Archangels' standards, he had an elfin quality to him; he looked like he could have stepped out of a story by Tolkien. The way he fidgeted in Jonah's presence rather undermined that impression, though. He saluted in the same odd way he'd seen Victoria do earlier, his hand held to his chest with the index, middle, and pinkie fingers extended, then held out the same hand for Jonah to shake.

'Captain Harrison,' he said. An accent Jonah couldn't pin down was clearly audible through the by-now-familiar glassy quality of Archangel speech. 'It's an honour. Victoria asked me to check on you.'

'Thank you, son,' Jonah replied. Of course, he had no way of knowing how old the Angel was in relation to him, but given the way he acted towards him, the diminutive term just seemed appropriate. 'Your name is?'

The Angel rattled off a slurry of syllables that he didn't know how to begin to parse; his implants' translation software kicked in automatically and rendered 'Ahkejuoksa Hartikainen' upon his field of vision.

'What is that, Finnish?'

'I'm Sami by heritage, sir; Martian by birth. Call me Aki if you like.' Aki gave him a small smile. 'I suppose you could say that living as a nomad in sub-freezing temperatures comes naturally to me.'

'Martian, hm? Colonisation was only just getting properly started when the *Prospice* set sail. I would have loved to have seen the Red Planet properly. We had to satisfy ourselves with a flyby.'

'You weren't missing much in the early days, before the self-sustaining habitats were completed. The dust got everywhere, no matter how good the filters were. It was like a fine film over everything, always in your mouth, nose, and hair, and nothing you did could completely get rid of it. It drove most of the colonists so crazy that they'd end up shaving every inch of their bodies, just to give the dust less surface area to stick to.'

'The frontier life has a certain romance to it though, doesn't it?'

Aki wrinkled his nose, a strange expression on a face otherwise marble smooth. 'Maybe it did in America's old west. Not so much when all of the settling is done under a sterilised dome, with the promise that the terraforming will kick in long after you're dead. I couldn't wait to get to Earth, to see the sky overhead without a suit on and breathe air that hadn't been filtered a thousand times. Almost made it, too. I'd been accepted to Harvard on a full scholarship, starting in the winter term of 2136, right before...' He gestured around, absently.

'Victoria told us there was fighting on Mars. You were there for that?'

The Martian's face darkened. 'I was a civilian during the siege of Arsia Mons. The Insurgency holed up there in 2139 while the Collective surrounded us on all sides. Commander Albrecht rigged the life support units with bombs and threatened to blow them if they tried to break in. The Collective's goal is to assimilate us, not to destroy us; they won't allow humans to die unless it furthers their goals in the long term. So, for a while, we held out. Almost three years.'

'But?'

'But "self-sustaining" is a relative term. They launched skirmishes against the exterior solar farms, the biofuel processing plants, and so forth—all the facilities that kept Arsia Mons above borderline. And there were more refugees inside the habitat than it was designed to sustain. Little by little, they starved us out. In the last days, the really bad days, I was so hungry I would have chewed off my arm if I'd had the strength for it.'

Aki looked pensive for a brief moment, then carried on. He seemed to talk very easily for one of his kind, like it was a relief for him. 'Eventually, riots broke out, and one of the bombs was triggered. The Collective took advantage of the chaos, and most of the half-million colonists were captured or killed. The Commander gathered up about a hundred of us, and we fought our way to the spaceport. We retreated to a base on Lysithea, and I've been with the Insurgency ever since, naturally.'

Jonah thought carefully about how to respond to all that. Aki seemed remarkably easy-going about sharing such a tremendous ordeal with him. His story probably wasn't exceptional among the Insurgency. Jonah suspected that Aki's boyish demeanour wasn't just a function of the eternal youth conferred by the Archangel frame. Albrecht portrayed himself as the leader of a well-organised army, but in truth, he seemed more like a paramilitary Fagin, taking in whatever castoffs and runaways escaped the Collective's grasp. Many of them would have been cadets in the ORC like Victoria—young men and women stranded when the fighting on Earth intensified, pushing the resistance towards space. For want of anyone else, they had rallied around Albrecht and found themselves following him indefinitely, trusting his judgment, obeying his orders, and yielding to his strength of will.

Jonah had known men like him in the RAF and the ORC: senior officers of seemingly unlimited fortitude, for whom ruthlessness and integrity were two sides of the same coin. He supposed he might have been one of those men himself, once, even if he'd never thought of himself that way—certainly during the dark years of the *Prospice's* voyage. Such men tended to inspire loyalty in their followers, but in the absence of any other authority, those followers had no opportunity to develop emotional autonomy. It explained why, despite being almost as old as him in objective years and possessing powers he could scarcely dream of, Aki and Victoria both seemed somehow adolescent. Jonah felt an unexpected pang of pity for the Archangels, as he began to appreciate the lives they had been robbed of.

'Have you always served with Victoria?' he asked.

'The Viper?' Aki pantomimed a shiver, grinning. 'Yes sir, right from the very beginning. She was my squadron leader for most of it.'

'How in the world did she get to be called "the Viper"?'

'You wouldn't think to ask that if you'd ever seen her in a dogfight. Holy shit, the way she moves! The Scarabs' combat algorithms get more sophisticated every year, and still, they never see her coming. It's strange— outside of battle, she's the most compassionate person I ever knew. It's like she stores up everything that makes her angry and lets it out every time she fights.'

'You sound like you're fond of her.'

'Quite, sir. We…' Aki abruptly averted his gaze, like he'd just remembered who he was talking to. 'We were actually an item, for a while. Long ago, now, decades. It's quite common among members of the same squadron. I hope you don't mind.'

Jonah couldn't help but laugh at the surreality of the scene; an immortal fighting machine, asking for his *ex post facto* blessing in dating his granddaughter.

'Aki, it's fine, you seem nice enough. I only wish I'd had the opportunity to get to know her as well as you have.'

Their conversation was interrupted by the sound of overhead sonic booms. He glanced upward; trails of flame highlighted the descending shuttles against the sky.

'We'd better go, Captain. Once the shuttles make ground, we won't want to delay for long. The Collective are still out there.'

'You go on ahead. I'm just going to try one last hail.'

'Will you be long?'

Jonah heaved a sigh, and contemplated the difference between making one's peace with something and resigning oneself to it. 'Did you leave friends behind, Aki, after the siege of Arsia Mons? Family?'

Aki nodded, his expression solemn.

'If you had thought there was a chance, no matter how slim, that you could have saved them, wouldn't you have stayed, right up to the last possible second?'

'It's not a hypothetical for me, sir. My brother, Oskár.'

'You have my sympathy, soldier. One of our groups was ambushed to the southwest a few hours ago. It included my daughter, Robyn, and my son-in-law, Patrick. And my granddaughter, Alyssa. Alyssa especially; if I could only talk to them one more time, if only for long enough to say "I'm sorry."'

Aki wore a peculiar look, more like puzzlement than empathy. He was looking in Jonah's direction, but not at him so much as over his shoulder, towards an unseen distance. 'Sir, there's life to the southwest, coming our way.'

'What?'

'It's faint, but it's distinct. The human body has obvious electromagnetic signifiers if you go looking for them, and there's one about eighty klicks to the southwest, heading our way at sixty kilometres an hour.'

A terribly exciting idea occurred to Jonah; a dangerous thought that took root at the back of his mind and grew uncontrollably. 'Aki – you couldn't tell if the body that's approaching is giving off the Collective's tracer isotope, could you?'

***

The shuttles, a dozen of them spread out across several square kilometres, loomed over the plain like Stone Age cairns. Jonah recognised the squat, bullet-nosed design; it derived from the old ORC low-orbit insertion vehicles, intended to carry the maximum number of troops out of Earth's gravity well at the expense of the minimum fuel.

The settlers were being hurried onboard by gesticulating Archangels – two at a time, Noah's Ark-like. Jonah disregarded them as he marched towards Albrecht, fists clenched and jaw set. The Commander was in silent conference with four of his lieutenants as Jonah approached, but turned to face him, probably alerted by one of the many varieties of Archangel ESP to his elevated pulse.

'We need to defer the launch,' Jonah announced. He didn't phrase it as a request. Albrecht blinked.

'I beg your pardon, Captain?'

'There's another survivor inbound from the southwest, a minor. Her ETA is one hour. I need one of the shuttles to hold off from launching until we have her safely onboard.'

'And I need a holiday, Captain, but that's never going to happen either. As we speak, there are swarms of Scarabs converging on our transport's position in orbit, and it will be difficult enough to get away without hanging around for stragglers. Now stop making a nuisance of yourself and get in the damn shuttle.'

Jonah took a step forward, angling his head upwards so he and Albrecht stood nose to nose. It was going to take a force greater than whatever authority the Commander thought he held to dissuade him this time. 'No,' he said, flatly. 'I am responsible to every one of these men and women, and for as long as one remains in peril, we're waiting. I will not abandon Alyssa to the Collective.' He must have started to raise his voice, because he noticed heads beginning to turn in their direction, settler and Archangel alike.

'Alyssa?' Albrecht frowned. 'How exactly did you come by this information, Harrison?'

His gaze flicked away from Jonah, towards Aki where he stood behind him, nervously bearing witness to the exchange. After a brief pause, he rounded on Jonah, now openly furious.

'You want us to defer the launch for the sake of a girl acting as a beacon for the Collective? And *you!*'

He pointed imperiously at Victoria, his amplified shout loud enough to make Jonah wince. Victoria swung around like a startled deer. 'You let your frame be compromised and yet you still led us here? I should have you burned on the spot. Take this traitor to his species and get him out of my sight. You deserve each other.'

'*I'm* a traitor to my species?' Jonah shouted back. 'You wouldn't know humanity if it stared you in the face, you fucking automaton. I know you served in the ORC, so you swore the same oath I did. Does the "no man nor woman left behind" part ring any bells? I'm holding you to that oath, right here, right—'

His speech was cut off by diamond fingers closing around his windpipe. Albrecht's arm had moved faster than he could follow; he now looked at Jonah with murder in his pale eyes.

Spots began to dance in his vision. Somewhere behind him, Eoin was shouting, but the voice of the *Prospice's* loudest man was curiously muted, as though from a receding distance. Jonah drove his forearm into Albrecht's elbow, calling upon the years of training he'd received from Rahman in *pencak silat*, but the blow yielded nothing but a dull *thud*, accompanied by searing pain that made him worry he'd bruised a bone.

He, and all the settlers, were like newborns in the Archangels' hands; they would live and die according to their mercy. Finally, just as consciousness threatened to fail him altogether, Albrecht threw him to the ground. He writhed weakly where he lay, choking and spluttering.

'I think you need your position here clarified further, Captain,' Albrecht said, composing himself. 'I came here under sufferance to effect a rescue mission, and if the best way to see that mission through is to knock you out and drag you aboard, I'll do it without a second thought. Or, if you persist in aggravating me, I may just snap your neck and leave you here, conserving the fuel we desperately need. Either way, my patience is at its limit.'

'I—' Jonah found himself racked by a series of retching coughs as he fought to regain the power of speech. 'I think you might find she has something to say about that.' He gestured towards Victoria, who had watched the fight in mute horror.

'How's that, Captain?'

'Victoria already got you to come here in the first place. She's already shown where her priorities lie, and if you force her hand, she can disrupt your little operation plenty. You're not leaving without her, and she's not leaving without me. And I—' (he pointed to the west) '—am not leaving without Alyssa. How's that for clarifying my position?'

'I see,' Albrecht replied, his tone turning icy. 'And what do you say to this, Lieutenant?'

For a few seconds, Victoria's gaze flicked back and forth between her grandfather, sprawled and bruised on the ground, and her Commander

135

standing over him. For one despairing moment, Jonah thought that his last ace-in-the-hole had failed him. Then his granddaughter met his eye, and a wordless understanding passed between them, deeper than the silent communication she shared with her comrades.

'It's as he says, Commander,' she said, her tone respectful but firm. 'We wait for my cousin.'

Albrecht stared at the pair of them, disbelieving. He snapped his arm up, and a beam of energy lanced out towards Jonah. He instinctively recoiled, covering his face with his arms, bracing himself for the split-second of burning pain he imagined would preclude his being disintegrated the way Marcus Lawson had been.

It didn't come; hesitantly, he uncovered his face, and was greeted by the smell of smouldering grass. A blackened furrow had been burned where Albrecht had pointed, half a metre to the left of where he lay.

'*One* shuttle. *One* hour,' Albrecht pronounced, then turned and stalked away. Jonah exhaled, unclenching muscles he hadn't even realised could be clenched. A silver hand extended down into his field of view; he looked up and found Victoria standing at the end of it.

***

'Pretty ballsy, Jonah,' said Will. He stood with him, watching eleven of the twelve shuttles taking off in unison, their combined power making the ground rumble like an earthquake. Their roar necessitated that his cochlear implants filter the doctor's voice from the cacophony. It had been centuries since Jonah had seen solid-fuel rockets used to escape a planet's gravity well – they seemed quaint, given the circumstances, a 20th-century anachronism when set against femtech miracles and insect-robot nightmares. Still, the iconic beauty of the vapour trails they left in their wake wasn't to be denied, especially not against the backdrop of TransTerra's sunrise. Watching them, he felt curiously at peace, a feeling he knew would be temporary, the brief elation of a minor victory, but he revelled in it all the same. The absence of shame was like a stone being lifted from his chest.

He had canvassed the settlers for volunteers, looking for fifty-seven to accompany him on the last shuttle to launch, with himself, Victoria and, he prayed, Alyssa filling out its complement of sixty passengers. Albrecht, Aki and the other Archangels were riding up on the other shuttles, with the intention that they would go on ahead to intercept and fend off the Scarabs in orbit, buying those on the ground as much time as possible.

To his relief, he had received more than two hundred requests from the settlers to be among those to stay behind, some that he'd had to firmly refuse after the quota of fifty-seven had been filled. Among them, gratefully, were Eoin and Rahman, his oldest and most trusted friends. Most of Eoin's copious family stood with him, making up almost half of their contingent's total number. Riley stood at their head, bold as ever.

'Twenty kilometres and counting,' Victoria announced, looking at the western horizon. 'On a day this clear, you ought to be able to see her in about five minutes if you magnify your vision.'

'Girl's driving like a maniac,' Eoin muttered. 'She'd better not be mistreating my beautiful motor.'

'You do realise,' Rahman retorted, 'that when the shuttle takes off, the rockets will probably slag the Humvee, regardless of what condition it's in?'

'All the more reason to treat her gently right now. You don't think the Vikings abused their longboats before lighting them on fire, do you?'

Rahman opened his mouth, then shut it again, deciding that arguing with Eoin's reasoning was more trouble than it was worth.

Victoria glanced skyward, sharply. 'Looks like the fighting's already started. The full vanguard of the Collective's forces in orbit are approaching along the equator from the east, decelerating to match the transport's delta-V. Two hundred and sixteen. And... oh, shit. They've sighted Velasquez.'

'Velasquez?' Jonah asked, although he thought he could glean a general idea of what the name meant from Victoria's reaction.

'Sebastián Velasquez,' she replied. 'He used to be one of the Insurgency's best aces, but he was captured and assimilated a few years ago. The Collective haven't managed to take many Archangels – we have too many countermeasures, and failing anything else, we can self-destruct rather than let ourselves fall into enemy hands. When they field one of our former allies in a fight, that's when they're serious, and Velasquez is the worst of them. We need to take off ASAP – I need to be there if there's going to be a straight dogfight.'

'I'm sorry for roping you into this, Victoria. It's just that–' His granddaughter cut him off with a shake of her head.

'No apologies. I made Alyssa a promise, too. Speaking of which…' She pointed towards the horizon, and the settlers turned to follow her line of sight. With his corneal implants on their maximum magnification, Jonah could just discern the outline of a vehicle against the brightening sky. Black smoke was billowing behind it.

***

The Humvee sputtered to a halt on the clearing ten minutes later; to judge from the noises it was making, the engine seemed ready to drop out if the ignition was ever turned again. Jonah sprinted to the drivers' side door before the vehicle came fully to a stop and wrenched it open. A diminutive figure half-stepped, half-fell out of the seat.

Jonah caught Alyssa in his arms. She seemed barely conscious, mostly dead weight, and yet he could hold her up without his ageing, aching joints offering much in the way of protest. Had she always been this light? She couldn't be any more than forty-five kilos.

'Lys?' Jonah held her by her armpits and propped her up so he could look her in the eye. When he saw her profile, a lump came to his throat. The left side of her head and neck were blistered with severe, second-degree burns; the beige T-shirt she wore was caked with dried blood on the same side. The Humvee's passenger seat was littered with plastic wrappers. He recognised them from the settlers' standardised medical kits, those used to package syringes of morphine.

'Jonah?' The word came out slurred; her eyes were glassy. 'I made it, that's good. You have to warn everyone. Mum and Dad, they're… they're…' She slumped forward against his shoulder. The gentle rising and falling of her chest told him she was just fast asleep.

'Right, no time to stand on ceremony,' said Victoria. 'If she's not in critical condition, get her strapped in now, and I'll tell the programmable matter in her torso to compensate for the effects of the g-forces. We've definitely outstayed our welcome on the ground.'

Looking back the way Alyssa had come, Jonah saw Scarabs emerging over the western horizon. Their limbs worked furiously, bearing them across the ground with a sinister, unnatural gait inappropriate to their size. They were adaptable for machines made to work in zero-g; they must have been going at fifty kilometres an hour.

'Does "now" mean something different in England?' Eoin barked. 'You heard the lady, let's go!'

***

It had been decades since Jonah had been under thrust of any kind, let alone the multiple g's required for escape velocity. His bones remembered that old ache, though, the feeling of being squeezed in a giant's fist. He gritted his teeth, tried not to swallow his tongue, and reminded himself that it was only a question of holding up for minutes; even at his age, with his elevated blood pressure, the risk of having a stroke in the short time it would take to escape TransTerra's atmosphere was pretty minimal. His worry was for the groundborn, particularly the infants among them. Before his family had left in one of the earlier shuttles, Jonah had seen Wulan Herianto, the youngest of the groundborn at eight months old, being swaddled in thick layers of inertia-dampening insulation. He prayed it would be enough to avert permanent damage to developing bones and tissues; yet another matter he had relinquished control over.

The settlers were strapped into their acceleration couches cheek by jowl, packed together in rows of four. Physically, he was stuck with his head pinned forward, incapable of speaking, with his field of vision occupied entirely by the headrest in front of him. To his surprise, though, the ship's antique design extended beyond its material structure to its computer systems; his corneal implants automatically synchronised with its firmware, giving him full access to the exterior sensors. He watched the ground drop away beneath them with shocking rapidity. In a matter of minutes, his view encompassed the entire Prometheid mountain range and the Mercanta Steppe beyond them. The planet he had called home for two decades, where he had spent most of his life trying to reach, was one he would never return to.

The blue of the sky faded away, replaced by the all-encompassing starfield beyond. Despite himself, he felt the familiar thrill of wonder at the universe and the technology that brought him this close to it. The acceleration slackened; with his chest unconstricted, he joined the chorus of settlers taking deep, gasping breaths of filtered air. The rumble of the chemical rockets subsided, leaving them with a momentary sensation of weightlessness, before the more subdued hum of the QF drive cut in. It would carry them the rest of the way to the transport where it sat in geosynchronous orbit.

Still amazes me, after all these years, he messaged Victoria over the shuttle's communications. She sat ensconced in the nose, where the manual controls were housed.

Look ahead on camera 17, she responded. **Enhance pixels from CY1280 to DH1356.**

He did as instructed and saw the transport cruiser, though it was really only evident in the negative sense; its presence was marked by the stars beyond it blinking in and out of view. He realised with a start that the hull had been entirely camouflaged in vantablack, with no exterior markings or sigils whatsoever. He remembered hearing about this tactic from Jean, used to cloak one-man insertion pods during the ORC's high-orbit raids. The idea of applying it to an entire cruiser astounded him.

Above and to the left of the vantablack silhouette, a portion of the starfield looked unusually active, full of sudden bursts and trails of light. As he watched, the area appeared to grow nearer, the flashes spreading out and becoming more luminous.

Typical Collective tactics, Victoria wrote. **They use missiles as suppressing fire while their allies flank us. We're sitting ducks in geosynchronous orbit. Once we're docked, we can manoeuvre. Rest while you can – more high-g flying soon.**

Wonderful, Jonah replied, hoping the dryness of his tone was evident in text.

***

The shuttle flipped and began to decelerate shortly thereafter. The ladar systems guided them to a docking port alongside the other eleven shuttles without a hitch.

The spectacle that greeted Jonah upon disembarking was of chaos. The transport was large by the standards of the ships he had known in his time, perhaps a quarter of the size of the *Prospice,* but it hadn't been built with a complement of seven hundred civilians in mind. Broad corridors with smooth walls left the passengers scrambling for purchase in their haste to get to safety, caroming off the decks and each other like ball bearings in a centrifuge.

'Hand her here, Jonah,' came the voice of Eric Carmichael. He gestured to Alyssa's still-unconscious figure, cradled in Jonah's arms. 'The sooner we get everyone squared away, the better a chance we have. They say we'll be pulling manoeuvres up to ten or eleven g's.'

'Is she the invalid?' The voice that hailed them came from an Archangel with an olive-skinned face and a severe expression thereupon. 'No, hand her to me, Captain,' she said. 'If she's unconscious, she gets priority under triage.'

The three of them were distracted by a wail from the middle of the corridor; Jack Nguyen had managed to get stuck, slowly rotating in place in the middle of the corridor, flailing for any handhold in reach. The Archangel grabbed him and roughly moved him back to the wall he'd drifted from. 'Though I'm not convinced being unconscious qualifies her as the slowest among you lot. Christ, can't you people do *anything*?'

'They've had their whole world upended in the last forty-eight hours, Sergeant Visconti,' Victoria emerged from an adjoining corridor. 'Afford them the same courtesy you would have wanted when we picked you up on Lysithea.'

'Lieutenant? I—' Sergeant Visconti jerked alert at Victoria's approach, and saluted. 'Yes, ma'am. I apologise, ma'am.'

'At ease, Sergeant,' Victoria returned the salute, and, after a moment's pause, the two of them embraced.

'Good to see you again, Rosa.'

'Good to have you back, Viper,' Rosa said, voice full of something akin to relief. 'You actually pulled it off, you madwoman. Eight hundred true-to-life recoveries. Things are going to change considerably around here going forward.'

'We're not out of the woods yet. Prep for launch; I'll take the stragglers from here.'

'Once more into the breach?'

'Hell yes, once more into the breach. I'll be right behind you.'

Jonah watched the sergeant go, gliding smoothly towards the airlock. He was still learning to read Archangel body language, but something about her bearing suggested she was straining at the leash to join in the combat now unfurling in the upper reaches of the gravity well. Not everyone, it appeared, shared Albrecht's consternation at what Victoria had done.

***

Arrayed in the cruiser's holds were rows upon rows of what looked like upright plexiglass coffins. Suspended within were the motionless forms of most of the settlers, faces obscured by breathing masks – the ones still ambulatory were nude and squeezing themselves into form-fitting bodysuits, preparing to climb into the remaining empty containers. The technology had been suggested in a rejected proposal for the *Prospice* – gel pods, which sealed their occupants in a thick, semi-liquid substance that served to absorb the effects of rapid changes in velocity while maintaining their vital functions.

Victoria moved Alyssa's sleeping form over to one of the few remaining pods. Handling a human body in free-fall was delicate work; any error could potentially send them floating away until their momentum was arrested by a hard surface. The Archangel frame's wings twitched with subtle motions, corresponding to corrective changes in Victoria's vector. Zero-g really was her natural environment.

Jonah drifted to his own pod, hesitating before situating himself inside. Victoria caught his eye as she was handling her cousin, strapping the mask over Alyssa's head carefully so as not to aggravate the burns.

'Go ahead and get strapped in,' she said. 'You did well on the ground, standing up to the Commander that way. I'll handle things from here.'

'Are you heading out to fight? After we're all stowed away?' He couldn't fully disguise the tension in his voice.

'Of course. The Commander's angry with me, but he trusts me that much, and he's hardly in a position to refuse help.'

'Well then, just in case things, you know, don't go our way. While I still can, I wanted to say–'

She raised a hand, cutting him off. 'Don't do that. I don't want us exchanging tearful farewells every time I step out of your sight. It's unseemly. Here's what we'll do instead.' Her eyes flickered for a split second, and a notification flashed up in Jonah's corneal implants; an invitation to remotely receive a TSI feed from Victoria during the battle ahead.

'For most of the settlers, the rest of the operation will probably seem deathly boring. Just floating in their tubes, getting jerked this way and that. If anything does go wrong, it'll be too late by the time they realise it. But this is your party, so you should get to enjoy the fireworks.'

'And you'll be able to operate like that, knowing I was watching over your shoulder?'

Victoria flashed him a broad grin. 'It was feeling like you were watching over me that got me this far, Starman. Now go and suit up. We fly out in five minutes.'

***

As his pod filled up with non-Newtonian fluid, squeezing and immobilising his body with a tightness that would insulate him from impact, Jonah accessed the feed Victoria had gifted him.

He jerked back, or tried to, cushioned as he was by the gel. He cut away from the feed, a wave of nauseating disorientation receding as quickly as it had come.

Sorry! A notification from Victoria popped up in his field of vision. **I forgot, your optic nerve isn't wired to receive front and rear vision feeds at the same time. Hold on; I'll configure it so that you can access them separately.**

Jonah waited a few seconds, then tried again. This time, his breath caught at the sight that greeted him, until an amber alert from his implants reminded him to oxygenate his blood. He had been on spacewalks before, countless times during his captaincy; he was as intimately familiar with the view of the starfield as any astronaut. But even in those moments, when he'd felt a sense of communion between himself and the infinite, he'd been aware of the visor and the suit between him and hard vacuum. What he experienced now, through

143

Victoria's eyes, was like a fighter pilot being allowed the perspective of a falcon, or a submariner that of a shark.

TransTerra shrank behind her as she rose, emerging from the shadow of the planet's gravity well and into the full view of the local star. Her wings blossomed to their full extension, orange light susurrating across every inch of their surface area, transmuting into energy her body's platelets greedily drank. She swelled to bursting, radiant in the sunrise, her frame humming with power.

Victoria's shoulder blades arched, and she dove, her frontal vision pivoting through ninety degrees. A split-second later, the space she had just vacated erupted in her rear vision; a nuclear detonation silently flaring a kilometre across in the dark.

Jesus, Jonah wrote. **How did you dodge that?**

That was nothing, Victoria responded. **Just a signal shot, a torpedo trying to flush me out. They're not trying to kill us, remember, they're trying to direct us, trap us. Right now, the battle is like the early stages of a chess game, all feints and bluffs. It's going to get a lot more manic from this point on. If you're going to keep spectating, Starman, no more texts, OK? I need to focus.**

Their view swung around and honed in on a patch of orbit above and west of them. At a hundred-and-fifty-times magnification, they could just make out a winged, vantablack figure drifting inert, a slightly darker hole in the darkness of space. **Distress beacon,** Victoria wrote.

When they reached the drifting figure, the reason for its distress became quickly clear; it was missing most of its right arm and wing, and beneath the shoulder, there was a crescent-shaped absence where there should have been a large part of its chest and stomach. Something that looked uncomfortably like tendons protruded from the wound. **Bastard tagged me,** came a message which the text overlay on Victoria's vision identified as being from Rosa. **I got sloppy, but Villeneuve drew the shooter away. Couldn't lend me some platelets, could you?**

I'm running low, but I've got some to spare, Victoria replied. She was cloaked in vantablack herself, so it was hard to discern what happened next, but Jonah could fill in the blanks from the time he had seen her heal Alyssa;

she laid her hand on Rosa's injury, and material *flowed*, like mercury coagulating on a countertop, from her body to the sergeant's. Where she touched, Rosa's frame swelled, regenerating itself. Their equivalent of a field dressing.

You were lucky, Victoria mused. **A tenth of a degree to your left, and they'd have split your core.**

Let's call it providence rather than luck. Thanks for the assist, Lieutenant.

Victoria withdrew her arm, her treatment seemingly complete. **You can owe me a favour when we get home.**

The figure stretched its regrown wing, flexed its regrown fingers, and Jonah imagined a wicked grin animating its featureless face. **Stay sharp; it seems they've updated their algorithms to counter the Herzfeldt-Bucholz attack pattern.**

Got it. Let's go hunting.

***

The battlefront took the form of a rough hemisphere, with the Archangels' resistance forming an umbrella over the cruiser as it accelerated away from TransTerra, whilst Scarabs dashed themselves against it. The enemy's power reserves were limited; if they could just hold out long enough, they would reach a critical threshold of velocity past which any pursuit or boarding action would become untenable. A readout in Victoria's HUD estimated how long they had to reach that threshold. It sat at 81.07%, and ticked upward, decimal by decimal, second by all-too-slow second.

A maser beam crackled past Victoria's left wingtip; a second passed beneath her, close enough that it might have singed her navel if there had been an atmosphere through which it could radiate heat. Before the attacking Scarab could get off a third shot, she closed the distance and clamped her palm over its faceplate. Her fingers swelled with programmable matter, digits extending talon-like and clenching like a vice over the robot's sensors. With her opponent blinded, she fired, gigawatts of energy coursing through her palm, reducing the Scarab's critical processes to dissociated, superheated molecules.

A second Scarab loomed from above (whatever 'above' was at this point; Jonah had long given up on trying to reconcile Victoria's orientation with any frame of reference). She arced away from it, into the path of a third, its six limbs splayed towards her like widening jaws. Victoria didn't miss a beat; she tucked her knees to her chest, folded back her wings, and shot downward like an Olympic swimmer pushing off the edge of the pool.

Two bursts of light registered in her wake in quick succession. Seconds later, Aki fell in beside her to her left, and Rosa to her right.

The Archangels' trap had encompassed the trap the Scarabs had laid for them.

They were outnumbered, their squadron of thirty to the Scarabs' two hundred and sixteen, but even at worse odds than six-to-one, from his limited vantage point, they seemed to be winning. Twice, he'd been dazzled by enormous explosions which momentarily brought the fighting to a halt, which he would learn later were evidence of the Archangel frames' antimatter cores being violated. Four times, he'd been violently reminded of his body's physical presence in the transport when he felt his bones being crushed under some sort of fifteen-plus-g evasive action that hurt even with the insulating gel to compensate. But into the battle's second hour, they were still alive and unmolested by the Collective, and he began to notice Scarab corpses cluttering the view of the planet below them. Their decaying orbits would have made for a spectacular meteor shower in a few days' time if there had still been anyone on the ground to see it.

Alone in his pod, Jonah smiled to himself. The Archangels belonged to a world he didn't recognise, but one thing he had always believed remained true: hard-won human skill beat machine-learned algorithms, any day of the week.

The counter read 86.73%.

We're close, Aki wrote. **We may just pull this off.**

Don't speak too soon, Rosa warned in response. She pointed towards the western flank of the battle. **They've been holding their ace in the hole in reserve.**

A silver streak was weaving and threading its way through the front. Cerulean maser fire struck out at it as it passed, but it darted hither and thither in sharp zigzags, none of them coming close. The streak came straight for

146

Victoria, matching her and her comrades' velocity. It resolved in shape as it drew near: an Archangel. His features were male, youthful and androgynous, much like the others, but somehow unavoidably distinct from them. He wore a smug grin, long brown hair swimming about a face harshly illuminated by the detonations all around him.

Miss me? came a message from a sender identified as 'Cpl. S. Vsqz.'

The Collective haven't made you any less of a smug prick, have they, Velasquez?

That was uncalled for. Tell you what: join us, and I'll take it as an apology.

I think you know how that will end.

Suit yourself, Vic.

Velasquez dove, gaining speed as he approached the transport cruiser. Victoria, Aki, and Rosa gave chase. He seemed to dart around his former comrades' shots with taunting ease. The Insurgency watched, as powerless as the settlers in their gel wombs, as a single, perfectly placed beam cut through the strut attaching the port-side QF drive. It remained attached, dangling by a single, tenuous metal limb.

Sorry for the inconvenience, folks. This time Velasquez's message was directed at the transport's communication array, visible to any of the immobilised settlers whose implants were synced to its mainframe. **Just hold tight; we'll have you out of those sarcophagi in a jiff. It's a shame you all had to be exposed to Albrecht's propaganda before you could learn the truth, but I'll see to it that gets corrected after we clear up here.**

Back in his body, Jonah felt a wrenching lurch. His exterior view of the transport fizzed and stuttered; the shot must have disrupted the ship's electrics, through which his signal to Victoria was routed. His body suddenly felt sickeningly light. The ship's interior was once again under zero-g, meaning they were no longer accelerating. When his view through Victoria's eyes returned, he saw that the starboard engine had shut off as well, a function of the autopilot to prevent them from going into an uncontrollable spin. Velasquez was gone, disappeared somewhere far off to the east where even the highest magnification couldn't find him.

Victoria's HUD readout was stalled at 87.86%.

Damn him, said Victoria. **I knew this was going too easily.**

Hartikainen, came a directive from Albrecht, **you're closest. Get down to the ship and patch up the damage as best you can.**

Yes, sir, came Aki's reply. Victoria's vision tracked his distant form as he headed towards the crippled transport. A heartbeat later, the space around him became incandescent with energy beams, forcing him to make a series of frantic, flapping course corrections and veer off to the south. The remaining Scarabs had focused everything they had on the lone figure trying to repair the damage Velasquez had done. **Shit! It's no good, sir. Can't even make it within twenty klicks.**

Two others, identified by the text overlay as Hauer and Villeneuve, tried and were similarly rebuffed. **Harrison,** Albrecht said, addressing Victoria now, **how many enemy units do you count remaining?**

57, sir.

I've got the same here. It gets worse, too: the ship's sensors just picked up reinforcements coming from the east. Two full platoons this time, 432 units. ETA 45 minutes.

Anyone attempting to match velocities with the ship to repair the damage is a sitting duck. And if we try to chase the remaining Scarabs off, they'll just retreat and keep taking potshots from a distance, drawing us out until the reinforcements arrive. We're between a rock and a hard place here, Commander.

Jonah had heard enough. **I'll do it,** he announced. **I can repair that strike in 20 minutes.**

A moment's radio silence followed his boast.

Out of the question, responded Albrecht. **You'd just be giving them another target to fire at.**

Kiss my arse, Commander, Jonah shot back. Albrecht was much less intimidating to deal with when he was a line of text coming from ten thousand kilometres away. **I captained the _Prospice_ for 211 years, and in that time I repaired more micrometeoroid strikes than you've had hot dinners. And I**

don't have to worry about approaching the ship when I'm already inside. Do you want to get into another pissing match until the Scarabs board us, or do you want to pop the seal on my pod so I can get us out of here?

Another moment's silence; then Jonah felt a sudden, shocking burst of cold air on his face as his pod opened, the gel surrounding him lazily floating into the cargo hold in viscous, greasy bubbles the size of basketballs. He yanked the breathing mask off his face, and severed his TSI connection to Victoria.

You're a very stubborn man, Captain, came Albrecht's text, impressed now upon his own eyes. I can admire that, up to a point. I'll guide you to the storage lockers on Deck 4. There are suits there that ought to be functional.

***

Jonah had finished pulling on the antique spacesuit and was just about done pressurising it when Velasquez made another pass. The deck above the storage lockers exploded without warning; the first he knew of it was the coppery taste of blood from his broken nose filling up his helmet after the pressure wave bounced him off the floor. He gave himself a shake, seeing double, but he didn't think he was concussed.

Are you OK, Jonah? came a message from Victoria. We saw him coming that time, managed to steer him away from his ideal shot. I don't think he hit anything important.

'Guess again,' Jonah groaned. He felt pain blossoming in his right thigh; glancing down, he saw an eighteen-inch shard of shrapnel emerging from his leg. The suit's systems rushed to compensate, applying an analgesic salve to the injury and inflating a partition that sealed off the depressurisation while also acting as a tourniquet.

Oh God, your vitals are going through the roof. Get yourself to the medical bay immediately, we'll find another way to fix the engine.

No, you won't, not in the time we have, and not while Velasquez is still out there, Jonah gritted his teeth. I'll be fine, it's just a leg. It's redundant in space, anyway.

Following Albrecht's directions, Jonah retrieved the tools he needed for welding and soldering from another storage locker. He made his way through the decks toward the port-side airlock as quickly as he dared, grimacing every

149

time he used his right leg to propel himself. He cycled the airlock and activated the electromagnetic limpet pads on his suit's hands, feet, knees, and elbows, that would allow him to move around the outer hull like a scurrying insect.

Throughout all of this, the analgesia combined with the zero-g and his general exhaustion (had it really only been a Terran week?) made him dizzy and nauseous. Three times, he had to stop and collect himself when he thought he was going to pass out. Each time, the same thought penetrated the fog of his brain, and each time he seized it, clung to it for dear life, and recited it like a mantra:

Unconditional love is a lie.

Anything worthwhile in the universe had to be earned, and anything that didn't have to be earned wasn't worthwhile. It had to take commitment, sacrifice, *suffering*; otherwise there was no point. And what could be more worthwhile than having a person who values your life above their own?

Victoria had risked everything for him. If Albrecht made good on his promise of prosecuting her, she may well have *given* everything for him. All of it based on... what? A handful of video messages he had sent over a century ago, that he barely remembered sending? Their entire relationship prior to this week amounted to maybe a cumulative five hours of video footage containing a pack of contrived banalities and platitudes.

If he passed out; if he handed off the responsibility of repairing the engine to someone else; if he got it wrong, or took too long before the Scarab reinforcements showed up, or failed in any of the innumerable ways he could fail, then she would be doomed, and the last thing she would know as a mind free of the Collective's control would be that the Starman had fallen short of the stories she had told herself her whole life. He would prove false the assumptions that had kept her going all this time.

Unconditional love is a lie. Earn hers, you son-of-a-bitch.

Watch it, Harrison. Albrecht's message jerked him out of his reverie. **Blue to blue. Screw up the wiring and you could short-circuit the whole cruiser's electrics. Not that I'd mind, but we have passengers who actually need the life support now.**

'I've got it, I've got it,' Jonah mumbled, mostly to himself. Velasquez's shot had neatly severed the bundle wiring running through one of the port-side struts, providing power to the quantum drives. The wires had melted and fused together where they had been cut – each one had to be picked free and soldered together individually. Jonah counted it as a blessing that the technology involved was fundamentally the same as that used in the *Prospice* – he let decades of muscle memory take over and his hands did the work for him. He doubted the Archangels could have done it quicker themselves.

OK, he announced, giving the last wire a tug to check the attachment was solid, **that should be it. Try the engine to make sure.**

A moment later, he felt the hull tug at him ever so slightly. It was only a split-second, but the impression of thrust was unmistakable. **Looks like you've got it,** texted Albrecht. **Only 23% efficiency, so there'll be a lot of excess heat building up inside the ship, but it should be good enough to last until we've made our getaway and we can repair her properly.**

'Don't flatter me too much, Commander, it might go to my head,' Jonah grumbled. 'What's the ETA on the enemy reinforcements?'

22 minutes. If we're burning hard before then, they won't catch us. Get welding, Captain, then get yourself back on board.

We have a problem, Victoria interjected. **Velasquez is coming fast from the north, about to make another pass. Moving to intercept.**

Jonah had finished reattaching the first of the severed struts and was working feverishly on the other when a series of lights pulsed overhead.

The Inverse Fei-Hung manoeuvre, Vic? Velasquez's name reappeared on the text crawl. **Honestly, I'm disappointed you think so little of me.**

Damn it! Missed him. Take cover Jonah, he's heading straight for you.

This is fun, isn't it, Viper? Like our training drills used to be. I get why you're stubborn, but if you'd just come over to our side, it could be like that again. Remember fun?

Remember me? A new voice: Rosa's.

What Jonah saw next happened so fast, he could never have sworn to it. Even so, a silver shape flashed past his vision; not more than a few dozen metres from where he was clamped, welding the final strut into place. Although it couldn't have been in his field of view for more than half a second, it seemed to him that he saw two winged figures grappling inside it, silver and black, falling together through space.

You don't have to do this, Rosa, wrote Velasquez. Jonah finished making the final seal and began to scramble back towards the airlock.

You're right, I don't, retorted Rosa as the airlock cycled, **but I want to.**

It's not even smart from a tactical perspective, Velasquez pleaded. Jonah wondered why he was being copied into all of this; it had made sense when Velasquez was boasting that he would want everyone in range to hear it, but it made no sense for him to make himself sound so pathetic. Then he realised that Rosa was routing a private communique between the pair of them to her allies. She was taking pleasure in hearing Velasquez trying in vain to bargain. **Look, I've got hooks into your frame, you'll be assimilated in a couple of minutes anyway. I care about you, Rosa, we all do. More than I used to. More than any of your Insurgency. Just let it happen, and you'll see.**

The airlock completed its cycle. Jonah yanked off the suit as quickly as he could while propelling himself through the corridor back to the cargo hold. In his hurried attempt to multitask, he hit a wall faster than he'd meant to. He jolted his injured thigh and involuntarily yelled out in pain. The analgesia was wearing off, and he realised with a plummeting sensation in his stomach that he'd be lucky if he didn't lose the leg.

Sorry, Sebastián, but I think I'll take option B.

No, don't— Velasquez was unceremoniously cut off.

Hey, Vic, Rosa continued. **Pour one out for me when you get to the FOB, OK?**

Roger that, Rosa. Victoria's reply continued after the briefest of pauses. It had, Jonah thought, the cadence of rehearsal to it; words that had been repeated frequently enough to become script. **Your sacrifice will not be forgotten, nor will it be in vain. It was an honour to fly by your side, Sergeant.**

Our hopes go with you, Viper. May you all see another sunrise.

Jonah was in the process of climbing back into his gel-pod and reattaching his breathing mask when a violent tremor reverberated through the ship.

***

The simultaneous detonation of two Archangel frame cores flooded TransTerra's upper orbit with hard radiation. The surviving Scarabs were repulsed by the deluge of alpha-particles, and the Insurgency used them as cover to mask their retreat to the transport cruiser. Jonah's repairs held true; by the time the Collective's sensors had recovered from the disorientation caused by Rosa's kamikaze attack on Velasquez, they were already too far away to do anything about it.

After losing themselves in interplanetary space with a few hours' hard burn, and they were a dozen AU out from TransTerra's local star, Commander Albrecht judged it safe to lay off the acceleration and allow the passengers out of their gel-pods. The cargo hold disgorged over seven hundred people all at once, noisily retching and complaining about their cold and hunger and general discomfort. It took a while for things to settle down. Miraculously, no-one had been seriously hurt by the vicissitudes the ship had endured; even baby Wulan had made it through with no more than a lingering cough.

A short commemorative service was held on the bridge, in honour of the Archangels who had fallen in battle. In the absence of bodies, talismans they'd nominated while they still lived were used in their stead.

As a synecdoche for Rosa's corpse, they ceremonially vented her commendation from the ORC. Jonah learned that she had once been a cadet at Kisangani station. To her memory, Victoria played the composition she had let Jonah and Alyssa hear in the caterpillar. It remained unfinished, but she had come up with a tentative title – she called it 'Words that Stay Unspoken.'

To the aft section of the transport, there was a full-length viewscreen displaying the space in the craft's wake. Three days after their escape, Jonah found Victoria standing there, gazing into the blackness with her all-too-unblinking eyes. He announced himself with a cough and joined her. TransTerra was less than a speck behind them, now; indiscernible even with his implants at a hundred and fifty times resolution.

'She was special to you, wasn't she?' he ventured when she didn't offer any sign of what she might be thinking.

'Precious to me, yes,' she answered, her tone betraying nothing. 'As precious as any of the rest of them.'

'I'm sorry. If not for us, then she might have—'

Victoria rounded on him. Her brilliant eyes met his and pierced where they fell. Half-unconsciously, he took a step back. 'Is that all you can do, Starman? Apologise? Rosa took an oath. She knew what she was fighting for. For humanity, free of their control. So don't you dare second-guess that she was right to do so.'

Jonah nodded, curtly, and let his granddaughter be. She turned back to the window.

He didn't need to ask to know what she was thinking; more friends whose friendship she had to prove herself worthy of. More sacrifices she had to earn.

PART TWO

THE HEDONISTIC IMPERATIVE

A.N. Milne

156

Chapter 11

December 7th, 2135 C.E.

Jean was an old man looking out towards the ocean from the forty-first floor of the Vancouver arcology. His name was Tobias Stanley; Toby to his friends. Seventy-five and too weak to stand without robotic assistance, he was in the final stages of pancreatic cancer, his body ravaged by round after round of chemotherapy. His doctor had given him three months to live; that had been in September. He'd been so afraid that each day might be his last. But no longer; now he was buoyed up by the millions with whom he shared every facet of his memory and imagination, and the assurance that his mind would persist within their cognitive manifold after his body failed.

Toby blinked.

Jean was a young girl. Her name was Angavu; thirteen years old, the oldest of four orphans, left to care for her siblings after their parents had died of radiation poisoning. They'd both worked 14-hour shifts at Yang-Mitsubishi's regional manufacturing plant in Nairobi. They'd known the plant was a deathtrap; YM had undercut their competitors by cutting corners on shielding for fissile materials, but they'd been the only jobs available to put food in their family's mouths. Left to face destitution, lonely, angry, and bereaved, Angavu had nursed fantasies of building a bomb and blowing up the accursed factory, taking herself with it in a final, spiteful gesture against the world. But no longer. Now the same executives who had been responsible for her parents' exploitation and her brothers' abandonment saw to it that she was well-treated. She could feel the sorrow and contrition in their hearts, and know that it was genuine, just as they could feel the forgiveness in hers.

Angavu blinked.

Jean was a middle-aged man on the streets of Hong Kong. His name was Leung, and his body was beginning to feel the chills and the nausea he knew to associate with opiate withdrawal. There had been a time when he would have done almost anything to relieve himself of these sensations. He had long since exhausted the goodwill of his friends and former associates; he would have had to do the degrading work of circulating among his fellow addicts, pleading until someone spotted him enough money to cover the price of just one more ampoule of the attenuated fentanyl they unloaded in the small hours of the morning in Victoria Harbour. But no longer. The compulsions of his chemical dependency would never again hold sway over him.

Leung blinked.

A network of millions of minds; millions of stories; millions of frailties absolved. Each consciousness was a node in a structure, each reinforcing and supporting the other. No longer would the inhabitants of the Enclave need to face existence alone. They could know each other – truly know each other – as they did themselves.

One node in particular stood out; the one at the centre of the structure.

Xavier Wong: that was his name. The man who had started it all; the genius responsible for the first Enclave.

There was no hierarchy within the Enclave; indeed, the concept of hierarchy was antithetical to everything it represented. The cruel borders between individual units of consciousness became blurred and porous, souls freely mixing and commingling. Even so, Wong's spirit had a kind of natural primacy amongst them.

On 21 October, 10.21 am in Hong Kong, he had been in his lab in Yang-Mitsubishi's Tai Koo offices. He had been one of the few who had refused to stay home from work that day, waiting for the news of the Body's diversion, successful or otherwise. Fifty-one years of age, he had been uncommonly free of personal attachments. He had no spouse, no children, and his parents had both passed away years earlier. The few friends he had weren't especially close, or at least not close enough to draw solace from in the face of mortality. He favoured distraction as a coping mechanism. He was a man who defined himself by his work at Yang-Mitsubishi, where he acted as a senior project manager in their research and development of practical applications for quantum entanglement. And thus it was that he had found himself at the precise intersection of the Body's vector with the Earth's surface at the instant of the Engagement.

White Scar Across the Firmament

The psychic reverberations that had been felt around the world had been more keen in Hong Kong than anywhere else, and while most of humanity had reported the effects as being muddled and unintelligible, there were a few thousand in the densely populated city who had experienced a clear connection to a distinctly alien intelligence. The Engagement was a broadcast of sorts; a cry of pain at the impact of the kinetic torpedoes resonating across the Earth, and their precise placement meant that they received it undistorted, like they were on the one clear sliver of radio frequency sandwiched between the white noise around it.

They had all been dismissed at the time, their reports either being lumped in with other unverifiable crackpot accounts by an unsympathetic media, or simply drowned out by the general chaos and confusion of the aftermath. But although the world didn't yet know his name, Xavier Wong had become the most important human being on Earth at that moment. In the space of six objective minutes, he had communed with a billion minds; accessed a billion memories; lived a billion lifetimes. The Body had been no mere comet, but an ambassador from a civilisation on the far edges of the cosmos, carrying with it knowledge and perspectives and sensations so far removed from human experience that neither English, nor Cantonese, nor any other barbaric form of auditory or written communication could begin to encompass them.

And humanity, consumed by its egotistical, lizard-brained fear of death, had seen fit to nuke it.

By the time the clock hit 10:27, the Body disappeared behind the Moon, and Wong's link with it was severed. The ecstatic revelation afforded to him slipped through his fingers like water; the primitive meat-computer in his skull, with its puny quadrillion synapses, was pathetically ill-equipped to retain the concepts he had been exposed to. All he was left with was the sure knowledge that those six minutes had been incomparably more meaningful and real than the fifty-one years that had preceded them, and that he would do anything – quite literally *anything* – to return to that reality.

He had staggered home to his one-bedroom flat and spent the next three days alternately catatonic and sobbing uncontrollably, the awful, aching sensation of loss crashing over him in great waves. Then he had resolved to do something about it.

Flashes of the communication he had experienced with the aliens remained. They were incoherent, piecemeal, a fraction to the negative-tenth power of the full thing, but they were enough to work from. Part of the knowledge imparted to him had been the specifics of how that communication was achieved; with great effort and concentration, Wong was able to put together the basics of how the aliens' mind-to-mind technology had been developed, facilitating their species' advancement into an interstellar, collaborative group-consciousness. It represented decades of progress in the field he specialised in, and which Yang-Mitsubishi was pouring billions of dollars into. His work over the following month made Carlos Alvarez's pioneering research look like it had been written in crayon; if he had seen fit to concentrate his efforts that way, a Nobel Prize would unquestionably have been his.

Instead, he had laboured for the next four weeks, tirelessly but quietly. His two decades at Yang-Mitsubishi had won him a spotless reputation as an employee, consistently delivering results that pleased the executives on-time and under-budget. He had been given a long leash for what was understood to be complex and difficult research, and the freedom to structure his team and his lab facilities in the manner that suited him. He requisitioned Unit 56 of the Tai Koo complex for the construction of a machine he nebulously described in his four-page message to corporate as a 'new tool to investigate the properties of paired particles.'

The engineers, technicians, and programmers he enlisted from his team to help him build his machine were kept in the dark as to its true purpose. He kept them segmented, working separate shifts, each focused on the specific task he had assigned them while deflecting any questions about how the larger project would mesh together. Wong himself practically lived in Unit 56 in those weeks, working for twenty hours a day, taking dangerous quantities of stimulants to keep him going. An investment in the future, he told himself.

On November 23rd, the machine was switched on.

A flood of paired particles invisibly poured out across five square kilometres of Hong Kong, tuned to the electromagnetic properties of the human brain. Without warning, throughout Tai Koo and North Point, thousands of people found themselves sharing each other's perceptions and thoughts. Wong was ready for the feedback of fear and incomprehension he received and turned his own mind outward to console them.

Don't worry, he thought to them, *a wonderful thing has happened.*

And after the birthing pains were over and understanding kicked in, they agreed, every one of them, just as Jean had. The Enclave was the Body's gift to the world. It had revealed a better way of being; a real, practical end to the grief and strife and suffering coded into humanity's DNA. Hatred, mistrust, and other such Neolithic concepts could be forgotten at last, subsumed by the boundless love that humans bore one another when no barriers existed between one mind and the next.

But for this paradise to be achieved, a certain ruthless pragmatism first had to be adopted. Jean realised it too, now, just how blinkered people really were. Their every waking minute was so suffused with subtle pains and anxieties that they convinced themselves they were worthwhile, tried to twist them into *meaning* something. They would resist attempts to save them; she would have done the same, before. Everything about the concept of a 'hive mind,' starting with the name, provoked an irrational repulsion from those on the outside looking in. If the Enclave revealed itself to the world, it would be branded a dangerous cult by the very people it wanted so badly to save. The international community would send its armies to quell the spread of their gospel, ending the best chance of salvation humanity had ever been given before it had a chance to take root. It was better to ask forgiveness than permission.

So, the Enclave set itself to infiltration. Wong's device had a small area of effect, encompassing only a couple of districts of a single city, but it represented a foundation to build from. The Enclave's first few thousand members withdrew inside the device's area of effect and cut off all communication beyond, giving the rest of the world something to puzzle over while they bade their time. Having thousands of minds to bend towards a task with no delay or flaw in their co-ordination meant that incredible advances could be achieved in no time at all. It was only days before they had a miniaturised version of the device ready, like the one the mercenary had injected at the base of Jean's spinal column in the Kisangani arcology. Freed to move outside the sphere of influence of Wong's original device, Enclave agents could move invisibly among the populace of Earth, swelling their ranks slowly but deliberately, ingratiating themselves with people in positions of influence or power.

People like Tony Liu, with the ear of China's intelligence service, who could quietly alter the course of his nation's policymaking. The attempted incursion into Tai Koo on the evening of December 3rd had presented a difficult wrinkle for him when Team Delta had penetrated deeper inside the area of effect than had been anticipated. Wong's device operated by the dispersion of charged gamma particles, which could be inhibited by several metres of rock. As a result, the PRC had come close to discovering the Enclave's nature. But Tony had twisted events to their advantage, convincing his superiors to keep the investigation into the anomaly on the Dark Side of the Moon out of official channels. The Enclave had leveraged the fear of sleeper agents against the world's governments, and in doing so, had given its sleeper agents back the advantage.

There was a feeling of building anticipation in the sensorium following the most recent accomplishments; a growing certainty of their mission's success. Their numbers would continue to multiply exponentially. Very soon, humanity would be saved.

***

The node of consciousness identifying itself as Jean Harrison returned to the body from which it had originated. She was in the back seat of a black SUV, making slow progress through the snow-choked streets of Beijing. Sensory deprivation gear was clamped over her eyes and ears; her implants' connection to the 'net disabled. The unsmiling agents who had greeted them at the vacuum terminus had insisted upon it, a precautionary measure against the civilian and foreign national learning their route. Tony sat next to her, silently relaying to her what he saw and heard through the mind-to-mind connection they now shared.

I'm concerned about David Manderly, Jean thought. *Before I was saved, I left him a voice message detailing what I had learned. It wasn't much, but it's possible that he could connect the dots back to Yang-Mitsubishi.*

The SUV pulled up to the nondescript grey tenement block which served as Tony's safe house. He had arranged to rendezvous with Secretary Koo, his nominal superior in the intelligence service.

Don't worry about it, the Enclave reassured her. *We have members converging on him even now. Nothing will interfere with our objectives.*

162

The sensory deprivation gear was removed, and the pair of them were led upstairs to a shabby apartment living room. Jean recognised Koo from the PNC debriefing days before. He had been middle-aged before telomerase supplements came on the market, to judge by his drawn, lined face and bald patch, but his countenance was alert and intelligent. He was pacing and, to judge from the overflowing ashtray, was smoking what must have been his seventh cigarette that afternoon. *Poor little man, who needs the stimulation of carcinogenic chemicals just to get through his day…*

'Mr. Liu,' he said in lightly accented Mandarin, 'please tell me you're bringing me some good news. I'm sure I don't need to tell you today has been the shitstorm to end all shitstorms.'

'I have news, sir. Whether or not it could be considered "good" is a question of perspective.' Jean was almost startled to hear him speaking out loud again. His voice in an auditory medium was markedly different from the one he presented in their shared sensorium – deeper, throatier. 'Our meeting with Alvarez yielded some insights into the nature of the radiation involved in the spread of the Enclave Effect. It involves research at the cutting edge of quantum physics. If you'll permit me access to a secure channel, I can give you the details of the effect in a dossier I prepared this morning…'

Koo pinched the bridge of his nose and groaned. 'Liu, you know I have the Prime Minister's office on the line every five minutes, screaming for answers on this? I don't have time to comb through forty-seven pages of technical jargon that neither you nor I are qualified to make sense of. Just give me the abbreviated version; do we know who's responsible, and how do we stop it?'

Tony heaved a breath. The Enclave's anticipation sharpened, a million minds poised to watch how this next misdirection played.

'It's the PNC, sir.'

Koo's head jerked around, his forgotten cigarette hanging limply from his lower lip. 'Pardon?'

'To give you the abbreviated version, the same previously unobserved paired-particle effect that Alvarez' instruments picked up coming from the remains of the Body on the Moon, we found coming from various PNC installations across the globe.'

Koo withdrew his cigarette and slowly stubbed it out. His eyebrows were arched, his eye-contact with Tony severe and unwavering. 'You do understand, Liu, that you sound like a conspiracy theorist right now, and it's only on the basis of your good standing with this agency that I'm willing to hear you out?'

'Only too clearly, sir, but those are the facts of the matter. I believe that the PNC, or a rogue faction within it, is responsible for the appearance of the Enclave Effect. The more Enclaves they generate, the more they can enforce their will unilaterally across the globe. It behoves the Chinese government to take possession of the Body's remains and expose the PNC's plans for what they are before the ORC beats us to the punch.'

'Mr Secretary,' Jean said, this time being surprised by the sound of her own voice in Mandarin, 'for what it's worth, I can vouch for everything Tony has just said in my capacity as an independent observer.'

Koo's eyebrows somehow rose even higher. '"Tony," is it? First-name terms? Ms Harrison, while your aid in this operation is appreciated, your editorialising at this point is neither necessary nor welcome.' He paused for a moment and kept pacing, looking thoughtful.

'This has disturbing ramifications, Liu,' he said, finally. 'It took China decades to establish itself as a leading member of the new international community. If we were to act against the PNC's mandate when it comes to a matter that concerns the fate of our species, it would do more than just jeopardise those relations; it would be construed as a declaration of war against every other nation on Earth. No. No, I will not sanction any such action at this time, not until I have definitive, independently verified proof.'

He slumped into a moth-eaten armchair, apparently exhausted by the day's mental exertion. 'That will be all, Mr Liu, and you, Ms Harrison, thank you.'

Tony inclined his head. 'Very well, sir. But I must stress, this is a time-sensitive issue. When you're ready to proceed, I have a shortlist of candidates for the mission already drawn up.'

***

The Enclave was already a miracle, a revolution in human experience unprecedented in the short history of their species. But Xavier Wong's creation

164

was nothing more than an echo; a crude imitation of a technology thousands of years more sophisticated than humanity possessed. To receive the true gospel from the stars, to grow from the pupa it was now, the Enclave needed the body of the god that had shown Wong a glimpse of what they could all become.

Koo was shrewd; his failure to accept the fiction the Enclave had concocted at first glance was a stumbling block, but not an unanticipated one.

Soon, his hand will be forced. The voice in the sensorium was Tony's. *After the next phase of the expansion, thirty-six major cities will have their own Enclaves, all of them cities with PNC facilities listed in the dossier. Koo has had the seed of doubt sown in his mind; he'll run the numbers, and he'll know that the odds of that happening by chance are microscopic. He'll believe what we told him today – after that, it's only a matter of time before the Body is ours.*

Jean drew a deep, shuddering breath of contentment at that reassurance; she felt herself brimming with nervous energy; excitement at the still-greater ecstasies on the horizon. That contentment rippled out across a million other minds, a million other pairs of lungs echoing the motion. It grew and grew, echoing back to her ten times as strong as the original emotion in a strange, wonderful feedback loop.

***

There were remotely operated cargo drones high above Hong Kong, emblazoned with the logo of the World Food Programme. Across the circumference of the original Enclave, they airdropped in rations of canned food. The packages, landing softly on rooftops and in streets by parachute, included messages from family and friends of the saved, offering heartfelt pleas for their loved ones' well-being and safe recovery.

At the perimeter of the Athens Enclave, kept at a safe distance by military cordons, a candlelight vigil was gaining traction. Thousands of citizens had gathered in the city's pedestrian thoroughfares, silently holding their small flames aloft as a sign of solidarity with their countrymen inside the cordon.

Lines of lorries were backed up for miles outside the Vancouver and London Enclaves, where the temperature was well below freezing. They were unloading mountains of firewood at the borderline of the Effect. Private enterprises had donated millions of litres of fuel; donation drives were coming in from the public with contributions of old wooden furniture to be chopped up and used for kindling.

In a matter of hours, the world had rallied in the face of this unknown phenomenon overtaking their cities. Many were afraid; traffic jams stretched from horizon to horizon with those fleeing to rural areas where they believed they would be "safe." Others were angry, seeing the efforts at humanitarian relief as giving succour to the enemy, almost tantamount to collusion with alien conquerors.

But the Enclave noticed these kind gestures and was moved by them. There were sides to human nature other than suspicion and fear of the Other. That nobility; that kindness; that very willingness to think of the welfare of another; those were the very qualities the Enclave cherished. The bodies of the saved in London and Vancouver were indeed cold. The saved in Hong Kong, after weeks being cut off from power and public utilities, were genuinely feeling the burden of hunger and malnutrition.

They bore their corporeal discomforts gladly if it meant others could finally share in their spiritual relief. Having thus been saved herself, Jean knew with absolute certainty that she wouldn't hesitate to swallow broken glass, pour boiling acid into her own eyes, or let every bone in her body be broken with a smile on her face if it meant one more person could feel the way she felt. The Enclave didn't only offer happiness – it had made her a better, more moral being. She shivered in anticipation of its power soon being amplified sixfold.

A sharp ripple of disquiet passed through the Enclave, disrupting its serenity. It was a new feeling for her, one she hadn't encountered so far in her brief time sharing the sensorium. It took her a moment to make sense of the fact that some of their members had been violently severed from their connection with the rest, either knocked unconscious or killed. Three – no, four; another went dark even as she was paying attention. *We're compromised, he knew we were coming*, thought a fifth voice, just before it too went dark.

The disruption in their connections was nearby, Jean realised – it was coming from Beijing. Of course; the six members who had been sent to neutralise David at his apartment.

Manderly, Tony thought. *The message your past-self left him must have put him on his guard. He's more resourceful than we gave him credit for.*

Even as he thought this, she saw David's gaunt face appear in the view of the sixth team member for a fraction of a second. His flat was in disarray, papers strewn everywhere, furniture overturned. Two limp bodies lay on the floor; blood oozed from the left one's temple. Then the butt of a pistol whipped into her field of view in a blur, and she was jerked back into her body as though yanked by a leash.

Let me go to him, she thought. *Even if he's on his guard, he won't suspect me when it was my past-self that tipped him off. I should be able to restrain him without the need for any more violence.*

The Enclave concurred. 'Change of plans,' Tony said out loud to the driver. 'Head to this address instead, at the best possible speed. It's urgent.' He uploaded the street address of David's state-owned flat building in Niujie to the SUV's navigation UI.

***

They reached Niujie inside of twenty minutes later. Snow lay thick on the ground, and the night was almost quiet for Beijing. This close to the centre of the city, the push among civilians to evacuate somewhere less conspicuous had been strongest. David's apartment block hosted maybe a hundred windows on the side facing the street, spread across twenty storeys. No more than seven were illuminated.

Having had her sensory deprivation gear removed, the SUV deposited Jean on the pavement outside and continued around the corner, where Tony and the two agents would wait in the underground car park. She unfastened the top two buttons of her coat, despite the sub-freezing temperature, to display her bruised throat from where the merc had choked her hours earlier.

The best lies have an element of truth, and hers was simple: Enclave sleeper agents had attacked her, the same as him, and she had successfully fought them off and made her escape. After getting out of Kisangani, she had hurried to meet him face-to-face, worried that her message might have made him a target. That ought to placate him long enough for her to get a chance to go for the base of his neck. In the pocket of her jeans, she fingered the syringe Tony had given her.

Reaching the eighth-floor corridor, David's apartment was immediately obvious from the splintered doorframe. Blue-grey smoke and the smell of cordite wafted from the entryway. She approached slowly with her hands raised in the universal gesture of placation.

'Dave?' she called, feeling she conveyed uncertainty convincingly enough. 'It's Jean. Are you OK?'

Gingerly, she stepped over the threshold into the apartment's hallway. Sprawled face-down in plain view was the body of one of the Enclave agents, entirely motionless. A pool of blood spread outward from it. Dread emanated from Jean's mind outward into the Enclave, and its amplified echo came roiling back. She turned the body over and was confronted by exactly what they all feared: glassy eyes divided by a .22-caliber exit wound.

She checked each of the small apartment's rooms in turn. It was the worst-case scenario: no sign of David, but five more dead bodies, all of them sporting gunshot wounds. Jean felt bile rise at the back of her throat, stinging grief for five brothers she had known and loved all too briefly. Their ghosts, their self-knowledge, liberated from flesh, would be preserved in the sensorium.

Find him, urged a million voices. *He can't have gone far.* Tony's voice emerged from the multitude. *He's not checked in on the virtunet. His state-registered car is still in the garage, and the snow at the front and rear entrances is undisturbed but for our own tracks. Best guess is he's still somewhere inside the apartment complex. Stay on...*

Tony's thoughts were interrupted by a metallic shriek and a sudden, shocking impact. When his senses became intelligible again, the world had shifted ninety degrees clockwise, and his cheek was resting against the SUV's passenger window. The pain Jean felt from him, second-hand, suggested that three of his ribs were broken. Something had impacted the SUV hard enough to tip it on its side.

Manderly. Manderly's here. Tony's thoughts were sluggish, probably concussed. *Jean, hurry, get down here...*

Another impact, this time accompanied by the shrill noise of shattering glass. Tony was dragged forcibly upwards through the vehicle's sunroof; Jean distantly felt his skin receive hundreds of lacerations, some of them deep. She bolted from the apartment and down the stairs, taking them two at a time.

Tony tried to struggle to his feet, his muscles refusing to do as they were told, until the same rough hands spun him around, bringing him face-to-face with David Manderly. His formal white shirt was soaked with blood; his eyes looked even more sunken than usual, blazing with fury. A fist powered by the same enhancements Jean had received came crashing down, and the Enclave was diminished by one more mind.

The floor numbers flashed past as Jean descended the stairwell – four, three, two. She burst through the door to the basement garage, almost breaking it off its hinges. 'David!' she yelled into the cavernous underground space. 'It's Jean! If you're there, they came after me too. I have friends downtown, they can get us to safety, so come out, okay?' She felt the syringe in her pocket pressing against her leg.

No response came.

The garage was large, but almost entirely empty; most of the automobiles it would ordinarily contain were now choking the G45 highway to the southwest in the mad dash to reach a more remote region of China. The SUV was immediately obvious – its crumpled husk lay in the northern corner, with the bonnet of a white sedan embedded in its chassis. Jean sprinted over to it and found Tony lying where David had left him. His face was as thoroughly ruined as the SUV, but through the bloody remains of his nose, he was still taking shallow, gurgling breaths. Jean exhaled, and the Enclave exhaled with her.

She heard a handgun being cocked behind her back, the universal signifier of an assailant wishing their presence known.

'Stand up, Jean. Slowly. Keep your hands where I can see them.'

She complied.

'Dave, listen, okay? It's me. It's just me. Settle down, and we can talk this through.'

'When did they get to you?' Judging from the sound of his voice, he was keeping a good six paces of distance between them.

'I don't know what you're talking about.'

'You send me a cryptic message about Yang-Mitsubishi, and when I try to respond, you've gone dark. Less than six hours later, a hit squad kicks down my door, and you follow in their wake with Tony Liu, ex-YM-lackey, the man keeping the investigation into the Enclave Effect out of public channels. Forgive me my suspicions.'

'David, I told you, they came after me, and I got away; that's why I'm here. For Christ's sake, put the gun away.' She could feel the shape of the syringe in her trouser pocket.

'Prove it,' David said, offering no audible indication he'd adjusted his firing stance. 'Prove you're you.'

Jean heaved a sigh. 'What exactly are you looking for here, Dave? My driver's license?'

'I don't know, but you'd better think of something fast.'

'My name is Jean Harrison, born January 14, 2090, to Jonah Harrison and Astrid Fournier. Commissioned by the Orbital Reconnaissance Corps on July 3, 2108. Graduated with distinction from Scolt Head Island, April 4, 2111. Mother of Victoria, born August 4, 2114, and of James, born August 30, 2117. Widowed, January 22, 2127. And I know that you, David Manderly, have a pair of small moles just above your right hipbone, and that the last time we had sex, you finished in three minutes, thirty-seven seconds. I know this because you time the main event in your implants and log the results in a lined jotter you keep in the top drawer of your bedside cabinet. That's not, for the record, the reason I broke it off between us, but finding that jotter didn't help. Will that do? Or do we need the details to get more embarrassing?'

David took a deep, shuddering breath. 'That's good, Jean. What Koo said was true: the spellbound from the Enclave can impersonate their former selves flawlessly. You would have convinced me if you hadn't leaned down to check on your friend, and I hadn't seen the same needle mark on the back of your neck I saw on the six I shot. Interlace your fingers behind your head.'

Jean feinted left, then darted right. The dark garage was illuminated by muzzle flashes; three in quick succession. The third shot punched a hole in her coattail as it whirled behind her.

She got inside the reach of David's arms before he could fire a fourth shot; she clamped her hands around the gun – one on the grip, the other on the slide – and twisted with all her strength. David's index finger was neatly snapped at the first joint by the trigger guard; he yelped in pain, and Jean wrenched the gun free. She ejected the Sig Sauer's magazine and the round in the chamber, stripped off the slide, and tossed aside the component parts.

'OK, Dave, you got me. Sorry it had to come to this.'

He offered no response. Grimacing, he wrenched the finger she'd dislocated back into place and adopted a guard stance, centre of gravity low, head ducked behind his hands. Jean mirrored the stance.

David didn't possess the pain endurance that she did, thanks to the influence of the Enclave, and he didn't use telomerase supplements. Unlike Jean, his body was actually that of an adult in their late forties; past their physical prime; their reflexes slowing. On the other hand, his sinewy frame made it obvious he hadn't relaxed his training regimen by much, even in his life as a bureaucrat; he outweighed Jean by a good twenty kilos, and his reach exceeded hers by ten centimetres. She couldn't trade blows with him; she needed to get in close and bring the fight to the ground, find a way to get the syringe's needle to meet his spinal column.

He had seemingly come to the same conclusion, and he led with a push kick, intending to keep her off balance and maintain distance. Jean sidestepped it and, taking advantage of the split-second he was off balance, she moved inside his guard. She planted one foot behind his left leg, placed a hand on his chest, and shoved. David's entire bodyweight pivoted around his midsection, and he crashed to the ground, landing on his upper back with the combined force of gravity and Jean's strength.

The move would probably have fractured the spine of someone without enhanced bones, and even as it was, she worried that she might have done him serious harm. Perhaps it was because of that worry that she moved in to consolidate her advantage more slowly than she should have. In any event, as she descended with her arms outstretched towards David's neck, she felt a vicious impact in her ribcage. The haymaker didn't break anything, but she found herself sprawling with her back to the ground. David straddled her and began raining blows down on her raised guard.

She had underestimated him; he wasn't cut from the same cloth as the hired guns her past-self had fought in Kisangani, and pain endurance or not, this was her second physical brawl in less than eight hours. The euphoria of The

Enclave had distracted her from it, but she was exhausted. Fatigue toxins were slowing her down, making her sloppy. She managed to grab hold of one of David's arms, pulling him down towards her and, with considerable struggle, wrapping her legs around his neck in a triangle choke.

Against an unenhanced opponent, this would have been checkmate. David, however, gasping for breath but undaunted, made her realise her tactical error too late. He rose to his feet; with all of his enhanced muscles' strength, he hefted her fully off the ground with him and smashed her down on top of the white sedan, hard enough to buckle its roof.

Seeing stars, she fumbled in her pocket for the syringe. Her right hand finding it, she lunged at him, trying for the back of his neck. David's eyes went wide; he twisted away from the needle and reached across his body with his right hand. He grabbed Jean's wrist and expertly manipulated it into a gooseneck. The discomfort the technique caused was comparatively insignificant, but Jean's body's autonomous reflexes betrayed her; her fingers opened, and the syringe fell to the floor, where David smartly kicked it away.

'I'm sorry it had to come to this, Jean,' he said, and brought his left hand down on her forehead in a crippling hammerfist strike. Jean's world turned dark and silent; somewhere far away, where it couldn't reach her, the Enclave howled in frustration at her severance.

A.N. Milne

Chapter 12

July 12th, 2326 C.E.

Jonah had awakened to learn he'd spent two days of transit in the cruiser's medical bay, under the influence of a general anaesthetic.

He wasn't complaining; any pretext for the sleep he had been craving was fine by him. A colony of nanomachines beavered away at the chunk of shrapnel in his thigh, slowly extracting it millimetre by millimetre while knitting the mangled sinew and bone back together in its wake, repairing the damage as finely as they were able. Jonah would keep the leg, but he would have a grisly scar to show for it, and he would walk with a heavy limp if he was ever to find himself in groundly gravity again.

When the procedure had been completed, he had been chastened to learn that the molecular platelets which had performed it – the same ones that comprised the Archangel frames – were a finite resource. Aki gave him the story of how they had been salvaged from a laboratory on Ganymede, where an obscure branch of ORC's R&D division had been conducting experiments with femtech back in 2135 before all hell broke loose. The Insurgency didn't have the resources to manufacture them *en masse*, and they inevitably lost some every time they engaged the Collective. The volume Victoria had shed to keep Alyssa alive represented an obscene spending spree on her part. Jonah had begun to bluster an apology, but Albrecht insisted that it was the least that they could do after the role he had played in the battle above TransTerra.

After being discharged from the medical bay, Jonah set himself to the task which, under less severe circumstances, would have been his first priority; grieving for Robyn, and for Patrick, and for Ilsa.

Alyssa had been discharged the day before he had; for the duration of the voyage, she was bunking with Jack Nguyen and his extended family, maybe two dozen bodies crammed into a space the size of his cabins on the *Prospice*. When Jonah entered her cabin, she was lying on her acceleration couch, unnervingly still but for the rising and falling of her chest. Only her open right eye betrayed that she was awake. The left side of her face and neck were covered by gel-plasters steadily releasing anaesthetic into her bloodstream. The burns she had sustained were consistent with those created by the superheated air from a maser cannon's near miss. Even shot full of painkillers, the burns would be aggravated if she moved.

Hey, Lys. Jonah routed the message to her corneal implants.

Hey, Jonah. Why are we talking like this?

I didn't want to cause you the discomfort of having to move your jaw.

Oh, right. Thanks.

Do you feel up to talking about what happened on the surface? To your mum and dad?

A long gap in the conversation followed. The text interface indicated that Alyssa was formulating a response before sending it. Jonah waited, letting her take as long as she needed to let the words come.

I ran, she wrote, finally. **The Scarabs dropped down all around us. Ilsa, she was so brave. She charged right at one of them in the caterpillar. And when that didn't work, Mum and Dad got out and went at it with their flamethrowers. But I couldn't stop thinking about Marc, that night in the clearing. I couldn't bear to look at them, I was so scared. So, I hid in the grass, and I crawled away. Everyone else fought to the end, and let themselves die standing instead of being captured. But I just lay on the ground and hoped they wouldn't notice me.**

The text feed paused, and Alyssa suddenly moved a hand to her face, pressing the heel of her palm into her eye. She was sobbing, Jonah realised.

I don't deserve to be here, she continued. **I don't deserve to be alive. Ilsa should be here, or Mum, not me.**

Jonah yanked her hand away from her eye and held it. **Alyssa,** he wrote, **never let me hear you say that again. No one else there had seen what you did, gone through what you did. After that first night, when Marcus died, no one could have expected you to do anything else.**

They were there because of me. I heard it from Villeneuve. The stuff in my chest, that's what led them to our convoy.

You couldn't have known that.

Everyone there died on my account. Mum and Dad and Ilsa. Just like Marc did. And I ran. I got in a Humvee and escaped while the Scarabs were distracted. How do I live with that, Jonah? How does anyone ever forgive me?

Jonah couldn't think of an answer right away, but he sensed that this was a situation where bromidic reassurances wouldn't be enough.

Did I ever tell you about your Aunt Jean, Alyssa? Victoria's mother?

Alyssa looked perplexed for a moment, then shook her head, gingerly. **I heard a bit about her from Mum and Dad, but you never spoke about her to me. Why do you bring her up now?**

Jonah took a breath. For so long, it had been a topic everyone around him had skirted. Eoin and Rahman and Ilsa, the members of his crew who knew him best, they knew. Whenever Jean's name came up in conversation, there would be a pause where they averted their eyes, and when the discourse resumed, it would be on other, more pleasant matters. Rumours and hearsay passed amidst the crew in whispers, but the full narrative, the story of the Captain's great shame, remained taboo.

Because I failed her, he wrote, and to say so in so many words felt cleansing.

Alyssa frowned, despite the fluid weeping from her burns. **How so?**

Her mother and I met while I was still a cadet in the ORC. Astrid: that was her name. A student from Paris. I was on shore leave from Scolt Head Island when she was patronising a bar in Oxford. What started as a one-night stand led to dinner. Dinner led to a long-term relationship, and from there to marriage. A home. A child.

I was twenty-six when Jean was born, Lys. Barely older than you are now. And I loved her, from the moment they let me into the postnatal ward, and for every minute after. Truly, I did.

But when you're a twenty-six-year-old man, and you come from privilege, and you've earned every commendation and qualification the world has to give, the universe just looks like so much potential. And I made my way as

an ORC officer during peacetime, and twenty-six slipped quietly into twenty-eight, and twenty-eight ticked over into thirty without ceremony. And I felt myself becoming a husband, and a father, and I saw the rest of my life stretched out ahead of me, and it looked desolate. Sterile. The same as everyone else's.

So when the headhunters from the Merantau Program came knocking, I said yes. I wanted to be different. I wanted to be special. I wanted to be the Starman. Jean pleaded with me not to go. She was six years old, and I slammed the door in her face. For the better part of two centuries, no one reproached me, Lys. No one told me I wasn't worthy as an officer or as a man. I'm telling you all this because you're criticising yourself far more harshly than anyone around you is. If you feel you've done something you need to be forgiven for, I can't tell you you're wrong. But that forgiveness isn't something you'll get from other people. The only one who has to forgive you is you. It's because you're still alive that you have the opportunity to earn it.

Alyssa turned her head to meet his gaze for the first time since the conversation had started, and he didn't know how to read what he saw in her eye. 'Thanks, Jonah,' she said, out loud.

Her words came slowly, the pronunciation mushy and slurred. 'Really, honestly, thank you. I wish I could believe that was true.'

***

On the third day of the voyage, once the engines had been properly repaired, the cruiser began to decelerate towards the Insurgency's forward operating base at a gentle tenth of a g. Albrecht wanted to minimise the possibility of their showing up on the sensors of any Collective scouts, however insignificant the risk of being found was in these thousands of cubic AU.

They were permitted to roam throughout the ship; these old transports had been designed to operate with the bare minimum of crew, and most of its systems were automated, contained between the inner and outer hulls. There was a limit to the damage the settlers could do through ignorance or carelessness. They were allowed as much glucose paste and vitamin supplements as the ship was fit to synthesise. Faced suddenly with a surfeit of free time and a deficit of free space, the settlers began to make a habit of congregating in the cargo hold where the gel-pods had been set up; it shortly became the ship's unofficial recreational space.

The tenor of the conversations Jonah overheard there was less despondent than the one he had shared with Alyssa, but not by much. The relief of the successful getaway following the days of restless fear was wearing off, and in its place was emerging the dreadful realisation that their lives as they knew them were effectively over. They were refugees, driven from their homes by a force they could scarcely comprehend and taken in by guardians who didn't particularly want them. He hated that nothing he could say would assuage their anxiety, and listening to them, he found his own anxiety growing apace. He spent as little time in the cargo hold as he reasonably could without feeling he was letting them all down.

He petitioned Albrecht hourly for updates on where they were going, and what was going to happen to them. Hourly, he was met with silence.

He bunked together with Rahman, the pair of them wiling away the hours with games in shared TSI space. Jonah won two games out of three at chess or checkers, but he lost nearly every card game they tried. Even rendered as a digital avatar, Rahman had an extraordinary poker face. On the fifth day, the two of them met with Eoin and Will, holding a brief, silent vigil to Ilsa's memory. The original senior staff of the *Prospice* felt diminished as a group in her absence, like a hand missing its ring finger.

Jonah didn't see much of Victoria. In truth, he wondered if she wasn't avoiding him intentionally. He was only beginning to understand just how desperate her position had been when she had come to TransTerra, how fatalistic her mindset. He had encountered more than his fair share of botched suicide attempts over the years on the *Prospice* following the communications failure with Earth, crewmembers who had tried to override safety protocols and flood their cabins with nitrogen or carbon monoxide. After being resuscitated, they had wandered around the ship for a while with glazed expressions, surprised at finding themselves still conscious, and burdened with the myriad little decisions and responsibilities that came with being awake. When he saw Victoria on the cruiser's journey, her manner reminded him of those men and women.

Eager to make up for Jonah's lack of communication with the other Archangels—almost obnoxiously so—was Aki. He had been just the right age growing up to have seen the original broadcast that had conferred upon him the 'Starman' nickname and the celebrity that had come with it. He and his brother had grown up thinking of him like a latter-day Christopher Columbus or James Cook, the ultimate frontiersman of his age. It was an occupation that had commanded particular respect in fledgling Martian culture.

He seemed deflated when Jonah told him that the majority of the time aboard the *Prospice* would have seemed rather boring compared to his life of high-stakes battle. Hazardous and difficult, certainly, but for the most part, shipboard life had been routine for him and the other settlers. After the buzz of excitement of the first few years wore off, and discounting the dark years following 2145, it had been a job; a series of logistical hurdles and problem-solving exercises with the promise of a sort of retirement and the assurance of a life well-lived when they arrived at their destination.

Jonah and Aki each tried and failed to convince the other of the mundanity of their last hundred and ninety years of life. Jonah flatly refused to believe that the existence of a relativistic demigod tasked with sabotaging the operation of an alien hive-mind could grow dull, and yet Aki steadfastly insisted that it was the case. It unnerved him, the way Aki spoke of the possibility of death in battle the way most people he had known talked about dying of old age.

'The thing is,' said Aki, sitting opposite Jonah, leaning forward and absently wringing his hands, 'the first two decades *were* scary. That was when the fighting was all contained in the solar system, when we were getting squeezed from outpost to outpost, moon to moon. I fought ground battles on Callisto, where the heat differential from our weapons caused huge steam explosions all around us. I was there when the Collective dropped an asteroid on Enceladus to flush us out of our underground shelter.

'But when we were pushed out to deep space, it all changed. The distances involved became a hundred times bigger, and we'd be flying for months between missions. Sometimes years, even in subjective time. And the Collective changed. It might seem strange from your point of view, but they actually got a lot more docile. In the early stages of the fighting, it seemed like they were fielding new weapons every month that we'd never even theorised before. But the Scarabs have been their standard infantry unit for most of two hundred years, barring incremental upgrades. And sometimes, when we show up at one of their asteroid bases or relays in force, they'll just pack up and leave without any fight at all. It's like we're beneath their notice.'

Aki shrugged, despondent. 'I don't know what's more dispiriting, an enemy who hates you, or an enemy who doesn't even care you hate it.'

**

On the tenth day, a tannoy announcement rang through the ship, addressed to settlers and Archangels alike. 'We will be docking at our forward operating base in approximately one hour,' spoke Albrecht's voice. 'You will be called according to your surnames by alphabetical order upon arrival. When called, please make your way in an orderly fashion to the airlocks on the starboard side of decks 2 and 4. Temporary accommodations will be arranged for you. That is all.'

Rahman folded in the game of baccarat he was playing against Jonah for virtual coins and withdrew from the shared TSI space. 'You'd better start getting your things together,' he said, looking apologetic. 'You'll be called before me. Sorry I couldn't spend more time thrashing you.'

'Not to worry, I had a crap hand anyway. We'll pick up where we left off once we're settled in.'

Rahman said nothing to that, and Jonah suspected that he was preoccupied by the same thing he was. 'Temporary' accommodations, Albrecht had said. How temporary was temporary? And where exactly would the settlers be expected to go after that period expired?

Gathering his possessions didn't take very long. Out of consideration for fuel/weight rations and the fact that they had been under attack, all he had brought with him onto the shuttle were a couple of changes of clothes and a blister pack of anti-emetic pills for his first foray into zero-gravity in two decades. He'd even left his telomerase supplements behind.

Linking his eyes with the ship's exterior sensors, he caught his first glimpse of the Insurgency's base of operations as a black mass, looming slowly larger as they approached. An interstellar asteroid was what he had heard from Aki; a few trillion tons of rock, meandering their way through the cosmos, selected for its low-albedo, carbonaceous composition. There were no exterior lights on its surface, but magnifying the view from the ship's docking port, Jonah could just make out the contours of a corresponding port extruding from the rock, the shaped metal faintly reflecting the glow of their engines. It would lead into an interior of criss-crossing tunnels like an ants' nest. It came closer and closer until it filled his vision, and finally, a deep *clunk* reverberated through the ship's structure, and the press of the deceleration died entirely.

When the letter 'H' was called, he exited his cabin and was surprised to find Victoria waiting for him in the corridor outside. She appeared to hover perfectly steady in the centre of the corridor, using her wings to orient herself in the absence of significant gravity.

'Hi there, stranger,' he said, covering his unease with a tight smile.

'Hi yourself,' she replied. 'Sorry I haven't seen more of you this last week. I've just had a lot of people to apologise to. You not least among them. I said some things, more harshly than I should have.'

He shook his head. 'Don't be ridiculous. We're all of us in your debt. Don't take any shit from your comrades, OK? Whatever you had to do to pull it off, just know that I'm grateful to be alive and be myself, and so are eight hundred other people.'

They accompanied each other down the corridor toward the elevator to deck 2, he taking long, bounding leaps from surface to surface. He had regained some of his old confidence operating under reduced-g in the past ten days.

'Alyssa didn't seem to feel that way when I went to see her,' Victoria said. Her tone was sombre.

Jonah winced. 'She was like that with you too?'

'She talked about wishing she was dead.'

'She's had it worse than any of us. She's seen friends and family slaughtered in front of her. It'll take her some time to come around, and that's if we do everything we can to help her. But I'm concerned about you, too. What's the latest on this court-martial nonsense?'

'The Commander has scheduled the hearing for two weeks from now, after we've finished getting the settlers accommodated.'

'You seem awfully calm about the prospect of being reduced to a spinal column with eyes.'

'I've been talking to some of the other lieutenants. Currying favour, I guess you could call it. I'm not entirely without a defence for my actions when Albrecht puts me in the hot seat. And even if that's what it comes to, I'll accept it willingly. What we achieved, getting everyone off of TransTerra, it's close to my best-case scenario when I set out in the first place. I'd do it all again.'

The airlocks disgorged the transport's passengers into the FOB. The corridors hewn into the dead rock of the asteroid had been heated and pressurised in anticipation of their successful return; Jonah recognised the characteristic, synthetic smell of oxygen distilled from water-ice.

Dozens of stolid Archangels lined the corridors, ushering the settlers through like anachronistic traffic wardens. Their androgynous faces were typically hard to read, but Jonah thought he had enough of a sense of the Insurgency now to recognise curiosity when he saw it. The majority of them wouldn't have seen flesh-and-blood humans in decades, maybe centuries.

One approached him, another of the slender, pale, fair-haired types that they seemed to favour. He offered Jonah the three-fingered salute he'd grown to recognise. 'Captain Harrison,' he said. As was often the case with the Insurgency, his voice identified him as male more than his face did (though Jonah supposed in bodies comprised of manipulable nanomachines, gender was more of an affectation than anything). 'Lieutenant Taylor Daniels, at your service. The Commander requests your presence in the command module, as soon as you're able.'

Jonah thought of trying to return the salute, then thought better of it, and simply touched his fingers to his forehead the way he was familiar with. 'Glad to be here, Lieutenant. I'm at the Commander's disposal, just point me in the right direction.'

'Yes, sir. Perhaps I'd better... one second, my apologies Captain.'

A file popped up in Jonah's vision with a signature from Daniels; opening it revealed a three-dimensional map of the station. Jonah groaned when he saw it

– there were hundreds of kilometres of tunnels snaking throughout the asteroid's interior, winding and intertwining irregularly according to the contours of the rock. A red dot flagged up the command module at the centre of the base. He tried to estimate how long it would take to get there from the exterior, propelling himself from surface to surface while trying not to hit anything with his bad leg.

'Thanks, Lieutenant. If you could let the Commander know I'll be there in a Terran day or so?'

'Ah, of course. Sorry Captain, I should have thought. Perhaps I can give you a lift?' He held out a hand for Jonah to take. Jonah sighed, clasped it, and tried to think of a way he could make being dragged through the station behind Daniels like a toddler look remotely dignified.

It wasn't as bad as he feared. Daniels conducted himself with exceeding politeness and deference, and if he bore any resentment at having to act as a chauffeur, he didn't show it. Jonah had noticed that he referred to his rank as 'lew-tenant,' as opposed to 'left-tenant,' the way he and Victoria did. When they got to talking, it turned out he had been an engineer in the US Air Force before the Body had appeared, based out of the Puget Sound arcology in Washington state. He had been assigned to repairs on one of the USA's orbital defence platforms when the fighting had started. 'I heard you lost some people on the ground before the evacuation. Sorry for your loss, Captain.'

'I appreciate it, Lieutenant. I wasn't there to see it, but it's my understanding they took their own lives rather than allowing themselves to be captured. My daughter was in their number. I suppose I should be grateful. As I understand, it was the lesser of two terrible fates.'

Daniels didn't respond, and Jonah realised too late the profound insensitivity of what he had implied. 'I apologise, Daniels. You had... *have* people left behind on Earth, don't you?'

Daniels nodded. 'My husband, sir. We were expecting our first child when it all went down. It makes me sick, imagining that my son has lived his whole life an appendage of the Collective, when I've never even seen his face.'

'There's still hope you'll see them yet.'

'If I didn't think so, I'd have checked out long ago, sir.'

***

Under the gentle propulsion of the QF drive in Daniels' frame, they arrived at the command module in just under an hour. They passed through a second airlock to get inside; to judge from the map he had been given, the module was a hermetically sealed metal sphere about two hundred metres across, the kernel at the heart of the asteroid. Jonah didn't need to ask to understand that the module would also have its own battery backup, maybe even its own engines to escape if the asteroid were to crumble around it. It was smart, conscientious design; much like the bridge on a battleship, the strategic nerve centre of the base could preserve itself autonomously if the exterior was to be breached.

Albrecht hovered in the centre of the hollowed-out space, flanked by three Archangel officers Jonah didn't recognise, in silent conference. Upon their entrance, he held up a hand and spoke aloud. 'Thank you everyone, but I need a word in private with Captain Harrison. Dismissed, for the time being. You too, Lieutenant Daniels.'

Daniels and the three officers saluted, and quietly made their exit, leaving Jonah and Albrecht alone in the spherical space. The walls were disconcertingly blank, with no decoration of any sort, and any electronic or information systems built into the command module weren't physically apparent. The chamber felt like an extension of Albrecht's mind: hard, expedient, and bare of unnecessary adornments.

'Very impressive setup you've got here,' Jonah remarked. 'How long did all of this take?'

'Only five years or so,' Albrecht replied. 'We have bases similar to this one spread throughout interstellar space between here and Earth. This is one of the newest; our engineers standardised the design decades ago, and the Archangel frames enable them to work around the clock.'

Jonah whistled. He didn't want to appear too impressed; both men were aware how entirely the settlers were now dependent upon the Insurgency's patronage, but it would do him no favours to call attention to it.

'I know you're tired from the journey, Captain, so I'll be as brief as I can,' Albrecht said. 'There's a cavern located close to the surface of the asteroid, where I'm having my people erect temporary housing. There should be more than enough space for your lot to live. The quantum fluctuation drives in the base can be put to work generating heat, and we have algae cultures that can be cultivated in the tunnels, with some effort. They'll photosynthesise oxygen and act as an edible crop. With the available surface area, it should yield a surplus of calories to keep eight hundred people fed. It will be a hard, hand-to-mouth existence, harder than you faced on TransTerra, but for the foreseeable future, I see no reason why you couldn't sustain yourselves in this base indefinitely.'

'That means a lot, Commander,' Jonah said. 'I realise that you took us in under duress, and that we have no right to expect as much help as you've already given us. Which is why I sense that there's a "however" coming.'

Albrecht grimaced. '*However*,' he said, 'I find myself in a difficult position, Captain. I would never force anyone to join our cause against their will. But I told you on TransTerra that you represent a tactical liability for the Insurgency, and as much as it pains me to say so, that fact hasn't changed. Our entire operation is predicated on the ability of the Archangel Frame to act as a guerrilla unit that can preserve itself in vacuum. If the Collective were to take this base – and I think it only fair to tell you that they *have* taken our bases before – we would need to have protocols in place to evacuate your wounded, to prevent depressurisation, to have a ship ready to leave at a moment's notice with a cache of the materials necessary to maintain organic life. All losing moves, expenditures of resources that strategically gain us nothing. So, my priorities remain. My people's lives come before yours, and if this base is breached, you're on your own. And if I have my way, Lieutenant Harrison won't be able to influence that decision next time.'

'Noted. I'm guessing that the *quid pro quo* you're hinting at is that we can have Archangel frames of our own if we agree to fight for you.'

'That's precisely it. If we had the materials spare to convert eight hundred men and women to Archangels and simply send them on their way, we would. But we don't, and we can't.'

'Look,' Jonah said, trying hard to keep his voice level, 'I get it. And if it was just me, I wouldn't hesitate to sign up. I want nothing more than to get even with the bastards who took my daughter and my friends. I know there are others among us who feel the same way.' He thought of Brandon Lawson, and his bloodthirsty outburst to Victoria on the surface. 'But there are children among our number. *Infants.* They're incapable of giving informed consent to having their nervous systems crammed into a fighting machine. And as long as even one flesh-and-blood human remains amongst our number, you still have your tactical dilemma.'

'True,' Albrecht replied. 'Nevertheless, we remain at an impasse. I never said it would be an easy choice, Captain. But we are leaders. Hard choices are what we get paid for. Figuratively speaking.'

'Finally, something we agree on. I'll give it some thought, Commander. Thank you for being honest with me.' He gestured towards the airlock. 'Could you...?'

Albrecht gave Jonah a gentle shove, sending him drifting towards the exit. 'Before you go,' he called after him, 'there's something I think you should know about your granddaughter. It concerns Corporal Velasquez.'

'Oh?' Jonah called back.

'The Corporal was assimilated by the Collective six years ago, during an attack on Pisces Station, a base similar to this one. Lieutenant Harrison's squadron was stationed there. Scarabs were converging on the command module in overwhelming numbers, trying to gain access to the database stored there. If they had reached it, all of our base locations, all of our planned operations would have been laid bare to the Collective. We would have been set back to square one.

'Standard procedure under those circumstances would be to evacuate the base and detonate an EMP device remotely, frying the circuits in the command module and keeping the information they contained secure. But Corporal Velasquez was late in evacuating, and he was trapped inside the base.'

Jonah thought he saw where this was heading. 'And the EMP device would also disrupt the Archangel frame's functions, correct?'

'Correct. Lieutenant Harrison had a choice to make; detonate the EMP and leave Velasquez immobilised when Collective reinforcements arrived, unable to defend himself against assimilation, even by suicide. Or spare her comrade that fate, and let critical information fall into enemy hands. She made the correct choice. The Corporal's rank meant that he had limited knowledge that would help the Collective find us. Even so; he had been her teammate for over a hundred years, and she didn't hesitate for a second. That's how much she hates them. That's how much she's prepared to sacrifice to hurt them.

'But not you. For you, she turned her back on her comrades and everything she worked for these past two hundred years.' Albrecht fixed Jonah with a curious look. 'I wish I could see what she sees in you, that makes you so special.'

Chapter 13

December 9th, 2135 C.E.

Jean was awakened by the throbbing in her skull. She squinted against the glare of the sun, pouring through the blinds of a room she didn't recognise.

Something in her head felt wrong. Her body was shaky and unresponsive. Her eyes and ears were working, but her brain couldn't seem to do anything useful with the information they provided, or place it in any meaningful context. Was she just massively hungover? That would certainly seem to correspond to the experience of waking up in an unfamiliar bed, with a gruesome headache in place of the memory of the last several hours. But no; she'd experienced enough hangovers to recognise the sensation, and whatever it was she was feeling now, this strange *absence*, ran deeper than that.

She shrugged off the sweaty sheets and staggered to her feet. The shabby, impersonal furnishings seemed to indicate a cheap motel room. Her inner ear disagreed vehemently with her head's decision to turn vertical. She stumbled into the adjoining bathroom, her vision blurring, and reached the toilet just in time to vomit, copiously and at length.

The throbbing in her forehead occupied her attention while she was kneeling on the linoleum floor, shuddering with the effort of expulsion, but she became aware of another persistent ache. An area on the back of her neck felt swollen, tender. She probed the spot delicately with the tips of her fingers, wincing at the sensation, and found a vertical slit in the skin about two inches long. The cut was still fresh, and had been inexpertly stitched together.

Her memory clicked into focus, and it became obvious what the absence she was feeling was. It was the silence where there should have been a million voices.

No. Fuck. No no no no no NO NO NO!

Panic like nothing she'd ever known closed around her heart. She jerked away from the toilet and back out of the bathroom on all fours, her physical distress all but forgotten. Fight-or-flight instincts resounded in her brain, even as her higher thought processes realised their futility. She couldn't fight, and she couldn't flee from this. She was trapped again, a mind isolated inside a few cubic inches of grey matter, tethered to decaying, mortal flesh.

She tried desperately to spread her mind out, broadcast her thoughts as loud as she could, hoping in vain that another mind would answer to tell her that everything was alright, that this was just a nightmare, or a transitory glitch in the Enclave's system. When that failed, she huddled in the foetal position in the corner of the room, eyes squeezed shut as tight as she could manage, hands clamped over her ears. It was bad enough to be imprisoned within her own skull. If nothing else, she could at least try to mitigate the ugliness and the brutality of the material universe. She willed herself fruitlessly towards a dreamless sleep; she wished she had access to some kind of opiate, anything that could take the edge off of being conscious.

It was all so unfair. She had only been allowed a few hours of real, true, unfettered life, before she'd been yanked back against her will into this sick parody of it. Having been allowed the briefest glimpse of what reality could be, the barbarous world had conspired to beat it out of her. The memory of the euphoria at being a part of the Enclave wouldn't leave her be; if she had been agnostic before, she was certain now that there was no God, or if there was, that he was a sadistic, insane despot. What benevolent creator would inflict *this* upon His creations and call it 'life', this absurd, pointless cycle of consumption and destruction?

She didn't know how long she sat there, but eventually, she heard movement; muted as it was by her hands over her ears, her cochlear implants picked it up and clarified it in spite of her. Muffled impacts whose rhythm corresponded to footsteps on threadbare carpet, followed by a creaky door opening. 'Oh, you're up,' said a voice she recognised. 'Welcome back to the land of the living, Sleeping Beauty.'

Jean cracked her eyes open as widely as she dared, just enough to bring the figure who had entered into focus. David stood in the doorway looking apologetic, a brown paper bag clutched in his left hand. 'Sorry I wasn't there when you woke up,' he said. 'I just stepped out to get some *chow mein*, and it took me a while to find a restaurant that was still open. You should eat. I ran some tests, and your blood sugar is awfully low after what you've been through in the last couple of days.'

'Put it back,' Jean's voice came out as a hoarse whisper. She hadn't noticed how dry her throat was.

'Hm?'

It was possible he genuinely hadn't heard her. She cleared her throat and tried again. 'The device you extracted from my neck.' Her voice quavered, but her enunciation was clear. 'Put it back where you found it.'

David glanced around, acting hapless and innocent, like they were still friends, and nothing had happened. 'Jean, I don't...'

'Put it back, you bastard!' she screamed. She lunged at him.

In that moment, all she felt was hatred. She hated David because it was his fault that she again found herself in this fallen, debased state. She hated herself for hating him, knowing that the very concept of 'blame' was a property of her petty, animalistic mind that the Enclave had freed her from. She hated the depraved reality that had contrived to set them in opposition this way.

Her sudden flurry of motion sent a new spike of pain shooting through the bridge of her nose, setting her vision to swimming. She staggered and tripped, the floor rushing up to greet her. David caught her, gently stopping her from falling on her face and propping her upright. Something about the contact of his arms, the simple, platonic tenderness and thoughtfulness of the gesture, gave her pause. It felt like some small measure of relief, a chip in the outermost wall of her prison of isolation. She relinquished herself to that meagre comfort; in the absence of mind-to-mind contact, body-to-body contact was the best compensation she could expect. She let herself go slack in David's grip, and held him in return.

Minutes passed like that, and he didn't make any move to push her away. How long they stood like that in the motel room's entranceway, in that sombre embrace, she couldn't have said.

***

191

'This is what your brain looked like according to your implant tune-up three months ago,' David said, 'compared to what it looked like while you were under the effect of that *thing* in your spinal column.'

Night had fallen in the motel room hours earlier. When her sense of balance had settled enough that she could eat without immediately vomiting again, Jean had realised that she was ravenously hungry. She had eaten all her portion of *chow mein* and most of what David had brought for himself.

'Given the circumstances, I'll set aside that China can apparently just access my medical records whenever it wants,' she replied, bitterly. She tabbed back and forth between the two MRI scans of her grey matter and accompanying vital statistics. Even to her neurologically untrained eye, the difference was obvious. In the 'after' picture, her cerebral cortex was lit up like a firework display.

'Your head was flooded – I mean, *flooded* – with oxytocin and dopamine. Carlos told me it was like nothing he'd ever seen before. The dopamine, maybe, in studies on the effects of heroin, but the oxytocin levels? Unprecedented.'

'You don't need to tell me the sensation was like nothing else on Earth, Dave. I was there for it.'

'It's horrifying!'

'It's paradise. You don't understand – these scans, the pharmacology of it, they're only the tip of the iceberg. Your entire sense of self is redefined, you become part of a higher order of consciousness. Pain and fear and insecurity, it all falls away to be replaced by bliss. It's like being part of the body of God.'

The more she spoke, the more disheartened she became by David's expression, and by how far her own words fell short of the thing she meant them to describe. This was exactly why the Enclave had to move the way it did, by showing people its wonders rather than telling them.

'So what about, I don't know... personality?' David said. 'Ambition? Aspiration? All the stuff that makes you who you are, that falls away too, I take it. That's what it would take for you to conspire against your friends and your family, your whole species.'

'You're not listening!'

'And you're not hearing yourself. The Enclave is either the most addictive drug or the most persuasive cult ever documented, or some combination of the two. The reaction you're having now is exactly like the symptoms of acute withdrawal, and you only felt the effects for a few hours. God knows what would happen if we tried to pull out one of the poor bastards who've been under the influence for days now.'

'How many ways do I have to tell you I didn't want you to pull me out?'

David looked away from her, covering his mouth, stroking agitatedly at his chin. It was a gesture she recognised; something he did when he was working himself up to an act of self-disclosure.

'Did I ever tell you about my father?' he finally asked. 'About his history?'

Jean was taken aback. She shook her head; no, he hadn't.

'He was a bohemian type, when he was young,' he continued. 'A flake, really, a real tortured-soul, starving-artist sort before my mother domesticated him. He was one of the ones who got hooked on neurostims in the late 70s, after the wetware was leaked but before the legislators cracked down on their potency. That was well before he had me and my brother, but he never really got over it as long as he lived. He used to say that the world seemed so intolerably grey compared to when he was wired. He relapsed a couple of times, once when I was in school and again when I was a cadet. Both times, he seemed... shrunken, afterwards. Smaller, quieter, older, like the stims had taken a part of his vitality with them.

'The reason I say this, Jean, is that the look in your eyes right now reminds me of when I saw him after his second relapse. You know why he stopped? Because he told me he hated the thought of me seeing him when he was wired. Eyes rolled up in his head, tongue lolling out, barely breathing. The idea of me seeing that haunted him so much he went cold turkey, no matter how much it hurt him.

'I know it's not your fault, Jean. You were forced into the Enclave, the bruises on your throat prove that much. But I want to know for sure: imagine how Victoria would react if she knew how you behaved after you were injected. Is there still some part of you that feels revulsion at the idea?'

Silence dominated in the motel room, the air filled with the smell of cold, congealing noodles and the weight of David's question. Jean probed her thoughts, feeling she at least owed him an honest answer. Confusion and indecision mingled with her residual nausea.

A knock sounded from the door, breaking the reverie. David stood to answer it. 'That'll be our ride.'

The door opened; standing in the hallway were two darkly clothed security guards, both wearing lapel pins identifying them as representatives of the People's Republic. They flanked a smaller figure: Secretary Koo irritably adjusted his rumpled suit jacket, snapping the fabric against his chest like it had somehow wronged him.

'Ms. Harrison,' he said, discreetly surveying the dried sick caked on the front of her shirt. 'Good to have you back. Mr. Zhen, please, if you would?' He gestured to one of his mute sentinels, who nodded and produced a pair of reinforced titanium handcuffs.

***

At David's insistence, Jean was allowed a shower and a change of clothes he had brought with him before being led from the room with her hands bound behind her back. Koo was very courteous, even apologetic, about the process.

'We owe you an enormous debt, Ms. Harrison,' he said, striding ahead of her down the motel's corridor with a businesslike gait. 'Your communiqué to Mr. Manderly two days ago was just the piece of the puzzle we needed to start to get ahead of this whole sorry mess. With a common factor like Yang-Mitsubishi, it wasn't hard to follow the thread to their research into paired particles and mind-to-mind communication. Dr Alvarez confirmed our suspicions once we convinced him we were on the side of the angels.' He shook his head in a gesture that could have signified either despair or appreciation. 'Radioactive brainwashing. Some of the propagandists I knew in my youth would have sold their souls for a technique like that.'

'Brainwashing? You think that's all there is to it?' Jean was unable to keep the reproach out of her voice.

Koo glanced at her as they stepped into the elevator. His gaze held more sympathy than she had ever expected to find from the impassive old bureaucrat. 'I have some notion of what you're going through, Ms. Harrison.'

'I doubt that you do, Mr. Secretary.'

'Oh, not from my own experience, not remotely. But we've interviewed a handful of other subjects whom we've removed the subdermal transmitters from, and they've all described the same feeling of deep loss. Agent Liu was one of them.'

'Tony's alive?'

'He's being treated for blood loss in Jishuitan Hospital, but the last I heard, his condition was stable.' He shot David a hard look. 'I think I prefer Mr. Manderly as a foreign liaison. His approach as a field agent is rather more savage than I would prefer.'

'Can I see him?' Jean was eager enough to ask despite her current circumstances.

'I think not. Not yet, anyway. I sincerely apologise for the ordeal you've been through these last few days, Ms. Harrison, not least at the hands of my government and my agency. But, for the time being, you have to be considered a security risk. In the short term, you'll be held under guard at a treatment centre. Your extradition to the United Kingdom will be considered, depending on your progress in your therapy sessions.'

Jean snorted. 'Therapy, eh? Is "re-education" a frowned-upon term these days? Spoken like a real lackey of a totalitarian regime. An aberrant, beautiful idea springs up, and all you can think to do is treat it like a disease.'

'Call me what you please, Ms. Harrison, I've been called worse. Maybe it's not entirely accurate to refer to the Enclave as a disease, but it's even more disingenuous to call it a political phenomenon.' Koo lit a cigarette and signalled his lackeys to take hold of Jean's arms as the elevator doors opened, clearly indicating his lack of interest in discussing the matter further.

Jean was frogmarched through the lobby, past empty vending machines and timeworn self-service check-in consoles. The only other inhabitant of the building she saw was a vagrant lying in the hallway, taking advantage of the building's warmth in the absence of any staff or paying customers who would

195

object to his presence. He watched their little procession go by with studied incuriosity.

The cold admitted by the automatic doors opening onto the street came as a shock to her frayed senses. She momentarily lost her equilibrium and would have fallen if Zhen hadn't caught her and propped her back on her feet. He held open the door to their waiting SUV, so deferentially that he might have been a chauffeur rather than a security escort.

The roads this far out from the centre of the city weren't heated, so despite them being nearly deserted, the SUV moved at a snail's pace over the freshly fallen snow. Zhen drove, and Koo took on the glassy-eyed look of a man conferring with his bosses in TSI space. The guard whose name she hadn't heard – she thought of him as Lazy-Eye, after his most distinctive characteristic – did her the courtesy of cuffing her hands in front of her during the car ride.

The silence inside the vehicle was painful. The lack of input from other voices and other bodies gnawed at her. Though she had composed herself somewhat since waking up, she still felt inwardly fragile, like a submarine abandoned and depressurised below crush depth. The outward world pressed inwards relentlessly and mercilessly.

**

They'd pulled onto the expressway on the south bank of the Xinfeng River, finally able to build up to a decent speed when it happened. Gazing forlornly out of the window, Jean was the first to see it by a margin of a split second; a stretch of the horizon, dominated by Beijing's vast arcologies, abruptly went dark.

The SUV was filled all at once with excited Mandarin, Jean's translation software struggling to keep up. '...three kilometres in diameter,' she overheard from Zhen, 'The UI estimates forty-eight thousand spellbound.'

'That's lower than our models predicted,' Koo remarked. 'The evacuation must have gone more smoothly than anticipated. What's the sit-rep on the other twenty-nine expected cities?' Twenty-nine, plus Beijing, plus the original six – Koo had figured out the Enclave's base-six fascination without needing to be told.

'Delhi; Jakarta; Bogota...' Lazy-Eye rattled through a list of other population centres across six continents. 'Twenty-seven out of the anticipated twenty-nine,' he concluded. 'Cairo and Santiago threw us.'

'Ninety-three percent is a hell of a lot better than we've managed until now. We're on good terms with Chile and Egypt; it shouldn't be hard to organise strike teams with their respective countries' spooks.'

'Speaking of which...' David made a significant gesture.

'Right,' said Koo. 'Can't be too careful.' From his jacket pocket, he extracted a piece of unidentifiable, translucent fabric, which unfolded to reveal a wire mesh woven into it. Koo draped it over his head like a skullcap and fastened it down with a chin strap. It looked absurd on his serious countenance.

The rest of the SUV's occupants proceeded to do the same. After fixing his own in place, Lazy-Eye produced a second and placed it on top of Jean's head without a word of explanation.

'See, the thing about the Enclave Effect,' David interjected before she could protest, 'is that it's awfully delicate. It's hard to detect when you don't know what you're looking for. But the other side of that coin is that when you do know what to look for, it's easy to disrupt. All it takes is a bit of electromagnetic interference - Alvarez threw these designs together in a matter of hours.'

Lazy-Eye finished attaching the cap, pulling the strap tighter than was comfortable, and then taking the extra step of attaching a miniature padlock that prevented it from being undone.

'What the hell is this?' she demanded.

David shrugged apologetically. 'Sorry, Jean. If I had my way, it wouldn't have been necessary, but the Secretary thought otherwise, and at the end of the day, he's still my boss. We knew the Enclave targeting Beijing was a question of "when" rather than "if". They've realised they've been exposed, and they're getting desperate, trying to spread the effect to as many cities as possible, as fast as they can.

'But Koo's been busy the last forty-eight hours, coordinating with other governments behind closed doors. These caps have been distributed to commando squadrons stationed in all of the cities predicted to be affected, and soon they'll receive the signal to move in and flush out the source of the effect in their locality. In a few hours, we'll see the most coordinated military action ever undertaken by the world's governments.'

'You sound proud.'

'I suppose I am. Humans can overcome their differences when it comes down to the wire, after all.'

'And you don't want me getting any ideas when Beijing's Enclave is within spitting distance.'

'Don't want you getting caught in the crossfire, Jean. Would you prefer we drugged you and threw you in the boot?'

'It would have the ring of honesty to it.'

***

Jean passed the rest of the journey in sullen silence, ignoring the conversation passing between the Chinese agents. Any tactics they spoke aloud in her presence, rather than through their comms, were unlikely to be worthy of her attention anyway. She occupied herself with the sight of the wedge of darkness in the Beijing cityscape. As closed as her mind remained, she imagined she could hear its siren call through the SUV's reinforced windows. She tried again to imagine the repulsion at what it represented David had described to her, that her past self must also have felt. Again, she failed.

She began to recognise the streets they were passing through from her last visit to the city. They were heading southeast toward the Huoxianzhen Trans-Pacific vacuum terminus, probably to connect to San Francisco, and from there to the PNC headquarters.

By the time they arrived at the terminus, the first hints of dawn had begun to creep over the eastern skyline. The deserted structure, closed days earlier to the public, squatted ominously against the sky's dark blue. Koo stepped out into the near-empty car park and lit a cigarette, fumbling with his lighter in the freezing northerly wind. Zhen gestured for Jean to follow, and gently but firmly repositioned the handcuffs behind her back. David produced a coat from the boot and draped it across her shoulders, the sleeves hanging loose.

Koo glanced significantly to the northwest. 'The signal's been given for the operation against the Enclave to begin,' he said, sounding reluctant. 'Quickly, please, Ms. Harrison. I'd prefer to be as far from the fighting as possible once it starts - I know your erstwhile comrades can get desperate when they're backed into a corner.'

Lazy-Eye made to grab her by the upper arm. Out of the corner of her eye, she noticed Zhen checking his lapel, a look of puzzlement spreading across his features. It would only be a matter of moments before that confusion mutated into suspicion. Nothing for it but to make her move now, then, before her last, best chance slipped by.

The handcuffs they'd used to hold her were a heavy design, titanium alloy reinforced with a nanotube mesh, popularised in the decades since augmented limbs had become commonplace. She'd used them herself, on enough members of the equatorial cartels, that she was intimately familiar with the four-tumbler, magnetically-insulated design. During her leisure hours, she'd become quite adept at picking the old-fashioned, analogue lock.

Adept enough that she could undo a pair of cuffs on her own wrists by touch alone, using, for instance, a People's Republic lapel pin, grabbed from Zhen's suit jacket when he had caught her outside the hotel.

Everyone needs a hobby.

She stamped on the side of Lazy-Eye's knee and felt it give in a direction the joint was never supposed to. He cried out, as much in surprise as in pain, and fell to the icy ground. Before Zhen, Koo, and David could react and train their sidearms on her, she had hauled him back up to his feet, the chain of the broken handcuffs wrapped around his throat. She drew him close before her, as a human shield.

The car park erupted with the sound of angry Mandarin, Lazy-Eye's curses bleeding together with Zhen's threats and Koo's ultimatums. Isolated phrases swam in and out of Jean's comprehension – 'crazy bitch!'; 'on the ground'; 'prosecution' – but she didn't care enough to listen. David hushed his colleagues and approached her, making placatory gestures.

'Jean,' he said in English, 'you're not thinking clearly, OK? The Enclave is finished; it'll all be over in a few hours. All you're going to do here is make your position worse. China and the PNC will grant you amnesty for everything you've done up till this point; the legal precedent for Enclave influence is being worked out as we speak. But if you keep carrying on this way, I can't guarantee—'

'Shut up.' She cut him off, and the unhinged strength in her voice even took her aback. She couldn't know what her own face looked like at that point, but Zhen and Koo seemed to see something in it that made them both retreat a half-step. 'Drop your weapons and back away. Any false moves, and I'll snap his neck.'

David blanched. 'Jean, I've known you too long to believe that. For God's sake, I've seen you pull innocent men and women out of burning debris. I saw you offer your own hazmat suit to the civilians on Erikson Station. You're not capable of murder.'

'You still don't understand what I know now. What you call life, isn't. I could put this man out of his misery and sleep soundly knowing it was a philanthropic act. So, unless you want me to illustrate what I'm capable of now, don't push me.'

She moved back as she spoke, slowly and deliberately putting distance between herself and the agents. Their eyes moved feverishly, no doubt placing top-priority calls for backup. But they didn't approach her, which was good enough.

She crossed the open clearing of the car park and rounded the corner of a storage warehouse, placing herself out of Koo and David's line of sight. With that taken care of, she increased the chain's pressure on Lazy-Eye's trachea. He thrashed and struggled against her iron grip, gurgling out choked threats and pleas which Jean summarily ignored.

She waited until he stopped moving and went limp, then a few seconds longer before slackening the pressure on his neck. She allowed him to fall to the ground in a tangle of limbs; his colleagues would retrieve him before he froze. She turned and sprinted for the city, prising off the Enclave-inhibiting skullcap as she ran.

***

The outskirts of Beijing were dead at five-thirty in the morning; even the looters who would have been busy ransacking local homes and businesses in the wake of their abandonment had called it a night.

It was minutes before she found something she could make use of – a parked car with a full complement of five youths inside. From the vehicle emanated sounds of merrymaking and the acrid, chemical smell of synthetic amphetamines. She caught the attention of the occupants without any effort on her part; a lone, bruised, Caucasian woman limping through the snowdrifts was a novel enough sight, and they were high enough that it didn't occur to them to regard her with the suspicion she warranted.

Their leader emerged from the driver's seat and approached her, idly twirling a butterfly knife in his fingers, an affectation he'd no doubt picked up from old movies. 'You look cold, lady,' he said, the residual smoke in his lungs lending a harsh burr to his accent. 'Why don't you come in with us and warm up?' He laughed loudly at his own wit, his companions joining in a half-step behind him.

Jean punched him in the throat. He crumpled to the road, silently clawing at his Adam's apple. His companions, two boys and two girls, piled out of the modified coupé after her, their invective stretching the limits of their vocabularies.

She only needed a few seconds and two or three snapped limbs to convince them she wasn't worth the effort. The ones she left able-bodied dragged the others away to lick their wounds; they left the keys in the car's ignition. The darkened portion of the horizon loomed broad and expectant in her view to the northwest, closer than she had realised. Only a couple of klicks and her nightmare would be over.

The going was slow through the unheated streets; the coupe's tyres were shallow-treaded and lacking in traction, persistently threatening to lose purchase and skid. Koo would be gaining on her. Even if it meant diverting critical resources from the Enclave incursion, she'd never be allowed to slip through the net without a fight. That they knew exactly where she was, she had no doubt – between satellite observation and the AI relay laced throughout Beijing's infrastructure, hiding wasn't an option. Fortunately, she no longer had any intention of hiding. Her brothers and sisters had been exposed to the world, so it was only right that she should be too. A zealous joy filled her at the clear-cut dichotomy: she would reach the Enclave's perimeter, or she would die trying. They'd never take her again.

A strange fuzz abruptly appeared in her field of vision, multi-coloured digital artefacts superimposing themselves upon surfaces both within and without the vehicle. It took a moment before she realised what it was – her corneal implants had rebooted themselves, a process usually reserved for when the user was asleep. Koo must have removed the block he had placed on her 'net access.

The reason why became clear when a text communication from David popped up in the middle of her view, almost causing her to swerve in the manual-drive relic she was driving. **Jean**, it read, **there's a Chinese VTOL approaching the car you commandeered right now, less than three minutes out. Commandos have been diverted from the incursion and they're blocking every available route between you and the Enclave. You won't reach it. Just turn around and head toward the vacuum terminus, and we can put this behind us.**

Ever the peacemaker, Dave, she fired back. **Being a bureaucratic lapdog suits you.**

They *will* shoot you, Jean, and if it comes to it, I won't be able to stop them. You really have no regrets about that?

The buildings around her were growing taller block by block; she was entering what she thought of as the urban foothills of the capital's financial district. The new Enclave Effect couldn't be more than a kilometre away. She rounded another corner and was dazzled by a light coming through the windscreen, far brighter than any streetlight ought to be.

The VTOL's searchlight held her in its gaze as surely as if she were a bug under the lens of an entomologist's microscope. She disregarded it and kept driving.

No, Dave, she replied. **No regrets, whatsoever. Shoot me, or let me through, but either way, shut up.**

A pause.

Fine, David replied at last. **I'd hoped we wouldn't have to resort to this, but you're forcing my hand.** He severed the communication without any further sign-off.

One more right turn, three blocks straight ahead, then a left, and finally there it was, before her – the visible divide in the middle of a city street. On the east side, streetlights and windows burned as they ought to. On the opposite side, there was the darkness of an engineered power failure. The boundary of the Enclave Effect, beyond which lay her only home.

Standing between her and her salvation, astride a makeshift barricade of sandbags, were four commandos in impact-resistant Yang-Mitsubishi armour. Their visored profiles turned towards her, alerted by the VTOL's spotlight. They raised their flechette rifles.

Something new flickered in the lower-right corner of Jean's vision. Her connection to the public virtunet had been restored, and with it came a torrent of new notifications. In the last three days, she had somehow accrued forty-seven audio messages to her private account, the one she didn't give out to clients or colleagues. The instinctual flicker of the eye to bring up the list of missed calls was nothing but habit, but she was momentarily halted by what she saw there.

Message after message, almost one every hour, all of them from Victoria. They began to play in chronological order, the first dated 10.21 am GMT on December 7th, less than an hour after Tony's hired hands had accosted her.

'Mum, when you get this, call me please? I'm seriously worried about Gran after what's happened in London.'

Jean minimised the list in her vision, relegating it to a pinpoint in the lower-right corner, but somehow, she couldn't bring herself to stop the autoplay function, even as the commandos bellowed amplified demands for her to shut off the car's engine. She slid low in the driver's seat and threw the coupe into gear, resolved to charge the barricade.

'Mum, wherever you are, call me right now, okay? This isn't funny.' December 7th, 12.34 pm.

Flechettes ripped through the windscreen and carried on right through the body of the coupé, exiting through the back window in a blizzard of brittle ceramic particles. The vehicle's roof was nearly torn off by the volley; Jean screwed her eyes shut against the noise and the broken glass. She felt a cluster of stinging cuts open across her forehead and cheeks. Despite it all, she held her foot down on the accelerator.

'Mum, look. I know there's something odd going on with you. Whatever there is between you and that Chinese guy, "Roy" or whoever, you can tell me. You can trust me implicitly, but please, just talk to me!' December 7th, 5.17 pm.

The roar of the flechettes dropped away, only for two distinct, far louder *bangs* to take their place. All of the gauges on the coupé's dashboard fell abruptly to zero, and the accelerator stopped responding. She couldn't see what had happened to the car's bonnet, but her tactical instincts meant she didn't have to. If she had been in Koo's place, operationally speaking, she also would have given the command for the car's engine to be shot out with a high-powered rifle from the VTOL overhead. A jet of orange flame surged upward from the coupé's punctured exterior, no doubt a fuel line punctured and then ignited by a white-hot bullet.

Jean threw open the door and rolled out of the car, her fall cushioned by the snow. The vehicle's ruined husk was carried forward by its momentum the remaining fifty-odd metres to the barricade. The commandoes scattered at its approach.

Jean had a brief hope that the burning wreck of the car lighting up their infrared spectrum would distract them from her cold presence in the snow. No such luck; the armoured figures ignored the remains of the vehicle and converged upon her, rifles once again raised, anxious for any new sign of sudden movement.

She stood, slowly. The Enclave boundary was maddeningly, tantalisingly close. She couldn't cross it and hope to live, she knew that now. Even without the headsets that would allow them access to the Enclave without becoming subject to its effect, there was no cover she could hide behind that would prevent the commandoes from taking potshots at her from behind the boundary.

And yet, there was still a chance, a chance that she could take them aback, duck and weave through the crossfire long enough to reach the edge before bleeding out from the maceration of flechettes. If she was reunited with her millions of brothers and sisters, even for a moment at the end, it would all be worth it. Her soul liberated from the confines of her flesh in a glorious instant, and borne aloft as a hero and a martyr in the Enclave's infinite joy, thereafter to be preserved within the multitude. What more could a person ask of their own end?

She coiled her muscles and readied herself for one last mad sprint.

'MUM!'

Jean froze.

An impact behind her, as something human-sized dropped from the VTOL thirty metres overhead. The figure stood up in the snowdrift where it had landed, and met Jean's gaze.

Victoria's inflexible doll's face was contorted to its utmost, in an agonising expression of entreaty.

'Mum, please. Please, don't do this. I can't lose you, too.'

A dreadful realisation took hold of Jean, worming its way through her mind and undermining her monomania.

The world was going mad. Tens of millions of people all around the world were displaced, afraid, uncertain. And yet from those unfathomable numbers, Victoria had chosen one and one alone to direct her efforts toward. One person among billions that she bent her whole will toward seeing safe.

If by some miracle, she made it across the boundary alive, and the Enclave had its way, subsuming all of humanity, and Victoria was saved as she had previously been, she would be nothing more than another voice in the multitude. They would be connected, yes, but in the fashion of two worker bees in the hive.

This child – her child – whose life was immutably a part of her own, who Jean had stood by after she had suffered so much, and who was now doing the same for her in turn. If she made her suicidal sprint now, she would die rejecting that connection.

All at once, the repulsion David had described became powerfully clear to her. As unbearable as the thought of never again experiencing the bliss of the Enclave was, the thought of doing that to her daughter was less bearable still.

In that moment, Victoria's plea ringing in her ears, she could imagine no greater failure, no greater crime, no greater depredation she could visit upon another person. Rape or murder would be more forgivable.

As gently and slowly as she could, Jean knelt back down in the snow, the bitter wind stinging the gashes on her face. The commandoes approached, weapons raised. Returning Victoria's gaze, unblinking, she laced her fingers behind her head.

Chapter 14

July 24th, 2326 C.E.

The drill punctured a gas pocket half a metre from Jonah's face, sediment billowing outward and then hanging in the microgravity. The pressure of the expulsion wasn't enough that the particles could cause him any harm, but they made him grateful for the meagre protection of the mask covering his eyes, nose and mouth. Twelve hours into his fourteen-hour shift, and this was the fifth such pocket he'd hit; the grime coating his goggles on the outside and the condensation on the inside were making it hard to see. He allowed himself a few seconds' respite to raise them and mop the sweat from his brow, welcoming the chill of the asteroid's pressurised air.

'Easy does it, Jonah,' came Aki's voice over his shoulder. It had taken some persuading, but the Archangel had finally come around to addressing him by his given name. 'You'll get a feel for avoiding them in due course. There's a knack to it, a difference in the way the drill kicks when you're on top of one.'

'Done a lot of ploughing in your time here, have you?' Jonah's retort came out sounding more bitter than he had intended, but Aki didn't seem to notice, or care if he did.

'Some,' Aki answered. 'Not for agriculture, obviously, but rigging bases like this with electric systems is an extensive project too. High-powered masers get the job done faster, but good, old-fashioned pneumatic power tools are more economical in the long term.'

Jonah didn't know for sure, but he suspected that the lad had lobbied to be the one to show the settlers the ropes when it came to organising their food production. He seemed terminally cheerful in Jonah's company, which made Jonah feel vaguely guilty about being constantly on edge and short-tempered.

'Fair enough,' Jonah sighed. He pulled the mask back down and resumed where he had left off, boring holes in the rock in a grid twenty centimetres by twenty. The cracks from each hole spread as he went, covering the circumference of the tunnel the way he had come. Five metres spinward,

Anahita Lajani followed in his wake, carefully trowelling the nutritive paste the Insurgency had provided the settlers with into the fissures.

The glucose-rich goo sustaining them since evacuating TransTerra would last no more than four months. Inside that time, they had to optimise the surface area available for crops to grow. There were hundreds of kilometres of tunnels crisscrossing the base interior, but even if they were all to be put to use growing algae and fungi, with eight hundred mouths to feed, the settlers would find themselves with a calorie deficit in short order. Jonah and most of the other able-bodied men and women had set to work drilling the tunnels to increase the available yield.

Between them, over the course of their shift, Jonah and Lajani had covered perhaps seventy linear metres of one tunnel.

***

'Not bad, Jonah,' Lajani said to him two hours later, sounding considerably more chipper than he felt. 'More ground covered than yesterday.'

'Not bad yourself, Ana,' Jonah replied with a forced smile. 'Get some quality bunk time; we've both earned it.'

'Yes, sir.' She bounded ahead of him through the tunnel and rounded a corner out of sight, managing her momentum in zero-g like an old pro.

'You too, Aki,' he said to the Archangel, gliding silently alongside him. 'Thanks for the pointers; it's appreciated.'

'My pleasure, Cap—er, Jonah,' he replied. 'Say, how would you feel about a game of chess? I know you play often with Lieutenant Rahman, and there's a 3-D variation that Hauer devised a few years back that I've been dying to try...'

'Another time, maybe? I really just want to get some shut-eye.'

'Right. Of course, it's been so long since I've been around organics that I still forget...' Aki trailed off, looking wistful. 'Well, rest easy, and I'll see you on the west side next shift.'

'No, you'll see me the shift after next. You'll recall the Commander wants me to appear on the transport in thirteen hours for Victoria's hearing.'

'Ah, right. Of course.'

He peeled away to coreward down a narrow tunnel on their left, but before he disappeared behind the tunnel's curve, he paused and looked back.

'I just wanted to say, sir,' he started, his gaze darting around the passageway, failing to commit to eye contact. 'It's just… having eight hundred new people in our midst, it's—'

'It's *what*?' Jonah snapped. He didn't mean to; but his shoulders, his chest, and his forearms ached. His jaw and his head ached. The wound in his thigh ached. Everything ached, and in that moment, the sight of this immortal war-machine acting like a nervous schoolboy filled him with resentment. 'Burdensome? A drain on the war effort? That's all been made quite clear by your Commander, Sergeant, thank you.'

Aki stiffened. All at once, he managed to make the eye contact he'd been avoiding. 'No, sir,' he said. 'I was going to say, I'm glad to have you. Most of us are. After two centuries with only each other for company, it feels like victory. And we appreciate the impossible choices you've been given. So, I just wanted to know if we can make life easier for you, in whatever limited capacity we may.'

They floated in silent synchrony for a moment, until Jonah broke eye contact. 'I apologise, Sergeant,' he said. 'That was unwarranted.'

Aki shrugged. 'I understand, sir. I actually, really do. After leaving Mars, I've come to know life in exile, and I know the toll it takes. Whichever choice you make when it comes to the Archangel frames, know that you have my support, either way.'

***

The cave that now housed the settlers was filled with prefabricated boxes serving as dwellings, built from standardised panels of aluminium and industrial polymers similar to the ones that had constituted Pilgrim's Progress, but squeezed together in rigid rows around the circumference of the walls, rather than the anarchic, naturalistic sprawl that had spread across the Mercanta Steppe. The sight of domiciles being erected on the floor and the ceiling at once was discomfiting, like the concept of a 'house' had been transplanted out of the gravity well where it had been conceived and into an environment that didn't welcome it.

The settlers themselves looked just as incongruous, and felt it. In the last week, Jonah's attempts at sleep had been disrupted by the sound of wailing and crying from the younger groundborn, giving voice to both the emotional pain of being wrested from their old home and the physical discomfort of their new one, with the constant nausea and vertigo of microgravity, and the airless, claustrophobic environs of the caves. For many of them, it was beginning to sink in that they might never again see a sunset or a storm cloud.

At the entrance to the cave, Jonah came across Rahman and Victoria, the pair of them deep in conversation, their voices low enough that he couldn't hear. They cut themselves off when they saw him approach.

'Morning, Jonah,' Rahman said, stiffly. 'Or should that be "evening"? Moot point, I suppose.'

'Let's say "evening," for my sake. In either event, Daniels is expecting you to report twenty degrees counter-spinward in about half an hour. Might want to get a move on for the start of your shift.' He glanced back and forth between Rahman and Victoria, looking for a cue from either of them. 'What are the pair of you conspiring about?'

Rahman moistened his lips, looking like he was stalling for time, which was most unlike him. He had always been reticent talking about his personal affairs, but Jonah had almost never seen him look nervous. 'About that,' he said at last. 'Jonah, I've been thinking. I'm wasted as a farmer, or a miner, or whatever it is we are now. Given that producing enough calories will be hard enough as it is, I was considering that I might best serve the community's interests if I took myself out of the equation.'

'You want to join the Archangels, don't you?' Jonah asked the question they'd all considered, softly, with neither encouragement nor reproach.

'I was getting the details of how it all works from Victoria. The process is slow; it takes months to sync the frame to your synaptic profile. But given my background, my combat experience, I genuinely might be of more use—'

Jonah cut him off. 'Eka,' he said, addressing Rahman by his seldom-heard given name, 'you realise you don't need to ask my permission, right? I'm not your boss, and I haven't been for a long time.'

'Of course, Jonah. But be that as it may, I've been following your lead for most of my life. I'd hate to put an end to that if I didn't think I had your blessing.'

'What do Maya and Nadia say?'

'They'll be fine,' he answered, gruffly. Like most of the senior staff, Rahman wasn't especially close with the children he'd sired mid-voyage. 'They're both able-bodied and strong; they can take care of themselves.'

Give us a moment, Vic? Victoria's eyes flickered almost imperceptibly at Jonah's private message, then she acquiesced and left him and Rahman alone.

'Eka,' he said, keeping his voice low, 'if it's what you want, I won't stop you. But if you do this, there's no walking it back, you understand that? If you go Archangel, you belong to their cause, for better or worse, forever.'

'"Their" cause?' Rahman repeated, raising his eyebrows.

'You know what I mean.'

'The Collective took Brandon from us, Jonah. You were there, you saw it. They took Ilsa. They took your kids, for God's sake.'

'I know all that, OK? I know.' Jonah held up his hands. 'It's just… do you see a future with them? With their fight?'

'As opposed to all the future there is for us here?'

Jonah wanted to argue further, but seeing his old friend's expression, further protest failed to reach his lips. There was a defiant heat in Rahman that he had seldom seen before. He'd grown used to his security chief in the past decades being dependable and compliant in equal measure; always the cool head; always prepared to back his decisions. For Rahman to push back against Jonah like this could only mean that he'd found a cause of his own. He wanted his captain's blessing; but he would move ahead, with or without it.

Jonah exhaled and extended a hand. '"I was ever a fighter, so—one fight more,"' he quoted.

'"The best and the last,"' Rahman finished for him, clasping his hand. '"I would hate that death bandaged my eyes and forebore, and bade me creep past."'

211

'I'll talk to Daniels about finding someone else to cover your shift. Go and talk to Albrecht, right now. With you in an Archangel frame, the Collective won't know what hit them.'

An awkward pause followed, and then the two men embraced, in the expectation that after two hundred years, they would never see each other again.

***

'If I recall, it was you who chose the Browning poem as the name of the *Prospice*,' Victoria said after Rahman had gone. Jonah shrugged, the gesture subtly altering the direction of his drift in the microgravity.

'It was really your grandmother who appreciated poetry,' he replied. 'For the most part, I never much saw the point of ornamented language like that. But when she'd read to me, when we were courting, something about Browning struck me differently from the ones going on about daffodils or pottery or whatever. He sounded strong. Resolute. When the Merantau Program directors asked me to christen the ship, it seemed like an attitude worthy of taking with us.'

'She always made you sound like such a Philistine,' Victoria teased. 'Who would have thought old patrician Captain Harrison was secretly an aesthete!'

'I hardly think I count as—'

'I'm kidding. I always liked the name, really. It sounded noble.' She fixed him with a stare – no matter how he tried, he could never get accustomed to those inhumanly unblinking, deep blue eyes. 'The way you recited those lines just now was almost reverential. It sounds like you want to join up just as badly as Rahman does.'

'Of course, I do! I relate to everything he said. After all the life I've lived, everything I've seen, the idea that it all ends *here*...' He made an expansive gesture with his arms, encompassing the entirety of their surroundings. 'We're like vermin, hoping just to survive while the sweep of history passes us by. What's "noble" about that?'

'So why don't you join up? Rahman isn't the only one. He isn't even the first; Albrecht's been approached by more than two dozen of your lot these last few days.'

'It's not as easy for me as it is for him. Like it or not, people still look to me as a leader. There are some who can't make the transition to Archangel, and I need to be here for them. And then there's...'

'Alyssa.' Victoria finished the thought for him. Jonah had nothing else to add. 'Well, anyway, you're tired. Sleep tight, Starman.' She made to float away.

'You seem awfully cheerful for someone whose court-martial hearing is due tomorrow,' Jonah called after her before she could leave.

'I have some cards I'm playing close to the chest, that's all. See you there.' She turned her back and flew away through a coreward tunnel.

***

Jonah had been truthful with Aki; his leg was aching from the pain of his shrapnel wound. His shoulders and biceps were livid from the day's exertions with the drill, and every cell in his body was calling out for the peace of a deep, dreamless, chemically assisted sleep, the sweetest sensation available to him in his current living conditions. But before he could thus indulge himself, he still had a duty to perform.

The Nguyen family had their domicile on the surfaceward hemisphere of the cave, seventy degrees to spinward. The whole household was crowded into the enclosed space during the brief window of the shift-change; crewmembers Amelia and Julian Nguyen; their four children; their eight grandchildren; their three great-grandchildren. The ripe, sweaty warmth that met Jonah when he entered, accumulated body heat, was stifling but nevertheless comfortingly organic after his hours in the dead grey rock of the tunnels.

Most of the Nguyens were strapped to sleeping mats attached to every available surface, either sleeping or trying to. Jack, in particular, was twisting and turning under his restraints, looking clammy and profoundly miserable. Some of the groundborn had taken to sleep in their new environment more easily than others, and he was one of the others. Over the last two days, the settlers had discussed the prospect of producing and distributing pads based on the gel-pods in the transport ship that would simulate the feeling of a mattress under the press of terrestrial gravity. It was one of dozens of such notions to better acclimate themselves to the asteroid interior that barely rose to the status of an 'idea,' never mind a 'plan.'

Two figures were hovering in the centre of the communal space – one was Jack's sister, Julie. The other was Riley O'Brien. The pair of them were huddled over Alyssa's motionless form strapped to a mat in the room's lower corner, given an extra few inches of clearance from the others for the sake of propriety. Jonah watched his granddaughter's body for a few moments, to confirm to his satisfaction that she was, in fact, breathing.

'Look who's deigned to join us,' Riley said upon seeing Jonah enter. She made the best mock-curtsy she could without propelling herself into the adjacent wall. 'Hope you've been keeping busy, Captain.'

'Riley, I'm really not in the mood,' Jonah snapped. 'If I could hover over Alyssa all day and night, I would, but I have about a hundred other things to attend to.'

'Naturally.' The pair of them glared at each other for a few seconds before Riley shook her head, signalling not so much that she approved, but that a fight wasn't worth her time or energy either.

'How's she doing?'

'Worse. Hasn't spoken a word all day. Will couldn't find anything physically wrong with her, beyond, you know, the obvious. He was in about as much of a hurry as you, but he thinks it's catatonia brought on by PTSD and severe depression. Can hardly blame her, poor thing.'

'Has she eaten anything?'

'She'll swallow that glucose crud if you put it in her mouth, if you call that "eating".'

Jonah peered down at Alyssa. Most of the settlers, himself included, were showing signs of wear by now. There were few reflective surfaces around the asteroid, but on the occasions he caught a glimpse of himself, he was startled by how lined and severe his face looked. And yet, compared to Alyssa, he was a picture of health. The girl he had known for eighteen years had been short, yes, but broad-shouldered, strong from growing up working in the fields during harvest season. He couldn't reconcile his image of that girl with the frail figure lying limp against her restraints in a sleep that might as well have been death, cheekbones protruding and eyes sunken. The burns that steadfastly refused to heal stood livid against the rest of her flesh, periodically weeping droplets of pus.

They was happening again: the dark years of his captaincy. In those days, he had seen what he thought was every reaction to stress and loss in the human lexicon, and he had hoped that he would never again be reminded how multifaceted human suffering could be. It was worse this time, though. This time, the people he was responsible for had had their future stolen from them just as surely as their past.

'I look around this place, Jonah, and I wonder why we're not all right there with her.' Riley gestured vaguely about at their surroundings. 'You're the one talking to high command. Tell me: is this all that's left to us? This... purgatory?'

Jonah sighed, the exhalation exciting the dust in the air. The dust was ultra-fine, the individual particles microscopically jagged from eons of having existed as part of an asteroid, not a planet where wind and rain and tectonic activity might have smoothed them out. He dreaded to imagine the respiratory problems it would cause, and the air filters and scrubbers installed by the Archangels could only do so much.

On and on and on, one problem to solve after another with no end in sight, and he felt so very, very old.

'I don't know, Riley. Maybe. But for now, let's just try to make purgatory work.'

***

Despite his exhaustion, Jonah woke after less than five hours of fitful sleep and couldn't settle down again no matter what he tried. After an hour of fruitless effort, he admitted defeat, washed and dressed himself, and left his domicile for Victoria's trial.

Albrecht had elected to hold the hearing aboard the same transport that had borne them out of the Collective's reach. The unspoken reason why was obvious – Victoria was popular with the settlers, who saw her as their saviour rather than a traitor who had jeopardised her cause for personal gain. Conducting her trial in a depressurised environment where the settlers physically couldn't reach quelled any possibility of civil unrest on her behalf before it began. Among the organics, Jonah alone would be provided with passage to the ship for his testimony to be heard.

Waiting at the airlock was Lieutenant Daniels, proffering a spacesuit rather more svelte than the antiquated one that Jonah had worn through Velasquez's bombardment. He helped him into it with his typical professional deference, paying special care not to jostle Jonah's injured leg.

'You're receiving me, sir?' he asked when Jonah had the helmet securely fastened, testing the comms.

'Loud and clear, Lieutenant.'

'Acknowledged, sir. Whenever you're ready, we have about three kilometres of vacuum to where the ship is berthed.'

Jonah extended a hand. 'I feel like an old woman needing help to cross the road.'

'I'll be discreet upon approach, sir.'

The airlock cycled and ejected them both into the darkness. With almost 200 astronomical units between them and the nearest star, the blackness of space was all-enveloping – Jonah needed to turn on his suit's lights just to see his own hand in front of his face. As always when he was in a vacuum, he became acutely aware of the sound of his own breathing and the barely audible hum of the suit's scrubbers recycling the carbon dioxide and water vapour from his exhalations.

'Daniels,' he said to the silver figure pulling him along, as much to take the edge off the silence as anything else, 'I hate to ask, but are you...'

'I'm going to be speaking in Victoria's defence,' he replied, finishing Jonah's question for him. 'There are more than a few of us who aren't happy with the way Albrecht runs things. Naturally, you didn't hear that from me, sir.'

'Naturally. It seems to me he runs a tight ship, though.'

'Too tight. So tight that it can barely move. He lost his nerve after being pushed past the Saturnian outposts. The stakes got to him. For all the time we've been in deep space, he's never taken any proactive action against the Collective that was less than ninety-nine-point-nine percent in our favour at the outset. It's all consolidation and holding patterns; eternal defensive manoeuvring and withdrawal. Even if we weren't doing it openly, there were plenty of us who were cheering Lieutenant Harrison on when she went after you. It was the first time in decades we felt like we were doing something other than playing hide-and-seek between the stars.'

'He's your leader all the same, though.'

Daniels glanced back to meet Jonah's gaze. The suit's lights reflected in his frame's eyes, making them shine eerily bright in the blackness surrounding them both. 'Of course, sir. It's not my place to fault the Commander, and I shouldn't speak out of turn. If we don't follow him, then who?'

**

Jonah wasn't sure what arrangement he had expected when they arrived on the transport's bridge. For some inane reason, he had imagined the setup of an old-fashioned courtroom on Earth, with Albrecht presiding sternly over a mahogany judge's bench. What he found instead was much what he always found where the Archangels congregated – a flock of them hovering silently in an irregular circle in the middle of an unadorned empty space. Victoria had claimed that the Insurgency valued culture and creativity, and while it was true that he had heard of literature and music in the base's tunnels, what culture the Archangels possessed was strictly limited to what could be stored on solid-state memory drives. They had no use for furnishings or ornamentation.

He and Daniels had arrived early, with only a half-dozen Archangels yet present of the thirty that were expected in total, none of whom Jonah knew by name. Others continued to drift in in ones and twos, the bridge slowly growing crowded with silvery bodies. Victoria showed up after Jonah had been fidgeting for twenty minutes and made a beeline straight for him.

'Hey,' she said over the comms, her tone curt and not at all nervous.

'Hey yourself. Listen, what's the plan here? I want to support you, but I'm still not clear what it is I'm actually meant to be doing.'

'It's simple, really. Albrecht knows that I have support. He could order to have me made an example of, strip me of my frame without giving me a chance to make my case. But he realises that there could be backlash against doing that – he could breed even more dissent among the rank and file who are already impatient and frustrated. So instead, he'll make a show of an "objective" assessment of my actions, like a cost/benefit analysis, then put the matter to a vote among his most trusted lackeys. See her, over there?' She jutted her chin in the direction of a female Archangel with African features, who glared back at her.

'That's Lieutenant Farashuu Kariuki. Albrecht's third in command, originally an ORC corporal before it all kicked off on Earth. She'll be brought on to talk about the operation she led to capture a passing comet for the hydrocarbons to fuel the shuttles, and how the energy expenditure from that operation could have drawn the Collective's attention. Later we'll hear from Trachtenberg, the base's head engineer, about the cost of the battle over TransTerra, and how irrecoverable the soldiers and the platelets we lost were. It'll all be very long-winded, show-and-tell stuff.'

'So, you just need me to give my version of events? Sell them on the righteousness of what you did, and the benefits of having eight-hundred more humans on the Insurgency's side?'

'Exactly. Tell the truth, but with a bit of... what's the journalistic term? "Spin". Do you have my back?'

'Obviously. More importantly, do you think you can pull it off if the vote is rigged against you?'

'I have reason to think I can. Watch and see.'

At that, a ripple moved through the bridge, heads turning to the door as Albrecht entered. A hush didn't exactly fall over the room, depressurised as it was, but his presence carried with it a similar effect. He surveyed the room, hard eyes ticking rapidly from one face to the next.

'All accounted for. Good. Then we can commence. We have convened to hear the facts in the case of Lieutenant Victoria Harrison, who stands indicted of contravention of orders and placing the Insurgency at undue risk, and with it humankind's best chance of renewal. The penalty for these charges is the withdrawal of her Archangel frame. We will hear the arguments in favour of pardon and those in favour of punishment in due course. First, I will cede the floor to the Lieutenant, who will lay out the basis for her defence.'

No one moved from where they hovered, but the bridge's collective attention palpably transferred to Victoria. She spread her wings to their full span, in what looked to Jonah like a pack animal's assertion of dominance.

'Thank you, Commander. And thank you for having the magnanimity to allow my grandfather access to these proceedings, as the single representative of the eight-hundred settlers liberated from TransTerra. If memory serves, the last time our ranks were boosted with so many potential recruits was prior to the evacuation of Europa, one hundred and forty-seven years ago.'

The Archangels didn't outwardly betray any reaction to that bit of passive-aggressive impropriety. Nevertheless, Jonah felt like there was a change in the atmosphere, in the room's unstated power dynamics. Suddenly, Victoria wasn't the only one on trial.

'I need hardly impress upon anyone, I'm sure, the way our numbers and resources have dwindled. That no matter how cautious we are, how careful to preserve our platelets, we are growing weaker. Year by year, decade by decade, we become less a threat to the Collective. I need remind no one of the calamities we've suffered, of the territory we've conceded. I need remind no one of Pisces station.'

***

Alyssa's eyes fluttered open, and the dream which had seemed so vivid seconds earlier – fire had featured prominently, and blood – suddenly seemed remote.

It felt early. The lights in the settlers' cave had been tuned to gradually brighten and dim over a twenty-four-hour period. It was a simple enough alteration made by Riley's great-grandfather, one which helped those of them accustomed to natural light to stay sane, and which actually saved the base power; a win-win innovation.

The domicile was half-empty – one side of the Nguyen family was on their shift already; the others were in their bunks, dead asleep, even those who had been having trouble with microgravity. She made an effort to be quiet while undoing her harness. Once she had, she tenderly pushed herself towards the door, fighting down her stomach's protests at the motion. As a guest of the Nguyens, it wouldn't do to vomit up a bellyful of glucose paste all over their living space.

Exiting into the cave proper, she welcomed the chill of the processed air on her face after the stuffy confines of the domicile. Room to breathe meant room to think clearly. If she hadn't got her days mixed up, then Victoria's court-martial would already have started. She hoped her cousin was shown leniency – whatever crimes she had committed in the eyes of her comrades, she had given everything she had, even a part of her flesh, to keep her alive. It was still keeping her alive; she could feel its strange density sitting in her abdomen. Surely the Insurgency would recognise the bravery she had exhibited. She could hope, at least.

'Alyssa!' A strangled voice to her right startled her out of her introspection. 'Look at you, moving about and—' The voice was cut off by a fit of coughing. Alyssa turned to greet its source and was met by a familiar silhouette, surrounded in a sweet-smelling fug.

'Jack, how in the hell are you, even now, smoking weed?'

Jack fought to stop coughing and compose himself. 'Oh, be quiet,' he replied. 'It helps me sleep.'

'No, I wasn't passing judgement. I mean, literally, how? The atmosphere in here is pure O2.'

'Well, one of the botanists working on the original Merantau Programme had a favourable opinion of *Cannabis indica's* therapeutic properties. He included it in the seed bank that left Earth on the *Prospice*. One day, a couple of years ago, I covered for Riley when her old man was on the warpath. In return, she showed me how to rig up a portable atomiser. I happened to have it on me before the settlement exploded, and I didn't think an ounce or two would really make a difference to our shuttle's fuel consumption.'

He blew a little in her face. 'See? It's vapour, not smoke. This is my second-to-last cartridge. After this and the next one, there won't be any more. I could be the last human ever to get stoned.' He held the cigarette towards her, clasped between his index and middle finger.

'Want to join me? That seems awful lonely, now that I've said it.'

'Sure.' Alyssa accepted and inhaled deeply. The vapour was rich and thick and almost immediately set her head spinning.

'More importantly,' Jack added, 'you're awake! I mean, that's great, obviously, but why now? What's changed?'

Alyssa took another drag and contemplated the question. 'I suppose I got bored,' she replied, eventually. 'Depression and guilt and self-loathing are fine for a while, but soon you start to get self-conscious. Other people can only take pity on you for so long before you feel the need to give something back. My grandfather and Victoria. Your whole family. And you, Jack.'

He looked startled, and then flustered, and then self-consciously aloof. 'I hate to tell you this way, Lys, but you've always been a bit short for my tastes.'

'Jack, stop it with the class clown bullshit for once in your life. I'm not propositioning you. I'm trying to tell you, as a friend, that I appreciate all the times you've been there for me. After the last few weeks, after Ilsa, and Marc, and... and my parents... I don't know. In a dark kind of way, it's made me realise how much I have to be grateful to the people around me for.'

'Shit, Lys. I don't know what to say. "You're welcome," I guess?'

She smiled. 'Don't stress about it. I came up with a couple of ideas this last week, for how to make my appreciation known.'

Chapter 15

July 2nd, 2326 C.E.

Alyssa remembered. She remembered the day her parents died with stereoscopic precision, with fidelity the equal of the TSI-sims she had consumed so greedily.

***

'Jonah, don't come here!' Ilsa Mendeleev cried. 'Get as far away from our vector as you can. God, there are dozens of them! We'll try to lead them away, try to buy you some—'

The plain erupted in a blaze around them. Maser beams from above carved swathes of flame in the grass to encircle their convoy. Ilsa startled and dropped the handset, swinging the caterpillar's wheel around to avoid the inferno that had bloomed in their path.

Alyssa felt a series of dull impacts reverberate through the floor in quick succession, like a cluster of large, heavy somethings had fallen to the ground close by. Through the windscreen, she glimpsed a shape emerging through the wall of fire, its dark exterior glowing a dull red but unperturbed by the heat.

It was happening again – another of the monsters that had killed Marcus; killed her. Victoria was klicks away. Her group was truly defenceless.

During her encounter with the original, damaged Scarab, Alyssa had been scared. How could she not have been? But under those circumstances, the fear had been a natural, healthy, appropriate thing, the fight-or-flight response working as it was designed to. What she felt now was something else entirely – overwhelming terror blended together with guilt, grief and despair in a toxic stew. It was what she imagined going mad must feel like.

She recoiled as far as she could from the one Scarab she saw, her body moving of its own accord. She scrambled from the cockpit into the cargo hold of the caterpillar, trying to make herself as small and invisible as possible. The din coming from outside and the shouts of the caterpillar's other passengers combined to drown out her screams.

'Hold on to something!' Ilsa's voice somehow made itself heard over everything else. The caterpillar lurched forward, its engine audibly straining to build speed. There followed an impact that threw everyone in the cabin forward. A corner in the back of Alyssa's mind that was still rational intuited what had just happened. Fully laden, the caterpillar massed over thirty tons – in motion, it was the most effective weapon available to them. Using it to bulldoze straight through the enemy and the fires made perfect sense. A glimmer of hope – Ilsa's quick thinking might yet mean they could escape.

The collision slowed the vehicle down momentarily, and it tipped over on its right side. For a precarious second, fire filled the view through the windscreen. Then the view cleared, and the caterpillar again began picking up speed.

Someone next to her let out an exhilarated whoop that was echoed by a couple of others. A few burst into nervous laughter, for want of any better response. It was cut short when a sickening metallic screech sounded from the caterpillar's right side. It shuddered, heaved and finally stalled completely.

'Shit!' Ilsa cried from the cockpit. 'Fine, they can have it their way. We go on foot. Everyone, arm yourselves.' There was an edge of steel in her voice, the authority of someone who had been placed in truly dire situations before that compelled everyone to do as she said, white-faced and shaking as they were.

'Robyn!' She beckoned over Alyssa's mother. 'We're going to split up the group, give them more targets. Lead half of them to the south, as fast as you can, don't look back. Hide in the long grass as best you can. I'll head north, and we reconvene to the east later, got it?'

Her mother said nothing; she looked like she was going to be sick. 'Hey!' Ilsa snapped her fingers in front of her eyes, breaking her out of her reverie. 'Pay attention. If even one person is captured, then every other convoy is compromised too. The Collective will know every one of their vectors. That mustn't happen, under any circumstances. Do you understand what I'm saying?'

From her jacket pocket, Ilsa produced a plastic pouch. Contained within it were dozens of pills; gel-caps, each red on one side and white on the other.

Cyanide capsules.

'You heard Victoria. If they catch you, they make you one of them; your mind screams while your body moves according to their will. If you're faced with the choice, choose death.'

***

The caterpillar deposited its passengers onto the plain, slinging flamethrowers and satchels of Molotov cocktails over their shoulders as they went. The Scarab they had run over lay inert under its body, two of its limbs mangled by the treads. They had made it barely two hundred metres from where the fires had encircled them – the Humvees that had followed them through the flames had been similarly abandoned, the families they held running to join them.

Behind them followed Scarabs. They moved unhurriedly, striding after the settlers through the burning grass, like nightmares crossing the veil into waking reality.

Alyssa knew with a clarity the others did not: the only way any of them would escape capture was death. Victoria had been adamant that it was the less objectionable fate – better by far, she had told her, to go to your end with dignity and pride than to live out the remainder of your days host to an alien parasite, watching in impotent horror as it used your body and mind as a vessel for its own proliferation.

But Alyssa had died once already, and at the time dignity and pride had been the furthest things from her mind. All she'd felt was all-consuming disappointment at the places she'd never see, the people she'd never meet, the things she'd never know.

It wasn't fair. Earth had come back for them, just as she'd always dreamed it would. The day Victoria arrived should have been the day her life truly began, the start of an adventure, not the parade of suffering it had become.

'Lys, we have to go,' came her mother's voice. She met her eyes, and she saw there the same expression that had greeted her when she had woken up in sickbay. The same tenderness, the love, the total selfless concern for her wellbeing that only a mother could bear their child.

It was in that moment that she knew she couldn't do it. If she followed the group, she would die, but first she would have to watch the realisation cloud her mother's face that her daughter was going to die, in front of her, again, and that she would have to let it happen.

'I'm sorry,' Alyssa whispered. She backed away, slowly.

'Lys, honey, what are you doing?' The wounded confusion in her mother's tone was more than she could stand. She turned and ran, tears clouding her view. She had no idea where she was going, just so long as it was away from everyone else.

'Alyssa, *no!*' The scream that followed her carried with it more pain than she had ever imagined a human voice could contain.

***

The tall grass on these plains grew according to the land's naturally occurring furrows, with rows of thick stalks that rose above head height separated by patches of shorter scrub. On foot, it felt like trying to negotiate a hedge maze, and in her blind panic, Alyssa doubled back on herself more than once in the dark. Within minutes, she saw columns of smoke rising from the way she had come. Terrible sounds reached her ears from those directions – foliage and soil being crushed under pounding mechanical limbs; yells of defiance turning to fear when the flamethrowers' inefficacy became clear. She thought—or imagined—that she heard choked, gurgling noises; the people she'd known slumping lifeless to the ground, the cyanide froth in their stomachs bubbling out from their mouths and nostrils.

She hoped, strangely, that she would meet someone else, anyone else, fleeing from the group as she was. At least then, she wouldn't be alone in her cowardice. But there was no-one, just more screams that would be followed by silence. Everyone else had done their duty to keep the other convoys safe. Everyone but her.

Two of those screams must have belonged to her parents. She couldn't tell which ones. Finally, she stopped trying to run and burrowed herself deep into the densest thicket of grass she could find. Curled into a ball, breathing as shallowly as she was able, she waited for the moment a Scarab would sweep aside her hiding place and expose her. She waited, and waited. Hours passed, and she didn't move, except to shiver violently. The awful noise of the

226

machines lumbering around her became gradually more distant. It began to rain. The smell of burning plant matter receded.

It had to be some sort of trick. With the kind of technology available to the Collective, there was no way she had been able to avoid detection. And yet… she was just a single, small body, huddled in the dark. If the Scarabs relied on infrared imaging to hunt for human bodies, the heat from the flamethrowers might have concealed her.

Finally, she dared to risk crawling out of the thicket. There were no monsters there waiting for her. She crawled a little further, and a little further still, as quickly as she dared. Her clothes were soon soaked through, and she was cold enough for her extremities to grow numb, but she hardly noticed.

Pushing her way into a clearing, a hulking, inorganic shape loomed over her. She jumped but collected herself when she noticed that it was motionless. She recognised it as the wreck of the caterpillar, the chewed-up remains of the Scarab still pinned beneath it. She gave it a wide berth – motionless or not, who knew what functions the monster still retained.

A thought occurred to her – the caterpillar was dead, but some of the Humvees might still be functional. If she could find one with the keys in the ignition, there was still a chance she could reach the rendezvous.

'Christ, what an almighty bloody mess.'

Alyssa managed to stop herself from screaming. She swung around, scanning the darkness for the source of the voice.

'Over here, dear.' It sounded male and spoke with an old-Earth English accent, not unlike Victoria's. It didn't belong to anyone she knew. 'Come closer, I promise I won't bite.'

She stood, frozen. Slowly, she unslung her flamethrower and, with trembling hands, levelled it at the darkness. She swivelled back and forth, searching for the speaker. Raindrops pattered softly against the raised weapon's nozzle.

'Ah, of course, you're scared. Apologies, I should try to be more sensitive to these things,' the voice continued. 'Tell you what – you don't have to do anything. I'll just approach, slowly, with my hands in the air to show you I'm unarmed. Sound fair?'

The voice must have taken her continued silence as acquiescence, because a human silhouette approached her out of the darkness, its hands raised as promised. He was a tall, thin Caucasian man, dressed in close-fitting black tactical gear. He appeared very old; late seventies, at least, by pre-telomerase supplement standards. Pallid, translucent skin stretched tightly over his skull, combined with thin hair, gave him an almost skeletal appearance. Nevertheless, he moved with the easy grace and latent strength of someone much younger.

'Stop where you are!' Alyssa cried, her voice cracking and betraying any authority it might have carried. The man obeyed all the same and stopped, his old face showing no hint of unease or hostility.

'As you wish, madam. Allow me to introduce myself. My name is David Manderly, and on behalf of The Collective of Humanity, I am deeply sorry for the things you've experienced these last few days.'

Despite everything, Alyssa felt her blood start to boil. 'You're *sorry*?' she spat. 'You killed Marcus! We lost everything because of you!'

Manderly cast a resentful look at the Scarab where it lay, crushed beneath the caterpillar's treads. 'These damned machines,' he muttered, almost as though he hadn't heard her. 'They were never meant to come into contact with a civilian population; they're programmed for combat and nothing else. At any threat of violence, they respond with lethal force; no protocol for diplomacy. If it wasn't for the Insurgency's interference, we would have sent human ambassadors to TransTerra in the first place and avoided this disaster.'

Any threat of violence.

She cast her mind back to that night, in the crater where Victoria had landed. She had been the one to take aim at the damaged Scarab that had shambled into view. She had been the one to shout at it.

'Why should I believe anything you say?' Her hands were trembling harder now. 'Victoria told us all about you. You enslaved humanity!'

Manderly shook his head, looking morose. 'I know she thinks that. Hell, I was standing right where you are now, once, and I thought the same thing. It's natural to find it repulsive when you're on the outside looking in. But the truth is, the Collective isn't an alien consciousness. We didn't conquer humanity; we *are* humanity. We're what humanity has always striven towards – an end to suffering.'

'You're lying!'

'Alyssa—it is Alyssa, isn't it? May I approach you?'

He took one step forward. When she failed to burn him alive with a jet of ignited methane, he took a second and a third, until he loomed over her.

Manderly closed a hand around the barrel of her flamethrower. In the dim light cast by the fires, she saw a metallic glint upon his knuckles. *A prosthetic limb?* He gripped the weapon firmly, with pneumatic strength that told her he could have yanked it out of her hands and dislocated her arms doing so. But instead, he just gently turned the nozzle aside, out of harm's way.

'What do you want from us?' Alyssa whispered.

'To save you,' Manderly answered, his voice hushed and grave. 'To save all of you, as we were saved. Not to conquer or to dominate, but because we remember. We *know* how it feels, to be naked and alone in the dark, with no one to help, no one to offer succour or comfort. We know all too well what it's like to lose the ones we love.'

Somewhere in Alyssa's chest cavity, something broke. She let the flamethrower drop from her hands; she sank to her knees, her whole body transmuted to lead, buckling under its own weight.

'I...' she stammered, 'I can't... I... fuck—!' Images of her parents, of Ilsa, of Marcus, of Victoria, flashed through her mind in a stroboscopic fever, confronting her with her abject cowardice, stopping her from vocalising the thought she wanted to express: *I don't want to be a person anymore.*

Manderly crouched and embraced her. His cybernetic limbs encircled her with a tenderness she wouldn't have thought metal capable of.

'It's unbearable, I know,' he said. 'But here's the thing that the Collective reveals: it's not your fault. It's no one's fault. It's the fault of the universe. Call it "God" or call it evolution, it amounts to the same thing. Whatever process created a unique, sapient being like you, and then put it in a position where you feel the kind of pain you feel now? That's what's at fault. That's what needs to be corrected.

'You can't possibly know how much we want to save you, Alyssa. It's why we built the relays, crossed light-years of distance, all in the name of preventing another person from feeling what you do now. So, Alyssa, will you join us? Will you let us help you?'

Alyssa wiped her eyes and forced herself to look up at him. 'You're saying you can make these feelings go away?'

'That's exactly what I'm saying.'

She made up her mind. 'Do it,' she whispered. 'Anything but this.'

Manderly smiled. He reached into a pouch on his belt and withdrew a small syringe. 'There will be a few moments' of disorientation,' he said. 'Ride it out; it'll pass.' The needle plunged into the base of her neck, between the vertebrae. The shock of the stabbing pain lasted barely an instant before being overridden by sensations far stranger. Her mind dilated; her perception became decoupled from her own sensory organs. Across forty light-years, on Earth, billions of minds welcomed her into their midst, and their combined compassion and love dispelled her grief like motes of dust in a hurricane. *Oh*, was all she could think. *I understand. I get it, now.*

There was work to be done. A few hundred still left to be won to their cause, and she uniquely positioned to make that happen.

David's one-man insertion shuttle, dispatched from one of the transports orbiting overhead, was embedded a short walk from the remains of the convoy. It wasn't much bigger than a Scarab, built to contain its passenger, the propellant needed to arrest its descent, and not much else. David, however, had brought one piece of luggage down with him; a handheld maser cannon.

Have to make it look convincing, he thought. *Can't have anyone thinking you got away too easily, otherwise it'll raise red flags.* He levelled the cannon, taking aim just to the left of Alyssa's face.

Her consciousness was swimming in the Collective, her body a dim memory. When the maser beam seared her flesh with second-degree burns, she scarcely noticed. *He's within our reach, at last,* the Collective thought as one. *The Starman.*

A.N. Milne

Chapter 16

July 25th, 2326 C.E.

'...Months of preparation. Sagittarius Station have had to pull eleven Archangels away from the relays, most critically the Xi-Omikron thoroughfare. Left unchecked, the Collective could use this opportunity to gain a foothold in the eastern ecliptic, and—'

Farashuu Kariuki's testimony cut off mid-sentence. Jonah looked about him; the Archangels hovering around the transport's bridge were visibly distracted. Some stimulus he wasn't attuned to had alerted them, interrupting the proceedings of the court martial.

What's going on? He directed a message to Victoria marked as urgent. She looked intensely introspective. It took her several uncomfortable seconds to acknowledge his hail.

The proximity alarm just sounded. A cluster of QF drives were just detected within 0.01 AU, on a vector intersecting with the base. We're trying to raise communications with them now. Best case scenario, they're unannounced Insurgency members from another station. She didn't need to clarify what the worst-case scenario was.

He began to wonder if their getaway from TransTerra might just have been too clean, after all.

All he could do for the subsequent minutes was float quietly in the middle of the room, feeling conspicuously useless. The Archangels' profiles gave nothing away, but in this case, he assumed that no news was bad news. If confirmation came that the base's unannounced guests were friendly, there would surely be some evidence of the tension pervading the bridge being relaxed. The more time that passed without any such relaxation in evidence, the more his stomach tightened.

Any doubt he still had evaporated when the lights on the bridge cut out to be replaced by dull red emergency lighting. He recognised it as an effort to minimise the ship's electromagnetic signature.

Not the best-case scenario, then? This time he included Albrecht in his communication.

The Commander shot him a hard look.

No response to our original hails. And now two more clusters as large as the first have appeared. We're still awaiting optical confirmation, but we have to conclude the Collective have found us.

***

In the next hour, Jonah received an object lesson on the firepower that an Insurgency base could bring to bear. With his corneal implants hooked into the transport's exterior cameras, he found that the outside surface of the low-albedo asteroid, just dark rock to the naked eye, was in fact bristling with concealed laser cannons. These fired staggered salvoes that could have slagged the full might of the ORC when Jonah had known it.

Ordinarily, Victoria assured him, this would have been enough. But the Collective troop transports and Scarab squadrons now approaching had built up a formidable momentum beforehand. Even though they were decelerating hard, their relative velocity within 0.01 astronomical units was still over a million klicks per hour. That was troubling for two reasons. For one, it meant that it became diabolically hard to compensate for their evasive manoeuvres. For the other, more seriously, it meant that the Collective had begun their approach vector from several AU away – much further than the base should have been optically detectable from. They must have had access to intelligence on the base's location which shouldn't have been possible for them to have.

It's strange, she messaged him, seemingly thinking aloud. **When they've attacked our bases in the past, their first move was to bomb the exterior from a distance. The torpedoes give us more targets to divert our concentration, and the ones that hit cause cave-ins and cut off our exits. Archangels are trapped inside where they can bore in and capture us at their leisure. But this time's different. There's no ordnance coming in. All they're doing is evading.**

Isn't it obvious? Jonah replied. **They know that you escaped TransTerra with a hold full of soft, fragile organics that they don't want to kill. I doubt they'd do anything to compromise the life support systems inside the base that they ordinarily wouldn't be worried about.**

The HUD on Jonah's vision fed him the ranging and targeting data that the base's computers were processing in real-time. He could only make sense of a fraction of it, but the results he could glean told their own dismaying story. A scattering of faint flashes could be seen in the magnified distance, each one a dying enemy unit, and more flared with each minute that passed. But the flashes were too few and too infrequent. The Collective QF drives they had detected numbered over a thousand. Given the Collective's love for base six, he guessed six to the fourth power: twelve-hundred and ninety-six. At the rate they were approaching, a quarter of that number would survive to make contact with the asteroid's surface. Once that happened, a breach was inevitable.

Twelve minutes before the first Scarab was projected to land, Albrecht ordered every Archangel still inside the base to hurry to the exterior airlocks and prepare for combat. His brief message was notable to Jonah for what it didn't say more than what it did. He approached the Commander and opened a private audio link.

'Albrecht—' he started, but before he could continue, Albrecht cut him off.

'The answer is no, Captain.' The Commander's voice bore no anger, just authority and finality.

Jonah pressed. He had to. 'There are eight hundred people in there! *My* people. We're under your protection. Don't you all have an obligation to head out there and evacuate them?'

'An obligation? Captain, this transport is cloaked, and I don't mean to expose it to the enemy for the sake of another foolhardy rescue effort. If you'll recall, we discussed my priorities in this situation, and those don't change simply because the Collective's timing is inconvenient for you.'

Jonah sent a couple of obscenities Albrecht's way, mostly just to make himself feel better. When they were summarily ignored, he severed the link and opened a new one to the base. To his immense gratitude, Eoin answered immediately.

'Jonah!' The connection didn't permit him a view of Eoin's face, but he sounded appropriately wide awake and unnerved. 'What the hell is going on? All of the Archangels just started heading for the surface, without a word.'

'Eoin, listen carefully, okay? Somehow, the Collective followed us from TransTerra, and now there's a swarm of them descending on the base. They'll be outside in ten minutes, and inside soon after if the Insurgency can't fight them off. I want you to gather everyone and head for the command centre at the core. You'll be safest there if it comes to fighting in the tunnels.'

There was a long pause at Eoin's end. He began to worry their connection had been broken, that he wasn't receiving any of the O'Brien family's trademark bluster and bombast when he heard a deep, weary sigh. 'Aye aye, Captain,' Eoin said. There was a quaver to the words. 'Jesus, these Collective can't give a body a break, can they?'

**

An hour and four minutes after the alarm sounded, the first Scarab vanguard landed on the exterior of the base.

There were twenty-six Archangels remaining inside the base, and even with the tactics and superhuman co-ordination Jonah had seen during the evacuation from TransTerra, this time the numerical difference was enough to tip the balance in the Collective's favour. Three-hundred and ninety-four of the Scarabs eventually made it past the laser defence grid. Half of them laid down suppressing fire at any Archangel who dared to approach, while the other half began probing for the concealed structural extrusions that would permit them entry to the interior – if not a docking port, then an exhaust or a generator.

The HUD flagged up the shapes that could be detected from the transport with gold outlines that distinguished their black armour from the black rock. The regimented way they crawled around the asteroid's exterior put Jonah in mind of the anthills he remembered from his childhood. He had once found ants swarming over the body of a dead hawk in a meadow near the house where he had grown up. The shivering mass of red insects had moved as though animated by one mind, swarming about the noble animal's carcass, reducing it to nothing, one feather and one morsel of flesh after another. In his mind's eye, he saw Eoin and Rahman and Alyssa suffering that same slow mastication.

The Collective's ranks were being thinned, here and there, but not quickly enough; a breach was inevitable, whether sooner or later. The additional thirty Archangels milling around the transport's bridge might have been enough to turn the battle's tides, but before Jonah could articulate the obvious question – why, God why, weren't every last one of them out there fighting the Collective off with every ounce of strength they could muster? – he found the answer in Albrecht's countenance.

He could see the arithmetic Albrecht was doing in his head. The base was valuable insofar as it contained intelligence and materiel. But the intel was backed up in other servers and could be prevented from falling into enemy hands with an EMP device like the one that had been used on Pisces station. And while resources could be replaced over the course of years or decades to follow, the Archangel frames could not. Rather than risk giving away the cloaked transport's position by fielding the Archangels aboard in battle, he'd have the Archangels in the station, who would need to be evacuated regardless, make a token effort at preventing the Collective's invasion. When that inevitably failed, he'd have them pull back to the transport and live to fight another day. Albrecht's *modus operandi*, as Daniels had described; retreat, preserve, consolidate, and then retreat again.

The fact that the EMP being detonated inside the base would knock out its life support systems didn't even enter into his equations.

***

A breach! 112 degrees to spinward. Aki's report placed the hole in the asteroid's crust on the opposite side of the rock from the transport. Jonah thought he could make out a plume of dust and debris emitting from over its horizon. He hoped it was his imagination; the Collective wouldn't allow the base to depressurise while there were humans inside worth assimilating.

The Scarabs turned as a mass and took off toward the breach, repelling the Insurgency's fire as they went. Even if they somehow sustained fifty-percent casualties on the way, there would soon be hundreds of the machines scuttling around inside that giant ants' nest.

'Eoin,' Jonah said, re-opening communications, 'please tell me you've got everyone to the core. You're going to have some company very soon.'

'I know. Maybe it was silent from where you were looking, but in here it made a hell of a racket.'

'Anyone hurt?'

'No, I did as you said. Most of the crew are already in the core, the rest are making their way inside. It's snug in there, but stacked cheek by jowl, we'll fit.'

Jonah exhaled. 'Good.'

'Not that good. Will's been taking a headcount, and there are two of our number unaccounted for. Jack Nguyen, and...' Eoin audibly swallowed. Even in microgravity, Jonah had the sensation of his stomach sinking.

'Don't tell me.'

'I'm afraid so. It's Alyssa.'

Jonah tamped down his frustration at his own impotence, and, although he hated to admit it, his anger at Alyssa. Finding oneself at the mercy of an all-powerful alien hive mind once could be regarded as misfortune; twice seemed like carelessness.

'Don't go looking for them, just get everyone you can inside. I'll arrange a search party at our end. Keep your head down in there, Eoin.'

'You too, Jonah. Looking forward to seeing how we slip out of this one.'

Jonah severed the connection. It wouldn't do the settlers any favours to realise that Albrecht thought them only slightly more worthy of rescue than the algae they'd been planting in the walls.

The Commander had made it abundantly clear that appealing to his better nature would get Jonah nowhere. There was exactly one person present who could challenge Albrecht's authority, and who was concerned enough about the fate of the settlers to do so.

New enemy unit detected, heading straight for the breach, Aki reported, disrupting Jonah's train of thought. Not Scarabs; they're smaller and they don't have any extrusions. They almost look like personnel insertion pods, but that would be crazy.

They are, came a response from Hauer. They're almost identical to the ones we saw on Callisto.

'Why would the Collective be putting assimilated humans in the firing line, now of all times?' Victoria wondered aloud. 'They've used machines exclusively for over a century. They don't want to place their hosts in harm's way.'

***

Half-an-hour later, they got their answer. A communication originating from inside the base was broadcast across all frequencies; Jonah received it at the same time as the Archangels on the bridge. The format was puzzling: a low-fidelity audiovisual recording, rather than a live feed.

The image he was met with was of a man who appeared even older than him, dressed in a matte-black environment suit. The man was looking directly at the recording device, unblinking. In the background of the shot, Jonah realised with a jolt, were the settlers' now-empty dwellings. Other human figures milled around behind the old man, all clad in the same uniform suits, most with some degree of visible augmentation. All of them were armed with an assault weapon Jonah wasn't familiar with.

It was subtle, but there was something eerie about their body language. It was apparent more in what was omitted than anything – they looked to be methodically searching the settlers' homes for any stragglers in two- and three-person teams. They carried out their searches without any verbal communication, or even eye contact exchanged, yet their interpersonal coordination was precise. They put him in mind of game pieces being manipulated by an invisible player somewhere far overhead. Truthfully, they reminded him of the Archangels in ways he wouldn't care to admit in their company.

'This is David Manderly, speaking on behalf of The Collective of Humankind,' said the old man, addressing the camera. 'I seek parley with Commander Hermann Albrecht of the Archangel Insurgency, and Captain Jonah Harrison of the *Prospice*.'

David Manderly – something about that name stirred Jonah's memory from long ago. He racked his brains, and it clicked. A man by that name had been one of Jean's suitors in the years after Victoria's accident. That the Collective had seen fit to send him, of all people, couldn't have been a coincidence.

239

'We are here with a special task and have no desire to see the situation escalate any further than it already has. We know that the eight-hundred settlers evacuated from TransTerra are being held in the core of the facility. It is our sincere hope to see these men, women, and children saved from the yoke of individual consciousness and join our brothers and sisters on Earth, as it is for all humanity.

'However, our experience of the surface of TransTerra has retaught us a harsh lesson on the Insurgency's ruthlessness. For as long as Commander Albrecht insists that death is better than the Collective's salvation, innocent blood will be shed.

'We are aware that any effort on our part to enter the core will prompt Commander Albrecht to execute the colonists inside before we can reach them. Therefore, we will withdraw and leave this base untouched if our conditions are met. One: the base's defences are powered down for the next twelve hours. Two: all of the Archangel units currently engaged in combat and those aboard the cloaked ship to which this communique is addressed withdraw to a point we will specify, zero-point-zero-five AU distant. Three, the most important: Captain Harrison will surrender himself to us within the next two hours.'

The bridge suddenly became very still. Jonah could feel thirty pairs of artificial eyes boring into the back of his neck.

'The Captain has something the Collective values very highly,' Manderly continued. 'Highly enough that we are willing to forgo eight-hundred souls' salvation to reach it. For my part, I also wish to speak to him face-to-face. It concerns his daughter, Jean, and the reason for her absence today. I have worked to keep this body alive all these years for this purpose.'

What the hell is he talking about? Daniels asked the question everyone in the room was thinking.

'I have absolutely no idea,' Jonah replied, hoping his tone communicated his honest confusion. 'Until a month ago, I'd never even *heard* of the Collective. I can't even imagine what information I could have that would be of use to them.'

'By way of additional incentive,' the recording continued, and the camera turned to show two new figures hovering to Manderly's left. Rather than the black environment suits of the Collective's footsoldiers, these were wearing the dusty, faded blue overalls common to the settlers who worked in the tunnels. Their faces came into focus.

The taller of the two was Jack Nguyen. The other was Alyssa. Both of them looked comfortable, even serene, floating there with the rest of the Collective.

Jonah badly wanted to vomit.

'Hey, Jonah?' Alyssa now addressed the camera. 'For what it's worth, I hope Victoria's doing OK, and that everyone sees she was in the right. Not that it makes much difference since we interrupted the trial, huh?

'I just wanted you to know, I'm sorry for deceiving you all. As with so many things the Collective does, it was the least of the evils available to us. That's the burden we carry; we do what we must to spread something amazing.

'If it makes it any easier, I'd like you to know that I chose this. Historically, most inductions have to be forceful, that's the way of it. But I was one of the exceptions. I wanted it, I came to it voluntarily, and I don't regret it.

'If... *when* you decide to give yourself up, you have my word that no one here will force you to join us. You'll be afforded every assurance guaranteed to a P.O.W. Hell, on Earth you'll be treated like the celebrity you are. I hope you do join us, if only so that you can know how much I've always admired you, and how I don't hold anything that happened on the ground against you. I'm all that's left of your family Jonah, so please... come home.'

The camera swung back up to Manderly. 'There you have it,' he said. 'We'll await your acknowledgement within the next two hours.'

***

A thick pall of silence hung over the bridge. Then a peculiar, staccato barking sound came through Jonah's cochlear implants. Albrecht was laughing, mirthlessly.

'So, that's how they found us,' he said. 'Of course it was. They got to her on TransTerra when she wasn't accounted for, and then when she was inserted among the other survivors, they followed her here. If I'd been enforcing any kind of rigour, I never would have let her aboard. Well, never again.'

He expanded the communication to the Archangels still taking potshots at the Scarabs on the outside of the asteroid. 'Everyone, withdraw to the transport at these coordinates. We're leaving.'

'But sir, we can't—'

'No arguments, Sergeant Hartikainen. I want everyone onboard in ten minutes, and stragglers make their own way. We're pulling back to Taurus station. The EMP will be detonated once everyone is a safe distance from the base. And what the hell do you think you're doing?' He jabbed a silver finger at Jonah.

What Jonah was doing, and had been doing while Albrecht was on his tirade, was rifling through the holds next to the airlock.

'I'm looking for a propulsion system compatible with this suit,' Jonah replied.

'And why would you be looking for something like that?'

'You're smart, Albrecht, I'll credit you with that at least. You can figure it out.'

'Humour me, Captain.'

Jonah turned to face him. 'My people are caught between the devil and the deep blue sea in there. Either the Collective breach the core and turn them into their sock puppets like Alyssa, or you trigger the EMP and kill them all.'

Albrecht floated, his back ramrod-straight, wings flared. He offered no rebuke to Jonah's accusation, that he'd be capable of mass murder.

'If there's a chance that I can defuse the situation by turning myself over,' Jonah continued, 'then it's worth a shot. Even if it means selling my soul, I owe them that much.'

'Good speech, Harrison,' Albrecht replied. 'It must be a quality that runs in the family. I'd even be impressed at your nobility if I believed for a second that you thought I would actually let you leave. But you know as well as I do that if the Collective values you as an asset, for whatever reason, then my highest priority is to prevent you from falling into their hands. We are leaving, and the EMP will be detonated to preserve the intelligence in the base's computers, so you needn't make a spectacle of your martyrdom complex. I'm truly sorry for the loss of your people. Grieve as you must, but do it onboard this ship, *en route* to Taurus station.'

'I can't accept that,' Jonah said. He tried to project defiance, but he knew now from experience how well confrontation with the Commander was likely to end for him. He could see the scenario in his mind's eye, where Albrecht became angry enough to snap his neck and throw him out of the airlock. He wondered if it might not be the preferable way to go out. It was true, it would do nothing to help Will and Eoin and Rahman and the Nguyens and everyone else waiting for him, packed into the core like sardines in a ventilated can. They would meet their end just as helplessly as he, hoping until the last that he would arrive with the rescue party he had promised. Pushing Albrecht to the point where it got him killed would mean nothing.

But he could conceive of the alternative just as clearly – if he stood aside and let Albrecht do as he pleased, then he would live out the remainder of his days knowing he hadn't done everything he possibly could to save his crew and his family.

It would mean he would be left as the last 'normal' human in the universe, the only one not assimilated or mechanised in one direction or the other. He remembered newscasts from his youth of the last emaciated polar bears clinging pathetically to rafts of ice; of the last African elephants laying down and refusing to move from the corpses of their herds.

Death was the end, he had always believed, but there was another, more final end. Extinction took everything from a species, robbing it of dignity, pride, and self-respect before the *coup de grâce* of oblivion. Extinction was something he couldn't walk into willingly, no matter the circumstances.

He began to move toward Albrecht, his fists raised.

'Look at the two big, strong men,' Victoria interjected. Jonah and Albrecht stared at her. 'Fighting over what flavour of surrender we should offer the enemy. Is this really what we've come to?'

'Lieutenant,' Albrecht said firmly, 'you will not contradict me over an open channel. You understand that your court-martial is still very much under consideration, regardless of—'

'Pipe down, Hermann.' There wasn't the slightest indication in Victoria's withering tone that she believed she was speaking to a superior, or even an equal. 'I've had enough. The retreats, the concessions, the day after day of stagnation and failure. Hell, I'd had enough a century ago. After Pisces, everyone else started to catch up to me.'

Her wings flared. She extended a hand, fingers splayed with the palm facing the Commander. Pale blue lines of light trickled along her forearm. The effect was something like an old-fashioned handgun being cocked.

Albrecht turned slowly to face her. 'What is this, Lieutenant?'

'This?' Victoria nodded towards her outstretched hand. 'This is a threat. I'm threatening you, Hermann. And you'll find I have others with me, willing to take the same stand.'

'Mutiny, then.' Albrecht looked around, surveying the room. 'After two hundred years, it all starts to crumble because you couldn't disregard your own needs for the good of the cause.'

The other Archangels looked to be in suspended animation, none betraying a hint of where their loyalties lay. Or almost none – Jonah shot a look at Daniels, who glanced back at him. Their eyes only met for a second, but in light of their odd conversation earlier, Jonah could infer the significance of what he saw there. Something like this had been scheduled to happen.

Albrecht raised his own palm to face Victoria. 'I've obviously been too lenient with you, Lieutenant. I wanted to give you the benefit of the doubt, that your last stunt was just desperation out of concern for your family. But now it's clear that you pose a danger to every one of us, every moment you remain active. For this level of sedition, suspension is too good for you.'

'Perhaps, Commander,' Victoria replied. 'But what do you intend to do about it? Our frames are evenly matched, and we both know how tricky the other is in a dogfight. If we were to fight it out, here and now, who knows who'd come out on top? But as much as I'd enjoy myself, we'd destroy the ship around us, and the Collective would know exactly where we are. No more tactical advantage. No more quick escape route.'

'True. But I'd get away, and so would most of the others. We've done it before, and we can do it again. I find the prospect preferable to whatever manner of suicidal madness you have in mind for the Insurgency next. And I've been flying since before you were born. You're talented, Harrison, but I wouldn't be quite so confident in your abilities if I were you.'

Seconds passed, agonisingly slowly, with neither Victoria nor Albrecht backing down from their stand-off. Jonah was all too conscious of the latent energy in the space separating them, the potential gigawatts of power that could start flying without warning.

Even in the cool, recycled air filtering through his suit, Jonah felt a trickle of sweat run down the nape of his neck. Victoria's declaration of war had ignored a point he felt was fairly crucial – if maser beams began flying inside the close confines of the bridge, he would certainly be vaporised inside the first split-second of hostilities. For all the mania that had consumed him moments earlier, he didn't actually *want* to die.

'Put it to a vote,' he blurted out, surprising no one more than himself.

Every head in the room turned toward him. Even Albrecht and Victoria, although neither of them wavered so much as a millimetre in their aim, looked at him with expressions of incredulity that Jonah could almost believe were spontaneous, even on Archangel faces.

'Excuse me?' Albrecht said.

'You're familiar with the concept of democracy? It's something the Greeks came up with about three thousand years ago, I think?' Sarcasm helped Jonah to project a great deal more confidence than he felt. 'I'm sure this is a matter every Archangel in this room and fighting outside feels strongly about, so let's ask them how they feel. Make this a nice, civilised mutiny.'

A small smile played across Victoria's face, an expression that read as some combination of mysterious and smug. 'Well, Commander, do you have any better ideas? A two-way, yes-or-no referendum. If you have the majority, we turn and run like cowards yet again, and abandon the people we worked so hard to rescue to the Collective. If I have the majority, we storm the base and bring them out.'

Albrecht glared at her a moment longer, and then, in perfect sync, they both lowered their hands, the glow in their palms dimming in concert.

'Fine,' Albrecht grunted, 'but no matter how this ends, I'll see that you answer for this, Lieutenant.'

***

The poll of the fifty-six total Archangels took no more than a couple of minutes, and the result was decisive – forty-one to fifteen in Victoria's favour. Most of the lieutenants present on the bridge cast their lots without hesitation, confirming what Daniels had insinuated: dissent in the Insurgency's upper ranks had been brewing for some time already. Kariuki and Trachtenberg were among the few who threw in with the Commander.

The delay, such as it was, came from the corporals and sergeants, most of whom were engaged outside the ship. The last vote to be cast, Jonah saw, belonged to Aki. The eternally gentle, oblivious boy had no idea of what was transpiring between his superiors.

'That seems fairly conclusive, wouldn't you say, Hermann?' Victoria asked, with feigned sweetness. 'No need for a recount?'

'Save your gloating for someone who's more easily impressed, Lieutenant,' Albrecht answered. 'Brief your grandfather on your plan while I make the preparations. I'm sure he'll be delighted to learn his place in it.'

Victoria grimaced and opened a private channel to Jonah. 'Nice move, suggesting the vote,' she said. 'Things could've gotten out of hand otherwise.'

'From where I'm standing, things already look pretty far out of hand,' Jonah pointed out. 'Granted.'

'You never intended to answer to Albrecht's tribunal, did you? You weren't nervous about the court-martial because you never would have abided by its decision anyway.'

'You don't approve?'

'It doesn't thrill me. How long has this been going on?'

Victoria paused. He didn't like the feeling that his granddaughter needed to measure her words before answering him. 'Like I said, there's been unrest among the officers since the capture of Pisces Station, losing both the base and Velasquez. Albrecht's order to retreat was premature. The numbers that we had there that day, we could have forced the Scarabs back.

'But it wasn't just Pisces. It's... telomerase supplements have a limited capacity to sustain life. Even if the Collective has developed better life-extending technology, it won't be perfect. Albrecht was already a widower when it all went down in 2135. He never had children. He doesn't get it. But for most of us here, what's driven us all this time has been the prospect of seeing our loved ones again. Parents, spouses, kids. There's the sense that time's running out, that if we don't win this war soon, it will all have been for nothing. A regime change has been a long time coming. What happened on TransTerra, and the attack now just sort of... catalysed things.'

'You couldn't have told me? That your rescue mission wasn't just for our sake, but the groundwork was being laid for a coup?'

'I thought it was best to keep you away from this as well as I could.'

Jonah shook his head. 'Fine. It doesn't matter at this point. All that matters is that we find some way to get everyone out of that asteroid. Tell me your plan, and bear in mind, I'm not leaving Alyssa in there.'

***

Victoria's frame was tuned to vantablack as she dragged Jonah behind her, through the few kilometres separating the transport from the exterior of the base. In the near-total absence of light, it was as though he had grabbed onto the darkness itself and found himself at its mercy. He relinquished himself to providence and forces beyond his comprehension or control, trusting that if he kept the faith, they would deliver his people back to him.

The asteroid lacked the necessary mass to hold a spherical shape. About ten kilometres through its longest cross-section, half as wide as it was long, its shape was an irregular oblong. It was pinched in the middle, on the axis around which it rotated, narrowing towards the equator and flaring out towards the poles—it had the approximate shape of a peanut shell.

In one respect, they had been fortunate—the Collective's intelligence either hadn't been comprehensive enough to know where to probe for the command module or, if it had, they had been forced to settle for a less-than-ideal breach point. They had entered into the northern bulge, the side of the base where the settlers' cave was. The core, where the settlers had evacuated, was ensconced at the centre of the larger southern bulge, where the rock provided the best insulation against space.

To make their way to it, the Collective units inside the base would have to navigate through a naturally occurring choke point. Individually, each of the bulges were rat's mazes, their crisscrossing corridors full of blind corners and hard angles. Engaging the Scarabs in there, where the Archangels' agility was nullified as an advantage, would be tactically hazardous at best, and downright foolish at worst.

However, there was only one tunnel connecting the two bulges through the equator, fifteen metres in diameter and two hundred and seventy-five metres long. A docking port connected that tunnel to space—it was the first one that had been installed when the base had been established five years earlier, the Archangels having bored into the asteroid at the thinnest naturally occurring point and then expanded the tunnel network throughout it to the north and south.

Victoria's plan was to establish a barricade at the northern end of the corridor. There, they could hold off the Collective at the choke point, while shepherding the settlers through the tunnels to the south. The transport would pick them up at the equatorial docking port, and make a hasty retreat once that was done. It was a plan that hinged on a lot of assumptions—that the Collective hadn't already infiltrated the Southern bulge; that the transport would be able to dock while eluding fire from the Scarabs still combing the asteroid's exterior. But it was something they could work from.

Of all the 'ifs' in play, Jonah was most anxious about the one concerning him. Victoria had assured him that the first Scarab he had encountered, the one that had vaporised Marcus and nearly killed Alyssa, had been malfunctioning. Its target acquisition systems had been damaged in its dogfight with her and the impact of its landing—otherwise, its protocols would never have permitted it to directly fire on a flesh-and-blood human being. He was glad she was confident, but he couldn't help but recall the smell of Marcus Lawson's superheated flesh.

All clear, came a notification from Daniels. Jonah's HUD showed his silhouette against the docking port, made discernible by a dim, gold outline. **Most of the Collective units have congregated on the north side, protecting their breach point. Looks like they must have sealed it too, because atmospheric pressure is reading as normal, give or take a few millibars.**

Good, Victoria replied. **Let's double-time it. I'd bet my frame that they have another force incoming as we speak.**

Please don't jinx it.

The delegation from the transport split into two groups; fifteen, led by Daniels, remained outside the docking port to guard the transport's approach, and later its retreat. The other fifteen, plus Jonah, made their way into the base as quietly as the release mechanisms would allow.

Their contingent included Victoria, as well as Albrecht, Kariuki, and Trachtenberg. The reason was unspoken but clear as day—Victoria wanted the Commander and his loyalists trapped inside with the rest of them when their presence was inevitably noticed, rather than outside where they might be seduced by the possibility of counter-mutiny and escape. Mutual self-interest was a good motivator for cooperation.

The passageway from the docking port into the base interior was narrow enough to force them to move in single file, but the tunnel it joined was the broadest to be found anywhere in the asteroid—if the tunnels were blood vessels, this was the installation's aorta. In the absence of a suit equipped with built-in propulsion jets, it would be very easy for a zero-g neophyte to get stranded in the centre, flailing around for something to push against.

The Archangels shed their vantablack cloaking once inside; Victoria's features resolved themselves from the indistinct hole in reality that Jonah had been holding onto. She gestured to two of the others. **No sentries is a good sign,** she wrote, **but we can't rule out the chance that they've already passed through here. If so, we'll need to prepare for tunnel-to-tunnel combat. Shimura, Edelstein, you two drew the short straws, so you scout out the southern bulge. Any sign of Collective presence whatsoever, raise the alarm. When and** *if* **you judge it to be all clear, bring the settlers out. Everyone else, fan out and form a barricade on the tunnel's north side. Groups of three at twenty-metre intervals. The variation in air pressure won't have gone unnoticed, so we don't have long until they're on top of us. The objective is to give the settlers safe passage to rendezvous with the transport. Hauer, you're remotely piloting it in, so for Christ's sake, be careful.**

The ease with which Victoria had snapped into the authority of command was impressive and a little frightening. Albrecht had given him the story of how ruthless she could be with the lives of her enemies and comrades alike, and seeing the brusqueness of her orders, he could believe it.

'As for you,' she said to Jonah now on a private line, 'Are you ready?'

'As ready as I can be,' Jonah replied. 'But if any better ideas occur to you at the last minute, feel free to speak up.'

She pulled him slowly toward the northern mouth of the tunnel, past the spots where her comrades—her subordinates, now—were getting into position.

In chess, there was a principle Jonah had used to beat Rahman on more than one occasion: that two kings could not occupy adjacent squares. In the late game, when the pieces on the board had been winnowed down and the kings were moving freely, it was a principle that players could manipulate in their favour. He had always found the idea to be curiously profound. The object of the game was to protect the king from being captured, and yet there were circumstances where the king's significance could be leveraged to protect other pieces in turn.

Manderly's video had been intended to look like an earnest attempt at appeasement. Perhaps it even was. But what Victoria had seen was a tactical mistake on her enemy's part; they had revealed the significance they placed upon her grandfather. Whether they needed him to come to them willingly, or they'd condescend to capture him against his will, or they even needed him alive at all, were all unknown factors. But for the first time, they had been given a glimpse of variance in the Collective's goals; an unassimilated human being they specifically valued more highly than others.

Jonah took off his helmet, exchanging the sterile air of his suit for the warmer air of the base, infused these past days with the musk of plant and animal life. Victoria deposited him at the northern head of the tunnel, leaving him to float right in its centre, and then backing away.

He was unarmed—indeed, their plan involved making a point of his vulnerability. He spread his arms and legs, fingers splayed, making himself as large and visible as he could.

When the Collective converged upon their location, he would be positioned at the locus point of the predicted crossfire. Without knowing why, he had been declared his side's king, between the silver pieces at one end of the board and the matte-black pieces at the other.

***

He heard the Scarabs coming before he saw them. The sound had the tempo of insectile scuttling, but low and resonant.

He bodily flinched when the first one came into view. He didn't think the black-armoured beasts would ever fail to inspire a reflex of repulsion in him, and the idea of letting one of them come close without making any move to defend himself set off alarms in the reptilian centres of his brain. He held his here-I-am, look-at-me posture despite the cold sweat beading on his forehead.

The featureless nub where its anatomy suggested there should be a face assessed him. He'd raised the idea of one of the Archangels imitating his appearance, rearranging the platelets in their faces to match his likeness, but Albrecht had shaken his head. The Archangel frame could superficially reshape and recolour itself, but even the most token radiographic analysis would see through a sham like that in an instant. For once, Victoria had been on Albrecht's side.

'I want to speak to my granddaughter,' he shouted at it. It remained fixed to the opposite wall, motionless, making no move to advance or retreat. He imagined it was sizing up both him and the tunnel full of Archangels behind him, with their palms outstretched and glowing, ready to burn him to cinders in a microsecond. 'You want the others? They're past us, and the only way to reach them is through here. Through me. You want to talk terms? Go back to your masters like a good dog, and bring her here.'

The Scarab still didn't move, just kept observing. Soon it was joined by another, then a third and a fourth. None of them made any move to attack more than the first had. Minute followed minute, and no sign of any human figures approaching from the north or the south. Objectively, Jonah knew that this worked in their favour; the longer he could stall for time here, the better the chances of escorting the settlers out. Privately, he didn't enjoy the feeling of being transfixed by the maser cannons of two warring sides any more than he'd imagined.

Finally, two dark-suited figures drifted into view, dwarfed by the bulk of the machines that flanked them. The pair of them removed their helmets. The taller of them was the old man whose face had greeted them on the ultimatum video – Manderly. The shorter of them was... some of the tightness went out of Jonah's chest. It was Jack Nguyen.

'Captain Harrison,' Manderly said, his mode of address formal but calm, almost relaxed. Only the rigidity of his posture seemed to demonstrate any sense of the situation's stakes. 'It's a pleasure to finally meet you, sir, although I'd hoped that the occasion might not warrant quite so much firepower.'

'I'm not interested in talking to you, Manderly, and I'm not interested in acting like your friend just because you screwed my daughter a couple of times two hundred years ago. I want to see Alyssa. Until you make that happen, I have nothing more to say.'

'She's *en route*. We do realise you're stalling for time, Captain. That's fine by us. We've waited a very long time for this encounter – you'll forgive us if we take the opportunity to savour it.'

'You're connected to her right now, aren't you? Mind to mind, shared perception, that's how your lot work, right? If that's the case, then hear this: Lys. I don't know if you really chose this like you told me you did. Or maybe there comes a point where there's no difference between choice and coercion. At this stage, it doesn't matter anymore. What I told you that day on the transport still holds true. You live with your decisions, no matter what. No one has to forgive you but you.'

Jack snorted at that. 'Very pretty sentiment, Jonah. What about leading your family members into a situation where they get mortally wounded and almost die? I'd be really interested to know if you've forgiven yourself for that, considering you make it sound so easy.'

'Enough, Jack.' Manderly cut him off before Jonah could. 'Alyssa hears you, Captain.'

'Fine. Until she's here, you and your machines keep your distance just where you are right now.'

'Of course. I'm not the one trying to escalate things here, Harrison. You could make everyone's lives a lot easier by coming over to us.'

Jonah considered pointing out to him that he could have made everyone's lives a lot easier and safer if he hadn't seen fit to breach the base in the first place, but thought better of it.

A notification came from Hauer: **Proximity alert was just triggered again,** it read. **More unidentified QF signatures approaching from galactic southeast, 0.01 AU away and decelerating hard.**

Just perfect, Victoria responded. **Get the cannons warmed up, and see if you can build the last swarm's evasive manoeuvres into their targeting solutions. Shimura, Edelstein, a little urgency would be greatly appreciated.**

Sweep's 27.3% done by volume, 25.1% by linear metre, came Shimura's answer. **No sign of the enemy yet, but we're working on it.**

'You're not curious at all?' Jack Nguyen's voice distracted Jonah from the scenario evolving around him. 'About why the Collective wants you so badly, I mean? No flashes of inspiration come to mind about what makes you so important, of all people?'

Jonah glared at him. Somehow, assimilation hadn't dampened the obnoxiousness about the boy he'd always found so wearying. 'I think the Collective are liars and saboteurs. I think you tell concealing half-truths and put a polite face on the fact that you're parasites. You're an invasive organism that acts like you're humanity's best friend, and that's how you lure us into your traps. And for the record, you little shit: no, I haven't forgiven myself yet. But I'll get there without your help.'

Jack smirked, and it was a smirk Jonah recognised. He'd seen it on Astrid when they had argued; the dispiriting smirk of someone certain they had the right of it, and that their opponent's argument was based on a faulty foundation. 'We've never been anything but honest with you, Jonah,' he said. 'Can you say the same for Victoria?'

***

Shimura and Edelstein's search was 81.6% complete by volume, 83.4% by linear metre when another black-clad figure drifted into view of the northern end of the tunnel. It floated into place between Manderly and Nguyen and removed its tinted helmet to reveal Alyssa's face. Whether the being that wore his granddaughter's face and which spoke with her voice was a being that

253

Jonah should address with her name was a question he was still grappling with.

'Here I am, Jonah,' it said. 'Are we ready to talk about this like grown-ups now, instead of playing at brinksmanship?'

He was tempted to rise to her goading, but it wouldn't be worth it. 'Here's what will happen,' he said. 'We will confirm that there are none of yours waiting in ambush at the southern end of the base. Once this is done, you will all, except Alyssa and Jack, withdraw a kilometre into the northern bulge. The Archangels will escort the flesh-and-blood settlers to a docking port where they will rendezvous with the transport that will take them away from this place. Once they are safely aboard, you will give us Alyssa and Jack. They will be restrained, gagged, and blindfolded, until such a time as an anti-Collective countermeasure can be administered to them.'

'Pretty bold parley,' Alyssa said. 'Why do you think we'd agree to any of it?'

'Because if you violate any of the above terms, the insurgents behind me will open fire, reducing my body to its constituent molecules. I'm guessing I won't be much good to you in that state. And when the Insurgency withdraws, the base's EMP will be detonated regardless of whatever else happens. Any settlers left inside will die. If you make any move that we even interpret as aggressive, the same consequences apply. We lose a lot, but you get nothing. We offer only this – the potential for another shot at me, in another place, at another time, somewhere far from here.'

'You're bluffing.' Alyssa said it with the absolute confidence that could only come with a lifetime's insight into another mind. 'You'd put yourself in the firing line, sure. But we know you too well to think you'd ever allow that kind of harm to come to your crew, Jonah. And we know Victoria and Albrecht, too. Even after their old comrades like Velasquez passed on, the memories they shared with us are still rattling around in here.' She pointed at her temple. 'Albrecht would never try anything this stupidly bold, so we assume it's Victoria pulling the strings now. I don't believe for a second she'd let her grandfather be turned into ashes in front of her. We've both seen where her priorities lie.'

'Well, whoever you are, I don't know you,' Jonah shot back. 'Whether you're my granddaughter or something else wearing her skin. But let me be absolutely clear – you'd be wise not to underestimate Victoria. Even if I wanted it to, there is no way for this situation to play out where the Collective takes any of us alive.'

'Even if you wanted it to? Do you hear yourself? You're the one being held hostage here, Jonah, not me.'

'Call it what you will. We've laid out the least-bad option for you, and for us. It's your choice if you want to take it.'

Alyssa fired her suit's manoeuvring verniers on their softest setting, enough for her to drift a little closer. She arrested her momentum after a couple of metres, the Archangels behind Jonah shouting warnings and threats in amplified voices, but the distance she closed between herself and Jonah threw her face into sharper relief, enough for him to note the glistening texture of her face's burned tissue. Her eyes shone with entreaty, reflecting the tunnel's harsh artificial light. If her emotion was feigned, it was a convincing forgery. It was the same look she'd given him when she'd planted her heels and demanded he and Rahman take her with them on the Hummingbird; the passion of youth, projecting a confidence it didn't feel.

'Hey, cousin!' she shouted past him, down the length of the tunnel. 'I don't expect you to understand this, but I have to try. Things aren't as black and white as you think. If you'd taken five minutes in the last two centuries to look past your absurd war on the rest of the universe, you'd have realised there are opportunities for something spectacular and wonderful if you'd join forces with us. The Starman holds the key to achievements greater by far than anything the Collective has attained. If he comes with us, he won't be harmed. He won't even be assimilated. Won't you help us, instead of insisting on even more pointless destruction?'

Jonah didn't dare chance a look over his shoulder – no answer came, from Victoria or anyone else.

'I didn't think so,' Alyssa sighed. 'You know,' she said to Jonah, 'there was a time we tried to approach them diplomatically. We'd come to them unarmed, broadcasting our friendly intentions, flying white flags every way we knew how. And Albrecht would shoot them down, every single time. So now, we do this instead, everything conducted from behind the barrel of a gun, no trust on either side. It's no more than we deserve, I guess. It's our original sin, coming back to bite us two hundred years later.'

***

Shimura and Edelstein's progress ticked over to 100% without incident, and they reported that the settlers were being escorted through the warren of tunnels towards the docking port. The Collective units still crawling around the base exterior were accounted for, and Daniels reported they were making no attempts at encroaching upon the transport. Hauer placed the encroaching reinforcements at seventy minutes distant; the cannons' updated firing solutions were keeping them at bay more effectively than the first contingent. Their window of escape would be tight, but more feasible than what they had already survived in TransTerran orbit.

'It's time,' Jonah announced, addressing Manderly again. 'Decide whether you want a bloodbath, right now.'

Manderly's face gave nothing away, but his bearing told Jonah everything he needed to hear – the Collective had no ace up its sleeve, no gamble it was willing to make that would risk letting Jonah and the other settlers slip through their fingers. Finally, he nodded. 'Have it your way then, Captain. But remember this – it's within your power to alleviate a grave injustice. When Jean spoke about you, she told me you were a conscientious man before you were anything else. I trust your conscience will lead you to us eventually, irrespective of Albrecht or anyone else. We'll meet again.'

He manoeuvred around and gestured to the Scarabs; they turned with him in unison and retreated, heading back toward the breach. Alyssa and Jack turned and went with them.

'Wait!' Jonah called after them. 'They stay. That was the arrangement.'

Alyssa looked back to address him. 'No, that was your ultimatum. Unless you want to be the one to start your bloodbath, you can come and find me yourself.'

'Lys, please don't do this.'

'You don't understand what you're asking, do you? The connection with the Collective can be broken, but afterwards? The severance is enough to

256

destroy any human mind. Only one person who's undergone it has lived afterwards. The rest have all taken their own lives.'

'You expect me to accept that!?'

'No. I expect you to come and find me.' Alyssa turned her back on him and drifted away, Scarabs flanking her exit from the stage. Just before she was obscured by the curve of the northern corridor, she paused, as though struck by a sudden thought. 'You know,' she said, 'I've learned certain facts since I was assimilated that add some context to the story you told me about Jean. Details it's curious Victoria chose to leave out of her tale. On that note, I leave you.' She fired her suit's verniers and drifted out of sight.

'Wait!' Jonah was frantic now. He knew he was being played by the Collective, allowing himself to be drawn in by their games, but he couldn't make himself disregard Alyssa's last parting shot. 'What do you mean? Goddammit, what happened to my daughter!?'

'Jonah.' Victoria's voice manifested behind him. It had an edge to it. 'We don't have time to linger. We need to move, now.'

'Can't you send someone after her, before they get away?' Even as he spoke, he was discouraged by the small shake of the head she gave.

'Anyone we send in pursuit would turn this into a shooting match.'

'So, intercept them at the breach point, find a way of grabbing her insertion pod.'

'All of the Archangels outside just now are occupied keeping them off the transport's back. Any move we make would jeopardise our escape. I'm trying to thread a very fine needle here, Starman.'

Bitter understanding dawned on him. 'You never expected to get her back at all, did you? You just agreed with me to get me to go along with you in this scheme.' Victoria gave him a hard look that he returned in kind.

From the southern end of the corridor, a procession of huddled figures emerged, propelling themselves along the edges of the tunnel walls with as much speed as they dared. At their head, Shimura was ushering them forward with gestures that recalled an air traffic controller, trying to maintain a facsimile of order while keeping them moving as quickly as possible. From the confused and scared babble of voices that grew louder as the crowd approached, Jonah could pick out Eoin's voice calling after him. He disregarded it.

'We've saved eight hundred people, Jonah,' said Victoria. 'Your people. We'll take you to a safe location, and this time we'll ensure we're not followed. Even if it doesn't feel like it, that's a victory. One we didn't think was achievable two hours ago.'

'What was she talking about, Vic? You told me you didn't know what had happened to Jean, if she was assimilated or killed in the fight for Earth. What did Alyssa mean about details you left out?'

Another of those infernal pauses. 'Alyssa's assimilated, Starman. You can't give credence to anything the Collective has to say. A lie repeated by a million tongues is still a lie. I hate to say it, but for all intents and purposes, your granddaughter is gone.'

'Then it's true what she said? About no one surviving the de-conversion?'

Victoria hesitated, then nodded. 'We tried it with captives we took in the early fighting, many times. Some lasted hours, some lasted weeks, but no matter what sort of therapy we employed, all of them went irreversibly insane after the severance. Failing anything else, they'd refuse to eat or drink.'

Jonah choked down the yell of frustration building at the back of his throat. 'Then what's this for? What's *any* of it for? How do you ever expect to liberate Earth?'

Victoria glanced back toward the docking port, where the settlers were being shepherded onto the transport, cramming themselves into the airlock in groups of fifty. Jonah briefly caught sight of Rahman in the throng – he was watching their exchange with a look of perplexion.

'Jonah, it's neither the time nor the place for this conversation. I interceded on your behalf earlier, so please, listen to me and get on the ship with the rest.'

He saw it clearly: there was no appeal he could make to either emotion or reason that would sway her. And without Victoria's support, his hopes of retrieving the person he felt more responsible for than any other moved from infinitesimal to non-existent. Any move he could make on his own would end with him captured, stranded or dead, or some combination of the three. Alyssa couldn't be more than a few hundred metres away, and yet she was more utterly beyond reach than any goal he had ever set his eyes on.

He mutely allowed himself to be dragged into line with the rest of the settlers, floating passively like so much interstellar flotsam. Jonah had spent too many years living surrounded by light-years of uncaring vacuum to place much stock in the idea of a higher power. Nevertheless, he felt again the sensation that had plagued him more and often since this had all begun; that he was being tested, and found wanting.

***

His group was the last to be ushered into the airlock; seventeen settlers together with the remaining contingent of Archangels. Hauer was sending periodic and increasingly fraught updates on the situation in the space outside, and the narrowing window of time they had to escape without another risky open battle. **Once we're inside, I need everyone in their gel-pods inside ten minutes,** she wrote on a general channel. **I'm expecting a ten-g burn initially until we're well clear of their sensors.**

The airlock finished its cycle, admitting the second-to-last group into the transport ahead of them. It began to whir again, the hermetically sealed hatch matching the base's interior pressure before opening to admit the final batch of travellers. Jonah was distracted by someone tugging at his elbow. He turned and found Julie Nguyen waiting for him, anxious to speak in a hushed voice. 'I got separated from Jack in the panic,' she said, her eyes bright. 'His comms aren't responding, and I couldn't find him in the core. No one seems to know where he is.'

The girl was keeping herself together well, but he saw the beginnings of frenzy in her expression. It wouldn't be conducive to the evacuation for her to go to pieces now, and telling her the truth would do nothing to calm her down. 'We ran into him in the corridors,' he said, the lie sour on his tongue. 'He was off on his own when the attack came and got disoriented. Good thing we found him before they did; he's safe onboard already.'

It was a flimsy story, but she seemed contented with it for the time being. She could resent him for it later. The hypocrisy wasn't lost on him; it was a small echo of the way he had been manipulated.

The airlock hatch finished its equalisation and hinged open, admitting the group into its cramped vestibule. The Archangels helped the settlers inside, most of them eager to get away as quickly as possible, but Jonah tarried. Victoria caught his eye and hovered slowly down to meet him.

'I know it's hard,' she said, softly. 'If I'd seen a way that things could have gone differently, that's what I would have done. For what it's worth, I liked Lys, in the short time I knew her. I would have wanted her to think of me like she would a sister, one day. But we can't get everything we want. It seems selfish, even cruel of me to say, but so be it: you matter more to me than she does.'

She extended a hand, and he allowed her to gently steer him into the vestibule. 'You remember what you said, the first time you laid eyes on her?' he asked. 'You said I'd always be able to trust you.'

'That's still true.'

'Then I wish it felt more like it.'

She had the good grace not to reply any further.

'All aboard?' Albrecht greeted them inside the airlock with a tone that would cause fruit to die on the vine. 'Let's get out of here, and into whatever fresh hell you've prepared for us next, Lieutenant Harrison.'

The hatch began to close behind them, and Jonah looked forlornly at the base that had so briefly been his home, being obscured in a diminishing crescent. This would make three times in his life he'd left a home behind with the certainty he'd never return. First Earth, and then TransTerra. Each time he had left pieces of himself behind. How many more until there was nothing left?

He made up his mind.

Jonah pulled his helmet down over his head, reattaching it to his suit. **Good luck with your war,** he messaged Victoria. She turned to look at him in alarm, but by the time she'd understood what he was doing, she was too late to stop it.

He drew his legs tightly up against his chest, performed a backward somersault that put the balls of his feet in contact with the airlock's inner wall, and propelled himself off from it with all the strength his legs had in them. He blew through the closing hatch in the split second before it sealed shut.

He collided with the tunnel's opposite wall with a crash that rattled his teeth. Pain shot through his bad leg from the exertion he'd asked of it, enough for his vision to blur. When he regained his senses, he saw Victoria's face pressed against the porthole of the hatch behind him, her beautiful features contorted by a mixture of confusion, fear, and rage.

Jonah knew the antiquated design of the airlocks used on the transport from experience. Unless the Insurgency had made some extensive modifications to the hardware (and he saw no reason why they would), once the process of atmospheric equalisation began, it couldn't be overridden before it was complete. Victoria could probably blast her way through the hatch, but not without unleashing enough heat and radiation to cook the flesh-and-blood humans inside with her. He had a hundred and ten seconds before she could pursue him. In that time, he would put himself where she couldn't follow.

***

The Collective were in the final stages of their own evacuation when he reached them. Only Manderly and two other helmeted figures remained, in the process of strapping themselves into their individual personnel carriers. The diminutive vessels suggested to Jonah that they had been launched from a larger craft being used as a staging post outside the range of the FOB's passive sensor array.

Manderly halted in his preparations when he saw Jonah approach, his face splitting into a wide grin. His delight looked genuine, for whatever that was worth.

'Captain. Now, this is a welcome surprise,' he said, beaming. 'We're so glad you've changed your mind.' He approached, proffering a hand to shake. Jonah raised his own hand, not in friendship, but as a warning gesture.

'Don't come any closer. Make any wrong moves, and I'll flood my suit with pure nitrogen.'

Manderly adjusted his trajectory accordingly and shrugged magnanimously. 'Fair enough. You needn't worry so much, Captain. I told you, we come in peace.'

'And you needn't mistake this as a gesture of trust. Using Alyssa to win me over was a cheap shot, and you know it.'

'She's overjoyed that you've—'

'Spare me,' Jonah cut him off. 'I'm handing myself over to you voluntarily, on three conditions. First, I will not consent to be assimilated. You promised it wouldn't happen, and I'm holding you to it.'

Manderly bowed his head in acknowledgement.

'Second: I want to be able to talk to my granddaughter, face to face.'

'Done.'

'And third: I want to know everything. No more games, no more cryptic shit. Tell me the truth about this conflict, and how I can end it.'

Chapter 17

December 12th, 2135 C.E.

After her escape attempt, the Chinese government was no longer affording Jean such indulgences as shabby motel rooms and mediocre carry-out food. When her restraints were removed and the opaque metal visor over her eyes unclamped, she learned that she had been sedated in sensory-deprived captivity for almost 36 hours. Her dreams had begun to bleed together with waking hallucinations, all abstract shapes and colours.

Any hopes that her unshackling spelt an end to her tribulations were quickly dashed. She spent the following eight hours being manhandled by staff in variously coloured scrubs, who barked instructions at her in combinations of English, Cantonese, and Mandarin. She obeyed every order, despite the encompassing weariness that pervaded down to her bones ever since her severance from the Enclave. It could only stand to benefit her at this point if she acted as meekly as possible.

Her surroundings appeared to be some manner of high-tech forensic laboratory, probably underground, to judge from the absence of windows and the sterile décor. Possibly somewhere underneath Beijing, but she had no way of knowing; she had been blindfolded and sedated by the commandos who had taken her into custody. For all she knew, she wasn't even on the Asian continent. She had heard rumours for decades of Chinese black sites scattered all over the globe.

She was subjected to every examination she had the vocabulary to describe – neurological, physiological, and some just plain illogical. MRI, EKG, CAT, and Quantum Resolution scans were made of her brain in triplicate. Blood, tissue, and bone marrow samples were drawn from her until her skin bruised and she felt physically diminished by their extractions.

The inquisition and violation went on for hours until she was led, limping, into a bare room furnished only with two steel chairs, one steel table, and one steely occupant.

'We really have to stop meeting like this, Jean,' said David. He rose when she entered, but didn't approach. She could hardly blame him, considering the course their last couple of encounters had taken.

'Dave. Do I have you to thank that I haven't already been buried in an unmarked grave?'

He sighed. 'Not quite. I'd like to think that my petitioning stopped you from getting vivisected, but the Chinese are smart enough to recognise that you're more useful to them alive than dead, without needing me to point it out.'

She opened her mouth to thank him, and to apologise for the behaviour which already seemed remote and implausible to her, the memory of it like something she was observing in the third person, of a woman maddened by rabies or lupus. Before she could begin, David raised a hand to quiet her. 'Don't bother, Jean. Whatever colourful insults you've come up with this time, I think I've got the gist.'

'No, I wasn't—'

'It doesn't matter. Look, I understand now, even after I removed that thing from your neck, just how much you weren't responsible for your own actions. Especially after the last few hours.'

Jean was grateful, hearing him dismiss her sins like that. Even so, the ominous quality of that last turn of phrase wasn't lost on her. 'What do you mean, after the last few hours?'

David grimaced. 'Let's start with the good news, shall we? First of all, Li Jun is alive and recovering.'

Jean racked her brains, searching for some significance to the name. 'Who's Li Jun?' she asked, giving up.

'The thief whose trachea you collapsed. He's in intensive care, but he'll make it through. Neither he nor any of his gang wants to press charges, on account of the fact that you caught them carjacking that coupé you wrecked. You're off the hook for manslaughter and several counts of assault.'

'And the bad news?'

'Probably better if you see for yourself,' he said, darkly. An icon blinked to life in the lower right-hand corner of her vision – her connection to the virtunet, stripped from her when she had been incarcerated, had been restored.

She was subscribed to updates from over two dozen news feeds, ranging from long-standing institutions like The Financial Times and The Guardian to independent, tech-savvy bloggers capable of up-to-the-minute coverage of live events all over the world.

Gory images captured from urban settings bombarded her, accompanied by similarly apocalyptic headlines:

'2 MILLION ESTIMATED DEAD'

'OCEANS OF BLOOD'

'THE WORLD WEEPS'

***

While she was being debriefed, the pair of them were joined by Secretary Koo, and if Jean looked like hell, then he was scarcely any better. Under his suit (the same one he had been wearing when he had accosted Jean two days ago, more rumpled than ever), his skin was taking on a worrying pallor.

As well it should be, Jean thought, though she kept her opinion to herself. He had, after all, co-ordinated the international incursion into Enclave territory. As David had been explaining, the operation had run without a hitch. Carlos' preventative measures against the effects of Xavier Wong's device had proven effective. Thus guarded, the special forces of more than two dozen nations had caught the Enclave completely unaware. They had executed their objective cleanly, isolating the devices responsible for the Enclave's propagation, and eliminated them with minimal casualties.

The spectacle that had followed after their objective was complete, however, had been the greatest humanitarian travesty in history.

From Jean's perspective, it was only too obvious what had happened. Everything she had felt upon her severance from the Enclave had been played out in the minds of millions of individuals at once; the fear and rage and loss, all the negative emotions that they had been liberated from flooding back in at once. All of those people experiencing the worst trauma imaginable, yoked together in some of the most densely populated areas on Earth. Of course, they had turned to violence, against themselves and each other.

It had manifested in different ways in different places, the outpouring of pain and self-destruction following different trajectories. In Delhi, the liberated citizenry had taken turns bludgeoning each other to death. In Jakarta, they had serenely joined hands and walked into the ocean.

The worst images of violence had come from Los Angeles – there, the violence had been directed against the squad responsible for destroying the device. The crowd had converged upon them, desperate to tear them limb from limb in a futile gesture of vengeance. The commandos had fired back, and when that only provoked the populace further, they had called for reinforcements. The crowd turned on the reinforcements, and the massacre had grown according to an exponential curve, until the USA had done the unthinkable and launched kinetic torpedoes on its citizens from orbital defence platforms positioned overhead. Los Angeles had been devastated; the city, which had weathered the rupture of the San Andreas Fault, was brought to ruin by its own government.

'Ms. Harrison,' Koo said. 'I'm sorry for the discomfort you've endured. I've spoken with your country's embassy. You'll be released from custody within forty-eight hours.'

'Just like that?' Jean was bewildered by the leniency she was being shown.

'I called in a few favours,' he replied. 'My tenure as Secretary of Security – as a functionary of the Chinese state, actually – will be over in a few days.' He lit a cigarette, his hand trembling a little as he did so. 'I fully expect I will be assassinated before my first week of civilian life is up. History will remember me as a monster responsible for propagating the worst massacre the world has ever known. I don't know that I can say that history will be wrong.'

Despite herself, Jean felt a swell of pity for the man, broken as he was by what amounted to a turn of bad luck. He'd done what he saw as his duty; he'd 'liberated' the millions of spellbound from the Enclave Effect. He, and the governments of Earth, had learned just what that liberation cost, in the harshest possible way. 'You couldn't have known,' she said.

He waved her forgiveness away as though it irritated him. 'I accept the responsibility,' he said. 'There are wrongs that can't be righted by saying "I didn't know." And in any event, I don't have the luxury of self-pity just yet. There's still work to be done, and I hope that you may be able to help us.'

***

Of the 36 Enclave territories which had been infiltrated, Koo explained, 35 of them had been captured successfully, with the devices at their hearts being accounted for and dismantled. The parts which had gone into building them had been confiscated by the PNC for the time being. Doubtless, the design of Wong's device would become a flashpoint in the international community in the days and years to come; it would be regarded as a new kind of superweapon, with nations and corporations alike eyeing each other with renewed suspicion, vying for control of its power. It was just one more way the world would never be the same, lines on the map soon to be permanently redrawn.

What was worrying Koo now, though, was the thirty-sixth device. 'Mr. Manderly, you ought to hear this too,' he said.

The team of AFEUR agents who had infiltrated the Enclave in Bogotá had done so with as much stealth as the other special forces units worldwide. However, negotiating the city's densely packed Barrios Unidos locality had cost them precious seconds in checking blind corners, and they had reached the city's regional Yang-Mitsubishi offices at 7:34 pm, local time on December 9th – four minutes behind the schedule Koo had laid out, and the latest of any of the 36 groups.

Koo had insisted the operations be synchronised for obvious reasons – with the Enclave being capable of instantaneous and silent coordination between its members, any lag would be tantamount to a tip-off. Sure enough, that was what had happened – the AFEUR had combed the building and found no sign of a device resembling the ones captured in other Yang-Mitsubishi offices. Satellite surveillance had observed six lorries emerge from the office's basement garage before proceeding to split up and head through the city streets, scattering themselves to the north, south, east, and west.

It was Koo's opinion, which both David and Jean agreed with, that one of these lorries contained the Bogotá device, the other five acting as decoys. It was a sensible contingency plan for the Enclave to have made against incursion. He had ordered the commandoes to give chase, to bend all of the resources of their agency toward stopping those lorries. But before they could do so, the same violence that had erupted in every other Enclave erupted in Bogotá. Walls of crazed bodies made their way out into the streets, and the frenzy of roiling motion had confounded any attempt to follow the vehicles, on the ground or from orbit.

Hours later, a lorry matching the dimensions of those observed in the satellite footage had been found abandoned by the banks of the Guayuriba River a hundred klicks to the southeast, hastily concealed in the foliage, its trailer empty.

Koo postulated that the device had been temporarily switched to a portable power supply with its effects reduced, enough to keep a handful of Enclave agents connected mind-to-mind within a radius of a few dozen metres. These agents would have been responsible for transferring the device to other means of transport cached throughout rural Colombia beforehand. Roadblocks had been erected around the country, despite resources being stretched to their breaking point trying to quell the destruction in Bogotá, and satellites had been scanning the hills for signs of camouflaged airfields or launch sites. So far, the search had turned up nothing, and Koo was pulling every string he could reach to prevent the knowledge of the lost device being leaked to the press.

'We've interviewed hundreds of survivors of the Enclaves,' he concluded. 'Most of them are some combination of inconsolable, delusional, or catatonic. Jean, as far as we know, you are the most lucid individual anywhere on Earth to have undergone severance.'

The weight of this knowledge pressed on her. 'Why me, of all people?' she asked.

Koo took a deep drag on his cigarette as he mulled over his response. 'The prevailing factor, I would suppose, is the circumstances under which you were severed. The majority of the spellbound were physically clustered close together when the devices were taken offline – I'd imagine that proximity with others experiencing those overwhelming negative emotions would be self-reinforcing, whereas you were in the company of non-spellbound like Mr. Manderly and your daughter, pulling you back to the light, as it were.

'But, although I'm no psychiatrist, there's another aspect. The descriptions of the experience of severance we've had from the survivors who've been able to talk mesh with yours. They characterise it as like bereavement, but amplified. I've seen your psych profile from your time in the ORC, and your personal history may also have equipped you for that sensation of loss.'

Abandoned by her father at age six. Widowed at the height of a happy marriage. Witness to her daughter being crippled for life. It was true; Jean had more education than most in the experience of abrupt, cruel loss – and more understanding of the significance of the connections that remained.

Mum, please. Please, don't do this. I can't lose you too.

Koo gave her a hard look. 'I've been in the intelligence business for nearly forty years, Ms. Harrison. I began at the bottom and worked my way up the ranks. Every spy's instinct I have tells me not to trust you. That your compliance in Beijing, your compliance now, is part of some greater plot, more Enclave subterfuge that I don't have the wit or the insight to see. But after the last two days, I don't believe in that spy's judgement anymore. And, frankly, I'm tired. I want this to be over, and I'll take any help I can get to arrive at that point. I'm taking a leap of faith, giving you this information, so please, if you can shed any light on where the device in Colombia went, you have to tell me.'

Jean racked her brain, willing herself to come up with something that would be of use to Koo. It surprised her to find how few reservations she had about abandoning her one-time brothers and sisters in the Enclave and working against them once again.

Had it really been only two days ago that she'd been one of them? So recently, their mission of conquest had seemed so obvious to her, so self-evident in its righteousness. Even now, the absence of those millions of voices gnawed; every moment of silence, every occasion to think, that feeling of *severance* made her want to curl into a ball and cry.

But then she thought of Victoria, there in the snow. Of how it might have felt to have chosen the Enclave over her. Or, worse; for Victoria to have become a part of the Enclave with her; to see that wilful, defiant girl she loved be hollowed out, made a part of that same all-engulfing hive-will.

No. They have to be stopped.

However, while the will was there, the ability was not. The Enclave distributed information amongst itself as though it were one mind, fragments of data spread throughout thousands of minds, which was only intelligible when they thought in concert. When Jean had been part of the system, she could have recited the name, age, shoe size, and blood type of every one of the tens of millions of others as though they were her own.

Now, though, all she could access was a multiplicity of non-sequiturs. Half a face here, a snatch of syllables there, half-imagined memories of sounds and smells with no context. Individually they were of no more use than single pixels when she was trying to assemble a high-res picture. She focused on the keywords and phrases she had – Bogotá; lorries; contingency plan – and she thought for a moment she glimpsed a handful of associated concepts that didn't spring from her own brain. But she couldn't be certain of anything she gleaned; couldn't be certain she wasn't imagining things.

She hadn't realised her eyes were closed until she opened them, and found David and Secretary Koo looking at her, anxiously.

'I'm sorry,' she said at last. 'There are bits and pieces, but nothing that would do you any good.'

'Tell us anyway,' David coaxed her. 'Any clue might be helpful.'

She obliged. 'A logarithmic function. A burst of orange flame. A rainstorm over a tropical jungle.'

Koo wore his disappointment plainly. 'That's all?'

'It's like trying to remember a dream, or a hallucination. The more I try to focus, the hazier it becomes.'

He stood, signalling that the interrogation was officially over. 'Another dead end,' he groaned. 'Thank you for trying, anyway.'

***

Her captors were true to their word. She spent a further two days in solitary confinement, albeit no longer hooked up to the sensory deprivation apparatus. Her connection to the virtunet was rescinded, and as such, she had nothing to keep her occupied but her thoughts. In the long tradition of recovering addicts, these tended towards the morose, but she was buoyed up by the anticipation of what she would do upon her emancipation from this whole sordid business.

David greeted her outside her cell when her forty-eight-hour wait was over, on the afternoon of December 14th. With him was a pale, well-groomed gentleman with deep bags under his eyes. Her lawyer, it transpired, representing her on behalf of the British government. He had spent the previous two days hashing out the terms of her probation and return to the UK.

The Enclave phenomenon and its aftereffects, he told her, existed entirely outside of legal precedent; the extent to which an individual under its influence could be considered culpable for their actions was a question which would dominate the legal profession for decades to come. The conditions required for a plea of insanity were judged to be unreasonable, given that millions of people had reacted similarly to the same stimuli. Taking the view that, prior to her assimilation (that was the term people had begun to use) and later severance, she had been a model citizen with no criminal record; that she had been instrumental in exposing the way the Enclave was structured; and that the crisis currently facing the world made it a waste of time and resources to prosecute her, China was prepared to waive any charges it could bring against her, under certain terms of probation.

First, she was to wear a tracker which would allow the UK to keep tabs on her location at all times, with a clause stipulating that any PNC signatory nation could petition for the information if they had cause to do so. Her right to privacy, nominal as such a thing was these days, would effectively be dissolved. She would have the right to appeal to have the tracker removed after eighteen months. Secondly, she was to attend sessions with a therapist on a weekly basis – this would serve the dual role of helping her come to terms with the trauma of severance and with helping the scientific community better understand the Enclave phenomenon.

Jean half-listened to all of this with glazed eyes, nodding her assent every time the lawyer indicated it was required. When prompted, she signed the documents he thrust under her nose. The conditions felt lenient, as far as she was concerned, and she couldn't find it in herself to dispute any punishment that came her way, regardless.

She allowed herself to be blindfolded once more, letting David guide her to the facility's exit. She was bundled into a car and driven for perhaps half an hour, after which the blindfold was removed.

The car – another of the black SUVs she had become thoroughly sick of by now – was parked on the curb outside an automated chain motel. She was handed an envelope, containing a credit chit to the value of 20,000 yuan and two tickets for a vacuum pod from Beijing to Dover the following morning.

This last surprised her a little. 'The vac-pods are running again?' she asked.

David nodded. 'The PNC lifted the travel restrictions yesterday, now that the back of the crisis has been broken. Seems perverse, doesn't it? They're clearing out bodies from some of the biggest cities in the world using industrial digging machines, and yet the main reaction I hear from people is relief that it's all over.'

'That's people for you, I suppose. It's easier for us to live with a terrible certainty than a dreadful uncertainty. I don't know what that says about us. Maybe nothing too flattering.' David nodded, looking as though he had more to say but was unsure of how to say it.

'Well,' Jean ventured, 'if this is my stop, then I suppose it's goodbye again, Dave.'

'Does it have to be, though?' he replied, meeting her gaze. 'Jean, I know you're strong. Maybe the strongest person I've ever known. But when I saw the state that you were in, in that motel room, it scared me. It put me too much in mind of my dad. And I thought it was important that you know you're not alone, not if you don't want to be.'

She arched an eyebrow at that. 'What are you trying to say, Dave?' she asked when his face failed to become any less lethally serious.

'Nothing in particular. But I know you, Jean, better than you think. You'll try to shoulder it all by yourself, all that suffering, like you've got something to prove. It's just about the worst impulse you could follow, believe me.'

'You're worried I'll implode? That one day I'll just melt down, pitch a screaming fit in the middle of the street and refuse to move until I'm committed?'

'Pretty much, yeah, if I'm being frank about it.'

They sat in silence for a time, contemplating the image. Jean had been sarcastic when she said it, but the more she thought about it, the less comical it seemed. Even at her calmest, there was a negative space in the back of her head ever since her severance; something pressing against the inside of her skull, a pressure longing to escape. In moments of quiescence, like the hours she had spent in solitary, she found herself fixating on that pressure, and how sweet it would feel to have it relieved. Expulsions like screaming or vomiting might take the edge off; the hole created by a bullet would be better still.

'I could take a leave of absence,' David said suddenly. 'After this is all over. God knows I have vacation time saved up, and I'd bet that the UK will recall its attachés from China any day now, trying to distance ourselves from this disaster. I could keep you company, you know. No commitment, no pressure, just someone for you to come home to at the end of the day.'

'You mean like a pet?'

'Jean, please don't joke.'

'You're right, I'm sorry. I appreciate the offer, Dave, and I'll think about it. Honestly, yeah, I'd...' she swallowed. 'I'd appreciate another warm body around the flat.'

'That's good enough for now,' he said. 'Go on, get some sleep. I need to be off; I'm expected in San Francisco tomorrow to give my report to the PNC's security committee.'

She climbed out of the SUV and gave him a small smile through the window. 'Sorry I tried to beat the shit out of you.'

He smiled back. 'Sorry you lost, more like.'

***

Victoria sat expectantly on the edge of the bed in the broom-cupboard-like room. The second that Jean entered, her daughter sprang to her feet and wrapped her in a hug that almost literally knocked her off her feet. Accustomed as she was to her prosthetic body, she still forgot her own strength sometimes.

'Easy, Vic,' Jean implored with a pained wince. 'I'm happy to see you too, girl, but I've taken a few beatings these last few days.'

'Oh God, Mum, don't ever, *ever* scare me like that again.' She pulled away, and her eyes widened when she got a good look at Jean's face. The lacerations from the shattered glass had been sutured while she was being held in the underground facility, and the bruises on her forehead and throat were beginning to fade, but she had caught sight of her reflection in the SUV's tinted windows on the ride over. It wasn't an altogether pretty sight.

Jean had steeled herself on the journey over to present a confident façade for her daughter's sake. She knew that she had put her through hell over the past few days; she had a responsibility to mitigate Victoria's worries as best she could. She had planned to pass off her assimilation and subsequent severance as nothing to get worked up about; a minor blip in her otherwise stable and reliable continued existence, no different than if she had been sequestered on jury duty or undergoing minor surgery.

But seeing the reaction on Victoria's artificial face at her appearance, she couldn't do it. She couldn't pretend otherwise; she had stood on the knife's edge between life and death, and it was only because of the strength of the love Victoria had shown her that she had been pulled back. Something that she had been holding steady inside herself ever since that moment, kneeling in the snow as the commandos surrounded her, slipped.

'I… oh Christ, Vic. I'm sorry. I'm so, so sorry.'

Her eyes blurred with tears, and she found herself returning her child's embrace just as fiercely as she had made it.

***

They spoke for the better part of three hours. The truth about the Enclave phenomenon was now a matter of public record, so Jean wasn't obliged to hold anything back about her exploits, save for the situation that was still unfolding in Colombia. Beginning with the offer of employment from Tony Liu and the creature that China had discovered on the Dark Side of the Moon, she walked Victoria through her story, which sounded increasingly fabulous even as she heard it emerge from her own lips.

For Victoria's part, she had contacted David over the 'net when it had become clear that Jean wasn't answering any of her hails. After their altercation in Niujie, David had left her a short response out of a vague sense of obligation to his ex-comrade's daughter. Hedging his bets as to what details of the operation would later be classified, his message had been light on details beyond the fact that Jean was accounted for and in Beijing. He had, however, used the word 'custody' to describe Jean's circumstances, and that had been enough to convince Victoria that she needed to be there for her. She had taken off from Kisangani station with neither a backward glance nor a solid plan of action for what she would do once she got there, deluging David and everyone else she thought might be able to help with messages all the while. David, sensing an opportunity, had scooped her up in the VTOL after Jean made her escape attempt.

'I meant to ask about that,' Jean said. 'The Kisangani elevator and the vacuum transit system were shut down. How did you even get to Beijing to begin with?'

Victoria averted her eyes, suddenly bashful. 'There were some Chinese diplomats on the station who'd been recalled via charter shuttle. I... convinced them to let me come along for the ride.'

Jean's eyebrows arched. '*Convinced* them?' That didn't sound like the behaviour of the Chinese civil servants she was familiar with.

'I suppose "bribed" them would be more accurate. Five thousand pounds. Um... using your credit details.' She fidgeted. 'I don't think they're very well paid.'

Jean's eyebrows rose a notch higher. 'And why do you have access to my credit details, young lady?'

Victoria squirmed. If she had been capable of blushing, she would have turned cherry-red by now, Jean knew. 'You gave me your PIN to pay for school supplies six years ago, remember? You said I'd know what I needed better than you would? The details hadn't changed since then. I promise, I never used it for anything else, but I figured, given it was an emergency...' She trailed off.

'And to think, people pay me to keep their valuables safe from thieves.' Jean grinned. She couldn't muster anything more than the gentlest mock-reproach. Victoria was probably hoping it wouldn't occur to her mother that she had gone AWOL in her devil-may-care rush to her aid. There had been a time when Jean would have been livid with her daughter for throwing caution to the wind, spending a not-inconsiderable sum of her mother's money without permission, and potentially jeopardising her career in the process. In light of her own actions, she almost found it cute that Victoria considered indiscretion with her mother's bank details to be worth fretting over.

Before going to sleep ahead of their return journey to England the next day, Jean sent messages to her mother and James, letting them know the crisis was over and that she and Victoria would be home soon. She also arranged to hire a car once they reached Dover. The Thames arcology had been at the epicentre of the London Enclave; obviously, no vac-pods would be ready to arrive or depart for some time.

Her mother's home was only just outside the area of the Enclave Effect itself, and Jean didn't like the idea of her being anywhere in the vicinity of the violence that had sprung up in its wake. Even Birmingham was nearer to the chaos than she preferred.

'Why don't we visit the old farmhouse at Fort Pierre for a couple of weeks, once things have settled down a bit?' she suggested. Victoria's grandparents had their resting place in South Dakota, where her father had grown up. 'You, me, James, and your grandmother. I think we could all do with getting out of the city for a while.'

'Good idea,' Victoria agreed. 'Plus, there's another treat around the corner. The Merantau Program's deep-space communication array? It got requisitioned by the ORC after the Engagement, so all outgoing messages have been on hold since October. But I heard through the grapevine that it's going back online on Boxing Day. We'll be able to record a message for the Starman, and tell him all about your adventures.'

'"Adventures" feels like the wrong word, somehow,' Jean said. 'God knows where we even begin to tell the *Prospice* about all this. They're bound to think everyone back home has lost their minds.'

***

That night in the motel room, Jean was visited by uncommonly vivid dreams. Not nightmares, as she might well have expected given her current frame of mind, but soothing, even pleasurable while they were ongoing; intense yet amorphous impressions of light, colour, and sound.

Victoria woke her at 8.30 am. She had unintentionally overslept, and they would have to hurry to clear security before her vac-pod departed at 11.15 –

the terminus would be manic now that the travel restrictions had been lifted. Still, she lingered for a few moments in the shower, trying to collate the nocturnal images.

She had no doubt they had originated from somewhere outside her skull – their texture felt like something from the Enclave, detritus left behind after her severance that her unconscious mind was working to parse. She had never been any good at hanging on to her dreams. For all that she tried to remember, all she could discern was a triptych of colours, cyclically repeating itself: cool azure, followed by burning red, and then verdant green.

She tried to push the matter to the back of her mind while she dressed and bolted a quick breakfast, then while she jostled her way through customs, and then on the three-hour journey to Dover via Paris. Still, that series of colours kept popping up unbidden, and she found herself distracted, contemplating them all through the morning and into the afternoon. It was only when the vac-pod emerged above the sea level of the English Channel, and the iconic white cliffs rose to greet her that she snapped out of her contemplation. She was finally home, after a time that could be measured far longer in experience than in hours and minutes.

The Dover vacuum terminus was a small one, built more as a stopover for tourists entering Britain from the south than as any kind of major transport hub. It lay perched on the edge of the cliffs, its most prominent feature a thirty-metre-high glass frontage overlooking the Channel, giving visitors a panoramic view of the coastline. It was manifestly unequipped to handle the increase in traffic generated by the closure of the Thames arcology, even with the bulk of travel being diverted to Birmingham or Cardiff. Their pod spent an hour and a half queuing before they were able to disembark.

They were also greeted by a familiar face she hadn't expected – Carlos Alvarez. He stood looking bewildered in the human throng of the terminus until he caught sight of her and waved as if he were flagging a taxi. 'Jeanie,' he said, greeting her with the same genial warmth she remembered. 'When I heard what had happened, I just had to see you were alright with my own eyes.'

Hesitantly, she embraced him. 'Glad to see you on the ground, Carlos. I should have known it would take the end of the world to tempt you out of your workshop.'

'I do make special exceptions for old friends and colleagues, from time to time. And Victoria – I heard there was a Cadet Harrison who pulled off quite a vanishing act a few days ago. Glad to find you alive and well.'

'Has Dr. Alvarez ever told you about his invention, the Archangel Frame?' Victoria piped up, hastily changing the subject.

'He might have mentioned it once or twice.'

'He says he's going to put in a recommendation for me to be in the first round of trials! Three cheers for nepotism.'

Carlos scoffed. 'All of the simulations we've run have shown you as one of the best suited for its controls. Finding someone with those natural talents from ORC's pool of cadets isn't easy, and it's rarer still to happen upon one who's already received extensive cybernetic enhancement. Nepotism has nothing to do with it.'

'Just good breeding, then. Got it.' Victoria winked at Jean, who returned the gesture. 'I'm afraid I have something I need to talk to you about rather urgently, Jean,' an edge crept back into Carlos' voice as he turned back to her. 'Vic, would you give your mother and me a moment in private?'

Victoria gave Jean a silent look that made it plain she would prefer not to let her mum out of her sight. 'Vic, it's fine,' Jean consoled her. 'Go and organise the hire car. We won't be longer than a few minutes.'

'Try to be quick,' she replied, and reluctantly made her way out of the crowded terminus.

'So, what's this about then, Doctor?' Jean asked.

'Something came up shortly after you were discharged in China,' he said, keeping his voice low. 'Secretary Koo's first impulse was to bring you back, but he thought your state of mind was fragile enough without being hauled back in for questioning. He reckoned it was best you get the request for help in person, from a friend. Believe it or not, I was on my way down the elevator just to call on you, when they asked me to contact you on their behalf.'

'And what's so important that Koo has you running errands for him?'

'Not here.' Carlos lowered his voice. 'Follow me. Better you see for yourself.'

***

They made their way through the crowded terminus to a discreet service exit, which admitted them out into a loading bay being pounded by freezing wind and sleet. Carlos rapped on the rear door of an articulated lorry bearing the logo of a local haulage company, parked a short walk away.

The trailer door raised a moment later – what lay inside wasn't cargo, but three men clustered around a fourth figure, sitting cross-legged and quiet on the floor. Two of the guards were Caucasian, and these Jean didn't recognise. The third was Zhen, she realised with a start, the man whose partner's leg she had broken. He gave her a look of distaste.

'He insisted on speaking to you directly, Ms. Harrison,' said one of the white men. His accent was Welsh; no doubt what she was seeing here was another ad-hoc arrangement between the governments of China and the UK, jury-rigged by Koo. 'Said he had something very important to say that only you would understand. Someone thought it was important enough that they chartered a spaceplane, so he could be here waiting for you.' He gestured to the silent individual sitting between them.

It was a man, she saw, dressed in the same kind of colourless overalls that had been issued to her in the black site beneath Beijing. He peered up at her, and when she recognised him, she flinched. The last time she had seen Tony Liu was less than four days ago, after David had dragged him through an SUV sunroof. For him to have undergone the transformation she saw before her in so short a time was nothing short of frightening. He looked like he had shed ten kilograms. His skin was drawn and sallow, covered in a sickly film of sweat, its pallor contrasting with his jet-black hair. He smiled at her, and it made the effect worse.

'Jean,' he said in English, 'I'm very pleased to see you.' He fixed her with an intense stare for a handful of seconds, before his eyes began darting back and forth around the trailer interior, seemingly having forgotten she was there.

'When we brought him in, he was near-catatonic,' Zhen said. 'He almost never spoke, and what little he did was incoherent, completely disconnected from his surroundings. He wouldn't even eat or drink unless forced. That all changed a few hours ago when he found out you'd been released from custody, and he started yelling at the top of his lungs. After he tired himself out, he talked about you non-stop. He was begging to be allowed to see you. At one point, he said "the world hangs in the balance," and apparently the Secretary thought that was worth paying attention to.'

Jean tentatively approached Tony, whose gaze kept darting around the cramped space, fixing on things no one else could see. His hands were manacled behind his back. No one present was wearing a lapel pin. She reached out and gently took hold of his chin, directing his gaze towards her own. His eyes immediately stopped darting around the room and fixed on hers with unblinking intensity.

'Jean,' he said, his voice pleading, 'you're here. That's good. You have to warn them: the ablative shielding in the silo is old, decaying. The exhaust ports are clogged with foliage. The heat build-up could be catastrophic. The second rebirth could be jeopardised.' He was switching at random between English and Cantonese, her implants struggling to keep up with the adjustments in syntax.

'Tony,' she told him, 'I don't have the faintest idea what you're talking about.'

'The *evolution*.' His voice was low but insistent. 'The next plateau. We're so close. Don't you remember?'

Jean stood up, repulsed by what she was witnessing. 'He's delusional,' she declared. 'Hallucinatory, suffering a psychotic break, who knows? I certainly don't. Gentlemen, if you'll excuse me, my daughter is waiting for me.' She turned her back on the group and made to leave the trailer as quickly as possible. Tony deserved better than this ritual humiliation.

'Blue. Red. Green.'

Jean froze.

'When I was young,' Tony said, 'I read these magazines. I always liked knowing the processes behind things, it's why I started working with tech. Anyway, volcanoes, right?'

'He's babbling again,' the Welshman sighed. 'Sorry for taking up your time, Ms. Harrison, I'll—'

'*No!*' The room jumped at the force of her exclamation. 'No. Let him talk.'

'Volcanoes,' Tony continued. 'Six hundred million years ago. The Cambrian explosion, when multicellular life started to take hold. It was the climate shift that allowed it to happen, brought on by volcanic chain reactions. Life was stagnant up until then, dormant. It was the eruptions that caused that to change, bringing about a new level of complexity. We need the same thing to happen again. We'll affect another change just like it, a paradigm shift as profound as the move from sea to land. It'll be beautiful.'

'Tony,' Jean said urgently. 'Where is this eruption going to take place? Please, tell me.'

'Jean, I know we have company, but you don't need to play-act for their benefit!' Tony laughed. 'You saw the same charts I did. I'm not much use now, not in my present condition, but you can get the message out. *They need to know about the ablative shielding.* It wasn't factored into the calculations, and if they don't compensate for it, it could go very, very wrong.'

Zhen, Carlos, and the others were watching this exchange with bemusement, tinged with alarm, but Jean ignored them. 'Tony,' she said, 'after this "eruption," what happens? What comes next?'

He looked at her incredulously, as though astounded she needed to ask. 'Then the rains come, Jean. The healing rains, to cover the Earth.'

Everything clicked into place. The blue display, showing launch vectors together with thrust-to-weight ratios and debris charts; to be followed by the burning red of a launch designed for geosynchronous orbit, and the rain that would follow, not of water droplets but of gamma particles, over a newly verdant Earth.

No. Oh God, no.

She rose and hurried out of the trailer, contacting Koo on her implants as she went.

The Secretary answered her summons almost immediately, and she didn't bother with the nicety of a greeting. 'Did you find any sign of the missing device in Colombia?' she demanded. 'Anything at all?'

'No, nothing,' he said, no more standing on ceremony than she. 'Did you learn something from our mutual acquaintance?'

'There's a mothballed Yang-Mitsubishi rocket silo in the Amazon rainforest, on the Brazilian side of the border with Colombia,' she said. 'It was used to deploy satellites into geosynchronous orbit before the space elevator was built. The Enclave had a contingency plan. If their operation was compromised, they'd use it to carry one of the devices to upper Earth orbit and broadcast its effect from there.'

A long pause preceded Koo's reply. 'My God. There was just a launch from the region of the Pico da Neblina National Park. It was registered with a local heavy manufacturing corporation as carrying freight for the large particle accelerator. It had all of the correct documentation filed!'

'Shoot it down!' Jean cried.

'I can't. The launch was three hours ago, and it was confirmed as having docked with the particle accelerator an hour and fifty-seven minutes ago. Ms. Harrison, I—'

'They're going to retrofit the equipment in the particle accelerator to project and amplify the device's effect. That was the contingency plan. Secretary, the accelerator has to be destroyed, at all costs. Nuke it, if necessary.'

'I—'

Jean was distracted from Koo's bluster by a cluster of notifications popping into her peripheral vision, her newsfeeds blowing up with real-time footage.

All of North and South America had just gone dark.

The Enclave had returned.

PART THREE

ONE FIGHT MORE –
THE BEST AND THE LAST

A.N. Milne

284

Chapter 18

July 29th, 2326 C.E.

'We've dispatched word to Taurus Station, Commander. Trachtenberg will attempt to hitch a ride along the Upsilon-Sigma relay chain, that ought to buy us a few extra objective weeks. It'll take a bit of elbow grease, but the station should be prepared to receive the settlers by the time they arrive.'

'Good job, Lieutenant,' Victoria replied. Daniels was the correct choice for her right-hand man; he had a knack for anticipating her decisions before she even knew she had reached them.

No doubt Trachtenberg had griped about being given the role of messenger boy, but she welcomed the pretext to get one of Albrecht's few remaining loyalists out of her hair. The sooner the preparations for her grandfather's crew and their families were complete, the happier she would be. She had pledged to see them safe, and so she would, but she bristled at the duty of playing nanny to them all, just as she bristled at the claustrophobic confines of the old freighter. She was itching to get back outside, spread her wings to their full extension and get back up to the 90%-of-c velocities she was accustomed to. That close to the speed of light, years became months, and months became weeks.

Time dilation was strategically disadvantageous, as the Insurgency had learned to its cost in the early years of the war against the Collective turning interstellar. A formation flying for six months at nine-tenths of lightspeed would arrive at its target, finding that its defenders had had fourteen months to prepare for their arrival. It was thanks to such a miscalculation that Hoyt had been captured over a hundred years ago.

Even so, she would welcome the effects of relativity now if they meant her anticipation could be assuaged any sooner. This close to her dream, she could swear she felt actual, palpable *hunger* for it, despite the sensation having been physiologically unavailable to her since she was a child.

'We'll need to make plans to hitch a ride ourselves,' Daniels added, tentatively. 'Taurus is the nearest station, and it's over a light-year distant. The transport's food supplies won't stretch anything like that far if we don't take any shortcuts. It's a risk, but obviously, it would be a waste getting Taurus pressurised and all, if the ship's full of skeletons by the time we get there.'

Victoria waved these concerns away. 'We're more than a match for any resistance we'll find at the Upsilon relay. Half the time it's unguarded anyway, and after the forces they fielded during that last attack, they must be stretched thin this far out in space.'

'Unless we're being followed.'

'Of course. Which brings us to our next order of business. The ship has been thoroughly detoxified?'

'Double- and triple-checked. We haven't found any sign of the tracer isotope anywhere.'

'Good. And I switched out my contaminated platelets back at the FOB, which leaves them just one more potential option for tracking us. We can't put it off any longer.'

'Right you are, Commander. I'll issue a notice for the settlers to gather in the cargo holds in two hours.' Daniels said. He lingered a moment longer, the pair of them hovering alone together on the ship's bridge. 'I know your mind's made up, Victoria. It's probably been made up for a long time, but still, I have to ask – are you sure you want to go through with this?'

'I can't afford you getting cold feet, Taylor. Not at this stage.'

'Of course not. Where you go, I'll follow, if it means an end to this. It's just hard, coming to terms with the idea that I'll never see him again.'

'The Collective is death, Taylor, for anyone touched by it. Not of the body, but the spirit. It's our failure to fully appreciate that that's cost us so much for so long.'

'But of course, you didn't have to make that choice, did you?' Daniels' tone was more indignant than she was used to hearing from him. 'Out of all of us, you alone got to have your cake and eat it. A few days with your family, an opportunity to speak with them before the end.'

'You think that made it hurt less?' Victoria answered, quietly. She met Daniels' eye, not reprimanding him, but silently daring him to consider what he was saying. To consider what it might be like to have what you'd yearned for, for two hundred years, and then to have it taken from you after a few cruelly short days. No, not taken, she corrected herself: to have it look you in the eye, and reject you.

'I'm sorry, Commander.' Daniels seemed appropriately chastened.

'Don't worry about it. Is there any other business we need to discuss?'

'Just the one matter. What we're going to do about the old man.'

***

Albrecht wasn't confined, in any traditional sense. The transport wasn't built to contain any Archangel who didn't want to be contained. If he had the inclination, it would have been a simple matter for him to burn through the hull and take off for the nearest station he thought might constitute safe harbour. The part of Victoria that was still generously disposed towards the Commander suggested that he hadn't broken out by force out of consideration for the ship's flesh-and-blood inhabitants. The same ruthless arithmetic that would have sacrificed them and fled the FOB, applied in this case, would have come down in the settlers' favour.

More likely though, he simply understood his position. Victoria had been sowing the seeds of unrest under his nose for years. She would never have dared to make the plays she had if she wasn't sure she had most of the Insurgency backing her. The resistance to his command that had manifested on the bridge of this transport wasn't just the work of a few dozen mutineers – it was a full-fledged *coup d'état*. Anywhere he ran and attempted to assert his command, he would find himself in the same vipers' nest he was now, where suddenly he found his authority was no longer recognised.

The power dynamics at play were different from those of historical military command structures. In the old days, when soldiers had fought for governments, churches or corporations, authority had only ever partially derived from a cause or an ideology. Recruits had followed generals and generals had followed kings because the kings held the land that the recruits lived on, that kept them fed and watered, that generated the industry that paid their wages. But Albrecht, uniquely, had been the head of an army which

287

didn't need food, water, or sleep. Every member of his army could survive, indefinitely, in a hard vacuum without support. The only currency a leader in his position could offer were results.

He had lasted as long as he had based on his credentials as a professional soldier that no one else left in the Insurgency could claim. His personality, his authoritative bearing, and the fact that no one had ever been able to offer a better alternative to his orders had commanded loyalty. But the years and decades had worn on, and they were further from Earth than they had ever been.

After Pisces station, Victoria had begun disseminating whispers among her closest peers, playing on their desperation. An alternative existed, she told them. Radical; perhaps once unthinkable. She was cautious about how she broached the idea, approaching it slantwise, letting her comrades reach the same conclusion she had without stating it outright. But after two centuries of failure, she had found them receptive to new ideas. Many were horrified at first, but came around to her reasoning. Some had confessed they had entertained fantasies of something like what she was suggesting and were glad someone had come out and said it.

Her flight to TransTerra had been a signal to her followers, her first open defiance of Albrecht. That the mission had succeeded had galvanised her supporters behind her. She had contented herself to play the humbled subordinate a while longer, but she knew that soon the charade would be over. Once word reached the other major stations of her heroism, the Insurgency would be hers.

Too late, Albrecht had come to understand this. Although he wasn't a captive, he behaved as though he was. He stayed confined to a cramped maintenance compartment, his transmissions monitored and filtered through the ship's systems before reaching anyone outside of his quarters. The only transmissions he had sent thus far had been clipped, dispassionate requests for information about their transit. Villeneuve had been posted outside his cell, reporting on Albrecht's behaviour directly to Victoria at the top of every hour. The former Commander had yet to cause any disturbance.

Villeneuve greeted her with a salute. He had been one of her earliest and most enthusiastic converts, and one of the most amenable to the notion of her as the leader. 'He's just hovering, Commander,' he assured her. 'Barely twitched in eight hours.'

'Good work, Sergeant.' She returned the salute. 'Give us a few minutes, would you?'

He looked uncertain. 'You're sure you want to be alone with him? What if he tries to pull a fast one?'

'He won't. And if he does, I'm ready for him.'

He shrugged, deferential. 'Fair enough. He's all yours, Commander.'

Albrecht had his eyes closed when she entered the dingy space, his body eerily still even by the standards of an Archangel. There was a meditative quality about him that she had rarely seen before. Upon registering her presence, he opened his eyes slowly, in no great hurry to greet her. 'Lieutenant,' he said, 'finally. I thought you'd never visit.'

'I don't answer to "lieutenant" anymore, Hermann. You wanted me stripped of that rank, so I suppose you got what you wanted.'

'Quite. Victoria, then. I hope we can be frank with one another, considering the circumstances.'

'Frank sounds good. How's this, to begin with: I'm in command here, now. You're out, I'm in.'

'So I'm given to understand.'

'I'm preparing to dispatch messengers to the Zodiacal bases, letting them know about the administrative handover.'

'If only there were an award for euphemisms.'

Victoria ignored the barb. 'More than eighty percent of the officers have already committed themselves to me,' she said. The figure was actually 75.4%, but he wasn't to know that. 'But the remaining few holdouts that still venerate you, the Trachtenbergs and the Kariukis, they could cause some difficulties. At this juncture, infighting is the last thing we can afford to have holding us back.'

'I quite agree, though it seems the irony is lost on you.'

'No, I see it, believe me. I initiated all this; I acknowledge that, and I make no apology for it. It's in service of what you might call big-picture thinking.'

Albrecht affected a sigh. 'What do you want from me, Victoria?'

'I want your last command. A recording, notarised with your synaptic signature, authorising the handover of control of the Insurgency from you to me.'

'Intriguing. And why do you think I'd be so ready to just hand something like that over, without any concessions from you?'

'It may not seem like it, Hermann, but I don't want us to be enemies. We've fought together for so long. I know full well you're sincere about doing what's best for the Insurgency, and for humanity, no matter what that entails. Well, now it's this. The Insurgency is mine. That's true under any circumstances. If the worst-case scenario comes to pass and it's civil war, I'll win, because I have the numbers.' She uploaded to him the records that proved she wasn't bluffing – six years' worth of recorded conversations and clandestine rendezvouses, demonstrating how she had bent the Insurgency's command structure to her will.

'But I don't want it to come to that,' she continued. 'I need as many Archangels for the plan as I can gather, and anyone lost over hierarchical squabbles is a loss to all of us.'

'And this plan would be?'

Victoria told him. When she finished, she took a small measure of satisfaction from his response. She had seen Albrecht angry on several occasions – she had never seen him shocked.

'You can't! It defeats the purpose of everything we've worked for.'

'Where has all that work brought us, Hermann? Two hundred years on, and how many people have we actually rescued from the Collective? None. Not a single, fucking one.' Victoria found herself hovering back and forth across the length of the room, her words directed as much at herself as at Albrecht. Dimly, she remembered the physiological symptoms of strong emotion; elevated heart rate; shortness of breath; tears and perspiration and an overall loss of self-control. She experienced none of these anymore, but the agitation had to be expressed somehow. 'They're dead and walking, being moved about like marionettes. They've procreated, these last two-hundred years: the bodies of the ones we've left behind. Do you ever stop to think of it?

Newborns are being ripped from the womb on Earth, and assimilated before the umbilical cord is cut. There's no saving them. We're all that's left of humanity.'

Albrecht exploded. 'Don't you think I know that?' He shouted it with his voice close to full amplification; Victoria could see the ripples in the transport's pressurised atmosphere from the force of the sound. She sent a furtive message to Villeneuve not to interfere. 'You don't think that's why I've led the way I have? Because I wanted to preserve humanity. Because we're all that's left, and we can't afford to lose it. There are worse things than détente, Victoria.'

'It was all a great big fiction then, was it?' she replied. 'The idea that we were soldiers fighting a crusade. All along, you knew that we would never take back Earth.'

'I couldn't allow us to despair,' he protested. 'Do you honestly believe that we would have lasted as long as we did if I hadn't kept that spark of hope alive?'

'False hope, Hermann. False hope, and lies. For God's sake, how much longer did you see this going on? A thousand years? Ten thousand? Would you have let them hound us all the way out of the galaxy until there were ten of us left? Then five, then one, then none? Is that how you envisioned the human race ending, with one individual, alone in interstellar space, floating there until their battery finally fails? That sounds a lot like despair to me.'

'And your way? Asking everyone to look straight at the place and the people they've had in their hearts when they fought, and telling them to throw it all away? That's not victory, it's just a different kind of despair. What right do you have to demand that of them?'

'I have every right.' Victoria stared Albrecht dead in the eye. Reflexively, she flared her wings, extending their span until their tips touched the walls. 'More than anyone else in the universe, I have that right.'

Albrecht shook his head, unintimidated. 'I still remember that day, you know. It's burned into my grey matter, same as yours. December 16th, 2135. I remember the way you raced to your mother's side, a child refusing to accept her bereavement. A hundred and ninety-one years later, and you're still that same child, with a child's sense of justice.'

Victoria felt an ache that didn't ache; an itch that didn't itch. 'You don't get to talk about my mother, Hermann.' She said it softly, without any amplification. 'You failed her. I won't.'

'This isn't how you'll honour her memory.'

'Yes, it is. And most of the Insurgency agrees with me. Review the recordings.'

Albrecht was silent for a moment, as he reviewed the recordings in fast-forward. Comprehension dawned on his face, just as it had done all the others.

'It's happening, Hermann. With or without you. This way, there won't be much left, but when the dust settles, humanity will have a toehold in the solar system again. From there, we can rebuild. No more détente. No more play-acting at resistance. We'll have a future again.'

He paused a moment longer to comport himself, then began speaking aloud to an audience that wasn't there. 'This is Hermann Albrecht,' he said. 'Effective immediately, I am stepping down as Commander of the human Insurgency, and instating Victoria Harrison as my successor. I have every confidence that she will lead with the discipline and competence the role demands of her.' He paused a moment longer, then sent the recording to Victoria. It was watermarked with his synaptic profile, verifying its authenticity.

'You know,' he remarked, 'I grew up in a rural mountain valley, in Bavaria. Two hundred years on, and I remember the contours of that valley more vividly than any of the moons or barren asteroids we've bled for. Perhaps it's irrational, perhaps I was buying into my own fiction, but I'd always hoped I might see that valley again, somehow, someday. When the dust settles, I suppose even that won't be possible anymore.'

***

In the communications she had received from the Starman when she had been young, Victoria had become familiar by proxy with his key crewmates, among them Lieutenant Eoin O'Brien. The *Prospice's* head engineer was respected and feared by his subordinates in equal measure. His temper was part of it, but it wasn't that he was known for being a cruel taskmaster, so much as for having an utterly phlegmatic approach to problem-solving.

He wasn't the most innovative individual who might have been selected for his post, at least not in terms of lateral thinking. Rather, he was known for achieving results in ways other engineers might have dismissed out of hand for their sheer laboriousness. One anecdote Victoria remembered keenly was of the time one of the *Prospice's* solar panel arrays had been scarred by a micrometeoroid on the ship's way through the asteroid belt. A certain amount of damage to the arrays had been figured into the *Prospice's* contingencies; replacement solar cells could be generated by epigenetically modified bacterial cultures kept on board for just such a purpose. But the losses they had experienced were an order of magnitude outside of the ship's planned parameters. While O'Brien's team had been panicking, trying to come up with workarounds to catalyse the bacterial cultures using the materials available on board, Eoin had simply rolled up his sleeves and begun assembling replacement solar cells by hand, one at a time. It was a mind-boggling way of brute-forcing the problem, requiring tens of thousands of man-hours. But he had done it, pulling shifts of up to seventy-two hours for three weeks and asking the same of his subordinates. Only after the *Prospice* was back up to the operational capacity it required in the early, crucial acceleration stages of its voyage, had the entire engineering staff gotten dead drunk together and then slept for two days solid.

It was this proclivity to take the long way around that Victoria was now butting heads with. 'I'm telling you, the same principle as we were going to put to use in the asteroid base can apply here,' Eoin said. He had barged into her quarters, insisting to speak with her ahead of the gathering of the settlers. Word had somehow reached him of the plan to hijack the Upsilon relay. 'I've double- and triple-checked the phytochemical specs of the algae we were planting. With a little prompting, it can be grown in fissures in metal just as well as in cracks in dead rock. And with the surface area available…'

Even as he spoke, Victoria was shaking her head. 'Maybe, Lieutenant,' she replied. 'Maybe with every single drop of reclaimed water, you could grow enough algae for your people not to starve. Which ignores the rather pressing issue of them dying of thirst considerably faster, instead.'

'We can solve that issue,' he maintained, dismissing her concerns over the settlers' dehydration as though they were an elementary technical problem. 'We don't need to live in the ship indefinitely, just the few years we need to get to — well, wherever it is we're going.' Though she didn't show it, it was a source of some relief to her that he didn't know their specific destination. If that information had been leaked, it would have been symptomatic of serious problems.

'*No*, Lieutenant,' she said, firmly. 'Your people's welfare aside, I need us to reach our rendezvous in a matter of weeks, not years.'

'Then for God's sake, let us have the ship, woman!' Eoin cried. 'Your lot can take off and do whatever you need to do in those frames of yours. We can fend for ourselves.'

'I'm sorry, Eoin, but that's out of the question, too. The fact of the matter is, if you try to make it to Taurus at sub-light speed, your population will be decimated by the time you get there, no matter what you try. And I don't just want you alive because I've pledged to keep you that way. Eight hundred potential recruits could make all the difference for the Insurgency.'

Eoin seethed. 'Here I thought you'd be different from Albrecht,' he said, darkly. 'But you're just the same, aren't you? Now that your dear grandad's gone, the rest of us are just a commodity to you. It doesn't cause you any grief to drag us all kicking and screaming into another battle, locked in those bloody gel-coffins, where we can't do anything but pray we make it through by your good graces. Do you even remember what it's like to be that helpless?'

Victoria glared at him. He didn't recoil, not quite, but he seemed to at least realise he had struck a nerve. 'I've had sufficient education in helplessness, Lieutenant. This isn't up for debate any further. Your concerns are noted, but we're going through the Upsilon relay. Suffice it to say, I have more faith in my people's ability to take it unscathed than I do in yours to survive five years in deep space on a cargo vessel designed to be staffed by a skeleton crew.'

'No,' Eoin went on, bullish in his refusal to concede to her authority. 'No, it won't bloody "suffice it to say." If Jonah were here—'

'But he isn't,' she snapped. 'And you aren't him.'

*****

Watching her grandfather through the porthole, Victoria had lost valuable seconds to sheer incomprehension, to the impossibility of the moment. When she had regained her faculties, molecular platelets had swarmed to the end of her right arm, her fist swelling to become a three-kilo bludgeon. She had smashed down on the airlock hatch, again and again, hard enough to buckle the tempered steel of the hull that still obstinately refused to give way. She had been prepared to blast her way back into the asteroid interior to go after him; it was only a cascade of warnings crowding her vision that stayed her hand, from her allies and rivals in the Insurgency alike (the settlers in the airlock with her would be cooked alive; she would jeopardise their escape from the base; the Collective would have their hands on Captain Harrison by now anyway, and if he wanted to go over to them that badly, then good riddance).

In the days since, she had spent her every waking moment – which, for her, was every moment – biting back violent, white-hot anger, directed at everyone and everything around her. Anger at the Collective, somehow further intensified even after all this time, for having taken the last thing in the universe she considered precious. Anger at the cowards and fools who surrounded her, whose hesitancy and risk-aversion had cost them everything. And strongest of all, anger at the Starman. *Grandmother was right about you*, she had thought, over and over, directing the accusation at the image of him in her head, grinning as he abandoned her. *Human attachments really do mean nothing to you. You'll take off without a moment's notice, and give no thought to the devastation you leave in your wake.*

For the first few days, she had meditated on her various hatreds, allowed them to compound each other and grow hotter and hotter until it was all she could do not to kill anyone who entered her line of sight. But then, in one of the fleeting moments she had alone, her secondary consciousness had chimed in:

Are you sure that it's not because of what you did? The half-truths you told?

Her grandfather's flight to the Collective's open arms wasn't so incomprehensible at all. Rather, it was a consequence of her failings, her naïve hope that the Starman would be her confidant and her friend, the way he had been on those recordings when she was a child. She had nurtured that futile dream of closeness within herself, and the fear that he would push her away if he learned the whole truth.

She had told herself that she was doing it for his benefit. After all, she and her comrades had taken two centuries to come to terms with the terrible knowledge that Earth was beyond saving. Bad enough to discover the existence of the Collective all at once, but to realise that there was no hope of humanity being restored as it once was? Better, she had thought, to let that hope linger a while longer; to let the Starman and his crew believe that the war could be won on terms they could accept. It wouldn't benefit them to despair.

Self-delusion, she realised now. She had been afraid that if he understood the full scope of her plans, he would denounce her, call her a monster. She had been afraid that if he learned the full truth of how she had been separated from her mother, he would hate her. She had seen an opportunity to present the ideal version of herself to her grandfather, implacably strong and virtuous. And in turn, her lies of omission had blown up in her face. No matter how she rationalised it, no matter how noble she had thought her intentions were, she had been the first to betray him. What did she have the right to expect but betrayal in turn?

This new understanding hadn't caused her anger to dissipate, but it had enabled her to focus and channel it, let it bubble to the surface as she deemed necessary. It was with this new self-assurance that she addressed the settlers in the cargo hold, gathered there by Daniels' summons.

'I understand that some of you have concerns about your immediate future,' she said to the massed crowd of ashen-faced men, women, and children, some of whom were already showing symptoms of malnutrition. 'It's true, the Insurgency is in the midst of a transitional phase, and a changeover in leadership. Nevertheless, let it be known that you are valued now more than ever. We will use the full resources available on this ship to see you safely to our destination.'

'Is that why you're dragging us into battle, yet a-bloody-gain?' Victoria scanned the crowd for the source of the dissenting voice and found it. The Lawson boy, the same one she had argued with in the Prometheid mountains.

'Brandon,' she answered, 'raises a valid point. Yes, we will be entering Collective-controlled space *en route* to Taurus. With the limited food we have aboard, this is a necessary evil. But rest assured,' (she raised her voice to be heard over the growing murmur of discontent) 'that this engagement will not be like the ones you have recently experienced. Scouts have been dispatched to the relay to take stock of the enemy's numbers, and we will adjust our tactics accordingly, but we don't anticipate any significant resistance. The Insurgency has made use of the relays for transit many times, and we estimate our chances of success at close to one hundred percent.'

'That's what you said about the last base!' Brandon carried on, undeterred. 'And we lost Jack and Lys there, and the Captain disappeared! Why should this time be any different?'

'Because,' Victoria said, now having to amplify her voice to make herself heard in the cramped hold, 'our operations were previously compromised by a Collective agent in our midst, Alyssa Cavendish, making our direction and destination known to the enemy. This was an oversight on the part of our previous leadership.' She pointedly didn't mention Albrecht by name. 'As such,' she continued, 'this information will remain confidential until every individual aboard this transport is screened for the influence of the Collective.'

The murmurs pervading the crowd grew to an uproar. She shouted over it. 'The process of checking is painless and non-invasive. If you have nothing to hide, you have nothing to fear.'

**

Three hours later she was in her quarters. Her primary consciousness was in the process of collating timetables, computing probabilistic options for how much materiel she was likely to have at her disposal when the operation began, based on the likelihood of her various messengers making it to their destinations unmolested. Her secondary consciousness was working on 'Words that Stay Unspoken.' Finishing the composition had become something like an obsession; she wanted it done before zero hour. The harpsichord melody kept eluding her – it seemed to have a mind of its own, determined to trail off into dissonance where she demanded harmony.

Can't you do anything right? She snapped, distracted by yet another discordant squeal in her hind-brain.

I can, sometimes. Can you? Her secondary consciousness shot back, as sullen as she felt.

She was shaken from her internal dialogue by Daniels, announcing himself at her quarters' hatch. His bearing was appropriately sombre; she had asked that she be disturbed under only one specific circumstance.

'We've found one?' she asked. Daniels inclined his head a few degrees in acknowledgement. He didn't need to ask one of what. 'Show me.'

Her quarters were located deep in the ship, insulated from the inner hull by half a dozen decks in every direction. She followed Daniels through the rats' warren of corridors and bulkheads toward the fore, where the primary docking airlock was located. She heard a commotion growing louder as they progressed; a steady stream of obscenities, the still air of the ship's interior doing little to dull their baleful edge.

Rounding a corridor, she caught sight of Eoin O'Brien, struggling against Aki's gentle but unyielding grip. When the engineer caught sight of her, he was seized by a renewed ferocity, both physical and invective. 'You *bitch*!' He possessed a bellow that, even unamplified, could command any space where he chose to deploy it. 'Conniving, traitorous, murderous *bitch*! I hope the Scarabs find you and gouge your fucking heart out! We're human beings, you can't do this to us!' He continued to howl after them as she and Daniels passed him by.

It's okay, he's already been checked, Aki assured them as they went. **He's clean.**

'They're going to riot about this, you understand,' Daniels said.

'Let them. Let them get angry – any sane person should be angry these days. They'll burn themselves out when they realise they can't do harm to anyone but each other, and then in due course, they'll understand who the real enemy is.' She paused for a moment to consider her prevarication, then shrugged. 'Or they won't. That's still a loss I can accept.'

She was met at the fore airlock by a pair of sergeants, hovering where they framed the hatch, a pair of silent sentries. Between them, they held by the arms a squat figure, the kind that could only have been reared in terrestrial-equivalent gravity. Its red hair drifted in zero-g across a face that showed neither defiance nor hostility, only a kind of weary acceptance.

'What was the Old Earth expression?' asked Riley O'Brien. 'Oh yeah, I remember – "it's a fair cop."'

'We found this on her person,' said the sentry on the left (Sergeant Heinemann, Victoria noted). He held between his thumb and index finger an inert, metallic insect. A Wasp. The diminutive cousin of the Scarab, more commonly found in swarms of hundreds or thousands like the one that had spotted their party on TransTerra.

'It must have slipped in past our front lines on the asteroid when we weren't looking,' Heinemann continued. 'It never occurred to us that they could be used as a subcutaneous delivery mechanism against flesh-and-blood types.'

Unfortunate, she thought, *but not unexpected*. It was in the nature of a contagion to find new ways to proliferate itself.

'You know,' Victoria said, levelly, meeting the gaze of the thing wearing Riley's skin, 'I can make this easy, if you like. One maser blast to the cranium. You won't even feel a thing. Just tell us where you've sabotaged the ship.'

Riley smirked. 'Sabotage? Why would we do that? It's not like we could do any damage to your people with any parts I could jury-rig here, and you know full well we would never hurt other humans. I was just meant to observe, keep an eye on you, figure out your vector if we could. And we did. We know you're heading for the Upsilon relay. Be our guest, ride it wherever you like. Now that we have the Starman, we're in a generous mood.'

'I'll remember you said that.' Victoria moved back and gestured to Heinemann. The sergeant nodded and roughly deposited Riley into the airlock chamber, closing the inner hatch behind her. As the airlock began to cycle, the Collective, looking through Riley's eyes, met Victoria's gaze through the porthole.

Riley's mouth moved, and though her voice didn't carry through the metal, plastic and fibreglass between them, Victoria's machine-assisted perception was quite capable of reading her lips. 'You're nothing but dust,' they said. 'Robotic motes of dust floating between the stars, trapped in your insular little existences of fear and hate and pain. Of course, you lie to each other and turn on each other; what else can you do? And even now, you claim it's us who aren't human?'

The airlock finished its cycle and the exterior hatch opened. A spume of gas, briefly made visible by the condensation, gusted into deep space, and carried Riley's body with it. It took several gruelling seconds for its lungs to rupture and the moisture in its cells to vaporise. It spasmed in the vacuum for a few minutes longer before going perfectly still. The transport wasn't currently under acceleration, so the body matched its speed through the cosmos. It would continue at 20% of lightspeed indefinitely, the fastest corpse in the galaxy, until it collided with an errant particle or mote of dust and shattered into a million frozen pieces.

Jesus, Vic, came a message from Aki. **That was pretty harsh, even for one of them.**

If we'd removed the device from her neck, she would have suffered infinitely more from the severance, Victoria replied. **If we'd let her live, she would have compromised us further than she already has. It might not seem it, but it was the most merciful treatment we could offer her. It's about time we all stopped being so damn sentimental and realised that.**

Victoria's gaze remained fixed on Riley's face right up until the last possible moment. She would replay the instant of execution back in her quarters later, frame by frame. Try as she might, she couldn't find a trace of fear or doubt in it. She'd looked positively beatific, like a red-haired, latter-day Joan of Arc.

The more she reviewed the scene, the more incensed she became. Who did they think they were, these usurpers making a pageant of human life and dignity? Of course, it was easy for one insect in a hive to appear serene as it expired, knowing there were billions of others to swarm in and take its place. But not for much longer, she promised herself. Soon, she would see that façade crack.

Chapter 19

December 15th, 2135 C.E.

All across the eastern horizon were distant plumes of rising vapour, almost luminescent against the darkening sky. They represented a last-minute, knee-jerk exodus; Earth's ultra-rich making a run for their private colonies in orbit, and beyond. As though they could expect that to save them from the entity poised to consume the planet. Its tendrils would grasp further and more greedily than they could possibly know.

'Do you think we have a chance?' Victoria asked her from the passenger seat. Jean was driving manually, following little-used B-roads and old dirt trails through rural Norfolk, heading for the coast of the North Sea. Much of the path she was taking wasn't acknowledged by the car's navigation system as a viable route, which suited her fine if it kept them out of the congestion which, by now, would have brought the world's highway networks to a standstill.

The world, minus North and South America, she corrected herself.

Jean bit her lip, unsure of how to answer. 'The Enclave has two options available to it,' she said. 'They could spread by land, sea, and air. Establish beachheads in Europe and Africa from the west and Asia and Australasia from the East, and advance across the world, one city and country at a time.

'In the long term, they'd probably win. They have over two billion people under their spell now, all working with perfect coordination and fanatical devotion to their cause. But it would be drawn out and arduous, and a lot of people would die before they were assimilated. That's why the Enclave favoured moving covertly in the first place, because that's what they were trying to avoid.'

'So, what's the other option?' her daughter pressed.

'They conquer the rest of the world from space,' Jean answered. 'The trick with the particle accelerator worked, but because it's fixed in geosynchronous orbit, its effect is limited to a fixed range of latitude and longitude. If I were them…' She stopped herself at the unfortunate choice of words. She had, indeed, 'been them' just days earlier. How else would she have gained such insight into their tactics? Victoria's artificial face betrayed no obvious dismay, but Jean was familiar enough with her daughter's robotised body language to notice it all the same.

'They'll try to establish a network of similar devices in orbit,' she continued, brushing aside her blunder of phrasing. 'Construct a series of satellites so that all the Earth's landmass is blanketed by the Effect. Orbit's a much more limited theatre of war, much less likely to result in the casualties they're trying to avoid. But it's also riskier for them. It's where we can fight them on even terms.'

'You think we can win? Humans, I mean?' Once again, where Victoria's emotions might have been inscrutable to others, they were transparent to Jean. She was poised, hopeful for reassurance that only a mother could provide.

Jean smiled at her. 'Yes, hon. I think we can win.' She was surprised to find that she meant it, too. It was a peculiar, pleasant sensation to feel self-confidence again. For the first time since her severance from the Enclave, there was a part of her that was content. It wasn't quite that she felt at peace; rather, she felt *needed*.

***

Snow had been falling persistently since they had moved inland, and now lay thick upon the ground – even with the hired car's four-wheel drive, progress across the countryside was ponderous. Night had fallen by the time they reached their destination, three-hundred kilometres from Dover. Jean pulled the car over a couple of kilometres from the coast at the head of a dirt path, evidenced only by a pair of faint divots in the snow, running in parallel toward the treeline concealing the shore.

They had neglected to bring torches, but the Moon was full, and anyway, Jean remembered her way by rote. They soon made their way through the trees to be confronted by a three-metre chain-link fence, topped with razor wire.

'If I remember rightly,' Jean said, 'there was a section of the fence somewhere near here where a tree collapsed on it. The ORC never had the time, money or motivation to fix it; that can be our way in.'

'Mum, remember who you're talking to,' Victoria said, with mock resentment. She sprang onto the fence, ascended to the top, and before Jean could protest, she stripped the razor wire away, her carbon-fibre palms indifferent to its bite. 'All clear,' she pronounced, not a little smugly, as she dropped down on the far side. Jean clambered over after her, trying not to let her mix of pride and bemusement show.

***

Jean had contacted James and her mother before leaving Dover, commanding the pair of them to head for the Fournier family's summer retreat on the Knoydart peninsula in northwestern Scotland. It was cut off from access by land and air, she reasoned; the crossing by ferry was treacherously icy in winter; the sparse local community had taken to stockpiling food from October through to March as the 21st century's climate had worsened. It was the ideal place to wait out an Enclave ground invasion should it come to pass, secluded enough to be beneath notice for a while.

Victoria had refused to go with them. She had argued, and when Jean had put her foot down, she had argued all the harder. Now, more than ever, she had protested, the ORC was needed. Her fellow cadets in orbit were being rallied as they spoke. For her to turn tail and hide in the deepest hole available was nothing short of treacherous, and she absolutely would not consider such cowardice. It was a stand on principle that Jean couldn't help but be humbled by, even when – perhaps especially when – she was the one the stand was being taken against.

And so, the two of them were here together, in the old ORC facility on Scolt Head Island, where Jean had been trained decades earlier. The structure the base was built around, the massive, antiquated mass driver, was just discernible in the gloom, stretching far out to sea. The linear, electromagnetic rail was shaped like a graph of a population explosion; its gentle upward curve extending for kilometres before abruptly sharpening at the end. It and others like it had been the favoured method of launching cargo to orbit in the mid-21st century until the cheaper, safer space elevators had rendered them obsolete. The facility had been repurposed for a time as a training ground for

ORC cadets, but in due course, political and logistical pressure had moved that operation to orbit too. The base had been decommissioned eight years ago.

Jean felt a pang of nostalgia, seeing the officers' mess and the cadets' sleeping quarters in such a dilapidated state. Still, she didn't have time to gawk. What they were looking for was located in the hangar, the hulking, boxy structure straddling the shoreline which the mass driver protruded from.

The weedy padlock on the personnel entrance to the hangar admitted them without much struggle. The ORC's budget didn't extend so far as to provide beefy security for a base where there wasn't supposed to be anything left worth stealing. The only people who regularly laid eyes on it were the local children who played games around the border fence in the summer, and the maintenance crews who made cursory inspections four times a year to make sure nothing was falling apart in such a way that might harm the local environment.

It was these maintenance crews whose palms Jean had crossed to look the other way, as well as calling in some old favours with the base administrators. It was the most egregious abuse of privilege for personal gratification she had committed in her days, but for all the 'poor little rich girl' taunts she had endured in basic, she felt karmically justified using a little of her family's good fortune to keep a sentimental token of her time in the Corps. She couldn't justify the cost of buying it outright, and where was the harm in just knowing where it was?

There it sat in the gloom of the empty hangar, covered in a waterproof tarp, looking oddly small in the cavernous space. Dragging the tarp away, her heart skipped a beat.

Her old orbital fighter plane looked the same as the last day she had seen it. The maintenance crews had been as good as their word – not a spot of rust. It was the old-style Y24 Neith model, since taken out of service to be replaced by the lighter, wispier Y31 Nephtis. Flying in a squadron of those, the two-seated Neith would resemble an osprey in a flock of starlings, which just made Jean appreciate it all the more. Let the ORC keep their flimsy little mosquitoes. She knew a classic when she saw one.

On its side, next to the serial number, was emblazoned the name *Melinda*; it had been Stephen's choice of name to give Victoria while Jean had been pregnant with her. The plane was configured exclusively to her synaptic profile; her relationship to it while flying was symbiotic. No one else in the world would experience the feedback from the control of this specific plane in the fine-grained detail she did; the arc of its orbital decay, the punch of its acceleration, the way it listed ever-so-slightly in the upper thermosphere. The thought of it being reconfigured to another would break her heart a little.

'Mum?' Victoria's voice jolted her out of her moment of reverie. 'Don't we have someplace we need to be?'

'Right you are, Vic,' she said. She flicked her eyes to open a communication channel. 'Hey, Secretary,' she announced, 'we've arrived. Time to hold up your end of the bargain.'

Koo's face appeared in her vision. There was a brief lag in the connection, suggesting he was already in space. 'Patience, please, Ms. Harrison. Perhaps you missed it, but the global community was just dramatically reconfigured, and the PNC is in disarray. I have to get creative when I'm pulling diplomatic strings.'

'Far be it from me to lecture you about statecraft, but it's one electromagnet, how bloody hard can it—' She was interrupted by the rising hum of electricity around her, long-disused power lines sparking to life. A moment more, and the hangar lights flickered on. The north-facing wall opened, exposing them to an icy gust from the sea.

'Okay,' she said. 'Good. Thank you.'

***

It was an hour longer before the mass driver was fully charged; in that time, Jean and Victoria had their work cut out. Jean performed a comprehensive systems diagnostic on the *Melinda*; her record time from her service was thirty-six minutes, but it paid to take extra care when dealing with a spacecraft that hadn't been flown in a decade, let alone undergone the rigours of escape velocity. An airfoil a degree out of alignment; a single frayed wire; one deflated cushion in the pilot's acceleration couch; any of it could be deadly when dealing with those kinds of speeds and G-forces.

For her part, Victoria booted up, and synced with, the base UI, and with Jean's guidance, carried out a safety check of the mass driver itself, ensuring that none of the millions of kilometres of wiring were misaligned, or the support columns bent.

In this, at least, providence was on their side; everything was within tolerances. Sixty-five minutes after the lights had come on, they were ready to make the launch to orbit, and from there, they would rendezvous with Kisangani station – the staging post for humanity's last stand against the Enclave.

Jean tossed Victoria a piece of fabric as she hopped into the gunner's chair, behind and above the pilot's. 'Make sure this is secure before we take off. Can't take any chances.' She affixed her own Effect-negating skullcap underneath her helmet – Carlos had kept a few of them on his person, and had let Jean take two to protect herself. *You'll need them more than I do*, he'd said, darkly.

'Ready for some real acceleration?' Jean asked. 'This will be a first for you, right?'

'I've done twelve g's on the centrifuge before,' Victoria replied, a note of indignation in her voice. 'I can take anything this thing can dish out.'

Jean smirked. The competition over who was the biggest badass in the face of inhuman G-forces was another thing she missed from the Corps. 'Just you wait, hon,' she said. 'The centrifuge is one thing. The mass driver's another.' She wasn't kidding about that, either. The sudden lurch at the end of the tracks, the redirection of momentum that blindsided you no matter how ready you thought you were, like a rollercoaster designed by a sadist. Even with her epigenetically edited resistance to nausea, she had felt weak at the knees the first time she had completed a launch.

'OK: let's scare some seagulls.'

The mass driver flung the *Melinda* to the heavens with such force that they pierced the troposphere in a matter of seconds. Jean heard Victoria emit a shriek that she would later deny had happened as emphatically as a defendant in a murder trial.

***

Launching at night, the shift from the atmosphere to space was visually subtle but obvious in how the *Melinda* handled. When the resistance of the atmosphere began to ebb and the sensation of zero-gravity kicked in, Jean made the switch to the plane's quantum fluctuation drive and charted a course south, toward the equator.

As they continued to ascend, more and more of the Earth's surface splayed out below them. In a matter of minutes, the shape of Britain's topography was discernible below them. Familiar as she was with the country's profile of city and vehicle lights, Jean had the peculiar impression of England having been smeared to the right by the mass eastward migration of the population, trying to put as much distance as possible between themselves and the Americas.

'Oh my God,' Victoria breathed. Looking toward the Atlantic, they received an immediate and visceral sense of what it was Britain was fleeing from.

A great mass was rising from North America, the continent itself seemingly having come alive like a protean giant. All across the curve of the horizon, feelers extended upwards, arcing southward toward the equator, following the same latitudinal trajectory as the *Melinda*. Magnified, they saw the feelers for what they were: innumerable chemical rockets. Tens, perhaps hundreds of thousands; a host without equal anywhere in history. Even Jean, who had briefly been a part of the Enclave, was dumbstruck by the demonstration, by the scale of the consciousness arrayed against them.

The *Melinda* pinged an alert into her inner ear. 'We have a transmission,' she announced.

'Where from?' Victoria still sounded overawed.

Jean checked. 'West.'

'Can you be a little more specific?'

'Not really, no. It's one transmission being broadcast on the same frequency, from every point on the far side of the Atlantic.'

Jean routed the transmission to her and her daughter's corneal implants. The face that greeted them was that of Morton Prowse, the sitting President of the United States of America. He had all the trappings of a statesman about him: he was formally attired, calmly authoritative, and standing at a podium in the Press Briefing Room in the West Wing of the White House. The sight was so familiar as to be bizarre.

'My brothers and sisters,' he pronounced, 'I address you today not as an elected representative of the United States of America, but as a spokesperson for The Collective of Humankind. And what a glorious day this day has been, that has seen the dissolution of all nation-states and corporations. That has seen, at long last, an end to all human strife and folly. To sorrow, and regret, and suffering, and in their place ushered in a boundless joy and love!' His composure was fraying, to reveal the mania Jean recognised as belonging to the newly assimilated. 'Have no doubt, brothers and sisters, we stand at the dawning of a new era. What began in Hong Kong, and took root here, in the Americas, will soon encompass all peoples, everywhere.

'We understand the fear that accompanies the prospect of radical change. But rest assured, in time you will join us in the light. In time, you will see this change not as a defeat, but as a triumph. Allow me to be the first to extend you our hand in greeting. May the Collective prosper and grow!'

The scene cut from the American President to the President of Mexico, who gave his address in Spanish, modified in its syntax and cultural identifiers, but fundamentally the same in its content. Each of the Heads of State of North and South America followed in turn, formally abnegating not only their respective countries' sovereignty, but the concept of statehood itself.

'They're really doing it,' Victoria said aloud, wonderstruck by the sheer, vast impossibility of what she was seeing. 'They're declaring war.'

***

When the *Melinda* reached the apex of the Kisangani space elevator, the sun had risen. Starbursts reflected upon the hulls of the hundreds of other craft that had congregated around it, forming a long, gleaming ribbon along the station's geosynchronous course. There was a waiting list for anyone looking to dock, but at Jean's hail, the *Melinda* was automatically moved to the front of the queue and assigned an approach vector.

Once they had come to a halt and the shuttle bay was pressurised, Jean floated free of the cockpit and was greeted by a face she hadn't seen in years. Captain Hermann Albrecht had a sour expression at the best of times; the imminent end of the world had shifted the corners of his lips downward perhaps a fraction of a degree.

'Jean,' he said, with as close as he ever got to warmth, 'Glad you could make it so quickly. Now you're here, the show can properly start. And Cadet Harrison.' He addressed Victoria now. 'It reflects well on your dedication to the Corps that you found your way here without needing to be told. If we avert the apocalypse today, I'll make a special point of it in my report.'

'Wouldn't dream of being anywhere else, sir,' Victoria replied, obviously grateful to her CO for not dwelling on her time spent AWOL.

'When do we start?' Jean asked.

'All the key crew have been assembled. The briefing is scheduled to begin in twenty minutes. I trust you have your notes in order.'

'Don't you worry, I don't get stage fright that easily.'

'Your stage fright is a long way down the list of things I'm worried about. Come on, let's get some gravity under us.'

They made their way out from the centre of the station to the outermost torus, jostling their way through the packed transitory corridors. Every living, non-assimilated member of the ORC had been recalled when the Americas had gone dark – serving; cadets; not-in-active-service. Sexagenarian quasi-retirees thronged together with terrified-looking seventeen- and eighteen-year-old recruits. Some of these seemed to know Victoria, because they tried to draw her aside as she passed them, petitioning her for knowledge of what would happen next. They moved on when they got an apologetic gesture from her and a stern look from Albrecht.

'I take it that it's China organising all this,' Jean wondered aloud. Albrecht nodded, confirming what she had suspected. There was no way an operation on this scale could have been organised this quickly on a multilateral basis.

'There was some sabre-rattling in the immediate aftermath. The President of the People's Republic had to twist a few arms when Russia and Japan made noises about forming a joint committee to oversee the response to the new threat from the Enclave. But that died down pretty quickly when they realised the writing was on the wall, and any bureaucratic wrangling would cost precious hours we don't have. The PNC is basically dissolved now, and the USA is spellbound, leaving one obviously supreme superpower. For all intents and purposes, the ORC and all its attendant resources are now under Chinese command.'

That this idea came as a comfort to Jean threw the severity of the situation into sharp relief. Not so very long ago, the disintegration of multilateralism and the consolidation of world power by the People's Republic would have chilled her to the bone. Now, it seemed like the absolute best-case scenario.

The crowd thinned out when they reached the outermost torus, which was designated as off-limits to everyone but officers and state emissaries (Victoria, in this case, was admitted with Albrecht's special permission). Centripetal gravity here was a quarter of terrestrial standard, making it possible to walk normally with a degree of care and boots with a frictional tread.

The briefing room was 140 degrees to spinward – the walk gave Jean time to review the reconnaissance of the Brazilian station, being updated in real-time. Her corneal implants were a clutter of more than two-dozen tabs. She flitted back and forth between them as she moved, making tweaks to her tactical proposition.

Waiting outside the briefing room was Secretary Koo, the man Jean suspected was behind the bloodless Chinese coup of the four remaining continents. If he had looked worn-down the last time she had seen him, now he looked positively on the brink of collapse, and enormously relieved at the arrival of someone who could take the burden of responsibility off his shoulders for a few minutes. The ban on cigarettes in an oxygenated environment looked to be wearing on him.

'Ms. Harrison,' he said, a strained note in the officious voice she had become familiar with. 'I'm sure I don't need to tell you that a lot depends on everything you say after you walk through that door. I hope I made the right decision, trusting you with this.'

'This is what I do for a living, Secretary,' she replied.

Koo coughed. 'That's true, I suppose, in *very* broad terms. Most of the key staff have already arrived; we'll give it a couple of minutes to allow for stragglers. I'll introduce you, and then you can take it from there.'

'Sounds good.' Jean turned to Victoria. 'Wait for me here, OK, hon? I won't be long.'

***

The staff crammed into the briefing room were the bulk of the ORC's squadron commanders, mostly lieutenants and captains. They were of diverse ethnicities, most somewhere in their mid-thirties or the post-telomerase-booster equivalent, split about 70-30 along gender lines, skewing male. A greater proportion than she recalled from her service were sporting visible augmentation, with cybernetic limbs, eyes and headplates on full display. She thought she even saw a couple of full-body cyborgs mixed into the crowd. Every one of them had their eyes focused on her with an intensity that could have bored a hole through the station's hull.

'Ladies and gentlemen,' Koo began. 'My name is Lionel Koo, Secretary of Security for the People's Republic of China, and in light of recent developments, the acting administrator of the Orbital Reconnaissance Corps. I'll be brief, as time is short. The counterattack against the Enclave – now referring to itself as The Collective of Humanity – will be led by the woman standing to my right, Ms. Jean Harrison. Some of you may know her; for those of you who do not, she served with distinction as an ORC squadron leader with the rank of Captain before taking an indefinite leave of absence in 2127. During her service, she led multiple, successful incursions into hostile territory.'

He swallowed; the next piece of information he would disclose about her was crucial, but he was visibly unsure of how it would play to the massed officers. 'She is also a survivor of the Enclave Effect; the most stable individual of whom we are aware that has previously been assimilated. This has given her a unique insight into the Collective's motivations and strategy.'

ORC officers held themselves to a high enough standard of discipline that they didn't murmur amongst themselves during a briefing, no matter how scandalous the information they heard might be; however, one woman's hand did shoot up. 'Please hold your questions for Ms. Harrison once she asks for them, Captain Arquette,' Koo said to her, but she ploughed ahead regardless.

'My apologies, Mr. Secretary,' she said, 'but is it really wise to entrust command of this operation to one who has already been spellbound? What guarantees do you have that this doesn't represent a grievous security risk?'

Koo sighed. 'The details of Ms. Harrison's severance from the Collective were declassified three days ago, and are now a matter of public record. You are welcome to peruse these records if you have not done so; however, having personally spoken with her at length both during and after her brief period of indoctrination, she has demonstrated her loyalty to the human race to my satisfaction. I will now give Ms. Harrison the floor.'

Jean appreciated the sentiment; she would have appreciated it more if Koo had sounded convinced, himself. She took her place at the podium.

'Ladies and gentlemen,' she said, 'you have seen the same reports of the forces massing at the apex of the Brazilian space elevator as I have. These reports confirm my suspicions; that the Collective intends to prosecute its expansion across the Earth's remaining landmass by means of Enclave-effect generators placed in geosynchronous orbit, using technology adapted from the Brazilian particle accelerator to amplify their potency and extend their range.'

She uploaded a series of diagrams into the station's UI, to be distributed to the corneal implants of everyone present in the room. 'Before the Collective can accomplish this, however, they must consolidate their hold on their current territory. This means guarding the one currently operative generator in the Brazilian station. The two billion spellbound men, women and children in the Americas remain thus only with its continued operation.

'There are two prongs to our counterattack strategy. Both of these rest on the principle of holding the Collective to ransom.'

They actually did murmur at that.

'In the first case,' Jean continued, 'a raiding party will mount an incursion against the Brazilian station at the earliest possible opportunity. By taking control of the device currently responsible for the continuance of the Enclave Effect in the Americas, we will gain leverage according to the principle of Mutually Assured Destruction. The spellbound fear severance more than they fear death; if we are in a position to threaten them with severance, this will enable humanity to dictate the future terms of its relationship with the Collective.'

Arquette's hand shot up a second time; reluctantly, Jean acknowledged her. She had expected someone would suggest what she was certain the captain was going to – she wasn't surprised, but she was disappointed.

'Why don't we just nuke the Brazilian station right now?'

Jean screwed her eyes shut and pinched the bridge of her nose. Even having expected it, the ignorance of Arquette's question made her blood boil. 'Captain,' she replied, 'I presume you've seen the news feeds that have come out of Los Angeles in the last few days? You do understand that you have just called, in a public forum, for what amounts to the massacre of a quarter of the human race?'

Arquette lowered her hand, slowly.

'Allow me to be frank,' Jean said. 'The people spellbound in the Americas, given a slightly different set of circumstances, could have been anyone sitting in this room just now. Yes, the Collective represents an existential threat to our way of life; and beyond that, to the sense of self that makes us what we are. But our objective must be to contain and mitigate that threat, *not* the unilateral annihilation of billions of innocent people. It's my hope in the short- to medium-term to establish an equilibrium with the Collective, however uneasy, so that in the long term, a method of humanely reversing the Enclave Effect can be developed. Make no mistake: in this mission, the destruction of the Brazilian station or the device inside is a fail-state. Anyone here who intentionally and maliciously pursues that destruction will be tried in accordance with the magnitude of their crime. Is that clear?'

There were a few scattered, furtive nods of acknowledgement from around the room.

'Good. The Brazilian station will be the objective of our main force. As we speak, it is surrounded by one thousand, two hundred and twelve Collective units, with more gathering from groundside by the minute. How many of these are effective fighting vessels is undetermined; however, our chances of successfully infiltrating the station diminish the longer we delay. I have drawn up squadron formations and attack plans that should be accessible via your corneal implants. If there are no pressing questions regarding how these plans should be implemented, I would advise that the concerned personnel excuse themselves and make arrangements to launch ASAP.'

No questions were forthcoming. 'You will be flying under the field command of Captain Hermann Albrecht,' she appended. 'Godspeed.'

Four-fifths of the room sidled out, taking care not to jostle one another, muttering under their breath the orders they would already be forwarding to their respective squadrons. 'As for the rest of us,' Jean continued, 'we will be responsible for the mission's secondary objective; a means of spreading our operational risk.'

She changed tabs to a new image and indicated that the personnel remaining in the room should do the same. The image was the one which, in the past 48 hours, had become the most viewed in history. The vast lifeform, something between cetacean and insectoid, lying inert in a newly formed crater on the dark side of the Moon.

'The Body – or rather, what remains of it – is the Collective's Holy Grail. The Enclave Effect as it currently exists, they believe to be flawed, something like an interstitial step to a higher understanding. It's the one thing they value more highly than their own unchecked proliferation. If we can reach it before they do, then we gain an alternative source of leverage by threatening its destruction.'

Another hand rose in the room, this one from a Lieutenant Akinosho. 'Is that really a threat we want to make?' he said. 'Leaving aside that it's… well, an *alien*, if it's the source of the Enclave Effect then it might be the key to its humane reversal, like you say.'

Jean nodded. 'It may. But then we're entering the realm of speculation, and for the time being, we can only be sure of one tactical advantage the Body has to offer. Capture it first; use it to tease out the mysteries of the universe later.

'I should point out that the Collective will have anticipated this move on our part, and as soon as they have sufficient forces in orbit, they will move as quickly as they're able to beat us to the Moon. In fact—' she consulted the latest real-time reconnaissance update. '—It looks like they may be making their move now.'

A small cluster of craft had peeled away from the main group congregating around the Brazilian station, moving into higher orbit.

'This is it, ladies and gentlemen. I'm sure I don't need to remind you of the stakes. Anyone who is inclined to pray, do so, but do so quickly. Assemble your squadrons, review your formation plans, and prepare for launch from the main shuttle bay in ten minutes.'

There was a moment; a handful of seconds when no-one dared to move, nor even take a breath, knowing that when they did so, the battle would have begun.

Jean had a view of Earth's surface from half a dozen different angles in her vision's tabs. Even now, how peaceful it looked; blue and green and white; still and quiet. The Overview Effect: she felt it now, more acutely than she had done in many years.

'May we all see another sunrise,' she murmured, almost surprised to hear herself speak the words aloud. The other officers in the room heard her. They stood, and saluted.

***

Victoria was waiting for her outside. Doubtless, she would chafe when she saw where she had been placed in the battle plan – Jean had her immediately under Albrecht, who would be directing the attack from the rear flank. Yes, it was nepotism. Jean didn't care.

'Vic.' She pulled her daughter aside from the crowd, speaking lowly. She had no intention of any maudlin goodbyes; it would feel too much like bad luck. Better to use their time together for contingency planning rather than insuring herself against grief. 'There's something I need you to promise me.'

'Name it,' Victoria said, without hesitation.

Her last recourse. The failsafe against the final failure. 'The Collective won't allow anyone out of its grip. Every human it knows of that isn't a part of it causes it a measure of agony. If it wins today, soon the Earth won't be enough for it. It'll turn its gaze further out, to the colonies. And then further than that.'

Only Jean could have perceived the shift in Victoria's body language, the minuscule backward recoil. Her daughter knew what she was saying. 'The Starman,' she whispered.

'Exactly. The communications array on the Bornean station is precisely tuned to the *Prospice's* vector. Across light-years, even a micron's deviation in its alignment would mean a loss of contact. And if the array were to be destroyed, and the data on the *Prospice's* course scrambled...'

'They'd be lost forever.' Victoria sounded faintly horrified at what Jean was suggesting.

'If the Collective gains control of the Bornean elevator too, they'll issue a phoney order to the Starman. They'll persuade him to abandon his mission and come back here where they'll be waiting for him. But if they can't reach him – if *no one* can reach him – then he'll be free. The settlers will be beyond their reach. And if it comes to it, if the mission today fails, then someone, somewhere in the universe will remember what it is to be human.'

'Some victory that would be,' Victoria said, sullenly.

'I'll take it if it's the only victory there is,' Jean countered. 'Promise me, Vic. Promise me, if things go to hell, you'll destroy the array.'

Victoria averted her eyes, but after a moment, she nodded. Jean embraced her.

'Give them hell out there, hon.'

'You too, Mum.'

Chapter 20

August 3rd, 2326 C.E.

The Collective, speaking through Riley O'Brien, had been as good as its word. The Upsilon relay hung abandoned in interstellar space.

The relay was built to accommodate the passage of entire platoons at once; perfectly circular, it had the proportions of a wedding ring scaled up over ten kilometres wide. It was an achievement of engineering that shamed even the architects of the space elevators on old Earth. For decades, the relays had been flashpoints for their conflict with the Insurgency; who controlled the relays, controlled the flow of information and materiel between the stars.

Albrecht's best military triumphs had been the operations he had co-ordinated to capture several of the relays in quick succession. For a few brief years – around 2254 to 2261, as Victoria recalled, the period she thought of as the Interregnum – the Insurgency had carved out a territorial niche for itself in the region between Earth and TransTerra, keeping the Collective at bay and rebuffing their attempts to leave the solar system. That short window had been the last time she had felt that turning the tables on their great and terrible adversary might actually be feasible. But the Collective's numbers had won out, as they always did. Denied access to the relays they had already constructed, it had simply shrugged and begun building new ones from scratch.

Upsilon was one of the old, obsolete relays from before the Interregnum, no longer paired with any of the relays being used by the Collective for their main supply chains. It was the cosmic equivalent of a station on a disused railway line, but it remained functional, periodically maintained by whichever side held it. In recent years, that had been the Insurgency less and less often.

Careful on the approach, Victoria ordered. **However much of a generous mood they're in, I don't trust them not to have left some kind of booby traps. The transport is to remain cloaked until I give the go-ahead.** Her thirty-strong unit of Archangels were spread across five hundred kilometres, all in vantablack camouflage, moving slowly so as to reduce their wings' warp signatures. The transport lay to the rear, its velocity null in relation to the relay. **Shimura, you're on point.**

Aye, Commander, came the response. Victoria's HUD showed Shimura break formation and head for the distinctive bulge on the outside edge of the ring. The control centre, from which a destination could be selected from a range of other paired points, light-years distant.

Shimura had been the cyberwarfare specialist in Victoria's squadron ever since the loss of Velasquez; she trusted him implicitly with the responsibility that always came with moving openly on a Collective-controlled relay. The giant machines functioned in much the same way as the Collective itself did; just as the paired particles in the brains of the assimilated allowed for the transmission of thoughts across space instantaneously, so too did the relays transmit matter as information. A body which passed through the ring would be analysed by a sensor suite down to the molecular level. This information would be sent to the selected terminus through a loophole in lightspeed (in this case, the Sigma relay, orbiting 300 AU distant from the Dog Star), which would reassemble the scanned body, molecule for molecule, at the far end of the transit. The original body would be obliterated after being scanned, creating the impression in the copy at the other end of seamless continuity.

Naturally, a process that relied on annihilation and replication held ample possibility for sabotage. The Collective, waging the condescending war that they did, wouldn't stoop to letting Insurgency members be annihilated without being replicated at the far end; that would violate their sense of fair play. But it was possible to install protocols in the relays' operating systems that could identify Insurgency members and, at the point of replication, to recreate an Archangel frame *sans* its quantum fluctuation drive, leaving it adrift in deep space. Or to delay the replication by fifty years. Or to change the transit destination, leading entire squadrons into a trap. Learning to identify these computational tripwires and keep one step ahead of them had become, in time, as crucial to the war effort as dogfighting prowess.

Looks clear, Shimura announced. **The code from our previous transit is still intact. Seems like Trachtenberg made it through ahead of us as well, so his message to expect the settlers will have reached Taurus in time. Only...**

Only what? Victoria prompted.

There's a recording, Shimura wrote, **addressed to you specifically, Commander.** An audiovisual file popped up in Victoria's vision – somewhat hesitantly, she played it. The image that greeted her was the face of her cousin, with its still-raw scar tissue. Alyssa, whom she had known, however briefly, as a creature of intense passions, now wore that same maddening, diffident smile as the rest of the drones. It made her look like she'd been hypnotised, or sedated.

'Hi, coz,' the face said. 'I assume if you're watching this, Albrecht must have rolled over for you. That's fine by us; if TransTerra was any indication, you make a much more interesting quarry than he does. But as much as we're enjoying this game of cat-and-mouse, I wanted to let you know that our invitation is always open. The Starman's here, and he badly wants to see you.'

The anger that Victoria had been effectively keeping a lid on until now, came boiling to the surface once again. The piteous inflection in the Collective's tone, the self-assurance of an animal playing with its food. It wanted them to know that, if not for its magnanimity, this war would have been over centuries ago.

I'll go through first, she announced.

You sure about that, Commander? Shimura replied. Conventionally, a scout would be the first sent through a relay to confirm the passage was all clear before the higher echelons.

Absolutely. Wait for my hail.

Victoria approached the ring. There had been a lot of philosophical pontificating amongst the Insurgency when the relays had first been observed, whether a replica that emerged after the original had been annihilated could be considered the same person. It had made many them queasy about using the machines.

Not Victoria, though. She didn't care about the cessation of her consciousness — she had been awake and aware for far too long. That her will persisted, and retained its ironclad integrity; that was the important thing.

***

She arrived at the Sigma relay unscathed; after the customary transmission back to Upsilon to confirm the crossing was safe, the rest of the unit followed.

There followed five days of acceleration at one G, and then another five of corresponding deceleration, before the transport finally arrived at Taurus station. Victoria was happy to be shot of it.

The station's officer-in-charge, Lieutenant Morrison, met her five kilometres above its surface. Taurus was a more established station than the FOB they had been using in the TransTerra system, built into an asteroid of similar carbonaceous makeup, but considerably larger and more spherical, its rotation slower. Its dark surface, scarcely illuminated by the dim glow of the Dog Star, moved sluggishly below them.

Commander, he addressed her. Morrison was one of her converts, but not one of her inner circle of die-hards like Daniels; his persuasion had been belated and hesitant. She was quite happy for him to be left to administrate the settlers while she attended to the real business of the operation. **We have the station prepared for flesh-and-blood inhabitants. Barely. You didn't give us much notice.**

Desperate times, Lieutenant, she answered. **Provided there's water, air, and heat, they can be relied on to take care of themselves. They've lasted a long time on their own.**

Morrison nodded his assent, although he still seemed uneasy. **Will you be staying?**

Not any longer than I must. I'll make the introductions, then I'm heading for the Sol relay with my people. You can keep Albrecht, and good riddance. He shouldn't give you any problems; he's formally recognised my authority.

If you say so, Commander.

I do. Prepare for docking in T-minus 20 minutes, and extend the perimeter alarm tripwires to 0.03 AU.

That'll stretch our resources very thin. Any wider, and someone could slip through the gaps in the net, even at relativistic speeds.

Just make it work. We need more reaction time than we had on the FOB. I don't anticipate another surprise attack, but the specifics of the plan are too consolidated now. Too many of us know everything to risk a leak, or it could all be for...

An urgent transmission burst into her consciousness, disrupting her train of thought. It was coming from the transport, still hovering with engines shut off five kilometres above Taurus, its inertia wedded to that of the asteroid, the two bodies drifting through the dark together as though joined by a taut cable.

Daniels' ID flashed into her vision, bordered by an amber alert. **Commander**, he wrote, **there's a situation on the bridge.**

Victoria immediately braced for the worst-case scenarios. **Albrecht?** she guessed. Or, worse... **The Collective?**

No, ma'am, Daniels replied. **It's the settlers.**

***

Victoria arrived back in the transport's bridge minutes later; there she found Daniels with a flesh-and-blood settler held in each hand. His wings were flared; his QF drive exerted just enough force to keep his captives pinned to the deck without injuring them. Aki flanked her as she entered.

She didn't know the name of the man writhing beneath his left hand; the woman beneath his right, however, she recognised when she raised her head and shot Victoria a baleful look. Julie Nguyen; the sister of the boy who the Collective had taken together with Alyssa. Nguyen said nothing, but the reason for the naked hatred in her expression was plain as day. *I know what you did to Riley O'Brien*, her face said without its lips moving. *Would you have done the same to my brother, if you'd laid hands on him?*

They burst in here five minutes ago, Daniels wrote by way of explanation, **brandishing those**. He indicated a pair of handheld weapons, fastened to a magnetised plate inset in the bridge's starboard wall, well out of the captives' reach. Victoria prised one of them loose and examined it; it appeared to be a modified version of the same kind of welding torch the Starman had used to patch up the transport's engines. The gas canister that ought to provide a steady stream of plasma to the nozzle had been retrofitted to lead to a chamber. The air in the chamber would be superheated and ejected through the soldered-on barrel. Tamped down inside the barrel, flush with the chamber's exit port like it was a muzzle-loaded, 18th-century flintlock, was a package of loose nuts, screws and rivets, wadded together in a scrap of ragged fabric, primed to be fired like buckshot. It was a precarious, cobbled-together design, good for maybe two or three shots before its components jammed or melted, but before that happened it could probably throw a few dozen grams of matter at close to the speed of sound.

There's only one person on this ship who could have improvised something like this in the span of four days, Victoria thought. Despite herself, she was earnestly impressed.

Of course, her secondary consciousness countered. *But what could he hope to achieve? Even if a weapon like this posed a threat to an Archangel frame, how would they expect to take the bridge? And even if they did that, where could they hope to go?*

All true... unless...

A diversion.

Sergeant Hartikainen, she wrote, turning sharply towards Aki where he hovered by the entrance to the bridge. **When you restrained Eoin O'Brien the other day, what did he say to you? More to the point, what did you say to him? Tell me exactly.**

Nothing, Commander. Aki's response came almost before she'd finished writing, so quickly it couldn't help but seem indignant. **I removed him to his quarters, and kept him there until he cooled off, as directed.**

Words were exchanged, no? Send me a recording of the time you were alone together, please, Sergeant.

Aki complied. The recording of his sensory impressions ran for four hours and fifty-two minutes of real-time. Victoria scrubbed through the timeline in forty seconds, her secondary consciousness combing the compressed data for anything salient. O'Brien had carried on roaring and swearing at Aki from his quarters for much of the first hour, beating his fists against the door. His enhanced strength wasn't enough to buckle it, but the reverberations caused such a cacophony that Aki finally pleaded with him to calm down.

Eventually, the old engineer wore himself out, and the noise he was making quieted. He stopped inventing new ways to tell the Insurgency to get fucked and die, and instead started asking pointed questions, through the locked door, his voice level and cold, lacking any of the boisterousness that was his default setting.

No, she realised: not *questions*, plural, but one question, over and over again, restated and rephrased in myriad ways for over three hours. It was just like O'Brien – not subtle; not clever. He'd just pick an approach and stick to it with endless, mulish tenacity. 'What's Victoria planning, Aki? She's staged a coup, and she's gathering her forces, any fool can see that. What's her endgame? What does she think she's going to accomplish, a few thousand of you against billions of them?

'Why did she need to do that to Riley, Aki? There's a strategy here, something she spaced her to protect.

'It's Earth, isn't it? That's the way she's heading, back to home sweet home.

'What does she do when she gets there, Aki? What's different now from two hundred years ago?'

He's fishing, she thought. Just speculating aloud, in the hope that Aki lets something slip. He has no way of knowing the actual plan.

For the full three hours, Aki never once rose to O'Brien's bait, remaining statue-silent the whole time. Only the soft hum of his wings, the static electricity they emitted in a pressurised environment, could even have evinced to O'Brien he was still there at all. At last, even the engineer's questions slowed and stopped. After close to five hours of confinement, Aki unbolted the door and ushered his charge back out into the corridor with a half-apologetic shrug.

O'Brien looked terrible. None of the settlers appeared especially healthy these days, but on his tall, broad frame, the steady weight loss and dry, ashen skin tone they'd all taken on looked particularly unnatural. He glowered at his captor, but said nothing; he'd rendered himself hoarse. He exited his quarters when prompted and separated from Aki, heading for the transport's hold, where the idle settlers congregated.

Aki had given nothing away; he'd been as good as his word. He'd leaked nothing of the plan that could stand to compromise them.

Except...

Victoria loathed her secondary consciousness sometimes, even as she'd come to rely upon it in all things. Always flagging up inconvenient nuance, making a mess of what she wanted tidy, disrupting her clear, smooth vision of how things ought to proceed. Infuriating, because the doubts and fears and second-guesses it brought to the fore were her own, and couldn't be brushed aside or ignored.

Except, that we're talking about Aki.

Aki; always exuberant, always talkative, always eager to please. After the settlers' successful extraction, he, more than any other member of the Insurgency, had taken real joy in it. He'd seen it as his first opportunity in over a century to make new friends. The settlers knew him; they knew this about him. For him to stay conspicuously quiet, to refuse to answer questions with open-hearted honesty? His silence might have answered O'Brien's probing questions as eloquently as words ever could.

Commander, Daniels wrote, **I've ordered the settlers to congregate in the hold, but there are twenty-seven who have refused to comply. Judging from the infrared signatures, they look like they're congregating at the stern of the ship.**

Yes, that makes sense, Victoria replied. **Follow me. I know where they're going.**

***

She, Aki, and Daniels were the only Archangels still inside the pressurised craft, but it made no difference; any one of them on their own would have been enough. After Daniels wrestled Nguyen and her compatriot into the nearest cabin and sealed the door behind them, the three of them made their way to the medical bay.

As they approached, Victoria started to notice traces of toxins in the air, stray particles of hot, ionised gas drifting according to the air currents. If she'd possessed mucosal membranes, they would have registered as an acrid, metallic smell, growing stronger the closer they got.

O'Brien and the handful of settlers he'd convinced this was somehow a good idea had clearly helped themselves to the welding equipment still left in the deck 4 storage lockers. They'd waited until the prime moment when the cruiser was at its least occupied. It had been a mistake, clearly, to let the settlers move around as freely as they liked while they were in her charge. She made a note to confer with Morrison before her departure on measures to restrict their freedom of movement and contain any further lapses in security. Curfews; surveillance cameras; limits on gathering sizes and discretionary bandwidth.

The medical bay lay at the stern of the cruiser, nestled between the engines, at the end of a long corridor. Rounding a corner into that corridor, they found it filled with settlers. Victoria performed a quick headcount. Sure enough: twenty-seven of them. Twenty-seven faces turned at her approach, displaying various degrees of fear and defiance. Behind them, the door had been forced open, the cooling remains of the lock an origin point for the greasy smoke.

Brandon Lawson hovered nearest to her; the fingers of his left hand clenched white-knuckled around the adjacent handrail. With his right, he braced the stock of another improvised bolt thrower against his shoulder.

The look on his face was nothing like what she'd seen in Riley O'Brien's. This was nothing like looking into the eyes of a child and having the Collective stare back, serene and condescending and implacable. The Lawson boy tried his utmost to project confidence, but his body betrayed him. His heartbeat was in excess of 120 bpm; he breathed rapidly through his nose, the exhalations coming sharp and ragged. Every part of him was quivering, despite how tightly his muscles were clenched. It was clearly all he could do to keep his conflicting impulses in check, his sense of duty warring with the urges to flee or fight or surrender. He was brave to face her down without blinking; but it was the brittle, impetuous courage of a child, one whose will the universe had not yet tempered and fortified.

She could sympathise. She could remember well how it felt.

Victoria slowly raised her hands, the gesture intended to mollify. 'Don't do anything foolish, Brandon,' she called, voice loud but level. 'Whatever this is, it's over. I understand why you're upset. You won't be punished; you won't be sanctioned in any way. I just need you to throw me your weapons, and...'

The jury-rigged gun discharged, catching her quite legitimately by surprise. A loosely associated wad of hot metal struck Victoria in the right cheek at about Mach 0.9; her frame hardened autonomously at the impact, but the shot still stripped away a few thousand platelets from the upper layers of her armour. It was a negligible fraction of her frame, barely a millionth of a percent of its total mass; but those precious few platelets were now irrecoverable and irreplaceable.

She affected a sigh. 'OK, then.'

***

O'Brien had seemingly directed his troupe of rebels to buy him whatever time they could for him to ransack the medical bay. If that had been the case, then all of their weapons, all of their scheming, all of their desperation bought him perhaps an extra few dozen seconds.

She, Daniels, and Aki broke through the defenders headlong, swatting them aside as they went. They struck hard enough to bruise or concuss, but not to kill. A few more shots were fired from the repurposed welding equipment at point blank range; between the three of them, they lost maybe a few million platelets. One of the guns misfired when its trigger was pulled, its leaky chamber bursting and scalding its wielder's hand. He jerked back into the ranks of his compatriots, screaming, sending them into greater disarray. He'd ended up more a hindrance than a help.

Victoria slipped through the broken door into the medical bay. The space was in complete disorder, stainless steel drawers and broken glass floating free amidst the thick fug of smoke. Cabinets and lockers hung open and empty, their locks smoking. In the starboard corner of the room, O'Brien crouched, using one hand and both feet to brace against the walls. He betrayed no sign of having noticed her presence, or the scuffle outside. His free hand was clutched close to his chest, concealing something from her view.

'Eoin,' she said, by way of announcing herself. 'Did you find what you were looking for?'

O'Brien, with no excess of haste, turned to face her, and removed the heavy mask he'd been wearing while operating the welding torch. He looked, if anything, even more haggard than he'd done in Aki's recording just four days prior, his hair and beard lank with sweat, his face rimmed with ashy residue.

'I did,' he replied. His tone of voice was uncharacteristically solemn, maybe even wistful. 'Heinemann told me it had been stashed in the medical bay. I wish I understood why you'd keep something so potentially dangerous, rather than blast it out into space.' He held up the prize he'd found; the lone Wasp that Heinemann had recovered from Riley, that had infected her. It was rictus-still now, its limited reserve of battery power long-since used up.

'Their power supply is full of transuranic elements,' Victoria said, by way of answering Eoin's curiosity. 'Berkelium; fermium; laurencium; all useful in antimatter refinement. The Wasps are small, but they're worth a million times their weight in gold. We try to capture every one that we can.'

'They're valuable.' Eoin said it tonelessly, as though chewing the words to sample their flavour. 'But my Riley, nothing of her was worth preserving was it? Not the iron in her blood, not the phosphorus in her bones, not the electrolytes in her cells.'

'I mourn for Riley too, Eoin. But you have to understand, I didn't kill her; the Collective did. The death of her soul; that's on its conscience, and its alone.'

'She was part of them, even if just for a moment,' Eoin said quietly. His eyes were downcast, and Victoria couldn't be certain that his words were still addressed to her. 'In the Collective, d'you suppose some part of her still survives? Some memory of her?' He rolled the robotic insect back and forth, between his fingers and his palm. The four-centimetre needle that tipped its lower body glinted in the light of the medical bay.

'It's inert, Eoin. It was only ever loaded with one subcutaneous device.'

He nodded. 'Yeah, that makes sense, I suppose. But here's the thing, Victoria. Right now, I'm not inclined to believe anything you say. I've had people I love taken from me, because they took you at your word.'

'What do you want from me, Eoin? This is war. We're both of us, soldier and refugee alike, together in a conflict where the deck is incalculably stacked against us. Things go wrong. People die. As horrible as it feels, there's nothing to be gained from trying to bring them back.'

'We took you at your word,' Eoin went on, as though he hadn't heard her, 'because you were Jonah's family, and he vouched for you. Do you know why I respect him? Why we all respect him? I'd been under his command a few years before I understood it myself. He's not the smartest guy I've known. Not the toughest, either. But what always set him apart was that he was honest. If he said something was the way it was, then you could trust that was the way it was, even if – *especially* if – it cost him something to say so. He never treated people like game pieces.'

He raised his eyes to meet hers, and there was a light in them. His muscles stiffened, and his pulse quickened. He was priming himself to do something foolhardy. 'What are you planning, Victoria?' He repeated the question he'd plied Aki with for hours. 'Give me the truth. *That's* what I want from you. Show me you're worthy of our trust.'

The implicit threat was clear. If he was to inject himself with one of the Collective's paired particle devices at the base of the spine, if he was connected to the hive mind for even a split second, all of his suspicions about her intentions would be instantaneously broadcast across light-years. He didn't know anything; he hadn't blundered into any specifics. But his suspicions alone could be enough to snap the one gossamer-strand of hope left to the Insurgency, and all humanity.

'Just throw me the Wasp, Eoin,' she said. She extended a hand, palm splayed. 'This doesn't need to get any worse.'

His arm flashed, his hand twisting upward in an arc to drive the Wasp's needle into the vertebrae of his neck. He was fast – faster than a man so old and so malnourished had any right to be. Still, not quite fast enough. Victoria fired an energy blast from her palm, tuned to a low wattage. The beam grazed the tips of Eoin's fingers as they moved, burning away a few layers of skin. He roared, reflexively dropping the Wasp that had been made red-hot inside a millisecond.

Victoria closed the distance between them before he'd recovered. Her elbow crystallised to hyperdiamond, she struck him in his nose, shattering it. Globules of bright red blood added to the general disarray.

His body went limp. Victoria held him by the ankle and dragged his unconscious form through the ship, back to the hold with the other settlers to await transfer.

***

The settlers were left to their own devices in Taurus three days later, with a skeleton crew of seven Archangels, headed by Morrison, to help them get oriented and begin the algae farming. Victoria headed back to Sigma relay, followed by her original unit which had now been bolstered by thirty-six of Taurus' staff. Fifty-one Archangels moving in formation through space, finally able to stretch their wings to their utmost 90% of c. The freedom and the exertion of it made Victoria feel capable of storming Earth right away, irrational as the thought was.

The Sigma relay was no less abandoned than it had been when they arrived, which was cause for relief and trepidation in equal measure. Was the Insurgency being baited? Or was the capture of the Starman such a paradigm shift for the Collective that all of their forces had been withdrawn to the solar system ahead of him, deep-space outposts no longer considered strategically worthwhile? Either way, she saw no reason to deviate from the plan.

With the customary precautions, they used the Sigma relay to make the jump to the Sol relay. Sol's name reflected more whimsy than accuracy; it deposited them in the inner reaches of the Oort Cloud, just under a light-year from Earth. The Sun was hardly brighter than any other star at this distance, its gravitational effects negligible. And yet, it felt tantalisingly close all the same. This was as close to the solar system as anyone in the Insurgency had dared come for decades. The cis-Neptunian relays were so heavily guarded now as to be impregnable; any Archangel who attempted to sneak through them would be immediately overwhelmed by a dozen Scarab platoons, most likely captured before they could get a shot off.

Even this far out, Victoria emerged to the signs of a battle hard fought. Scarab carcasses littered the zone surrounding the Sol relay for a thousand klicks in every direction, and traces of anti-neutrons and positrons suggested more than one Archangel core had been ruptured before they arrived.

The unit from Sagittarius station had beaten them to the punch, she learned, when she was hailed by Lieutenant Rebecca Ngo. Her unit of forty-seven had been greeted by an ambush upon transmitting into the system, being thrust immediately into a dogfight against a full Scarab squadron. They had won quickly, but not before Corporal Vennam and Sergeants Koenig and Watkiss had been forced to sacrifice themselves to avoid capture. Victoria authorised and presided over a brief service to their memory, in which she gave her thanks for their long service and the sacrifice which had made their rendezvous possible.

Over the subsequent hours and days, more Insurgency forces arrived through the Sol relay in dribs and drabs. Each of the Zodiacal stations were represented by a squadron or two, with individuals and pairs drifting in from the smaller bases.

After three days, the tide slowed, and Victoria took stock of the forces available to her. She counted eight hundred and ninety-six Archangels, including herself, with twenty-five transport carriers. It was the largest host the Insurgency had gathered since they had fled the moons of Saturn. And yet at the same time, it felt like so few. Eight hundred and ninety-six men and women. At the very end, was this really all humanity could bring to bear?

It would have to suffice.

She gestured towards the Sol relay. **Destroy it**, she ordered. At her word, a hundred beams lanced from a hundred hands. In the absence of explosive components, the relay's end was unspectacular. The heat of the maser fire simply caused its superstructure to soften and melt, the fine-tuned electronics it relied on being rendered non-functional.

The Collective would be prevented from sending reinforcements to attack their rear, at the unprecedented cost of the Insurgency cutting off its own retreat to friendly territory. There was, in a very real sense, no turning back for them now.

The Oort Cloud was populated by a great many trans-Neptunian satellites, and it didn't take Victoria's small army long to find what they were looking for. The Insurgency had become adept at the interception of stray comets over the years, being as they were an invaluable source of fuel. The one which caught her eye was approximately eight-hundred metres in diameter, massing somewhere in the region of two billion tons. Its vector placed it on a near-direct course into the heart of the solar system, making it easier to guide.

The Archangels immediately set themselves to attaching the quantum fluctuation drives being carried by the transports that would propel it to nine-tenths of lightspeed. The work was painstaking, requiring the comet's mass to be reshaped and its spin brought under control. Balance was key; at the velocities and the distances they were working to, a fraction of a degree or a few grams' worth of asymmetry could send them a million klicks off-course, missing their one and only shot. The army toiled without rest, straining the limits of their frames' physical and computational capabilities to turn a chunk of ice into a bullet aimed directly at the surface of the Earth.

For all the Collective had expanded into deep space, the hive mind made its home in human bodies, and with the exception of TransTerra, there remained only one biome in the known universe that naturally hosted sapient life. By necessity, the vast majority of the Collective's infrastructure and population was concentrated on Earth.

In one fell strike, all of the infrastructure that allowed the Collective to maintain its hold on the human race could be destroyed, at the price of the Earth's surface being rendered uninhabitable for a geological epoch. The assimilated hordes that resided there, the billions that had been spiritually murdered long ago, would be euthanised.

A fragment of the Collective would survive – the fraction of a percent residing on the surface of Mars and the Jovian and Saturnian colonies, and the autonomous orbital habitats. But its ability to wage war would be crippled; the Insurgency, far from being the fly buzzing in the ear of a bull it had been for so long, would be in a position where it could actually win. They would move on those extraterrestrial colonies and retake them, wiping out the devices there that propagated the Enclave Effect as they went.

More assimilated would inevitably die; the ones who didn't would be left in a state of irreversible insanity. But they would provide the pool of genetic material needed for a program of *in vitro* fertilisation. Enough for a seed population to begin the human race afresh. And in TransTerra, there was a garden world forty light-years distant that had been proven to be hospitable to life.

Victoria had read once that during the ice age, the total human population had been reduced to no more than a few thousand. It was what accounted for the species' relative lack of phenotypic diversity. But in due course, humans had sprung back, numbering in the billions only a few short millennia later. The harder humans are pushed by their circumstances, the harder they retaliate; it was that tenacity that had made them conquerors. They had weathered that calamity, and she would see to it that they weathered this one.

In 2135, the sight of an approaching comet in the sky had marked the beginning of humanity's long nightmare. In 2327, the same sight would mark its end.

Chapter 21

July 29th, 2326 C.E.

For the first two days he spent among the Collective, Jonah fought hunger and thirst and fatigue.

'I meant it, Manderly,' was the first thing he said when the airlock had finished cycling and he was ushered onboard their ship. 'I want answers. Not later. Now.'

Jean's once-upon-a-time boyfriend just smiled his wan, apologetic smile, that made his face look all the more like a fleshless skull. 'You'll have them, Captain,' he said, with the infuriating cadence of a kindergarten teacher placating a stubborn toddler. 'We'll attend to you shortly, but for the moment, we need all hands on deck.' With that brush-off, he and the other Collective crewmembers dispersed, with abruptness and coordination like they were following a stage direction.

He was left with an assimilate who didn't give a name, and who communicated only in hand gestures. When she placed a hand on Jonah's shoulder, as though in a friendly gesture, Jonah slapped it away. The assimilate recoiled from the explosive motion, but after half a second, she regained her composure. She led Jonah through the craft's brightly lit hallways to a spacious, freshly prepared cabin, leaving him a respectful metre of personal space after her first attempted gesture of familiarity. Throughout, she wore a warm, open, tranquil expression that made Jonah queasy whenever he looked upon it.

**

The ship accelerated to two g's and three-quarters, putting distance between itself and the FOB's defences. Jonah remained buckled into the gel-mattress in his cabin throughout; even in this prone, insulated position, the pressure on his injured leg was agonising.

He remained in his spacesuit, keeping it pressurised; within hours his primary oxygen tank had depleted, and his auxiliary tank a couple more hours after that. Grudgingly, he switched his suit to equalise with the ship's atmosphere so he could continue to breathe. He programmed his filters with a standing order to alert him if they detected any exotic ions or radioactive materials permeating his helmet. He had no idea what devious means the Collective might have to propagate itself.

The hours wore on, and the pressure of the acceleration didn't slacken, and Jonah was given ample time to question the wisdom of his recent choices.

If his new hosts wanted to assimilate him, couldn't they do so whenever they wanted? But then, they needed him intact; perhaps they were simply waiting for him to leave himself vulnerable, ready to renege on their word as soon as he offered a window of opportunity.

He started to take stock of what information he had on the Insurgency's movements that his assimilation might compromise; of what harm he might do to Victoria, Eoin, Will, Rahman, Aki, and all the others he'd abandoned. He considered what it might feel like to have control of his own body and mind wrested from him by an intruding consciousness. He shuddered.

And yet: he'd made his choice, and set the attendant wheels in motion. He reflected at length on what had prompted him to it, clarifying his thoughts to distract himself from the pressure on his leg.

First: a Scarab, an unmanned Collective fighting machine, had killed Marcus Lawson, grievously wounded Alyssa, and attempted to do the same to him and Rahman. This had led him to give credence to Victoria's original warning that there was an extrinsic threat to the safety of the settlers of the Mercanta Steppe. He had later learned that this was not the typical behaviour of a Scarab, that the aggression of the machine they had encountered in the clearing was an aberration most likely caused by damage to its target acquisition software.

Second: Victoria, whose testimony he had trusted implicitly by virtue of her being family, had told them the story of an alien parasite capable of taking over the minds and bodies of humans; that this was what had happened to the population of old Earth, causing the cessation of communication with the *Prospice* in 2145 and the attendant, historical trauma to the crew; and that the

Collective was ruthless and relentless in the pursuit of its own multiplication. This story had gelled with his experience of the Collective up to that point (re: the encounter in the clearing) as an invader. Victoria had later proven to be willing to take liberties with the truth, about her own objectives and about the broader goals of the Insurgency, casting doubt upon her characterisation of the Collective.

Third: the Collective had indeed proven itself to be capable of, at the very least, forcibly altering an individual's personality; he had the testimony of his own senses to back that up. The way Alyssa and Jack Nguyen had acted after they had come into contact with it was hard to explain except by way of their higher mental functions being co-opted.

Fourth: the Collective needed him. In Alyssa's words, he was the key to achieving its endgame. This, combined with his newfound understanding of the futility of the Insurgency's cause, made it seem to him that there was at least a chance of doing some good with the remaining years of his life, where there was none if he remained with the Insurgency, to be passed around as a hostage and/or bargaining chip as and when Victoria or Albrecht required it.

Fifth, last, and the detail that had clinched it: the Collective claimed to know what had become of his daughter.

Whether his choice had been the right one, he still wasn't sure. But at the very least, there was context he had been missing, having been out of the loop for two centuries. After all, if a hypothetical caveman was unfrozen from a hypothetical glacier on old Earth in the 21st century, and the first people he encountered were a hypothetical cell of jihadists, no doubt that hypothetical caveman would quickly be poisoned against western democracy. That didn't exonerate western democracy of all wrongdoing; but it likely wasn't the monolithic evil the hypothetical caveman understood it to be. The truth was probably closer to somewhere in the middle.

***

After fourteen punishing hours, the acceleration began to wind down, gently decreasing to a level, single g. The same assimilated woman who'd guided him to his quarters entered, carrying a tray. Jonah rose to meet her, heaving his protesting limbs out of the gel-mattress and failing to suppress a groan as he did so.

335

'We imagined you would be hungry, Captain,' the woman said, in the same polite, blandly warm monotone as ever. 'Please, eat.'

'I don't need food,' he objected. 'I need answers. When can I—' He cut off when he saw what she was holding. On the tray were two plates; on one was a salad, made with tomatoes and courgette and garden rocket, sprinkled with goat's cheese and fennel honey and pine nuts. On the other was a steaming fillet of trout, daubed with butter. Adjacent to both plates was a long-stemmed glass, filled with a generous pour of white wine.

The richness of the meal being presented to him affected him far more than he could have expected. For most of his life he'd sustained himself on simple combinations of fungi and root vegetables and vitamins synthesised from stardust. He hadn't eaten anything derived from an animal since 2096. Being presented with such abundance all at once made his stomach lurch. He was hungry; all at once, he realised he'd never felt so hungry. Yet at the same time, being plied with food like this, food that made him want to open his visor so that he could inhale its scent, he grew nauseous. His gag reflex activated, and he gulped it back, tasting acid.

'Please, eat,' the assimilate said, placing the tray on the floor. 'Your wellbeing is important to us.' She made to leave.

'Wait!' Jonah made to grab her arm, but his thigh cramped as he moved, and he stumbled as he did so. She turned back to support him, taking some of his weight. 'I need to speak to Manderly.'

'David is needed just now,' she replied, her voice still with that same utter lack of tension or urgency. 'The ship is still on amber alert, and he's manning the controls. Don't worry, you'll see him soon.'

'Hold on, look, Ms... I'm sorry, what's your name?'

He thought he saw a look of puzzlement flicker across her face, before the same beneficent expression as always reasserted itself. 'I've no name, Captain. You can address me as you would any of my crewmates.'

'Fine. *Collective*, then: you all speak with one voice, isn't that right? Can't you answer my questions?'

'I'm afraid I can't stay, sir. I also have to get back to my post.' The assimilate bowed her head apologetically, and backed out of the room like a geisha who'd been dismissed.

'No!' Jonah called after her. He limped to follow her, but the cabin door closed and sealed as she left, leaving him imprisoned. He turned and kicked the tray with his good leg, sending thousands of calories of lovingly prepared food spattering against the cabin wall.

***

Time ticked on. It was 12.39 am, July 27th, 2326, Greenwich Meridian Time. His implants had kept him right for centuries, and they'd yet to let him down. His head drooped. He jerked it back upright, blinking rapidly. 12.40 am. He wouldn't sleep. He mustn't sleep. If he slept, he would be utterly at their mercy. He stood, and paced about the cabin, trusting the motion and the circulation of blood to rouse him.

The exercise helped him maintain consciousness for a little while, but after a time, his thigh started throbbing. His eyes itched, and he dearly wanted to open his visor so that he might reach inside his helmet and rub them. He didn't let himself look at the congealing remains of the meal in the corner.

Eventually, he sat back down on the gel mattress. The pain in his thigh had taken on a burning quality, and he had to stop. His implants read 2.21 am.

Again, his head drooped. Again, he jerked it upright. Now the time was 5.26 am. Against the opposite wall slouched Manderly.

'I believe you wanted to see me, Captain?' he said. There was no trace of irony in his voice. 'You had some questions?'

Jonah opened his mouth to answer, and coughed. His mouth was terribly dry. He took a sip of water from the suit's filters. 'Why—?' he choked out.

'Why keep you waiting like this? A show of goodwill, Starman. A hand across the aisle. You must realise there are any number of ways we might have assimilated you by now. We hope the fact that we haven't counts for something when you hear what we have to say.'

Jonah did his best to compose himself, as groggy and disoriented and depleted as he felt. He straightened his back, and looked Manderly in the eye. 'Alright then,' he said. 'What is it you have to say?'

'We can imagine what Victoria told you about us. About our – shall we say – missionary zeal. We deeply regret the way you and your people have suffered. We do bear at least part of the blame for it. Let us offer an olive branch. Let us give you our account of how the Collective began.'

***

Manderley's chronology of the Collective's history began in the same way Victoria's had, with the appearance of the Body in the sky on the night of October 18th, 2135, the coordinated efforts of the world's governments to destroy it, and the psychic fallout that had followed. Where his account diverged from – or rather, added to – information Jonah already had, was with the story of Xavier Wong, the scientist-turned-prophet who had received the gospel of the Body, and whose efforts to replicate the vision of unified consciousness bestowed upon him by the alien visitors had formed the crucible of the Collective as it now existed.

'Those early days were… tumultuous,' Manderly said. 'We came very close to failure, numerous times. We made a great many mistakes, none greater than the way we chose to multiply. You heard Alyssa call it our "original sin," and that's how we've come to think of it since. The subterfuge, the dirty tactics, treating our revelation as though it was a trap to be sprung on the world – no wonder we were hated and feared by the non-assimilates. I was among the ones who fought against it before being saved, if you can believe that. I should know better than anyone.

'Our only defence is that in the early stages of the Effect, the honeymoon stage, there was an extraordinary *fervour*. It was like evangelism, or lust. The need for others to share the joy of its revelation was desperate, overpowering; we felt vindicated in doing so by force or by trickery. In the long term, that made us lasting enemies.'

'Based on what I've seen, you're still not above the application of a little force and trickery,' Jonah retorted.

'If you mean Alyssa, she came to us of her own free will, just as much as you did. We were truthful about that.'

338

'She'd just seen her family die. She was in no fit state of mind to make decisions about anything. And the way you used her to track us down...'

Manderly shook his head. 'Extraordinary circumstances. Regrettable, but the Insurgency is far past the point of listening to reason. And now Victoria's staged her coup, we fear they'll be further gone still. If we hadn't seen fit to apply some leverage, we would have missed our best chance to retrieve you.'

'Which rather brings us to the crux of the issue, doesn't it?'

'What makes you so important?' Manderly apparently intended it as a rhetorical question, but it came out sounding legitimately quizzical. 'Well, that takes us back to the beginning again.'

He described the alien visitor that had emerged from the Body to crash land on the dark side of the Moon. The first and most obvious detail was its size. Three thousand, five hundred and twelve metres from nose to tail, limbs splaying across a diameter of four kilometres, massing over a million tons. The creature, wherever it had come from, couldn't have evolved in the gravity of a planet.

Indeed, further investigation had indicated that it hadn't 'evolved' at all, at least not in the sense that a biologist might define the term. Its hide was curious in just how familiar it was. Samples chipped away from the exterior suggested a cellular, carbon-based invertebrate; not related to anything on Earth, obviously, but recognisable in its construction on the scale of micrometres.

Portions of the creatures' exterior, however, appeared to be cybernetic, including components that seemed for all the world to resemble those one would find on a starship; heat fins, sensor arrays, even engines, comprised of metals and alloys which carbon-based biology simply could not account for. A species making cybernetic modifications to its anatomy was, by itself, nothing remarkable; humans had been doing it for over a century at that point. What was remarkable was the way that the Collective could find no join between the creature's organic and cybernetic components, in much the same way that a screen displaying a gradient from red to green had no definite point where one pixel stopped being 'red' and started being 'green.' Samples of the tissue surrounding the cybernetic portions were observed as containing greater and greater quantities of iron, silver, nickel and so forth, until an indefinable point where it was no longer recognisable as 'tissue' at all.

This discovery cast doubt upon the categorisation of the creature as something organic or synthetic; it was seemingly the result of processes that precluded a distinction between the terms. What appeared to be simple living tissue was governed by different physical rules, suggesting a command of femtotechnology far greater than the comparatively crude programmable matter that made up the Archangel frames. It was presumably what prevented the creature's cells from imploding when exposed to vacuum; what allowed it to manipulate and even disregard inertia, the way it had been observed to on its approach to Earth.

It was in making these observations that the Collective had arrived at a new, exciting hypothesis – despite the absence in the creature of any visible movement, of any kind of metabolism, of the generation of the exotic radiation it had swamped the Earth with, its physical mass remained intact, refusing to freeze or necrotise, as though frozen in time. If it carried information through a medium beyond the Collective's grasp, the Body's passenger could, in fact, still be conscious, if not technically 'alive.' Dead but dreaming, as it were.

The Collective had refocused its efforts from trying to analyse the creature to trying to communicate with it. And they had succeeded.

The exterior sensors had been key. They had appeared powered-down, not receiving any input. But the Collective had delicately spliced in exterior power sources, taking surgical care to damage the surrounding structure as little as possible. They had connected to what they gleaned to be a simple optical sensor, and input a simple on/off pattern of electrical impulses.

The hope with that first connection had simply been to generate some kind of response, whatever it might have been. The Collective had expected it to be the work of generations to create an actual, comprehensible rapport with the creature. But they had received an answer immediately, in straightforward binary denotation that a student of computer science would learn on their first day at school.

And the message they had received from the envoy from another world? 'I will speak only with the Starman.'

They had tried again. They had tried the technique on other sensors, used different modes of stimulation, addressed the creature in different languages, both computational and linguistic. The creature would answer in the corresponding medium, but the content of its message had remained stubbornly identical for two centuries. 'I will speak only with the Starman.'

Jonah gaped. 'Me?'

'Yes, Captain. You.' Manderly looked grave, the Collective's customary smile nowhere to be seen.

'But why?'

'We were hoping you could tell us, if we're being honest.'

'But it doesn't make any sense! You could scarcely find anyone in the universe who knows less about the Body or its passenger than I do. Christ, I'm hearing all of this for the first time, what does that tell you?'

Manderly's expression moved beyond serious to looking actually pained. 'We believe that it has something to do with your daughter,' Manderly said.

Here it was, at last. Jonah's mouth was dry.

'Jean.' he finally said. 'What is her involvement in all this? Is she alive? Assimilated? Please, tell me. What happened to my daughter back then?'

The fathomless, communal sadness of a billion souls etched itself upon Manderly's withered face. In tones of regret and long-unspoken agonies, the Collective told Jonah the story of his daughter's final hours.

Chapter 22

December 16th, 2135 C.E.

Jean's rear display showed the Kisangani station shrinking behind her at a pace that would seem unintuitive to one accustomed to atmospheric velocities. The *Melinda* was pulling a steady ten g's, but its engine was purring like it was brand new; coupled with the lack of air resistance and the absence of any other close-by points of reference, the craft gave the deceptive impression of being still, rather than moving at forty-thousand klicks per hour and climbing.

Does anyone have a visual on the bandits? Jean put the question to her unit, using text rather than vocalisation to spare her larynx the extra strain on top of what the g-forces were already inflicting.

Negative, *Melinda*, came a chorus of responses. Surrounding her were a total of 91 spaceplanes, all Y31s except for hers, bristling with armament. It was a larger unit than had ever been entrusted to her during her original service.

To judge from their warp signatures, they're actually gaining on us. This from the squadron leader on her left flank whom she had designated her XO, one Sergeant Esteban Velasquez, callsign *Belladonna*. Jean reviewed the data showing the subtle redshifting of light passing through the wake of a quantum fluctuation drive, and cursed. If it was to be believed, the Collective craft they were meant to intercept had put a thousand more klicks between them and their pursuers since they had launched. At this rate they would never catch them.

Roger that, *Belladonna*. Christ, they must be pulling over 12 g's and holding steady.

It made sense, of course; the enemy pilots, in addition to having bodies enhanced in the manner of the ORC's elite, would have the added advantage of minds with the disregard for pain conferred by the Enclave Effect. The only countermeasure left to them was sheer, bloody-minded gumption, in the best human tradition of the gung-ho and the foolishly brave, reserved for soldiers and astronauts. The men and women flying with her fit those criteria.

All pilots, she announced, **brace yourselves and increase acceleration to 15 g's. Close the gap.**

Roger, *Melinda*, came the 91 replies, with only a fraction of a second longer delay than they had acknowledged her orders thus far. She gunned her own engines accordingly, and the weight sitting on her chest graduated from 'Clydesdale horse' to 'African elephant.' She could feel her eyes being pressed back in their sockets; even issuing orders through her corneal implants would become a struggle. But when she checked the warp signature data again five minutes later, she saw that the abuse she was inflicting upon herself was not going unrewarded. The gap between them and their quarry had reduced by 800 klicks. Barring a further escalation from the Collective, they would catch them before they could reach the Body's resting place. If her entire unit didn't black out or suffer cardiac arrest, first.

She thought gratefully of the doctors at Scolt Head who'd implanted her augmentations. The weeks of agonising recovery she'd suffered were paying off; her enhanced musculature kept her diaphragm inflating; the titanium filaments in her bones kept her ribcage rigid.

The Y24's rear display alerted her to a series of pulses of light against the face of the Earth, along the equator at around 40 degrees longitude. For them to be visible at this distance, the explosions' yield must have been in the range of kilotons.

God, they're already using nukes. It shouldn't have shocked her; she herself had authorised the use of tactical nuclear strikes to thin the ranks of the armada surrounding the Brazilian station – it was a level of firepower the Collective would be reluctant to bring to bear. Hell, she had urged Koo to sign off on the decision. Even so, nuclear weapons were so mythologised that their use in anger felt like a line in the sand. Her species had crossed a threshold it had deigned off-limits since 1945. Even considering everything that had happened, there was a finality to that decision.

Movement. Bandits 2, 3, 7. The update came from the *Belladonna*, the text creeping across Jean's field of vision, the pause between each character pregnant and infuriating. Velasquez used abbreviated text to offset the delay the acceleration's press was putting on his eyeballs. **Breaking. Engage.**

Sure enough, three of the enemy warp signatures had peeled off from the main group, and were making an about turn through a wide arc to face their unit. *The nukes must have thrown a scare into them,* Jean thought. *Made them realise that we're just as serious as they are.* **Evasive manoeuvres**, she replied, the characters emerging from her own interface with the same maddening sluggishness.

Bandit 2 led the tearaways, approaching the central squadron of Jean's unit – her squadron – accelerating at nearly 15 g's. Its delta-V combined with theirs was something terrifying, in the high hundreds of thousands of klicks per hour. Visual contact was established; a Y31, no different from the ones in her own unit. Had she been expecting it to be emblazoned with a skull and crossbones? No-one in this battle was flying a flag.

It launched a volley of eight dovetail missiles, the whole of the Y31's meagre payload, aimed straight for the central squadron – Jean's squadron. Upon seeing the missiles flagged by her HUD, she yanked the *Melinda* southward as hard as she thought it could withstand. The dovetails were dumb projectiles, lacking any kind of guidance systems; they compensated for that lack with a warhead that would iris open and issue forth a thousand tungsten pellets, just larger than ball bearings, across a wide dispersion range. At the terrifying velocities the Y31's under-wing railgun launchers could manage, the impact of just one of those pellets could pierce the *Melinda's* cockpit and exit through the other side, having left a viscous absence where its pilot's head had once been.

The Collective's lag-free, mind-to-mind communication might have given its pilots an additional edge, but its tactics were almost disappointingly uncreative. The dovetails were meant as a crowd-dispersal weapon, intended less to disable than to force a squadron to scatter. Having abandoned formation, they would then be picked off at will by maser fire and guided asp missiles.

In practice, the idea that a single Y31 could face down a full, six-strong squadron of experienced paramilitary flyers and expect to prevail with textbook manoeuvres was naïve, bordering on ludicrous. The pilot of Bandit 2 was recently spellbound, Jean realised; whoever they were, they were possessed by the same heady euphoria she had known when she had been within the Collective. It was that same euphoria, that sense of immortality that had led her to get into a fistfight with Dave Manderly when she was close to exhaustion. The same overconfidence that had led her to lose.

The asp missiles came, and she was ready for them. Their targeting protocols hadn't been exposed to anything more than incremental firmware upgrades in the time she'd been away; to her eye, their trajectories looked like a first-time chess player trying to lure their opponent into a scholar's mate. A carefully timed hard deceleration led the one marked for the *Melinda* to soar harmlessly by, missing its two-klick proximity trigger by a healthy margin. In her head, Jean offered a silent apology to the spellbound pilot, and returned fire in kind. Of the four asps she launched, two of them found their way inside their proximity trigger. The burst of shrapnel and flechettes reduced Bandit 2 to a loosely associated cloud of metal and fibreglass on a trajectory that would lead it to burn up in the thermosphere in a few hours.

A cluster of similar flares of light in the surrounding few thousand cubic klicks told her that other such engagements had resolved themselves in concert with hers. **Squadron leaders, report**, she ordered.

Bandit 3 destroyed. No casualties, came the report from the western flank.

Bandit 7 down, came Velasquez's report. **One casualty – *Typhon* caught a dovetail pellet. Sheer bad luck. Everyone else accounted for.**

Acknowledged, *Belladonna*. Resume original heading and get after them.

About that…

The Collective's craft had split up. Her HUD showed individual warp signatures pulling away from each other in erratic directions; all ascending to higher reaches of orbit at punishing accelerations, but dispersing across apparently random longitudinal and latitudinal bearings. She counted twelve bandits remaining.

New plan, Jean observed. **They want to draw us off on a wild goose chase, spread the odds of one of them slipping the net and reaching the Body before we do.**

So call their bluff, CO, Velasquez replied. **Head straight for the Moon and ignore them. They'll expect that too. If we take the shortest route to the**

Body, they'll re-converge and flank us, now they've seen they can't take us head-to-head. She mused for a second longer, weighing the odds.

Squadron leaders *Belladonna, Colossus* **and** *Ariadne,* she wrote, deciding. Those were Captains Velasquez and Zikri, and Lieutenant Bezzerides. She had singled out their service records as having the greatest aptitude for spatial combat among all the personnel at her disposal. **You'll pursue the remaining bandits. Disperse your squadrons as necessary, but remain in radio contact at all times, and be careful. Everyone else, on me. Brace yourselves, we're resuming the hard g's.**

***

Little by little, the Moon swelled in the front of her vision, and continued swelling. Geological features in its face that barely registered as a pixel from groundside proved to be ridges and divots as wide and deep as the English Channel. Its gravity – the same gravity that gave Earth's oceans their tides – started making itself known to the *Melinda's* handling, first faintly, then with progressively greater insistence.

A transmission came through from Albrecht. The main sortie against the Brazilian station had begun, 200,000 kilometres below them. Light took almost a full second to reach her from geosynchronous orbit. The two-second lag that resulted was just enough to throw off the natural rhythms of conversation.

'CO.' Jean chose to interpret Albrecht's typically unreadable intonation in a no-news-is-good-news sort of way. 'You should be aware that there are more Collective vessels headed your way, in far greater numbers this time. Some fighter planes, some civilian craft launching from the surface that are bypassing the Brazilian elevator entirely. There are too many for us to shoot down – you'll need to deal with them as and when they arrive.'

'Appreciate the heads up, Captain,' Jean replied. She was now pulling only a modest 8 g's, and the pounds per square inch being exerted on her body had slackened enough for her to be able to talk. 'How's the operation proceeding at your end?'

'We penetrated their lines of defence after the nukes went off. Set up multiple breaching points around the ring of the particle accelerator – plenty of good surface area there to make use of.'

'Assuming they don't turn the damn thing on while your people are inside. Even individual atoms of lead or uranium can do serious damage when they're moving within a fraction of a percent of c.'

'I wouldn't worry about that, CO. Preliminary X-ray scans show that the equipment powering the particle accelerator has been disassembled and moved to the core of the station, to boost the effect of their device. Tactically, the Collective is well fortified, right at the centre of a wheel-and-spoke pattern. Every corner and aperture works against us.'

'Exercise extreme caution. The Collective essentially works to a kind of extreme utilitarianism. It will avoid casualties on either side, right up to the point where it thinks casualties are the only way to ensure its continued existence. Past that point, the spellbound will fight like rabid dogs.'

'Roger that. I'll keep you hooked into a real-time feed of the operation as it progresses. T-minus three minutes until the breach. How's it going at your end?'

Jean consulted the field reports from her squadron leaders, chasing the scattered bandits hither and yon across high orbit. Six of them seemed to be bound for the poles with no return forthcoming; two of the others had headed west and east. The remaining four were the ones that concerned her; they had reached the surface of the Moon, and were now hugging its surface as closely as the Y31s' quantum fluctuation drives would allow against the pull of lunar gravity. Fighters from the *Belladonna, Colossus* and *Ariadne* squadrons fought to keep up; the bandits kept dipping in and out of visual contact, intermittently hidden behind the Moon's horizon.

'I'm working on it,' Jean summarised. 'Just keep an eye on your people for now. The next few minutes will be critical.'

***

The breaching of the particle accelerator was relayed to Jean through three-dozen sets of eyes divided among four teams (she fought down the sense of *deja vu* harkening back to the events of December 3rd). The shaped charges arranged on the structure's exterior were detonated in unison, creating roughly circular holes wide enough to admit the intruders, bulky as they were with their matte-black, armoured environment suits and heavy flechette cannons.

They waited a few seconds for the air to gust out as the structure depressurised before moving in.

The techniques the squads used were familiar to Jean from when they were still being devised, the time when she had led the assault on the Silva cartel; create as many environmental ruptures as possible, taxing the enemy's life support systems on multiple fronts while also forcing them to spread out across their controlled territory.

The accelerator's lighting had been cut, rendering the torus interior pitch-black on the visible spectrum. The breaching squads switched over to night-vision, the interior loop being dimly illuminated in shades of sickly green in the feeds Jean was receiving.

Of the four teams, designated Victor, Yankee, Tango and Zulu, the first of these had their uplink immediately severed as soon as their leader made his way through the hole. The feed automatically transferred to his second-in-command, affording Jean the grisly view of him floating back out the way he had entered, or what was left of him. His torso had been riddled with flechettes; his impact-resistant armour had repelled most of the super-fine projectiles, but at such close range (the shooter couldn't have been more than a few metres from the breach hole), they had found the weak points in his armour's joints and exterior lenses. If the flechettes themselves didn't kill him, he would be quickly finished off by the ruptures in his suit exposing his skin to vacuum.

'Shit, Benjamin's been hit!' his second-in-command cried.

'Lay down suppressing fire,' Albrecht responded. 'Team Zulu, you're closest; follow the torus sixty degrees to counter-spinward, back Team Victor up from inside. Once the torus has been secured, form up at the southern corridor.'

Jean bit her tongue. She was tempted to countermand Albrecht's textbook approach to a breach-and-clear scenario, which saw the intruders consolidating their gained territory one corridor and room at a time, watching each other's backs all the while. Correct procedure for a cartel raid; less so, she thought, when the future of the world hung in the balance. If Team Victor could draw the Collective's fire at the rim of the station, then they might free up the other teams to reach the core unmolested. Albrecht, she knew, wasn't a gambler by nature; zero-sum situations made him uneasy.

She didn't voice any of these thoughts aloud. With two seconds' delay in any feedback she could give, her reactions to what was going on in the station would be too laggy to be of much use. Even if that weren't the case, there were few things more counterproductive for a soldier than to be exposed to two sets of conflicting orders during a combat operation. She had set up this chain of command, so she would respect it, and place her faith in Albrecht to see the operation through.

'Acknowledged, CO. We're on our way.' The response to Albrecht's order came from the leader of Team Zulu, one Captain Arquette; the officer who had twice challenged Jean in the briefing. The one who instinctively saw no issue with destroying the Enclave Effect device, despite the unimaginable fallout that would result.

Her presence in the breach operation made Jean much more nervous than Albrecht's orders did, for precisely the opposite reason.

***

The fighting for control of the Brazilian station was fierce, and bloody, and underhanded on both sides. The Collective had entrenched itself at the coreward end of every corridor, access hatch, and air duct between the outermost torus and the device. Liberal application of explosives was off the table on both sides; a grenade tossed along an unlucky trajectory ran the risk of destabilising the station's equilibrium and sending it into a decaying orbit, which would raise a whole new set of problems. As such, the battle for the future played out in a series of room-to-room firefights.

Albrecht's Y24 (he was as old-school as Jean was) was parked a thousand klicks away from the action, from which vantage he directed his teams' movements, unaffected by the terror and stress of the muzzle flashes and maser beams permeating the station's dark interior. All four of his teams suffered losses. They encountered booby-traps; laser tripwires that released jets of scalding steam; remotely activated digital viruses that targeted their suits' life support systems. And at every bulkhead, the Collective had dug in with jury-rigged defence platforms, each teeming with the largest-calibre weaponry they could risk deploying without being certain it would throw the whole station off its axis. Jean was startled when the Tango team leader rounded the corner into the southern corridor linking the outer torus to the inner, and was immediately struck by a series of rounds from a mounted anti-materiel rifle. His body armour dampened the impacts enough that he lived, but he was taken out of commission and forced to fall back, his ribs and breastbone not so much broken as powdered.

Every enemy strategy they encountered, Albrecht took stock of and incorporated into his contingencies for the next room, co-ordinating the four teams' progress as carefully and methodically as game pieces. Not much of a gambler, it was true, but an incredible multi-tasker; he did all of this while simultaneously managing the squadrons remaining outside the base, preventing any more Collective forces from docking and joining up with their friends.

Steadily, the centripetal gravity of the outer torus gave way to the microgravity of the inner station. Reconnaissance had suggested that the device would be located in the main hangar bay, the only space in the station large enough to contain both it and the additional equipment needed to boost its signal.

Their suspicions were proven accurate when Team Zulu's approach to the connecting passageway was cut short. The entry hatch was blown outward; ten-centimetre-thick titanium burst apart in the shape of an opening flower's petals. The projectile that penetrated it left a discharge of static electricity in its wake. Looking through Captain Arquette's eyes, Jean winced at the sight of one of the soldiers under her command, identified as a Private Zierler, who had been laterally bisected by the blast.

'Jesus. That's a fucking railgun,' Arquette sounded almost awed at the brazenness of using such ordnance indoors.

'Do not approach, Zulu leader,' Albrecht ordered. 'Link up with Team Victor and find an alternative route to the objective.' Another depleted uranium round ripped through the corridor, preventing the teams from advancing any further.

'No point, CO,' Arquette replied. 'Four entrances to the hangar, north, south, east and west, same as on the Kisangani station. It looked like a shot from one of the Y31's cannons, so they're probably detaching them from the craft in the hangar. They'll have all four entrances covered the same way. We get through this way, or not at all.' She looked down at her own chest; Jean didn't get a clear view, but she unclipped something the size of a fist from her armour's utility belts. New holes were being blown in the surrounding station architecture around her every few seconds, as quickly as the railgun could recharge.

'Captain, don't tell me that's what I think it is,' Albrecht's tone was level, but dangerous. 'The use of EMP devices is prohibited. If it interferes with the power supply to the device and the Effect is disrupted, the mission is a failure. Find another way.'

'It has a highly limited radius of effect, less than ten metres,' Arquette was carrying on as though she hadn't heard her CO. 'Should be enough to force the railgun to reboot. The device won't be affected.'

'Captain, this is an order, *do not* —'

Arquette, having gained a feel for the shots' rhythm, timed her overarm throw perfectly to take advantage of the weapon's refractory period. The EMP grenade sailed down the forty metres of corridor straight and true, with accuracy and speed that would have done a major-league baseball pitcher proud. For a few seconds, Jean's heart stopped.

The rhythm of the railgun's fusillade was interrupted, to be replaced with a torrent of retaliatory flechette and maser fire from Team Zulu. When the storm of transmissions that would have indicated the collapse of the Americas didn't manifest itself, she allowed herself to breathe again.

'Captain Arquette,' Albrecht said, 'that last stunt will appear in my report when this is over. I will see to it that you are court-martialled and held to account in a criminal tribunal. For now, finish your job.'

'Roger that, CO,' answered Arquette, who could scarcely have sounded less concerned.

***

We have a problem, *Melinda,* a transmission from Velasquez jerked Jean's attention back to Lunar orbit and her immediate surroundings. *Ariadne* **Squadron lost track of Bandit 4 above the Mare Nectaris. It pulled some kind of insane high-g deceleration manoeuvre; by all rights it should have**

knocked the pilot out. It put itself between the pursuing planes and the sun and then killed its drive. Visual contact lost; no warp signature to speak of. We have no idea where it is.

Roger that, *Belladonna*, Jean answered. At the very least, we know where it's going. Keep your eyes and ears open. Same goes for everyone else; keep your railguns warmed up and in roving mode, and be on the lookout for Bandit 4 approaching on an unknown vector.

A chorus of **Rogers** came from her full unit. The *Melinda* and the three accompanying planes in her squadron were now parked in high lunar orbit, following the equator eastward (east relative to the Moon, that was, which was west in terrestrial terms; the *Melinda* reoriented its guidance systems to a lunar frame of reference when the effects of its gravity kicked in). In a matter of minutes, they would round the corner to the Dark Side.

The plan at that point was to park themselves in a synchronous orbit above the Body, and remain there with every asp missile remaining to them trained on the alien creature where it lay. It was a tenuous position to place themselves in, but it was a foundation they could consolidate later. If they could hold the Collective's holy grail to ransom in the short term, then there was a chance that the situation groundside could be stabilised. If they could do so in concert with the capture of the Brazilian station, then the bargaining position of humanity's remaining governments would be all the stronger.

200,000 kilometres below, the breach teams had broken the back of the Collective's resistance; the fighting had proceeded to the main hangar bay, where the remaining spellbound were mounting a desperate but ferocious final stand.

The hangar was open to space, its aperture directed toward the surface of the Earth; South and Central America sprawled beneath. Ensconced in a scaffold hastily welded to the walls of the hangar and pointed groundward, there sat the smuggled Enclave device.

Jean was, of course, familiar with what Xavier Wong's creations looked like from her time as part of the Collective; she had seen them during her proxy inhabitation of the minds in the Yang-Mitsubishi offices where they had been erected. At the time, her perception of the machines had been coloured by the hive-mind's awe and reverence for them as the crucible of their salvation.

Seeing this one by means of an ordinary audiovisual feed, she was struck by how inconspicuous a piece of equipment it was, for all the lives it held sway over. The paired-particle generator was a regular icosahedron of composite metal panels, no more than four metres in diameter, mounted on a podium that served as its control unit. In atmosphere, it would have generated a faint hum of particles that would flood its surroundings; in vacuum, there was no outward evidence of its numinous power.

The transmitter mast that had been constructed around it, by contrast, dominated the cavernous space of the hangar bay, an enormous pylon fed by thick cabling that had been wrenched from the surrounding superstructure. The arrangement created the impression of a mechanical parasite, embedded in the tissue of the Brazilian station and leeching off its energy. The power consumption necessary to continually blanket the surface area of two continents with tuned gamma particles boggled the mind.

In the presence of the device, neither its defenders nor the breach team were willing to risk the use of projectile weapons. They resorted to hand-to-hand combat, both sides making use of microvibrating knives.

In the decades since ORC had been established, interpersonal combat conducted in microgravity and in vacuum had developed its own set of principles that had been honed and refined, and were now drilled relentlessly by every fledgling cadet in the Corps. What had started as a grab-bag of techniques derived from Sambo, Krav Maga, *Pencak Silat*, and Brazilian Jiu Jitsu had alchemised into their own art form, specialising not in breaking joints or exploiting pressure points, but in finding and guarding against the weaknesses in armoured environment suits; using edged weapons to expose your opponent to vacuum, and defending against attempts to do the same.

Jean had selected the 36 members of the breach teams, in part, for the superior proficiency in these techniques mentioned in their personnel files, and in the melee that ensued, she saw that her decisions had been the right ones. There were casualties on both sides, and the breach team were outnumbered two-to-one. But despite the intruders' tiredness, despite their stress, and despite the pain tolerance the Collective conferred upon the spellbound, for every one of their number who fell, they dispatched more than three defenders. After several long, frenzied minutes, they won.

***

Arquette ripped her combat knife free from where she'd plunged it into the Collective's final defender, into the nest of blood vessels in his armpit. The atmosphere in the assimilate's suit escaped through the puncture in a crimson plume, the force of it sending him cartwheeling uncontrollably through the space according to Newton's second law. He jerked and spasmed, struggling to right himself, until his back collided with the central pylon hard enough to break his spine.

She heaved a sigh, and voiced her report to Albrecht, who forwarded it to Jean a light-second away. 'All hostiles eliminated. Hangar is secure.'

'Affirmative, Captain,' Albrecht replied. His toneless voice offered no hint of either reproach or relief. 'Get those charges set, double time. There's been a change in the movement of the Collective craft outside, they're becoming agitated. I need our position fortified before any further complications arise.'

'Roger that,' answered Arquette, a note of bitterness in her words. She looked around, taking stock of the survivors. Eight members of the breach teams remained, picking their way around the corpses now drifting listlessly around the hangar. Eight, out of an original thirty-six; barely twenty percent. There had been a time a casualty ratio like that would have made Jean sick. Now, it made her sick that she felt relieved.

'We'll take care of the bombs, CO,' Arquette said. 'You get to work on the ultimatum.'

'Affirmative.' Albrecht took a moment to comport himself, seemingly unaware of how well-suited he was to be issuing a ransom demand. An inspiring public speaker he was not, as Jean knew, but she could imagine no-one better to issue a threat to a quarter of the globe.

'This is Commander Hermann Albrecht, addressing the so-called "Collective of Humankind",' he announced at last, directing his transmission on an open frequency to any device able to receive it. 'On behalf of the Pan-National Coalition and the nine billion remaining unassimilated human beings, we do not submit to your control. The indoctrination mechanism housed in the Brazilian space elevator terminus has been captured and will be destroyed if you fail to comply with our demands. Your forces will stand down and await further communication from the PNC, regarding the conditions of a ceasefire and de-escalation of tensions. Any further incursions on your part beyond the boundaries of minus-thirty degrees of longitude to the east and minus-one-hundred- and twenty-five-degrees longitude to the west, whether by land, sea, air, or orbit, will be treated as a failure to comply, and met with appropriate reprisal. Further combat engagement with our personnel in Earth or lunar orbit will be treated as non-compliance. The erection of backup Enclave Effect generators on the ground will be treated as non-compliance.'

***

Three long minutes passed with Albrecht's demands going unanswered. The task of setting and programming the bombs was laborious for the remaining breach team personnel. The charges had been carried by the members who had been killed during the fighting, and had to be fished from the utility belts hanging off their corpses, a task that would be unpleasant in any circumstances, made especially awkward in microgravity.

Arquette was in the process of attaching the first charge to the exterior of the device with foam epoxy when she and it were shaken loose by a violent reverberation in the station. 'What the hell was that?' she said aloud.

'A spellbound civilian craft just collided with the outer torus,' Albrecht replied. His voice sounded slightly fraught, which Jean found alarming; 'slightly' fraught for Albrecht corresponded to 'extremely' fraught by anyone else's standards. 'Brace for further impacts, there are more like it inbound.'

'Why would they... aren't you shooting them down when they get close?'

'Of course, but their movement patterns have completely changed. They're no longer attempting evasive manoeuvres; just barrelling towards the station like we aren't here.'

Another impact, harsher than the first. 'I don't understand,' Arquette said. 'They're going to knock the station off its axis at this rate. I thought that was what they were trying to prevent.'

Contact.

The transmission from Velasquez cut through the drama unfolding in terrestrial orbit.

Bandit 4 just blew right past us, heading north. Christ, he must be pulling 17.5g's. He's heading right for you, CO.

The warning from the *Belladonna* scarcely had time to register before the *Melinda's* sensors flagged a livid warp signature, with visual contact following seconds later. Bandit 4 had abandoned the stealthy approach. Its vector was incomprehensible to her targeting systems; it zig-zagged through space, making sudden shifts in direction that ought to cause any human pilot to vomit, black out, or both.

A volley of dovetail missiles screamed towards her squadron, forcing her to pull a hard 8-g acceleration to escape the spread of hyper-fast pellets. She escaped their radius, just; one of her squadron-mates was less fortunate, half-a-dozen of the tungsten ball-bearings ripping his plane apart and throwing what remained towards the surface of the Moon. Bandit 4 blew past them, too quickly to be seen by the naked eye.

The *Melinda* alerted her to a transmission coming from the direction of Earth; like the Collective's first announcement, it was being broadcast from all across North America, the sight of which was now disappearing behind the curve of the Moon's surface. The image being transmitted was again the visage of Morton Prowse; unlike last time, his expression wasn't one of euphoria, but of barely contained rage. 'To Commander Hermann Albrecht,' he intoned, his voice composed but his face taut. 'The Collective of Humanity hears your ultimatum, and elects to disregard it. Our cause is righteous, and our goal is noble. We represent the elevation of humanity to a better, more enlightened state; we cannot and will not be dissuaded of this cause by threats of force, any more than you would consent to be dragged back into the primordial soup to exist as amoebae. Other Enclave Effect generators exist on the Earth's surface. More are being created hourly. Our proliferation will continue, even if you are willing to allow the unprecedented suffering that the severance of two billion will create. We will not bow to your will, not now, not ever.'

The transmission ended.

CO, this doesn't make any sense, Velasquez implored. **There's no way they'd let us wipe them out, is there?**

Jean didn't reply immediately. She realised, too late, her fatal mistake.

The Collective was, in effect, a macro-organism, the accretion of all the minds belonging to it. The spellbound, its individual members, responded to external stimuli according to the cumulative emotional state of the entire organism. When she had been a part of that organism, the emotional state she had experienced was the default euphoria, the giddy revelation that she was no longer alone inside her head, that there were now others who knew her as well as she knew herself. That feeling created a feedback loop, compounding and intensifying itself the more members the macro-organism added.

What she had failed to anticipate was that there was more than one state of mind that could be compounded by that feedback loop mechanism. The Collective had *moods*.

Not in the sense that individuals had moods; human instances of happiness or sadness or fear or excitement were transitory, effervescent things, brief flare-ups of certain chemicals in certain corners of the brain. The Collective had moods in the way the Earth had changes in its environment, like the ocean's transition from El Niño to La Niña, or the beginning or ending of an ice age. Their onset was not prompted easily, but their effect was lasting and transformative.

And now, the Collective was angry. Albrecht had prompted the fury of two billion people, organised as though they were one; and right now, that wrath was compounding and intensifying itself, whipping itself into a frenzy that could boil oceans and crack continents.

She had imagined that the Collective would respond rationally to their ransom, their demand for a ceasefire. She had been mistaken. The Collective, in a state of anger, would gladly cut off its nose to spite its face. She had sought to emulate the mutually unacceptable failure state that had seen the world through the Cold War. Instead, she had recreated the Cuban Missile Crisis.

'They're calling our bluff,' said Arquette, back on the Brazilian station. 'CO, I can end this right now. Say the word, and I'll destroy this goddamned machine right now.'

'Negative,' Albrecht replied, a split second ahead of Jean's rather more emphatic '*no!*'

'CO, the bastards are boarding us. I can see the heat signatures of the bodies coming our way through the station. They're forcing our hand; so fucking be it, we've been forced.'

'Captain Arquette,' Jean said, forcing herself into the exchange. Chain of command be damned, she wasn't going to let this happen quietly. 'Do not, I repeat, *do not* take any action that will damage the Enclave generator. Remember, we still have our ace-in-the-hole. I am minutes away from having the Body in my crosshairs. The Collective might consider the device expendable, but the Body is irreplaceable to them. When we have captured the Body, they will back down, I guarantee it.'

Two seconds' lag before she received a response. Within that brief window, Bandit 4 reappeared on her monitor. Six asp missiles launched toward her squadron at blistering speed. She dove to avoid them, only to discover it hadn't been her in the crosshairs, but her two remaining wingmates. Bandit 4 swooped past her once again, her keel-mounted railgun's automatic return fire missing by a pathetically wide margin.

'You're tilting at windmills Harrison, any sane person would realise that.' Jean couldn't see the sneer on Arquette's face, but she knew it was there. 'They're not backing down when we threaten to destroy them completely; you think they'll back down if we threaten their religious icon? Don't make me laugh.'

'Think about this, Arquette. You're talking about having the deaths of two billion people on your hands. Two billion *bad* deaths. Entrench your team where you are now, hold the spellbound boarders off. The moment I have a target lock on the Body, we've won. No-one else needs to die.'

Two seconds' lag.

Bandit 4 had tasted blood in the water; it executed a stomach-turning braking manoeuvre, flipping and accelerating back toward the *Melinda* in a near-instantaneous reversal of momentum that appeared to defy the laws of physics. Never mind what it must have been doing to the pilot; the Y31 itself was ill-equipped to handle those sorts of stresses. Another few moves like that and the svelte craft would tear itself apart.

'I'm talking about saving the human race, Harrison. We'll never get this chance again; if we let it slip through our fingers now, they'll dig in with backup Effect generators on the ground and we'll never prise them loose. I know the thought of your old friends dying breaks you up, but if you can't be trusted to do what's necessary, I will. Albrecht can lock me up after, I don't care.'

Arquette cancelled her transmission.

Bandit 4 released all of its remaining ordnance straight at the *Melinda*; four dovetails and two asps. Jean tabbed over to the viewpoint of the single surviving member of Team Yankee – in the feed coming from his viewpoint (one all-important second behind real-time), she saw Arquette unholstering her maser cannon, her gaze fixed on the Effect generator.

Jean made a snap judgement. Any evasive manoeuvre she could take now would be well in excess of 15 g's. The pressure would mean it would take several seconds longer than she had to send the transmission she needed to send.

She remembered the names and personnel files of each of the surviving breach team members and settled on the one she judged would be least likely to hesitate. Private Gunther Gershwin, the junior of the two Tango survivors; he was an American family man who had been stationed in Kisangani when everything had kicked off. Three surviving grandparents and both parents, a wife, a young daughter and a second child on the way - all of them currently among the two billion spellbound.

'Private Gershwin,' Jean shouted. 'Shoot Captain Arquette. If you value your family's lives, SHOOT HER!'

Two seconds of lag – one for her transmission to reach its mark, one for his response to return to her. Immediately after her final screamed syllable, she hauled the *Melinda* forward and downward in a nosedive toward the lunar surface, praying the gravity well would work in her favour against the asps' guidance systems. She eluded the dispersion cone of the dovetail pellets by the skin of her teeth; despite the vacuum surrounding the plane, she swore she could imagine a high-pitched whistle as the closest of them passed by her, mere metres away.

One of the asps sailed harmlessly by, the *Melinda* avoiding its proximity triggers by a similarly fine margin.

Unfortunately, in a dogfight, it's the 0.01% of shots that connect that matter, not the 99.99% that miss.

The other asp found its way inside the two-klick radius that indicated to its guidance systems that their work was done. The concussion and the accompanying shrapnel hit the *Melinda* from behind like a freight train. Its QF drive was mangled; its wings were torn off; its electrics haemorrhaged and died. The Y24's ruined corpse plummeted to the surface of the dark side of the Moon.

In the last split-second before Jean's head impacted the console, hard enough to crack her suit visor and knock her out cold, the last image her eyes beheld was of Private Gershwin drawing his sidearm and emptying its clip into Captain Arquette.

Chapter 23

August 30th, 2326 C.E.

Jonah's voyage to Earth passed with little enough incident that it made him vaguely rueful. After all the blood, sweat, and tears that had been shed on the outward journey to TransTerra, the return journey was treated by his hosts as no more consequential or troublesome than a leisure cruise across the Pacific. He spent his days alternately resting, reading, exercising, and eating.

After two weeks, he had regained the weight he had lost following the ordeals of the Mercanta Steppe. Another week, and he had begun to overshoot the mark, developing – to his surprise – the beginnings of an unwelcome paunch. He tried thereafter to rein in his caloric intake, asking for the portion sizes of the rich food the Collective plied him with to be cut down. He would soon be back in terrestrial gravity again; he wanted to keep as much weight off his bad leg as he could.

When the troop transport bearing them made its first trip along the quantum relays, from Upsilon to Sigma, the effect startled him. It was neither pleasant nor painful; the impression the transit created was of going from total lucidity to utter unconsciousness in an instant, one state giving way to the other with the immediacy of a switch being flipped. Then, with the same suddenness, consciousness returned to him, leaving him awake and alert as he had been beforehand, with no sense of any length of time having passed.

Having it explained to him how the relays functioned, with matter being analysed at one end and reconstituted at the other, caused Jonah no small amount of agitation in the days that followed. It was one thing to know that he had thrown himself upon the mercy of the Collective; it was quite another to imagine that he had bequeathed to it the right to obliterate and remake what he was, molecule-for-molecule. His memory told him that he had left his friends and his crew on the FOB, that he had come here of his own free will. But what if his captors had dragged him, kicking and screaming, and the relay had reconstructed him with just the tiniest alteration to his synaptic configuration? What if his remanufactured grey matter was telling him he was a willing participant, when in fact he was a prisoner?

In time, he concluded that he was too old for epistemological angst. That it was possible such an idea could have been built into him by his hosts was, itself, encompassed in the idea (here, Jonah recalled what Victoria had said about framing complex thoughts as a dialogue with oneself).

He had had sufficiently many occasions in his life to ponder, 'how did I get here?' Enough instances to imagine what might have been had he chosen a different course. That line of thinking was a rabbit's warren; no more productive than wondering if you were the same person when you woke up in the morning as you had been when you went to bed the previous night. He knew who he was, and what he thought, however he had arrived at that point. That would have to do.

There were two further relay transits separating them from the solar system beyond Sigma, each separated by a little over a week of sub-light speed travel at a gentle half-g burn. It was in this time that Jonah became reacquainted with Alyssa.

She visited him in his quarters the day after the transit from Sigma. The difference in her from the girl he remembered pre-assimilation was striking, now that she was making no attempt to conceal it. The Alyssa he had known had been every inch a teenager; nervy, volatile, prone to flights of whimsy and passion. This Alyssa wore the same face, and could call upon the same memories, but her temperament couldn't have been more distinct. She was courteous yet reserved; familiar, but distant. She seldom moved her head or her hands when she wasn't using them to demonstrate a point. She blinked less often than seemed appropriate. In all of these regards, and a thousand other tiny ones that hovered on the threshold of perception, she reminded Jonah of an Archangel. He was only grateful that she didn't wear that damnable, mask-like smile the other assimilates all shared. Perhaps the Collective, in its wisdom, had realised the sight of it on his granddaughter's face would make him uncomfortable.

'I was starting to think you'd never show,' Jonah said, doing his best to appear as though he had his emotions about her in check. 'I'm glad you did.'

'Well, it was on your list of demands,' she retorted.

'Even so. I'd hoped we might have a chance to speak, properly, without guns on both sides.'

'Guns the Insurgency brought to bear.'

'Hence why I'm here, and they're not. Please, will you sit with me a moment?' While the carrier was under thrust, they were able to make use of the basic furniture bolted to the surface in the direction that temporarily constituted "down." He gestured to a table and two cushioned chairs arranged at the foot of his bunk. Alyssa shrugged, and settled into one of them. Jonah lowered himself gingerly into the other. When she didn't appear to be forthcoming after a few seconds, he tried to say his piece.

'I made some accusations, back on the FOB,' he said. 'I was coming from a position of ignorance, and after what happened there... after the things you told me... I'm not sure any more what I believe, or who. You said that you'd approached the Insurgency in the past with white flags flying, but that they refused to listen. Well, here I am, white flag on full display. Please, help me understand what the Collective really is.'

'What is it you think the Collective is?'

'What I *thought* it was, was a parasite. An alien mind that hollowed out its hosts and replaced them replicas. Imitations that walked and talked like the originals, but whose minds were those of the alien.'

'And you think this because Victoria told you?'

'Right. You heard the same speech that I did. Or did you? You look like Lys, but at the very least, I think we can agree that there's something different about you. So, who am I addressing just now? My granddaughter? Or the Collective?'

'Both,' she answered, immediately. 'There isn't a distinction to be made.'

'What do you mean?'

'Think about it. Even you aren't an island, Jonah. You were a British citizen. You were in the Merantau Program. You were married. The nation of Great Britain; the Merantau Program; a marriage; those are all organisations of people, just on different scales. Every individual within them adds to them, becomes a part of what defines them. But the organisation takes on its own character, and its own dimensions, separate from the individuals that comprise it. And in turn, the identity of the whole colours the identity of its members. It's a two-way street. I am the Collective, in the same sense that you were a citizen, or an officer, or a husband.'

In her tally of the bonds Jonah had formed in his life, he noted that *grandfather* was absent. 'So, you're telling me The Collective is a nation? Nothing more complex than that?'

'The Collective is a nation, sure. At the same time, it's a religion, and a family, and a group project, and a party. It's a confessional sacrament and a sexual tryst. It's all things to all people; the Omega point of human belonging. The free exchange of thought and sensation via the use of paired particles makes assimilates entirely transparent to one another. There are no secrets between us, and no taboos. When you have access to one another's deepest thoughts and impressions, "selfhood" becomes an obsolete concept. Like a printing press in the age of the parallel processor.'

'You don't talk like Alyssa,' Jonah observed. 'Is this network of minds you're connected to furnishing all of these colourful metaphors?'

She smirked. 'You're starting to get it,' she said.

'One thing I want to know, though,' Jonah pressed. 'Alyssa saw… *you* saw your parents die. All of the pain you must have felt at that – was that shared as well? Did you grieve together with a billion strangers?'

'It was what made it bearable. It was what let me survive it.'

'And when I spoke to you later, on the transport, *en route* to the FOB? You told me that you wanted to die, then. About the guilt you felt. The Collective reached you on the surface, so you were already assimilated by then. Was that all an act?'

The lack of a reflex in Alyssa's expression confirmed what he had suspected. 'Of course I mourned them. Any life that ends without an opportunity to experience the Collective's revelation is a terrible waste.'

'Is that all?'

Alyssa pursed her lips. 'Jonah, I don't regret what I did. The choice I made in that clearing, I'd make again. Can you say the same? Is there really no regret in your life that you don't want absolved? No pain you wouldn't alleviate if you could?'

***

46 terrestrial days after the evacuation of the FOB on the outer limits of TransTerra's star system, the Collective troop carrier and its Scarab escort materialised in upper Earth orbit, through the Gaia relay, suspended 1.5 million kilometres above the planet's surface at the L2 Lagrange point.

Jonah had his corneal implants tuned to the carrier's exterior cameras within moments of their transit being completed. He didn't know what he expected to see upon his return to his home planet following more than two centuries away. As was so often the case with long-awaited reunions, the aspects that were recognisable were all the more remarkable for what had been transformed.

The first and most obvious change was to the Earth's orbital infrastructure. When the *Prospice* had set out in 2096, a mere two space elevators had been completed; from this altitude, they might have appeared as tremendously fine threads of silk, if they caught the sun from just the right angle. Now though, the Earth appeared to have accrued a ring system; a halo surrounding its equator, dense enough to be perceptible with the naked eye. The structures that had begun as the equatorial space elevators had spread out from their points of anchorage like a cosmic spider's web, strands stretching and splicing together around the planet's horizon. A glimmering megalopolis hung in geosynchronous orbit, engirdling the world.

Zooming in, Jonah could discern some of the symmetry that caused the enormous structure to function. Combinations of equally massed strands at lower and higher elevations, one's more rapid orbit counterbalancing the other's slower. But there were so many, layered atop one another, the strands sub-dividing and ramifying in fractal patterns. He could scarcely comprehend a small part of its multi-dimensional complexity before he began to feel dizzy. The full structure was an astonishing piece of craftsmanship – Jonah wished Eoin had been with him to see it, if only so the old engineer could give him a more educated appreciation of its impossibility.

It saddened him to realise that back in his time, such a construct that flaunted borders and nations and continents would have been doomed from

367

its inception, not just logistically, but politically. A terrorist attack or act of sabotage on any part of the structure, disrupting its equilibrium in even the smallest degree, could have brought the whole edifice crashing down. This orbital halo was an indication of an advanced civilisation in more ways than one. It could only exist in a world where war was an impossibility.

From where they had emerged, they directly overlooked East Asia. The carrier lowered itself gently into cis-lunar orbit, following an eastward course. Slowly, the planet grew beneath them as they circled. Hours passed, during which time they fully circumnavigated the world. The landmasses were as Jonah remembered them from his youth; the long archipelagos of Indonesia and the Philippines; the scattering of Pacific Islands; the hard wall the ocean ran into at the west side of North and South America, extending thousands of kilometres on both sides of the equator, blocking atmospheric and oceanic currents alike. It seemed Middle America was enjoying a hot, dry summer. There was little cloud cover over the continent, and the snowpack in the Rockies and the Cascades was negligible.

In fact, the whole planet appeared healthy. The borders of the Amazon Rainforest, near critical collapse in 2096, had swollen again. The glaciers in Canada and Alaska had been reinvigorated. The globe resembled the most wildly over-optimistic predictive models of the carbon-trapping proponents he recalled from the tail end of the 21st century.

As they descended further, another surprise; as the environment had been revitalised, the teeming cities of the northern hemisphere had receded. Jonah could still pick out the outlines of the Bay Area, Seattle, and Vancouver on the west coast, and of New York, Toronto, and Miami on the east. But in each case, the urban sprawl looked far less extensive than he remembered, the overgrown man-made landscapes having withdrawn like melanomas in remission.

Jonah expected that the carrier would dock with the halo structure eventually; instead, it carried on its eastward course, smartly skirting the ring and making its way beneath the geosynchronous threshold. They made another full circuit of the Earth, passing over Europe, Asia, and the Pacific a second time. The carrier breached the thermosphere over North America, the view from the exterior sensors obscured by the corona of flames. When these lifted, the view outside of the craft placed them under a canopy of deep blue sky, miles of flat land not so unlike the Mercanta Steppe stretching from horizon to horizon, rushing past them at speeds diminishing toward the subsonic.

Jonah's heart jumped. He knew this landscape, better than he knew the gnarled backs of his own hands.

The rolling plains and fields of Stanley County, South Dakota splayed beneath them, divided from northwest to southeast by the Missouri. On the outskirts of Fort Pierre, the carrier finally came to rest on a pristine landing strip a couple of klicks long.

The carrier disgorged its few dozen inhabitants with a hatch-and-ramp arrangement, worthy of a UFO in a cheesy, retro-themed TSI sim. Alyssa, Manderly, and the other assimilates went ahead of Jonah. Disconcertingly, they formed a pair of columns at the base of the ramp, lined up on either side with heads turned expectantly towards him, as though he was a visiting dignitary from a foreign royal court.

To judge from their behaviour, Jonah might have expected to be greeted by a massed crowd of thousands gathered on the Stanley County plains. But only one newcomer appeared to be there to greet him. The lone figure waiting there saw Jonah tarrying at the head of the ramp, and beckoned him down. Jonah obligingly approached.

The figure resolved itself as he drew closer; it was a man, he saw. White; about his own height, though slimmer than he; middle-aged, by pre-telomerase standards, with a creasing face and grey hair receding towards a widow's peak, though his upright posture and steady stride suggested he was in good health. Unlike most of the assimilates he had come to know on the carrier, by face if not by name, this man didn't appear to boast any augmentation, and was dressed in a perfectly nondescript shirt and jeans that wouldn't have looked out of place in the 20th century. The man's apparent plainness was the oddest thing about the whole scenario. And there was something else Jonah couldn't put his finger on about him – a familiarity that seemed somehow of a piece with the memories evoked just by seeing his childhood home again.

'Well, the Starman falls to Earth at last.' the man announced. His accent, incongruously, was London English. 'No, I take that back. You never cared much for that name, did you, grandfather?'

369

Jonah's breath caught. The sense of familiarity he felt upon seeing this man resolved itself; he saw in him an echo of his own facial features; the same prominent brow and deep-set eyes and heavy jaw. He could see in him the emergent result of the boy he'd seen in the periodic video messages sent from Earth, who he'd watched become a man in monthly increments until the severance of contact. Jean's son, and Victoria's brother.

'James?' The name fell out of him as he allowed himself to exhale. 'You've grown.'

***

Fort Pierre was a little more than three klicks from where they had landed. James suggested that he request a carriage to bear them to the old farmhouse, but Jonah declined. He did, however, accept the use of the walking cane he was offered. His limp was pronounced without it, and even with it, his leg started to throb before they had walked half a klick. He didn't particularly mind; James matched his slow pace, and he needed the time to adjust to his surroundings. Everything about the landscape, from the muddy, muggy smell blowing in from the Missouri, to the particular quality of the heat from the late-August sun beaming down from a cloudless sky; the specific hummocks and divots in the fields his parents had given him free reign to play in on weekends; the specific trees disrupting the regularity of the horizon; the colour and quality of the flattened grass and earth on the beaten path they followed south from the landing pad. They added up to a nostalgia so powerful it bordered on vertigo.

Jonah was unaccustomed to homecomings. His life, for as far back as he could remember, had been characterised by relentless movement, interrupted by only temporary pauses for breath. He was struck by the disconcerting sense that his childhood had never ended; that he was still seven years old, and that everything that had transpired since he had left this place had been an unusually long and vivid dream. His service in the RAF; his marriage to Astrid and becoming a father; the voyage on the *Prospice* and the loss of contact with Earth; the establishment of the settlement on TransTerra and the nightmare of aliens and monsters that had uprooted it; all of it took on the quality of an apparition here, the figures who populated it hazy and unreal.

Irrational and stupid feelings, he knew; more than that, he was quite certain that the Collective had chosen this place to land to elicit exactly these feelings.

The same reason that it had selected Victoria's brother as its representative to greet him upon arrival. Its overtures to his better nature were far from subtle. He fought with himself, trying to maintain perspective. His hosts were trying to sway him, because they needed something specific from him. Knowing that he was on the receiving end of a sales pitch made him wary.

'You live around here?' Jonah asked, in an attempt to break the ice. James gestured vaguely toward the east. Looking the way he pointed, Jonah could make out a small cluster of one- and two-storey structures in the distance.

'I've stayed there for the last twenty years or so. It's a small commune, only two hundred assimilates or so at any given time. People drift in and out from year to year, according to the Collective's moods.'

'Not you, though?'

'Not me.'

'I seem to remember your mother took you and your sister to visit here, once or twice, when you were kids. You still feel an attachment to this place, is that it?'

James gave him a small smile. 'I'm an assimilate, grandfather. I don't look to specific places for a sense of contentment or belonging. The Earth is covered with my brothers and sisters; anywhere they reside, I can call home just as easily. No, the reason I've stayed here as long as I have is because the Collective has been anticipating your return for a long time. It took us a great deal of time to find the Prospice, after the relay's astrogation data was corrupted; longer still to reach it, with Albrecht's Insurgency delaying us. But we knew that one day, we'd find you, and when you came back to us, you should be met by a familiar face.'

Jonah met his gaze as they walked, uneasy at the implications of what he was saying. 'James,' he asked, 'how many assimilates are party to us talking, right now? How many others are looking through your eyes?'

'Oh, very close to all of us,' James replied, nonchalantly, as though there was nothing remarkable about the notion at all. 'Barring some of the very young, around seven billion, all told.'

Jonah tried to wrap his head around that number and failed. The cognitive dissonance of it was profound. On the one hand, he was strolling with his long-estranged grandson on a balmy August afternoon. On the other, he was holding an audience with an entire species.

'I'm that much of a celebrity, am I?'

'You have no idea.'

They reached the perimeter of the small town of Fort Pierre. Jonah had expected that they might meet other assimilates here, but he was mistaken; the town he remembered had been abandoned, and was well into the process of being reclaimed by two centuries' worth of nature. Streets and buildings were close to unrecognisable beneath the encroachment of vegetation. 'Why would the Collective leave a town like Fort Pierre to decay,' Jonah wondered aloud, 'only to build a commune a few klicks away?'

'Pre-assimilate towns were built with a pre-assimilate mindset,' James replied. 'They were wasteful, even small ones like Fort Pierre. Individualism gives rise to excessive production and consumption; when every person is independently responsible for fulfilling their own wants and needs, food is grown that no one eats. Hydrocarbons are burned to generate power that isn't used, to carry people on journeys to places they don't need to go. Entertainment is produced to distract people from the stress of all their toil, and then half of that goes unread and unwatched. The psychogeography of old human settlements reflect the soul-sickness of the people who constructed them. When the Collective was born, one of its first judgements was that the infrastructure of the world needed to be reoriented. Most of the human race lives in agrarian communes like mine.'

'And yet there are still cities,' Jonah observed. 'I could see them on the descent from orbit. Smaller than they were, granted, but you must still have some use for them.'

'There's still a need for industrial production,' James allowed. 'For as long as we have a presence in space, it can't be completely done away with, though much of the heavy manufacturing has been automated and moved to orbit now. But it's our hope that one day soon, we can do away with these as well.'

Whatever Jonah had expected Collective society to look like, post-industrial agrarianism hadn't been it. Was this really the same culture that had constructed the relays? The Scarabs, for that matter? 'Is that what you need me for? To complete your reversion to some sort of pastoral utopia?'

'Partly.' James stopped walking and turned to face Jonah directly. He gently took hold of Jonah's shoulders, the expression on his face grave. 'Grandfather, you have to understand. Humankind exists in a fallen state. Something went badly wrong with our development after we learned to walk upright. We developed ego. Our intelligence was misdirected, and it twisted us into vulgar, venal creatures, obsessed with power and ownership. Individuals sought to dominate each other's bodies and thoughts, in the same way they sought to dominate the land. We were driven apart from one another. Every societal and technological "advance" we devised, from agriculture, to feudalism, to industrialisation, to computation, served to trap us more completely in our own heads. We entertained the delusion that by virtue of attainment, we might finally feel complete, and we broke ourselves and everything around us, chasing that mirage.

'It took the arrival of the Body to make us understand. Only contact with a real, alien consciousness that developed along different lines from ours made us understand where we had gone wrong so long ago. And now the Collective is close, Jonah. We're so close to rectifying the fundamental error in human cognition. We're still reliant on the Enclave Effect generators to suppress it, but if we can communicate with the Body's passenger, we're confident that we can finally reverse-engineer a totally new and perfect form of consciousness. A true fix, not just a band-aid. Homo Sapiens is on the threshold of Nirvana, and you're the key that will unlock the final gate.'

Jonah was silent for a moment. He gently prised James' hands from his shoulders, which had tightened in the Collective's soteriological fervour. 'If this is something you need so badly,' he said, quietly, 'and I don't want to put ideas in your head, but why haven't you assimilated me by force? Why try to win me over, rather than just unmaking me? What is it you want from me?'

James let go and took an apologetic half-step back. 'Our original sin weighs heavy on our mind,' he said. 'Forcing our revelation on another is too much like an assertion of dominance. It's symptomatic of exactly the kind of egoism we abhor, a pre-assimilate relic. We fear it's this behaviour that closed the Body off to us in the first place. We firmly believe that, in due course, even a non-assimilate will see the righteousness of our cause. In time, you'll see that humanity is better for having followed the Collective's path. We want you to live amongst us. See us at our best, rather than our worst. At your own pace, and at your own discretion, you will help us. We're sure of it, Jonah Harrison.'

Jonah considered. 'I have one precondition,' he said, at length. 'It needs to be met before I'll consider helping you on any terms.'

'Go on.'

'End the conflict with the Insurgency. Completely. Recall every Scarab from deep space. Leave the settlers and the Archangels in peace. TransTerra will be declared a DMZ, and the Merantau settlers will be given safe passage to return and recolonise it. I realise that you hate the thought of leaving other humans beyond your reach forever. Too bad. You have your seven billion. If you want to open the gates to Nirvana, letting a few thousand go is the entry fee.'

James chewed his lip, weighing the proposal. 'It's not a *completely* unreasonable request,' he said, slowly. 'But what makes you think they'd listen? The Insurgency has thrown every attempt we've ever made at parley back in our faces. And besides, Victoria's been off our radar for a month. She amassed a huge force at the Sol relay in the Oort cloud, then for reasons known only to herself, she destroyed the relay behind her. She's adrift in deep space, light-years from any outpost.'

'She'll pop back up,' Jonah said, adamant. 'It's what she does. And when she does, she'll listen to me. If I can send a message that reaches her, combined with proof she'll accept that I'm unassimilated, I'm sure she'll end her crusade. Show her you're acting in good faith, and she'll respond in kind. End this war. That's the first step toward atoning for your original sin.'

James was silent for an uncomfortably long time, his eyes glassy. He had the look of someone in TSI space. Normally, the Collective spoke with one voice, without any apparent delay or lag time. For a decision of this magnitude though, Jonah supposed even it must need time to confer amongst itself. 'Very well,' James eventually said. 'We'll withdraw the Scarabs. We'll send your message. It's a fair price to pay. We just wish we had your confidence that Victoria will be as magnanimous as you think.'

***

On the southern edge of Fort Pierre, one lone structure had been maintained and cared for over the past two centuries, kept free of weeds and freshly painted, its roof regularly re-tiled and its gutters kept free of leaves shed by the ancient American Elm tree growing in its front garden. The four-bedroom, two-storey farmhouse was actually in better repair now than when he had last seen it.

When he and James arrived, there were four smiling assimilates waiting to greet them. Two women, who went by Nora and Jane; one man, Barry; and one boy in his mid-teens, who called himself Tim. All four had been born into the Collective, so their names had been created strictly for Jonah's benefit; they had no need for them amongst themselves. They spoke slowly, with careful enunciation, their jaws and tongues unaccustomed to verbalisation. In the farmhouse where he had grown up, Jonah came to live with James, Nora, Jane, Barry and Tim for thirteen months.

The house's exterior was as he remembered it, which he supposed meant it had been painstakingly restored, over and over again across the centuries, as part of the Collective's attempts to woo him. The interior was bare and impersonal though, for which he was grateful. If the Collective had tried to restore the decorations as he remembered them from his boyhood (his father's collection of etherpop SSD drives; the paintings his mother had laboured at on weekends; the holographic posters of historic spacecraft he had blanketed the walls of his own room with), it would have crossed the line from nostalgic to perverse.

There were, however, two ornaments that were unfamiliar. A pair of urns adorned the mantelpiece in the living room, which Jonah learned had been provided for his benefit. The one on the left, James told him, contained the cremated ashes of Astrid Fournier, *nee* Harrison. She had been assimilated in the initial struggle for Earth, but assimilate or not, the bowel cancer had been terminal and beyond the scope of contemporary medicine at the time. She had died only a few months later.

The urn on the right belonged to Jean.

The rhythm of his days was similar to that of his time on the Mercanta Steppe, although he was burdened with far less responsibility. His caretakers, together with the nearby commune James belonged to, tended to a 40-hectare plot of land used to grow maize and ochre. Harvest season began in earnest shortly after he arrived, and though he wasn't asked, he insisted he be allowed to help in the fields through the long working days in September and October. His labours were kept light; on account of his leg, he was forbidden from anything that might require him to crouch, which mostly limited him to carrying picked crops from the fields to the granary in wicker baskets.

The people he worked with in the fields for those two months arrived at six in the morning and departed after eight in the evening. Jonah remembered the autumns in Pilgrim's Progress, when the groundborn and younger shipborn had emerged onto the fields yawning and grumbling, dragging their heels until a sharp bark from Eoin compelled them to pick up the pace. The contrast was apparent. Here, no-one grumbled, and no-one yelled. Often the assimilates, prompted by a stimulus Jonah wasn't privy to, would burst into harmonised, wordless song which set the tempo of their work. Jonah wasn't made aware of any daily quotas, but his baskets were filled quickly and regularly. The stockpiles he saw in the granary suggested they were looking at a bumper harvest.

Initially, Jonah wondered why anyone worked the fields by hand at all, when the Collective plainly had access to the technology that could automate all the tasks the assimilates were performing. But he remembered what James had said about the Collective's disdain for human aspiration. To the Collective, making life easier or more convenient for itself wasn't a goal in which it saw inherent value. He began to develop a sense of the hive-mind's priorities, recognising in its behaviour the values James had espoused to him. It lacked the impetus towards growth and change that prompted the actions of the humans with whom he was familiar. Its members had no need for the expansion or intensification of their experiences. They didn't want to climb ever-higher mountains, build ever-higher towers, design ever-faster cars. They found satisfaction simply in the fact of being alive, the processes of eating, drinking, breathing, sleeping, waking, and being in one another's company. The *is*-ness of being was enough to make them content.

He studied the faces of the men and women he saw engaged in hard labour, day in and day out. Was there something in them to be envied? He wasn't sure.

In due course, the harvest season ended, and the temperature, as it was wont to do in the Midwest, dropped sharply towards and then below freezing with the onset of winter. Snow began to fall in thick drifts. Jonah, James, and the four assimilates busied themselves through the day with the upkeep of the farmhouse and the maintenance of the attendant machinery and equipment.

Jonah helped to cook and clean, made sure the pipes stayed unfrozen and the firewood remained amply stocked. The chores he remembered from when he was a boy came back to him easily. But even with his attempts to busy himself, the pace of life through the winter reduced to a crawl, and he found himself growing restless and morose when he lacked distraction.

He regretted leaving the other settlers the way he had. Whatever he might have accomplished by doing so, he had abandoned the men and women he had led for the bulk of his long lifetime, without so much as a cursory fare-thee-well. It rankled to know that Eoin and Rahman and Will were still out there somewhere, and that even in the best-case scenario, he would never see them again in the years left to him.

Also: he was bored. It seemed a shameful thing to acknowledge, but it was true. While the assimilates might lack such afflictions as a longing for novelty in their shared sensorium, he wasn't so lucky. In his hours of downtime, there were only so many books he could read and sims he could access from a pre-assimilate era before they began to lose their lustre. And Nora, Jane, Barry and Tim, despite being considerate housemates, were dreadful conversationalists. He would try to coax them into discussion of his history and theirs, and they would oblige him, but they were hampered by their lack of experience in the linguistic exchange of ideas. Every question he asked had to be remotely parsed by the rest of the Collective before they could engage with it and respond in terms he could understand; it was like talking with an invisible translator as an intermediary.

He did learn a little more from them about the Collective's nature and function; for one thing, how the Effect generators placed in orbit that had originally enabled its proliferation had later been dismantled and replaced by the miniature subdermal relays implanted in every assimilate at the base of the neck. This reduced needless power output, spread the risk of catastrophic system failure, and was what made it possible for Jonah to walk around on the planet's surface without always wearing an Effect-nullifying device on his head.

Still, the process of talking to them was laborious enough that he always tuned out after a while. And when they weren't talking, and they thought he wasn't looking, he found they stared at him with an expression awfully like hunger. James would often flash him a similarly pointed look at the end of a day, not quite impatient, but reminding him of his purpose in being here. Each time, Jonah would respond with a small shake of his head. *No, I haven't decided yet.*

He must have voiced these frustrations aloud at some point, because the Collective took two measures to accommodate him. The first: one morning he awoke to find Barry gone without ceremony, and in his place, Alyssa came to live in the farmhouse, taking on all the same duties Barry had been tasked with.

The second: one day in November, Jonah was gently steered aside when his group broke for lunch. A four-wheel-drive SUV waited outside the house; by the driver's side door, an assimilate Jonah hadn't met before greeted him with a smile and a small bow.

The assimilate called himself "Nick." He was dressed incongruously smartly compared to the field-workers Jonah had been mingling with for months; he wore an ironed, collared white shirt, pressed trousers and black shoes that had recently been shined.

'We thought that it would be a productive exercise if you were to see a larger sample of the Earth as it now exists,' Nick said. 'If you're amenable to the idea, we've made preparations for a tour of the American continent.'

Jonah found that he was, in fact, amenable to the idea; if nothing else, it would ease the monotony for a couple of weeks. He gathered a few changes of clothes, and they set off that afternoon, Nick driving, Jonah splayed in the SUV's back seat, watching the frost-hardened Midwestern landscape as it zoomed by. They crossed the Missouri and travelled due east, following the course of what had once, very long ago, been the I-90 interstate. Even in Jonah's childhood, roads like these had been falling into disuse, made obsolete by vacuum tunnels and the region's depopulation; now, it was little more than the ghost of a road, the remaining asphalt choked with weeds and patterned with cracks like spiderwebs.

They didn't see another soul all afternoon, their vehicle the only one in the silent expanse between horizons. If not for the empty settlements that punctuated their progress, he might have been back on the Mercanta Steppe. He challenged himself to remember the names of these small towns he'd known in passing, two-and-a-half centuries ago. He got a few of them; Chamberlain; Kimball; Mt. Vernon.

They stopped at sunset in a commune adjacent to the remains of the city of Sioux Falls. The commune was much larger than the one in Fort Pierre; home, at a guess, to a few tens of thousands of assimilates. They ate in one of the commune's mess halls, a looming structure like a giant's barn. Inside, assimilates sat at long tables, a hundred abreast on wooden benches. Upon his entry, every face in the hall looked up from its plate and turned to look at him, just for a couple of seconds, then turned back, and quietly resumed their simple meal of corn, green beans, and soya curds.

***

They slept that night in the communal dormitories, and the morning after, travelled on. Over the next few days, they progressed through Minnesota, Wisconsin, and Illinois. They skirted the perimeters of Minneapolis, Milwaukee, tracing the perimeter of Lake Michigan; in the distance, Jonah glimpsed the remains of Chicago's famous skyline, its late 20th century skyscrapers gracefully crumbling, plant life climbing its central arcology.

There were more communes as they drew further east; they would pass them on an hourly basis. Each night, they were welcomed in a mess hall hosting hundreds of assimilates, who would greet them smiling and eager to share their simple, organically grown fare.

There were still billions of humans on Earth, Jonah realised; but they had made themselves unobtrusive. Part of its ecology, not conquerors of it. Everywhere he looked, he saw signs of nature recolonising the spaces it had been driven from. In Illinois, they paused to let a herd of bison cross their path. In Minnesota, a pack of grey wolves loped beside their SUV for a while, as they crossed the plains of Chippewa County.

The Earth Jonah had left behind in 2096 had seemed such a hectic, chaotic place, even from a privileged vantage like his. Every day, a new crisis reared its head, or an existing crisis worsened. Ecological catastrophe; economic meltdowns; war and disease; rampant anxiety and depression. The news only ever seemed to get worse, and no-one ever seemed to offer a solution. He wondered if that had been part of what had drawn him to join the Merantau

Program in the first place: a desire to escape the Earth, with its background ambience of despair, and sail away in his own little bubble universe.

This Earth wasn't the Earth he remembered. Every face he saw looked contented. Here, there was no war. No crime. No social stratification according to wealth or race or gender. No sense that it was all hurtling toward imminent collapse.

One night, while they were staying in a commune north-east of St. Louis, Jonah received an object lesson in just how the Collective's society worked. He took his evening meal in the mess hall, as usual. Facing him opposite was an old man – in his eighties, to look at him. The old man was intently focused on his plate. He slowly speared leaves of lettuce with a fork held in his trembling right hand, pausing between bites to massage his chest with his left. His breathing was shallow, Jonah noticed. Perspiration had started to form on his brow.

'Are you OK?' he felt compelled to ask.

The old man turned his face to him, and smiled, serenely. 'Don't worry, Captain,' he said, his voice thin, and hoarse. 'This body has reached its limit, that's all...'

The assimilate spoke like he had more to say, but instead, he started wheezing. He clutched his chest, eyes rolling back up into his head, and crumpled backward off the bench, his slight frame collapsing to the hall's earthen floor with a soft *thump*.

Jonah jumped over the table, sending dishes flying, ignoring the protestations from his bad leg. He crouched at the assimilate's side, holding his ear to the old man's sunken chest.

'I can't find a heartbeat,' he announced. Old instincts pertaining to medical emergencies took hold of him. He started compressing the man's chest, searching for the rhythm that might resuscitate him. 'Help!' he shouted. 'For God's sake, send help!'

Around him, the assimilates had paused eating and turned to look at the spectacle Jonah was creating. Their expressions were blank; none moved to assist him.

Jonah's efforts were fruitless; the old man lay utterly still where he'd collapsed, no trace of breath or pulse to be coaxed out of him. Eventually, a pair of assimilates arrived wearing medical fatigues, and quietly ferried the body out on a stretcher. The mess hall resumed eating, as though nothing had happened.

'A pulmonary embolism,' Nick muttered to Jonah under his breath, as he resumed his seat. 'Very quick. He didn't suffer much.'

Jonah said nothing. *So*, he thought, *this is the price of peace.*

It made perfect sense, of course, now that he considered it: the way the others at the table had reacted to the old man dying right beside them. They had immediate sensory access to thousands of other deaths like it every day; a constant, live feed of mortality, intimately experienced from within the senses of the victim as their faculties failed them. The old man would not be mourned, any more than a body would mourn the loss of a single skin cell.

***

Their journey returned them to Fort Pierre some weeks later, and there Jonah waited out the winter, ruminating. The days grew longer, and planting season began, and steadily his hours became fuller again. Days began to bleed together, and months and seasons started to pass him by without him noticing. He found himself becoming more and more accustomed to the ebb and flow of life on the New Earth. Even without having been assimilated, it was easy to relinquish oneself to, a gentle, welcoming numbness.

Still, he remained conflicted.

He found that he increasingly kept to himself in the evenings. Rather than trying to lure the assimilates into conversation, he contented himself to sit amidst them, in silent reminiscence. It felt oddly thrilling, an adolescent act of defiance, as impotent as it was brazen. *Here I am, having thoughts you can't hear. Here are a few cubic centimetres of grey matter you're cut off from.*

More and more often, he found himself in the living room before tiredness carried him off to bed, contemplating the two urns on the mantelpiece. He didn't do so intentionally; they simply drew his gaze when his mind wandered, twin sentimental relics at odds with the otherwise utilitarian décor of the farmhouse.

His patterns of behaviour didn't go unnoticed. The Collective scrutinised him closely, and it could interpret his various hangups and neuroses without needing to be told. One day, in the September of 2327, James sat down next to him on the living room sofa, disrupting the code of discretion Jonah had taken to be mutually understood.

'We thought you should know,' James said, quietly, 'that we have done everything in our power to locate and communicate your message to Victoria and the Insurgency. All of our combat-ready Scarabs have been withdrawn. For over a year now, we've combed every supply line and every relay chain, beamed our acquiescence into every charted sector of interstellar space. But…'

'But space is a big place,' Jonah finished for him. 'I realise that better than most.'

'If there's ever an answer, you'll be the first to know,' James assured him. 'But for now, she's missing. For whatever reason, she doesn't want to talk to you.'

'I'd imagine she has a great many reasons not to want to talk to me. The women on your side of the family are wilful, James.'

The Collective seemed to consider its next words carefully. 'Jonah, this can't go on forever. Eventually, we do need an answer.'

'What if – and understand, I'm speaking hypothetically – what if my answer is "no"? What then?'

James didn't answer straight away, but his expression told Jonah all he needed to know. The Collective's magnanimity, and its commitment to self-determination, only extended so far. If it were forced to choose between his personal autonomy and the revelation it had pursued for two centuries, the Collective would take what it saw as the least-bad option. At least he had the consolation of knowing it would feel bad about it.

'I see,' he said. 'Heads, you win, tails, I lose.'

'Don't talk about it like that,' James snapped, in a tone more waspish than he had ever heard from an assimilate. 'What more is it you need to see, grandfather? What evidence will be sufficient, that our course is the right one?'

Jonah sat for a moment, and thought. It wasn't a bad question. There were, surely, advantages to the way of life he had seen demonstrated this past year. So, what was it he could see that would quell his unease?

He nodded toward the urn on the right side of the mantelpiece. 'I came here with your mother once, you know. Just once. She was barely three years old at the time, I don't imagine she would have remembered it in later life.'

'She did,' James replied, softly. Jonah shot him a reproachful look. Jean had briefly been an assimilate before she had died, he recalled. Of course, she had shared her most private memories to all and sundry before she had passed. 'It was the first time she'd been away from the light pollution in Britain. The first time she'd ever seen the stars.'

It was true, Jonah realised. Of course, it was true. The look in his daughter's eyes when they had reflected the light of Polaris for the first time – how was it that it hadn't registered for him until now? How was it that he had been so oblivious to the significance of that moment for her?

'Was there any ceremony?' Jonah was surprised by his own question, which seemed to bubble up from his subconscious. 'Did anyone say any words, offer any kind of tribute to her memory? Or did you just burn her and scoop her ashes into a jar, on the pretext that one day I might show up and see it?'

Another long silence, during which the Collective, with all its billions of minds working in co-ordination, couldn't seem to conjure an answer he would find satisfactory.

'I want to give her a proper funeral,' Jonah said. 'I want her to have the dignity of that much, at least. I think she would have liked her ashes to be scattered on the Missouri.'

'And afterward?' James was looking at him with that same hungry expression he had seen on the faces of the other assimilates, making no attempt to disguise it now.

Jonah sighed. 'Fine. Grant me this one last request. One last opportunity to say goodbye. Then you'll have my answer.'

***

383

Two days later, he rose earlier than usual. At 4.30 am, at this time of year, not even the barest hints of the dawn were yet visible on the eastern horizon. He dressed in the clothes the Collective had prepared for him beforehand; black shirt; black tie; black jacket. They fit more snugly than he would have preferred, but he took his time, readjusting his collar and cuffs three or four times apiece before he was satisfied with the reflection he presented in his bedroom's mirror.

He made his way downstairs slowly as he ever did, tightly gripping the banister. Waiting for him downstairs were Alyssa and James, attired in the same sombre hues as he, their expressions appropriately mirthless. James presented him with the urn, and Alyssa with his cane. He was surprised by the weight of the former. In his memory, Jean was still a child. The morbid thought came unbidden: *How did she produce such a weight of ash?*

The three of them were greeted outside the farmhouse by a procession of mourners, headed up by Nora, Jane, and Tim. They led the way down the beaten earth track from the farmhouse to the bank of the river. They carried electric lanterns, dimmed to their lowest setting; just enough to find their way by. They set their pace to be considerate of Jonah's limp.

He must have gone through a dozen drafts in his head of what he would say when he reached the bank of the Missouri. Somehow, every variation he had practiced seemed to ring hollow. He had found himself recycling words from the wakes he had presided over for Ilsa, and Robyn, and Marcus. It was, he mused, one of the hallmarks of such a long life, that it was punctuated with goodbyes. After a few dozen, the solemn and sanctified language used for the occasion no longer seemed up to the task.

The truth was that he had no idea what Jean had felt in her final moments. He had seen her grow up in increments, fragments of video spaced months apart, curated postcards amounting to the barest sketch of the person she had been. He didn't know her, not really. She would have had her own accomplishments and her own regrets separate from his knowledge, her own moments of heartbreak and triumph, her own friends and enemies and lovers and rivals in love. The short time he had spent as her father accounted for only a meagre part of the woman she had been, with innumerable facets and flaws that were now beyond his ken, forever.

Jonah had realised, later in life than he should have, that he was a selfish person. He resented it about himself, and he fought it. He had tried to lead a moral and honourable life, tried to consider the needs of his family, his friends, and his crew before his own, but it was always like someone born left-handed forcing themselves to use their right. He had never, for one waking minute, forgotten himself. He was now two-hundred and sixty-three objective years old; the longest-lived person in all history. And in all his three centuries, he had never met anyone whose needs he had instinctively, unconsciously thought of before his own.

Jean had deserved better than him.

The procession crested a rise, and on the other side was a short, rugged slope down to the bank of the Missouri. The morning was upon them now; the day was muggy and humid, the sky overcast. Jonah's leg throbbed, and he leaned heavily on his cane with his right hand. He began to pick his way down the pockmarked and boulder-strewn hillock, ready to be done with this.

In his eagerness, he stubbed his bad leg. Not particularly hard; a younger, more able-bodied man would have stumbled slightly and regained his balance right away. But the barb of pain that shot through his thigh made him lose his equilibrium, and he found himself falling forward, downhill. Out of pure reflex, he turned his left arm to cushion his fall, in the elbow of which he'd crooked the urn. He landed heavily, and felt a brittle crunch beneath him.

The procession stopped behind him; Alyssa hurried to help him to his feet. He was winded, but unhurt. The urn, however, was shattered. The velvet bag inside spilled open, its grey contents billowing into the open air. Jonah looked down at himself – his dark mourning garb was coated with the ashes. The fine, carbonised bones and tissues of his daughter stood out on his clothes like a pale accusation.

Jonah's first impulse was to brush the ash off, but he stopped himself, caught somewhere between horror and nihilistic mirth. He emitted a sound he couldn't be sure was a laugh or a sob. The whole Collective could see him, he realised. Seven billion voyeurs, privy to his bathetic absurdity. Captain Jonah Harrison, interstellar voyager, the Starman himself. Incapable of carrying a fucking jar of dust down a hill.

This is my fate, then. It was clear, at last. He could rage against it, gnash his teeth at it, beat his fists and head and heart against it, all to no avail. He couldn't change what had been decided long ago, or walk back to the fork in the road he had taken. He was a failure, to all those who were important to him. He was unworthy to look them in the eye, and call himself human, and worthy of their respect.

Alyssa must have seen some of that despair manifest on his face, because she reached into the pocket of the black blouse she had worn for the occasion, and withdrew what he recognised as a hypodermic syringe.

'Jonah,' she said, softly, 'we could make it better, you know.'

He recoiled a half step from her, but for a split second, he was ready to take the Collective up on its offer of salvation. He thought, at last, that he knew what Alyssa had felt in that burning clearing on TransTerra a year earlier. How sweet it would be, not to be trapped in his skull with himself; to dissolve into the multitude, and in dissolution be forgiven.

He staggered away, his cane shaking in his grip. The black-clad procession let him be.

***

He wandered in a blind daze through the undergrowth that stood chest-high along the riverbank, for how long he didn't know. The moisture in the foliage soaked into his clothes, trickling down through his shirt and trousers, pooling in muddy puddles in his shoes, carrying the ash with it.

I'm sorry, Jean.

He reached a clearing, and here, his leg throbbing fiercely, he sat for want of any better ideas for where to go or what to do. He had grown up barely a mile away, and somehow he had never been more lost. He was in the world, but not a part of it. He had the acute sense that he had become a phantom sometime long ago, and had only now realised it. Or, perhaps, that he was the lone living person left on a planet of phantoms.

A world of benign ghosts, inviting him to join their number.

And why shouldn't he? No-one would judge him for it. Far from it, he would be welcomed with open arms, and lead out the remainder of his days in the gentle, peaceful bliss he had observed on the faces of all those he had known this past year. At the price of... what? What was it in him he guarded so jealously, that he couldn't stand to share it?

And yet, still there was something in him that balked at the notion. Pride or stubbornness or sheer, reactionary opposition to change; whatever it was, it planted its feet and said firmly, unequivocally *no*. This was *his* humiliation; *his* failure; *his* pain. No-one but he had a right to it.

His corneal implants sprang to life, unbidden. He started; they hadn't been used for all the time he'd been on Earth, there had been no need for them. The flattening effect the UI had on his surroundings caused him a moment's disorientation. When his eyes refocused, they registered what he was seeing as a text scroll. A message directed to him specifically.

Jonah, it read. **I have to be brief. I shouldn't be contacting you at all, but my conscience wouldn't bear it if I didn't try something.**

You'll remember the molecular platelets that ejected the shrapnel from your thigh. Well, Albrecht didn't think you needed to know, but after the operation was over, he assigned a few to be left inside your body, just on the off-chance we needed to reach you. They're inert most of the time, not even enough to trace your position. But if an encrypted transmission were to reach them, they hold the Insurgency's active encryption key, which they'd use and then route the result to your eyes. So, if you're reading this, it means you're alive and on the surface of the Earth.

The other gamble I'm taking is that the Collective, for whatever impossible reason, kept to its word and left you unassimilated. If I'm wrong, I've just thrown a wrench into our whole operation. But if I'm right, and there's a chance you can still be saved, then I have to do it. I still remember leaving Oskár behind, and that's weighed on me for a long time. Never again. Not if I can help it.

Victoria has directed a comet from the Oort cloud into a collision trajectory with Earth. She's going to wipe the Collective out in one strike, reset everything to zero. At the time I'm composing this message, we're about to cross into cis-Martian orbit, a little under 1.5 AU from Earth. You

have maybe 8 hours to get into space. The higher, the better; the impact will throw debris clear of the gravity well.

It was an honour and a pleasure to have known you for the brief time I did, sir.

Your friend,

Sgt. Ahkejuoksa Hartikainen (Aki)

Chapter 24

September 4th, 2327 C.E.

The comet roared silently through the darkness, its two-billion-ton mass piercing the interstellar medium at the maximum velocity the overclocked QF drives could output.

At the cusp of Neptune's orbit, the border of the inhabited solar system proper, Victoria yearned for the journey to be over. For four subjective months, the comet's path had required constant monitoring and microscopic corrections. Encountering a single particle even a micron thick would have the potential to throw it catastrophically out of alignment. She had rotating shifts of Archangels flying ahead of it, monitoring for obstructions large enough to need to be burned away with maser fire, acting like sweepers on the universe's longest curling sheet. There was a good reason the engines on starships like the *Prospice* hadn't been designed for 0.9 of c.

It was around halfway through their voyage that the army had flagged a broadcast emanating from the direction of Earth. Given the distance it had travelled, it would already be several months old. Victoria's primary consciousness was in the middle of its sleep cycle, but her secondary registered the ripple that passed through the ranks, a surprised blip in the ambient comms activity from Archangel to Archangel.

Commander, Daniels wrote, after a pregnant pause, **you may want to give this your full attention.**

It was an unencrypted video message, addressed to her personally. The image it showed was of her grandfather, sitting at a burnished wooden table. His face was fuller than it had been when she had last seen him, and he had shaved his beard.

'I suppose I should start with an explanation,' he said. 'While I regret the way I had to do it, I won't apologise for what I did on the FOB. The Insurgency has gone down a dark path, Victoria. I believe that it started out as a fight for human liberation, but somewhere down the line, that changed. It lost sight of its strategic goals; it forgot how to engage the Collective by any means other than combat. The way you were headed, there was no hope. This way, there could be a little.'

He explained at some length what he had learned from Manderly about the nature of the Body's passenger, still lying on the dark side of the Moon, and the bizarre connection it had to him. From the sound of it, the Collective was fixated upon it. All of its will was bent upon unlocking its secrets.

'As a pre-condition for my co-operation, the Collective has agreed to grant amnesty to the Insurgency and the remaining non-assimilated humans. It guarantees safe passage through the interstellar relay network to TransTerra, which will henceforth be declared off-limits to Collective forces. An extrasolar, free human society will be allowed to prosper and grow without interference.

'This message will be distributed along the relays and broadcast into every sector of charted space. I have to trust it will reach you sooner or later. However long it might take, Victoria, I implore you; it's within your power to end this, if you can just make one gesture of trust.'

The message was accompanied by another file; a synaptic signature, showing the profile of her grandfather's brain, with a timestamp alleging that it had been made in concert with the recording. She supposed it was intended as a token of good faith, meant to demonstrate to her that he remained unassimilated, and had recorded the message of his own volition. Not that it necessarily meant much. It was hardly beyond the Collective's means or tactics to forge a synaptic signature.

There's still time, her secondary consciousness piped up. It had been doing that more and more often the closer to Earth they drew. Victoria had begun to resent its presence, that of a petulant adolescent in her cerebellum, but she needed it if she was to function as a leader.

No, she shot back. *No, there really isn't.*

The other Archangels all saw the transmission, just as she did. The longer she hesitated, the more it would look like indecision on her part, and so her hesitation lasted no more than seconds.

Disregard everything you just heard, she ordered on the shared channel. **The operation will proceed as scheduled.**

Commander, Daniels responded, he on a private channel, **are you absolutely certain? This could potentially be our best-case scenario. We could get everything we were hoping for on TransTerra, without the need for mass destruction on Earth. If you'd decelerate the comet a little and permit me to go on ahead, in a diplomatic capacity...**

No, Lieutenant. Victoria determined to shut down this line of thinking before it could gain any traction. **Even if we assume that the message was made in good faith – and that's a giant 'if' – there's no way for a ceasefire to be enforced. A human colony on TransTerra would exist at the Collective's mercy. Maybe they'd leave them be until the Starman dies, or for a generation or two, but you and I know that it wouldn't last forever. And when it decides it's hungry again, what then? Besides, we tried bargaining with the Collective in the first battle for Earth. You remember that, and I'm damn sure I do. We've only reached this point because we didn't do what was necessary then. If we tip our hand now, we risk losing everything, forever.**

Yes, Commander. You're right, of course.

In truth, she had expected something like this. She wasn't surprised, only disappointed. Her experiences since TransTerra had given truth to the old adage – it was never a good idea to meet your heroes.

She had witnessed both of her parents die, and both times she had been powerless to stop it. She had watched her planet be subsumed beneath the tide of the Enclave Effect. Comrades had died and been assimilated; bases captured, and squadrons routed. Nothing in her existence was fixed, or assured, save for one thing: the Starman.

She had thought of him after fleeing Arsia Mons. She had clung to the idea of him after the loss of Callisto. She had drawn strength and regrouped after the failure of the Interregnum, because he was still alive, still innocent. She had destroyed the Merantau relay, and corrupted its database, as per her mother's final request. For all the time since, she had counted it the best thing she had ever done.

When all of her comrades had looked toward Earth with fear and dread, she had thought instead of the *Prospice*, moving through deep space where the Collective couldn't reach it. There was someone out there, she knew, who was free from the curse of this conflict, that drew in everyone and everything around it as inexorably as a black hole. That man knew her name, and her face. Had praised her violin recitals and had wished her luck in her exams. There was someone out there who cared about her.

Though he had never known it, their relationship across light-years had been a symbiotic one. The TransTerran settlers had remained free for as long as they had, in part because she had made the Collective bleed for every inch of space it expanded into. And she had dredged up the strength to do so, decade after decade and light-year after light-year, because she knew that somewhere far away, the Starman remembered her as a child, and cherished the memory.

And then she had spoiled all of that by meeting him.

Jonah Harrison was an honourable man, and courageous. But he had ceased to be the guardian angel that she had imagined for two centuries. He was as human as anyone else, capable of great deeds by the same token he was capable of folly. He was no traitor; she was confident of that. He had been acting in what he thought were humanity's best interests when he left them on the FOB. He was, simply, a fool. He knew nothing of the Collective, and in the ancient tradition of fools everywhere, that made him think he knew best. He was susceptible to its lies and its flattery. He hadn't been there when it had stolen his daughter.

Even if he hadn't been assimilated when the message had been recorded, in all probability he was now, in which case he was as good as dead. And even if, somehow, he still wasn't when the comet reached its final destination... well, Victoria would mourn, but she could live with herself.

He was right about one thing, though, whether he knew it or not: it was within her power to end it. Not with a gesture of trust, but one of force. Love had failed her.

From here on, hatred would guide her hand.

***

Shortly before entering cis-Neptunian orbit, the comet and the army escorting it began to decelerate. The reason for this was twofold – first, the vacuum inside the solar system proper was positively choked with particulate matter compared to the interstellar regions they had traversed until now, and the odds of the comet colliding with micrometeoroids went up exponentially. Second, Victoria had no intention of completely obliterating the Earth from the cosmos. In the vision she had of humanity's future, they would one day, eons in the future, be able to reclaim their homeland. An impact of only fifteen million klicks per hour – still a hundred times faster than the comet that killed the dinosaurs – would be enough to render the planet temporarily unfit for organic life, without being so violent as to disrupt the oblate spheroid's integrity as a chunk of rock.

The mood throughout the ranks was sombre, here in these final hours. Victoria knew well how her soldiers felt, for she felt it too. This tiny corner of space, a meagre sixty AU across; for decades it had been their battleground. It had seemed so vast, then, at the beginning. Even the greatest celestial bodies had been like motes of dust suspended in a cathedral. The Insurgency had shrunk by increments, driven to ever more remote outposts, humanity fighting tooth and nail for every barren rock and frozen moon, until only those few privileged to receive Archangel frames were left. Now it all rushed past them so fast; crossing the orbits of Uranus, Saturn, and Jupiter, they relived their greatest failures in reverse order.

> 2172. The Collective had dropped an asteroid on Enceladus, flushing them out of their hiding place.

> 2158. A Collective infiltrator had sabotaged their heat sinks on Io.

> 2150. The rout of Ceres, the conclusive defeat in the months-long battle for the material resources of the asteroid belt.

So close now. They were set to cross the orbit of Mars at an obtuse angle, moving now at a mere twenty million klicks per hour. Their velocity was near-stationary by the standards of interstellar transit; in the inner solar-system, it was preposterous, lunatic speed. The Earth swelled ahead of them; what started as a single blue pixel at her vision's maximum resolution became recognisable as the planet of her birth in a matter of hours, the outlines of the continents shimmering into focus. If their calculations were correct – and having come this far, there was no reason to suppose they weren't – the comet's point of impact would be somewhere in the Pacific Ocean.

The simulations they had modelled showed it gouging a hole clear through the crust and deep into the mantle before its momentum was arrested.

Hundreds of trillions of tons of matter would be thrown loose, most of it to rain back down on the surface in a chain reaction of devastation. Low orbit would be choked with debris, frustrating any evacuation attempts the Collective tried to make. The shockwave would radiate from the point of impact at the speed of sound, boiling the oceans and blackening the land as it went, until the blue, green and white sphere was transfigured into an angry red and black. Even the tectonic plates would be defaced beyond recognition. The Seventh Extinction would be the worst.

Victoria spent the final approach canvassing her soldiers, performing last-minute diagnostics of their frames, taking platelet counts, scanning for misfires in their neural pathways. It was all redundant, all just reconfirming data she already had, but if there was anything, any possibility of a misstep at this late juncture...

She came, in due course, to Aki, who she examined with the same fastidiousness as every other member of her throng. He kept his eyes averted throughout.

Is he OK? he sent her while she was conducting his platelet count.

Is who OK? she sent back.

You know who I mean. Even through the limited medium of text, she detected petulance. She went a few seconds without answering.

Eoin. Eoin O'Brien. Aki wrote the name like it was an admission.

Recovering, last I heard from Morrison before we left.

Victoria almost asked what had brought on this late pang of concern for the engineer, but she thought she knew. Aki's gaze was angled away from their shared trajectory, towards Mars, just a few hundred million klicks away.

2139. The siege of Arsia Mons.

Mind on the operation, Sergeant. We can pick up the pieces after.

A pause.

Affirmative, Commander.

It was just as he wrote those words that an alert snapped her attention towards Earth.

The whole army registered it at once; a subtle, but immediately detectable, redshift in the wavelength of the light emanating from its surface. The tell-tale signifier of a QF drive; but for it to be noticeable at this distance, the space-compression had to be on a massive scale, at least as large as the signature of the overclocked engines attached to the comet. The signature they picked up was diffuse, but larger than theirs by a couple of orders of magnitude. The equivalent of tens of thousands – no, hundreds of thousands – of individual Scarab units. All of them converging on their location.

Ten minutes later, now just an AU distant from Earth, they received another broadcast. Like the Collective's previous communique, it was an audiovisual recording from Jonah, addressed specifically to Victoria. He appeared haggard and panicked. For some reason best known to himself, he was dressed in filthy funeral garb.

'Victoria,' he said, his voice low and his breath heavy. 'Aki warned me. I know what you're trying to do, and I understand why you're trying to do it, but *stop*. If not for my sake, or for humanity's sake, then for yours. You're not a murderer, but if you do this, you'll never be able to take it back. It's not too late. Please, I'm begging you.'

She looked at Aki, horror brewing in her heart. He looked back at her, and there was a hardness in his eyes she wasn't used to seeing there.

I'm sorry, Commander. I had to believe there was still a chance to reach him.

He'd always been so open; always so guileless. She'd envied him that; his willingness to believe the best of the people around him. It was the quality that had led her to think, once, long ago, that she'd loved him. And now it might just have destroyed everything.

She flexed her palm where it was splayed against his armour. One shot, and she could be rid of this latest liability, one more foolish idealist poised to jeopardise humanity's future.

No, her secondary consciousness chided. *It's not worth it. The damage has been done already*.

And for once, she agreed. It would avail her nothing to remove a soldier from her ranks.

To the vanguard, Sergeant. Rest assured, when this is over, we will have a very unpleasant conversation.

Aye, Commander. He immediately accelerated.

Victoria took half a second to calm herself down. This was, she reminded herself, a contingency she had prepared for. As they approached Earth, their chance of detection approached 100%; a force this size couldn't hope to make it all the way to the solar system's interior undetected, even with the best luck in the universe. That was fine. This confrontation was inevitable; it was just a question of sooner, rather than later. It was why they'd come prepared for a shooting war.

All Archangels form up, she ordered. **Accelerate ahead of the comet in an arrowhead formation. Keep it tight, 1000 klicks dispersal from wingtip to wingtip. Don't let even so much as one Wasp through. It's your time to shine, ladies and gentlemen. Everything's led to this.**

She moved to the front of the formation, appointing herself both the tip of the arrow and the hand that guided it. She took a moment to compose a brief message to her grandfather, her last before the battle began. 'I hear you, Starman, and I'm sorry. Understand that I don't bear you any resentment. I told you back on TransTerra that I never once stopped loving you. That hasn't changed. But, sadly, you're wrong. It is too late. It's been far past too late, for a very long time.'

***

At their present velocity, millions of klicks per hour of relative delta-V rather than tens of thousands, the principles of engagement here were different from orbital dogfights. Rather than Archangels and Scarabs buzzing around each other like angry insects, exchanging maser fire at distances where they could see the whites of each other's eyes, this was something closer to a game of chicken; victory and defeat were determined by precision, timing, and nerve. Combatants would pass each other at such speeds that they only ever appeared to one another as a flash, a blur in the other's sensors for a fraction of a second. It was in this near-instantaneous window that the respective Archangels and Scarabs had their opportunity to land a single, perfect maser shot, incapacitating or destroying their opponent.

The Scarabs had the advantage in reaction time; the latest models the Insurgency had captured boasted sensor suites with refresh rates they hadn't yet been able to retro-engineer. In that regard, the Collective had been the beneficiary of the relativistic arms race, with years to make strides in technology where the Insurgency often had only subjective months. Their enemy's image of them in the micro-instant of passage was clearer than theirs. But the Archangels had an edge of their own. Human brains working in concert with algorithmic combat protocols had the potential to zig where a Scarab might expect a zag. Spontaneity was an Archangel's best friend.

They entered a formation in the shape of an inverted 'V,' not unlike a flock of geese migrating south for winter. The Arrowhead formation, a tactic perfected over decades of raids on the relays. The Archangels in the front of the formation would take their shot; any targets that were missed would be mopped up by the second row, or the third, or the fourth, each successive row's chances being improved by the data on the target's movement patterns being passed back along the 'V.' Using this formation now allowed them to form a protective cone around the comet's course. Any Collective unit intending to reach the comet would need to force its way through that cone. Their numerical advantage – over a hundred-to-one – would only do so much to avail them here.

The first wave of Scarabs they encountered, two hours after they had started to mobilise, was five platoons strong – one-thousand and eighty individual units, launched from the Moon. They were spread widely, probing for a gap in the arrowhead formation.

The conflagration when the two opposing sides passed one another lasted seconds, but would have been visible from the surface of the Earth, three-quarters of an AU distant. The storm of maser fire enveloped the surrounding space like a supernova, punctuated by explosions and the flood of anti-neutrons and positrons that symptomised ruptured Archangel cores. Victoria scored two hits on Scarabs herself, and counted three near-misses from shots fired at her.

The butcher's bill ticked across her HUD after the engagement was over. Four-hundred and ninety-one Scarabs destroyed. Sixty-seven disabled. The remaining five-hundred and twenty-two had blown past them without opening a gap in the cone. The comet's course remained unaltered, and the

Scarabs which had passed them by would never be able to reverse direction and accelerate quickly enough to catch up to them.

The bad news: fifty-nine Archangels had been killed – much more than she was comfortable with in the first engagement. Among the number of the dead was Tetsuya Shimura; in the microseconds before he had died, he had broadcast a recording of his last few moments to the rest of the army.

The recording told a story in no more than three frames; Victoria discerned a Scarab's silhouette, taking precise aim at Shimura's centre mass, its maser beam striking him perfectly in the middle of his torso. A fluke shot, perhaps? No, she didn't think so. This explained the unexpectedly high death toll on their side. The factor they had failed to accommodate for; the Collective was no longer pulling its punches. For so long, the Insurgency had been used to fighting an enemy that was cagy and squeamish about killing; that had made every effort to disable and capture Archangels rather than destroy them outright. They had factored the expectation of this treatment into their evasive manoeuvre protocols.

Now though, they had forced the Collective's hand. She had finally put it in a position where it had been forced to fight them seriously, lest it be eliminated. Though she knew she should mourn Shimura and her other fallen comrades, she felt a swell of pride at this knowledge. She had already achieved more than Albrecht had managed in centuries. At last, their enemy did them the signal courtesy of shooting to kill.

***

The subsequent waves of Scarabs came thicker and faster after the first. Just as Earth's governments had emptied their caches of nuclear ordnance back in 2135 when they had been spooked by the approach of the Body, the Collective now spent itself with abandon against Victoria's approach. The Scarabs were hurled at them as recklessly as ammunition. Thousands upon thousands of them shot past the arrowhead into deep space, flying by into tactical irrelevancy.

Some left wounds as they passed; however savvy the army was, and however much it had drilled for the final conflict and been hardened by previous engagements, the attrition of the Collective's sheer numbers took its toll. With each wave, it left in its wake a dozen or a score of core detonations,

398

overwhelming her sensors with the fury of particles and anti-particles being mutually annihilated.

She herself escaped destruction by a hair's breadth, more times than she cared to keep count of. She found, only a little to her surprise, that her brushes with death didn't bother her at all anymore. Whether or not her body died was of little consequence when her will was in motion behind her, all 2 billion tons of it.

By the time her comet had made its way within 0.1 AU of Earth (only an hour from its final resting place now), her original complement of eight hundred and ninety-six Archangels had been whittled down to just over four hundred. Hundreds of comrades, people she had known for most of her long life, threw themselves into the line of fire on her behalf.

And she was happy.

Gleefully, manically happy. It was a feeling she had known only a handful of times over the centuries; the singular moment when the past and future ceased to exist, and only the rightness and exhilaration and vindication of the present seemed real. She had felt it when she had earned a standing ovation for her recital in Oxfordshire that fateful night when she was twelve years old. And she felt it now, at the cusp of her ultimate assertion of dominance, where she had challenged the universe, and the universe had been found wanting.

Less than 0.1 AU. Their final victory was all but assured. The Scarabs' flight patterns became more erratic and more desperate, the Collective fully aware that the comet was nearing the point where no disruption they could introduce would prevent disaster.

Victoria's attention was diverted to their right flank, in the direction of the Sun. Another swarm of Scarabs was approaching from an angle that shouldn't have been possible, at an equally implausible delta-V. No; she corrected herself. The warp signature was enormous, large enough to be mistaken for a full platoon. But its shape, she realised, was that of an Archangel frame with its wings at full extension, trapping the formidable solar winds to be found this close to a yellow star and channelling them into thrust.

Something was off about it, she thought. The redshift aura was too strong, and it was misshapen. The Rorschach blot in space presented four bulges, rather than two: less avian than lepidopteran. She realised what she was seeing

– the Archangel approaching them from sunward was attached to a pair of auxiliary QF drives, like the booster rockets on the old-Earth space shuttle. In concert with the power of its wings and its antimatter core, it was generating a truly fearsome acceleration – thousands of klicks per second per second, curving toward the path of the arrowhead. More specifically, her own path. Not intersecting it, but on course to merge with it.

It's going to match our vector, she realised, with something like awe. 15 million klicks per hour, and in the space of less than 0.1 AU, their adversary had managed to circle behind them and catch up to them. They wanted a dogfight that badly.

She hailed the nearing silhouette. **Well played, Hoyt,** she wrote, **but it's too little too late. What do you think you're going to achieve?**

The Archangel that had once been Corporal Abraham Hoyt, reconnaissance specialist and captured during a botched raid on the Phi relay in 2232, did not reply to her. The Collective's answer, however, was all too clear. Another wave of Scarabs was approaching from ahead – the largest yet, ten full platoons this time. It would meet the tip of the arrowhead in a hundred and seventeen seconds; the same moment that Hoyt's vector would converge with hers. With an enemy Archangel amidst their ranks spreading havoc, the Collective's chances of one Scarab or more slipping their net and detonating something heavy close to the comet's surface became significant.

Her first impulse was to tighten the arrowhead, denying the enemy a gap through which they might slip and reach the comet. But the arrowhead could only be tightened so far before the formation became counterproductive. Too far ahead of the comet, and they offered it no shelter; too close, and the detonation of an Archangel frame's core within a thousand klicks or so ran the risk of throwing it off-course even now.

The alternative was that she take the initiative and give Hoyt the one-on-one fight he was angling for. She didn't need much persuasion.

Daniels, you take point at the fore of the arrowhead.

Aye, Commander. Daniels moved in to fill her position, and Victoria spread her wings wide, to their single-molecule thickness. She decelerated hard, directly into a collision course with Hoyt.

You won't stop us, she pronounced. Hoyt could give her the silent treatment all he liked; he could hear her, and as such, the Collective could hear her. They would see her face in her moment of triumph, and know that they had finally reaped as they had sown two hundred years ago. **Humanity endures. This is our world, and we will drive you out.**

Hoyt retracted his wings and detached his frame's boosters right as their delta-V aligned. He twisted beneath her and loosed a salvo of maser shots. She was forced to evade in a corkscrew motion before she could return fire in kind.

The dynamics of a dogfight were as familiar to her as the contours of her own frame, and she remembered Hoyt's style from their time as squadron-mates. Still, something was different about this particular dance. He didn't move like Velasquez had in TransTerran orbit, teasing and taunting. He hounded her relentlessly, crowding her with maser fire that scarcely gave her space to breathe, let alone retaliate. He was the avatar of an organism in its death throes, and through him, the Collective fought like a cornered beast.

She dodged and dodged again, searching for the opening that would offer her the one shot she needed to drive a lance of killing light through her one-time comrade's heart. She twisted and weaved, calling upon every trick and every feint she had ever known. At last, after eons contained within a few berserk seconds, she found a window of a few microseconds when her crosshairs converged upon Hoyt's centre-mass.

Just as she thought she had secured a checkmate, the darkness whirling around them caught fire.

The ten-platoon swarm had arrived, and with it came the electromagnetic deluge of the largest single engagement the Insurgency had ever fought. Archangel frames detonated in brilliant conical plumes of radiance, surrounded by the criss-cross of ten thousand maser beams and a thousand Scarabs being reduced to slag, all in the space of less than five seconds. Name after name turned grey in Victoria's HUD.

Distracted by the energetic vista, her killing shot missed Hoyt by a fraction of a degree, maybe singing his outermost left wingtip, but no more. It was only minutes later that Victoria discovered Hoyt's shot had been luckier than hers.

Her sudden disorientation and displacement reminded her of nothing so much as the accident when she had been twelve years old. One moment she was in one place; the next, she was in another; the transition between the two states being marked only by a split-second of light, heat, and noise. She found herself tumbling in a gyroscopic motion, the Earth intermittently flashing into view below her as she spun.

She tried to right herself and only made the motion worse. She realised that she was short one wing, along with the attendant arm, shoulder, and a good chunk of her chest. The damage report came in from her secondary consciousness: fully a quarter of her platelets had been blown away, vaporised by Hoyt's parting shot. Her spinal column had been momentarily exposed to space. Billions of platelets had swarmed in to prevent the damage of the near-absolute zero temperatures of vacuum spreading to her brain. She had been unconscious for two hundred and fifty-seven seconds while her frame worked to revive her.

A figure moved into her field of vision and helped her right herself. The winged shape at first caused her to start, but then its gentle motions assured her that she was among friends. **What happened?** She could think of no more precise question to ask of her rescuer. **Hoyt made it through,** Daniels replied. **Before we could tighten the arrowhead, he slipped into the gap the Scarabs created. Dodged past the shots from any of our number savvy enough to tag him. He reached the comet, Victoria.**

Her mangled body rebelled against this notion, and Daniels had to steady her before she sent herself into another gyroscopic fit. Surely not? Surely not when they were this close? Not even the universe she was familiar with had such a cruel sense of irony.

And?

He suicided – blew his core less than three klicks away from the comet. Split it clean in two; there's one fragment estimated at six hundred million tons spiralling off toward the Sun. The larger chunk, the 1.3-billion-ton one, is still on course to enter the Terran gravity well. It'll still collide with Earth – at an oblate angle, and it'll generate only about a fifth of the force we originally planned. But still enough for us to achieve our end goal.

Victoria felt like laughing. The Collective had made its last, best Hail-Mary move, and it had failed.

We win. We win. We fucking win, Taylor. Lend me some of your platelets, will you? I'm a bit lopsided here.

Sure thing, Viper.

On a public channel, she might have chastised him for using the nickname she had once resented. Right now, she took pride in it.

What's the butcher's bill?

The arrowhead is down to 327. But the Scarabs aren't coming as fast and thick now either. That last gambit with Hoyt was the best they had to offer. 52 minutes to impact.

Daniels wrote this as he touched his hand to the gaping wound in Victoria's frame. There came a sense of relief as her mass was replenished, trillions of platelets flowing from his frame to hers. The chasm in her shoulder filled itself in; her missing wing unfurled, and her arm regrew according to her body's default archetype. She flexed her silver fingers, checking to her own satisfaction that they retained their dexterity.

She was no longer accelerating or decelerating, but her momentum remained – despite the impression of stillness, she continued to tumble Earthward at fifteen million klicks per hour. The arrowhead formation, reduced in the same way she was, fought on next to her, its velocity matched to hers, guarding the larger of the two fragments. The engines they had bolted to the comet had been irreparably ruined by Hoyt's kamikaze run. It was no longer under their direction, but it would find its resting place, nevertheless. Another conflagration momentarily lit up space; a few more names were greyed out on her HUD.

No matter. The battle was as good as over, and thereafter, it would be her war to lose. She would have work to do after this; much more work, systematically flushing out what remained of the Collective on their moons and asteroid colonies.

The half-remembered verse bubbled up from one of the corners of her memory she had long ago decommissioned – *And miles to go before I sleep. And miles to go before I sleep.*

She would savour the moment, here at the watershed, with centuries of chaos behind and centuries more to come. Surely, she thought, she had earned at least that much.

The Earth was so large below her now. With her eyes on their maximum resolution, she could distinguish mountain ranges and patterns of clouds. There was a hurricane forming in the Gulf of Mexico, she saw. A category-4, at least – in a few days, it would be battering the coast of Louisiana.

Or rather, it wouldn't. It would be swept away before it ever reached the coast, subsumed by a far, far larger storm.

A dark shape obstructed her view – the Moon, she realised, upon reducing the zoom function a little. She saw something there that gave her pause. A warp signature – a tiny one, drifting slowly across the Moon's dark side, decelerating towards its surface. It couldn't be more than one troop carrier.

She had a good idea of where it was going, and of who was aboard. What they hoped to accomplish with him now, she could hardly guess. Certainly, nothing that could make a difference to the outcome today.

She thought she had made her peace with it. Her grandfather had gone one way, and she had gone the other; what more remained to be said? But still, with him so tantalisingly close... what would she do if she saw him again? Would she berate him, accuse him, call him a traitor? Would she forgive him?

Would he forgive *her*?

It would weigh on her forever if she didn't take the last opportunity she would ever get to find out.

Daniels, you take point for the remainder of the operation.

But, Commander...

Don't worry, I won't be gone long. I'll rendezvous with you and the others in trans-lunar orbit in two hours, after the impact.

She flared her wings to their maximum extension and accelerated ahead of the formation, the Moon in the middle of her forward vision. The crater where the Body's passenger lay was where she had left it. In the centre, the Collective had constructed an enormous white structure around the cetacean giant, obscuring it from her sight. A research facility, she guessed, or a temple to their dreaming god, or some hybrid of the two. The troop transport whose warp signature she had glimpsed docked there. The place where her world had been torn apart. The place where the Collective had initiated her in hatred.

She would never forgive them. Today, the ignited atmosphere would be her mother's funeral pyre; the Collective's wail in a billion voices, her mother's elegy.

Chapter 25

December 16th, 2135 C.E.

Jean was awakened by the high-pitched drone of a low-oxygen alert, its repetitive pulse exacerbating the throbbing in her forehead. Considering the alerts that were flooding her HUD, she felt like she ought to be in considerably greater pain. It took her a little time to piece together where she was, and how she had come to arrive there.

The *where* was simple enough. She was still seated in the cockpit of the *Melinda*, canted to its left side at close to ninety degrees. She could perceive gravity, but she wasn't under thrust. By process of elimination, that could only mean she was on the surface of the Moon.

The *how* was harder, but with some concentration, she was able to retrace events back to the point when she had lost consciousness. After Bandit 4's last asp had detonated and her head had collided with the console, the cockpit UI had registered her blacking out and assumed emergency autonomous mode, its top and only priority being the pilot's life.

The *Melinda*'s nosedive into the lunar surface had been irrecoverable; it had neither functioning engines, nor the wiring to make use of them even if they had survived. The cockpit, however, was a different story. Its life support had its own backup power supply and independent, closed-circuit control systems. In the direst emergencies, it could be ejected from the rest of the craft and function as a hermetically sealed unit, supplying its pilot with up to an hour of oxygen. Within seconds of the explosion, a series of shaped charges would have severed the cockpit from its housing and a pair of rocket boosters would have thrown it loose from the wreckage. It was just one reason she favoured the Y24 over the Y31 – the Nephtis model had eliminated this safety feature in favour of compactness and manoeuvrability.

If she had been flying in-atmosphere, at that point a parachute would have deployed and she would have drifted softly to the ground. If she had been flying in almost any sane orbital path, she would simply have drifted, the cockpit UI emitting a distress beacon requesting recovery by friendly forces. What the Y24's designers hadn't accounted for – and honestly, it was a forgivable oversight – was a situation where it might be shot down in the presence of gravity but no atmosphere.

The 'chute would have done no good whatsoever slowing her descent to the Moon's surface, so instead the cockpit UI's only recourse had been to burn through all the propellant available to it. Lunar gravity was far weaker than terrestrial, but the boosters built into the cockpit were scarcely more than Vernier engines, with neither the thrust nor the equilibrium for a safe landing. The best the UI could manage was a controlled crash landing, with the emphasis on 'crash.'

Her head swam. She tried to raise herself from her seated position and failed. Her flight suit's left sleeve was caught on something. She gave it an irritated tug. The obstruction, whatever it was, refused to budge. She looked down at her arm.

Ah. That explained one of the more urgent medical alarms blaring into her HUD.

The cockpit's exterior hadn't been breached upon landing, but it had buckled inward at the impact. In one of the folds where the metal had crumpled, her left arm had been caught and crushed. Her suit had inflated a partition at the shoulder, which was acting as both a tourniquet and a seal against vacuum. It had also flooded her system with analgesics, which went some way toward explaining her lack of panic at her present circumstances.

The low-oxygen alert informed her that she had twenty-seven minutes before the cockpit's meagre reserves were exhausted. Probably closer to twenty, if she started hyperventilating, which gave her a powerful incentive to remain calm. After the cockpit ran out of breathable air, her suit would take over life support duties. Unfortunately, her visor had a spiderweb crack spreading from where it had impacted the console. If her suit was pressurised, it would immediately start bleeding air. She wouldn't last five minutes.

The console still seemed to be alive. That was good news, at least. '*Belladonna*,' she said aloud, hailing her squadron on an open channel, 'this is *Melinda*. Mayday, I was shot down over the dark side. In urgent need of extraction. What's the situation overhead?'

There was a pause before she got an answer. **Acknowledged,** *Melinda,* Velasquez wrote. The crawl of the text suggested he was under massive acceleration. **Situation dire. Collective craft making impossible moves. All we can do to keep flying. No chance of extraction. Over.**

Shit. It seemed she would have to take care of herself.

There was a storage compartment in the cockpit that included a standard ORC survival kit, providing for the event of crash landings in remote or hostile terrain. She had checked it was added to the plane's inventory before taking off from the Congolese station. Among the sundries it included were an inflatable life-raft; cold-weather gear; a maser cannon with fifteen single-use charges; ten litres of electrolytic drinking water; three days of military rations; fifty metres of nanofibre rope and carabiners to match; gauze; sutures; antibiotics; two canisters of compressed air; and a roll of adhesive tape.

It was these last that she was interested in. If she could patch the cracks in her visor, she could buy herself a few hours. But stretch as she might, her fingertips came up a few maddening inches short of the release hatch. All her exertion just lost her more precious minutes of oxygen.

That left her with only one option; the one she had very much hoped to avoid.

Jean had known her share of amputees during her time in the Corps. It was an unfortunate truth of combat in vacuum – arms and legs made up a large part of the exposed surface area of a spacesuit, and needed to be lightly-armoured compared to the torso and head to preserve mobility. Often the slightest nick, whether from a flechette or an errant piece of debris, was enough to write off a limb. It was a serious enough problem that the ORC offered tantalising packages to potential recruits with cybernetic limbs, which wouldn't be disabled by exposure to space, and bonuses to serving men and women willing to get them.

If, by some miracle, events turned in humanity's favour, she was definitely going to insist she was compensated accordingly.

She withdrew her knife from the sheath strapped to her suit's outer-right thigh, and clumsily activated the blade with the switch just below the quillon. Her arm was trapped just above the elbow, but her suit's partition had deployed all the way up at the armpit. She made the cut as close to the partition as she could, taking extreme care not to accidentally puncture it. Her knife's edge was inset with ten thousand microscopic, serrated teeth, vacillating a few microns back and forth several thousand times per second. When activated, although it appeared to be a normal combat knife to the naked eye, its blade of tungsten carbide had cutting power equal to a high-powered rotary saw.

When the knife's edge met the flesh of her arm, her vision flashed red, the throbbing in her temples accelerating and growing more acute, harmonising with the muscle and sinew tearing in her bicep. Her local analgesics were potent, but there was a threshold beyond which they couldn't reduce pain and still keep her conscious. Her suit detected the elevated heartrate and nociceptor activity; her vision narrowed and dimmed. She regulated her breathing and fought through the haze.

The tissue and nanofibre mesh of her musculature gave way to the blade like hot butter. The bone of her upper humerus was more of a challenge, the knife sticking in its titanium weave like it had encountered a knot in an oak bough. The high-pitched whine of its microvibrations audibly lowered a few octaves. The temptation was to press harder, but Jean resisted it; that would only get her truly stuck. Finesse, not force – she angled the blade back and forth, in an almost gentle motion. Gentle enough that she could just about forget that *I'm cutting my own bloody arm off OH CHRIST…*

She paused, and took a few deep breaths, disregarding the oxygen warning for a few seconds. It was just an arm. It ranked pretty low in the hierarchy of things from which she had been severed. A little more pressure, and the bone gave way. The rest of the skin and sinew yielded like slow-cooked meat, and then she was loose. Her stump jerked free, with only a treacly dribble of dark blood thanks to the tourniquet. Paying it no mind, she lunged for the release hatch, and the treasures that lay in the ORC's standard-issue survival kit.

***

Ten minutes later, she was content that she had averted her most immediate crisis. The adhesive tape had proved challenging when she was working with only one suited hand, but with some trial and error, she had patched up the cracks on her visor and, for good measure, covered up the hole where she had cut open her left suit sleeve. Suit partition or not, she didn't want the cold of the lunar surface leeching into her chest cavity through her dead stump.

She had shattered her orbital bone when her head had collided with her visor – a distant second on her list of the day's grievous injuries. Her suit had given her unconscious body a cocktail of analgesics that reduced the pain of it to a throbbing equal to a bad hangover. In due course, it would hurt like a bastard, she knew. As long as it didn't bleed into her eyes just now, it wouldn't prevent her getting updates from her squadron.

'*Melinda* here,' she said, 'Crisis averted. *Belladonna*, status update, please.'

Glad to hear you're OK, Melinda. Velasquez's reply scrolled faster than his previous one, and his sentence construction wasn't omitting prepositions, which suggested he was under less pressure than he had been during his last transmission. **We're above the dark side, and holding our own, but we can't get a steady target lock on the Body's landing place. The bandits are still hounding us, and there're Collective reinforcements inbound. I can see your landing place. You're 6 klicks away from the Body.**

Jean barked a laugh, in the best tradition of 'if you don't laugh, you cry.' Six kilometres. After all of the distance she had come, she was separated from her target by six kilometres. That was like running a marathon only to collapse a foot from the finish line.

'Route me through to Albrecht.'

Aye, Commander.

There was a delay as the transmission was relayed around to the Earthward side of the Moon, and from there down to geosynchronous orbit. Several seconds later, Albrecht's voice found its way back along the telecommunication bucket brigade to her cochlear implants.

'Jean,' he said, 'please tell me you have better news for me than I have for you.'

'Well, Hermann, I'm marooned on a dead, airless satellite, my squadron's been decimated, and I just cut my arm off. I know what I want for Christmas, by the way.'

'I'll keep it in mind,' he replied, sounding unmoved by her effort at gallows comedy. 'The operation at my end is a failure. After Gershwin shot Arquette, the Collective stormed the Brazilian station and killed the remaining Tango, Zulu, Victor and Yankee squad members. Or maybe assimilated them, it's hard to be sure. As for now, I'm trying to put the plans together for a counter-counter-incursion, but the strategic situation tips more in the enemy's favour each minute. More and more craft are launching from the Americas and taking up defensive positions around the Brazilian station. It's like the spellbound have taken every jury-rigged, barely functional craft that could escape the gravity well on two continents and sent them against us. It'll take blind luck or divine intervention to penetrate their defensive line now.

'I have to tell you, Jean – opinion groundside is turning more and more towards destroying the Brazilian station outright, whether with surface-to-orbit or orbit-to-orbit nukes. Koo wants to believe you. He wants, more than anything, to avoid another Los Angeles on his hands. So, he's fighting it. But he's a public servant, at the end of the day, no matter how much rope China gives him, and eventually he has to bow to the will of nine billion people.'

'He can't!'

'He can, and he very probably will, if events don't turn in our favour soon. Even the nuclear option will be off the table in a few hours, if it isn't already. We have satellite reports of new Enclave Effect generators being constructed in the Americas, and reconnaissance suggests that some of the craft we're seeing coming into orbit are carrying equipment necessary to replicate the Brazilian station's success at other degrees of longitude. Unless you can pull a rabbit out of a hat, Jean, and soon, genocide is going to be the only recourse left to us.'

Jean took stock of her situation. She was battered, weary, and recently dismembered, riding high on a cocktail of drugs that she would shortly be coming down from. However, she had two working legs; a high-powered, handheld maser cannon good for fifteen shots; and she was six kilometres from the enemy's Holy Grail.

Just six kilometres, and in lunar gravity, at that. With no enemy boots on the ground blocking her way.

'Tell the Secretary from me that he can expect a rabbit within two hours. And that until he hears from me, he cannot – *must not* – countenance the nuclear option any further.'

***

When she had pressurised her suit, double- and triple-checking until she was satisfied that her adhesive-tape seals would hold (and then applying a second layer just to be sure), Jean sent the command to the cockpit UI to open the hatch to the lunar elements. What little air remained in the cockpit flooded out, the backdraft admitting a flurry of fine, grey moondust.

The *Melinda's* hatch opened part-way, maybe a foot wide before the mechanism jammed against the buckled metal on its left side. Jean lay back in her acceleration couch, chambered her legs, and administered a couple of stout kicks to open it the rest of the way. Even under the effects of anaesthesia, her enhanced strength hadn't deserted her. The aperture quickly widened enough to admit her exit.

She withdrew the maser cannon from the survival kit. Thankfully, the designers of this particular model had been aware of space combat's propensity for dismemberment, and had worked to accommodate for either a right- or left-armed amputee user. The fifteen charges were loaded like an old-fashioned pump action shotgun, with the exception that the loading portal could be locked open, allowing the shots to be easily inserted with one hand. Similarly, the stock featured a hook that allowed it to be braced against one's shoulder, aimed, and fired, compensating for the absent steadying action of a second arm.

Courtesy of Velasquez, Jean downloaded a map of the terrain separating her from the Body's passenger. The shortest course would lead her across two small craters in the surface, both couched in the basin of a larger, older crater. Though the patterns were different, formed by the impact areas of ancient meteoroid strikes rather than wind, it wasn't unlike hiking across the sands of the Sahara Desert. As with the nomads who followed the sand dunes there, her course would be faster, even if it was longer in linear klicks, if she followed the crater rims.

She took her first step, and stumbled. Lunar gravity – one-sixth of terrestrial. She was unaccustomed to this particular midway point between normal weight and no weight at all. The closest analogue was the outermost torus on the Congolese station, but without the telltale dizziness of the Coriolis Effect. She tested herself with a second step, and then a third, each time adjusting a little further to the bounce caused by her gait. By the fourth step, she was confident she had it.

The dark side of the Moon, it seemed to her, was a misnomer. The Sun shone brightly overhead, almost blindingly so in the absence of atmosphere. The contours of the surface were defined by the sharp contrast of monochromatic shadows; if not for the heavy tint of her visor, snow blindness would have been a real issue. As it was, the surface of the Moon appeared to her to possess a phantasmal clarity, its desolation rendered with such definition that each grain of dust was distinct.

Or perhaps that was just the drugs in her system, preceding the inevitable crash. Who knew. The solar light overhead was punctuated by explosions, generated by much closer sources. The space battle from which she had been forcibly retired was ongoing, and had only grown in ferocity. A dovetail missile released its payload barely a dozen klicks above her head; she could tell by the plumes of moondust erupting at regular intervals along the horizon. Which side the missile had belonged to, she had no idea.

The going was slow. Not because she was heavily laden – she could happily have carried two hundred kilos in this gravity before she started feeling taxed – but the dust beneath her boots was so fine that it gave way at the slightest pressure, affording her no steady traction. Climbing a slope was a frustrating exercise; it took her twenty minutes to reach the crest of her first crater rim. She fell to her knees twice, and once stumbled badly enough to fall to her knees. Her equilibrium was shot, and she was too acutely conscious of her own raging pulse, her own arrhythmic breathing. The universe external to her suit appeared remote, like she could only see it through the porthole in an antique diving bell.

When she got to the top, already sweating from the exertion, she had to take a moment to stop and boggle at the vista laid out to the lunar northwest. The creature she had seen in the image taken from the Olympus Mons Observatory had been imposing in a purely conceptual way. But the wall of organic matter lying six klicks away now was visceral and overwhelming in its impossible presence. Jean experienced a moment of vertigo, instinctually

414

convinced that this vast aberration in the landscape must be a hologram, or a matte painting.

The Body's passenger, lying still, inert. It seemed appropriate as the thing from which all of the madness enveloping the world had emanated, this inscrutable monster or god or whatever it was. It was all the more alien for its chimerical morphology, the merger of an insect and a whale that appeared obscene to Jean's mammalian eye. Of the three legs on the side of the creature she could see, each individually more than a kilometre long, one of them seemed to point at her where she stood on her crater rim, its gargantuan claw either accusing or inviting.

I'm going to take that thing hostage.

***

She trudged closer to the giant, and as she did so, the battle overhead faltered and slowed. She was monitoring it in real-time, her implants linked to her squadron through the *Belladonna*. Velasquez kept her posted with status updates, which grew increasingly curt and infrequent as he reported his wingmates being shot down one by one. Eventually, he neglected to update her at all, and finally the connection itself was severed, with nothing but static where her XO should have been. She thought she could discern the flash reflecting against the moondust that corresponded with the *Belladonna's* expiry. At the moment of his last report, there had still been four bandits of the original complement remaining.

Ninety-two elite ORC pilots, brought low by fifteen Collective agents. Was the hive mind's passion truly so much greater than theirs? Did its will to survive eclipse theirs by such a wide margin?

The remaining planes in lunar orbit paid her no mind. She plodded on, cursing the lunar dust with every step. It was finer than dry sand, and gave way underfoot more easily. She kept losing her balance, unaccustomed to her newfound asymmetry. When she inevitably fell, multiple times, she tried to ensure that she landed on her right side. Her body was nearing the limit of the analgesics her suit could safely administer, and the throbbing in her shoulder-stump was intensifying.

Half an hour passed; then an hour; then an hour and a half. The Body's passenger crept imperceptibly closer.

Jean was startled enough that she almost fell yet again when she picked up a radio transmission. It was on a general frequency, she realised, not directed at her specifically. Ensuring that her implants were receiving but not transmitting, she listened to what it had to say.

'Jean.' It was David Manderly's voice. She bit down on the expression of dismay that was formulating itself in her throat. Of course – he had been in San Francisco for his PNC debriefing when North America had been occupied.

'We can see you there on the surface, Jean. Your environment suit is bright orange, did you really think we wouldn't notice in this quality of light?'

She didn't answer. There was always the possibility he was bluffing, that they were baiting her to give away her position with an ill-judged reply. She had more professionalism than to be goaded into freely communicating with the enemy in any event.

'What is it you think you're going to accomplish, Jean? You have a flechette pistol, a knife, and maybe a maser cannon if the ORC survival kit survived the landing. You think that small arms can realistically do serious damage to an object that size? One that already survived an impact with the Moon at astronomical velocities? If you had a nuke, or a cluster of asp missiles to bring to bear, we might take you seriously. As it is? One injured woman, on foot, with a diminishing oxygen supply and no reinforcements? Jean, it's all over. Come home.'

It's not over. She dialled down the volume of her cochlear implants; David's voice was making the throbbing in her skull worse. The Body's passenger, whatever it was, had a weak point, something that allowed it to maintain its integrity in vacuum. She would cut it open and dig around inside its guts to find it, if that was what it took. When she did, and only then, would she announce herself to the Collective with a broadcast from her corneal implants of her holding it at gunpoint. Her first demand would be a supply drop of replacement O2 canisters, to be followed by the Collective's immediate and unconditional withdrawal of its forces. She could still do it, and if they were taking the trouble to call her out on comms, they knew she still represented a threat.

'Fine,' he continued. 'Be like that. You were always headstrong, for better and for worse. But if you won't listen to me, there's someone you might be more interested to hear from.' A pause, followed by the replacement of David's frustratingly genial, reasonable voice with another; young, female, and unsure of itself.

'Mum?'

Oh my God, Vic. You didn't.

'I overheard Albrecht saying you were still alive, somewhere on the dark side. After the last of Velasquez's squadron got shot down, I couldn't reach you through a secure channel, but I had to know. I contacted the Collective directly, Mum. I'm sorry.'

They're simulating her voice. That was what it had to be. Victoria's voice was computer-generated to start with; the firmware that created it was bespoke, but surely not difficult to duplicate. The bastards were putting words in her daughter's mouth, as a gambit to get her to respond.

'We nuked the Brazilian station, Mum,' *No, we didn't. We couldn't have. It hasn't been long enough.* 'Koo tried every trick he knew to stop it, but the Chinese Premier overrode him. It barely made a dent. They must have been building backup Effect generators on the surface faster than we anticipated.'

She sounded upset now, even tearful. *Nice attention to detail.*

'The fallout was confined to an estimated few million dead, mostly in the rural regions of South America. More craft are still launching from the surface. The Americas are lost for good, and soon they'll be deploying the orbital generators faster than we can shoot them down.'

Not if I have anything to say about it, they won't.

'I just wanted to let you know, Mum, that I've done that thing we talked about. You know, before we set out. Our mutual friend is safe.'

Jean slipped and fell again. *Shit.* There went the voice-simulation theory. That was just specific enough that Victoria could only have been referring to the contingency plan to keep the *Prospice* out of the Collective's reach.

'There's a horde of Collective craft *en route* to your position, Mum. They'll be on top of you within the hour. Not just fighters either; there are troop transports, loaded with manned insertion shuttles. Albrecht's dispatched a complement of fighters to pursue them, but it won't be enough to fight them off.

'I talked to Dave, Mum. He's willing to bargain. If you just throw down your weapons, and move away from the Body, you can have amnesty. He promises me that he'll give us free passage to retrieve you. We'll send you down an insertion shuttle so you can rendezvous with one of our troop carriers. It's going to be OK.'

That is an extremely bloody circumscribed definition of 'OK.' What was significant, though, was what Victoria was implying without expressly saying. If the Collective was willing to bargain, then it regarded her as enough of a threat to bother with. That perception mattered more than whatever real harm she could do to the Body's passenger.

The throbbing of her stump was making her eyes water. Her suit showed her remaining O2 at 42%. She soldiered on, silently.

***

The Collective craft Victoria had warned of appeared overhead just as she reached the tip of the Body's outstretched claw. The lights in her peripheral vision suggested that a multitude of insertion shuttles were descending upon her position – she clocked at least eight. When they landed, the Collective's agents would have to catch up to her; lunar gravity didn't put up much of a fight, so the thrust needed for a safe landing wasn't that great, but Jean couldn't see the Collective wanting to spew white-hot exhaust within a kilometre of their god's resting place.

The claw, she could see up close, was actually less insectoid than crustacean in its anatomy, divided by a joint into two segments that accounted for most of its length, with a short, barbed point coming above a second joint like a witch's hooked fingernail. It was spindly in terms relative to the creature's main mass, but those terms were very relative. At its widest point, the appendage must have been over thirty metres in diameter. Where it lay in the furrow it had carved in the lunar dust, it stood as high over Jean's head as a four-storey tenement block.

The material it consisted of puzzled her. It appeared at first glance to be some kind of mottled cartilage or bone, warping and swirling in patterns of lighter and darker grey. The colouration was similar to marble, though the texture was coarser and duller. Flecks of something shiny stood out from the rest of the mass – could it possibly be threaded with metal filaments, like her own bones, or some unearthly equivalent?

As she approached the hulking mass, she had the intangible but growing sense of a living, present mind. She was almost certain it wasn't some side effect of the drugs in her system. It was more like the animal awareness that preceded a thunderstorm; a primordial corner of the brain that recognised the latency in the charged stillness. Of course, this creature had psychically touched nearly every person on Earth in the Engagement, across millions of miles of vacuum – the sensation she was feeling was to the Engagement as static electricity was to a lightning strike.

She was quite certain it was still, in some capacity, alive. Was it attempting to communicate, and having its efforts stymied by the anti-Effect cap she was wearing under her helmet? Or did it simply excrete paired particles as unconsciously as she might sweat, blindly groping for another nervous system? The answer, she suspected, lay at the creature's centre. She marched on, following the claw towards the middle of the crater where it lay.

Two of the Collective's insertion pods landed a klick and a half to the south. The flare of exhaust that announced them was shortly followed by a pair of figures bounding over the crater rim, traversing the lunar surface in great flying leaps rather than Jean's ungainly steps. Each leap was accompanied by a gaseous expulsion, like that of a Vernier engine. They were using jump-packs to hasten their passage, and they were coming straight for her.

The moment the two were in range, they announced themselves with a maser blast. The starburst it produced upon her helmet sent a barb of pain up into her cranium, and she lurched away. It sailed harmlessly over her head to diffuse out in space. *A warning shot. Those condescending pricks.*

Give it up, Jean, came an ultimatum from one of the two suited figures. **We have this position surrounded. You're outgunned, and you're running out of air. Leave the Body be.**

She pushed herself falteringly to her feet. Her vision blurred; her ears rang. She prompted her suit for another shot of adrenaline and analgesics; after she swiped aside two layers of dire warnings in her HUD, it was grudgingly administered.

Just a few more minutes of performance; a few more minutes that she could exert her will over her body. That was all she asked; everything else would follow.

Her back was to the enormous claw; any shot they aimed at her in anger would run the risk of gouging into the flesh of their god. Was that a risk they were willing to take? There was one good way to find out. She trained her own cannon on the assimilate on the left, taking care to judge the arc of their jump, and timed her retaliatory shot to coincide with the second they came into contact with the ground.

The cannon's single-use charge packed more than a gigawatt of stopping power, its efficacy improved in vacuum where there were no ambient particles to act as dampening refractors for the beam. She caught the assimilate squarely in his centre mass, reducing most of his body instantaneously to ash and plasma. His end, whoever he might once have been, would have been painless.

The second leaping figure immediately dove to one side. If he was hunting for cover, he wouldn't find any – the crater in which they stood was only months old, there hadn't been time for it to be disrupted by more meteoroid strikes, which meant no ridges for either of them to hide behind. He settled instead for a zig-zagging pattern, altering the height and angle of his jumps randomly to confound Jean's attempts to get a bead on him. At eight-hundred metres distant, and unused to firing one handed, she wasted four more shots that went far wide of their mark. She forced herself to slow down and conserve her ammo. Only ten charges left, and she would have more than this one to deal with soon.

The assimilate circled around to her east flank, and apparently contented himself that he had a clear shot that wouldn't endanger the Body. He suddenly fired a beam in a broad arc at the height of his jump, tracing a line across the lunar surface intersecting with Jean's position. She jerked out of the way by pure reflex; the motion, which would have thrown her to the ground in terrestrial gravity, instead left her suspended for fully two seconds, helplessly sailing through vacuum. Her opponent would have ample time to line up another shot, this one sure to be lethal. She twisted in the middle of her arc, bringing her cannon to bear on what she guessed was maybe, possibly her enemy's position, and fired before she hit the ground. She fully expected she wouldn't strike her mark; she just needed to buy a few seconds to get back on her feet and reoriented.

She landed on her stump; a distant jolt of something that ought to have been pain tugged at her torso. The Sun caught her visor, and she winced away from it. Everything was so awfully bright.

She rose to her feet, eyes streaming from the impact, just in time to flinch away from a second maser shot sweeping the ground from above. It passed close enough to her this time to leave violet streaks on the insides of her eyelids, but she didn't lose her balance.

She looked up – her opponent was, quite literally, almost on top of her. The arc of his boosted jump was carrying him bodily right towards her. He was lining up a third shot; at such close range now, there was no way he'd miss this time.

In the time it would take her to bring the cannon around, rack it one-handed to eject the spent charge, aim, and fire, she would already have been dead for at least a second and a half. She didn't think, just did what came naturally; she dropped the cannon and jumped towards her opponent, colliding with him in mid-arc six metres off the ground, right as he pulled his cannon's trigger.

The impact knocked the wind out of her, but the move had caught him completely off-guard. They spun together above the lunar surface, his maser shot tracing through ninety degrees in the moment he had his finger on the trigger. About the only thing it didn't hit was Jean, now that she was safely within the reach of the weapon's barrel. Denied the application of her left arm, Jean wrapped her legs around the assimilate's torso.

The pair of them crashed to the ground, tangled together; he trying to push her off; she refusing to be dislodged. Quickly, fumblingly, Jean withdrew her combat knife from its sheath on her thigh and activated it. She cut two quick punctures at his left and right shoulders. His suit's partitions activated, sealing off the depressurisation; he dropped the maser cannon, his limbs rendered useless by the exposure to vacuum. Having both literally and figuratively disarmed her enemy, she raised the knife overhead and plunged it with all her strength through his helmet's visor.

He stopped struggling.

When she wrenched the knife free, it was red almost to the hilt for a few seconds, before the microvibrations shook the droplets of blood loose to freeze.

Gasping, Jean heaved herself upright. Her HUD's readout was showing 18% oxygen remaining. She would have to swap in the spare O2 canisters from the survival kit soon, and the procedure to do so would leave her vulnerable when the rest of the assimilates showed up, alerted by their comrades' severance. The last adrenaline booster was wearing off. She felt sick, bone weary, and worse, on the cusp of genuine despair.

Humanity has lost.

This plan is ridiculous.

You will never see your family again.

She kept moving.

***

Her opponent's last, errant maser shot had hit the Body's passenger. It had burned a furrow about a klick long, roughly parallel to its limb, and as they had twisted in mid-jump, it had briefly struck the 'flesh' of the central, cetacean part. The hide hadn't been deeply penetrated – the beam had swung across the creature's girth too quickly to have cut more than a few inches into whatever material it was that comprised it – but what the shot had exposed gave Jean occasion to stop and stare when she finally reached the scorch mark.

The creature's innards had been exposed to vacuum. There was a layer of something very like the fatty blubber of a seal or a whale immediately beneath the mottled grey skin, white and slimy where it hadn't been charred black by the maser's heat. Hundreds of litres of the soft white offal had spilled out of the wound, together with pink and red organs and tissues beneath, the function of which Jean could only guess at.

These tissues pooled and steamed on the crater floor, but failed to freeze as they ought to have done this close to absolute zero. The creature's flesh reacted appropriately to the application of heat, but appeared to disregard the effects of the cold, in defiance of physics and common sense.

In amongst the organic tissue, there were inorganic components visible in the creature's flesh. Jean probed the wound, plunging her arm inside it all the

422

way up to the shoulder, grateful all the while that she could smell none of what was going on outside her suit. She yanked out something that she could have sworn was a circuit board. It clung to the surrounding tissue by fibrous strands of sinew that obstinately refused to snap. Where the fibres ended and the circuit board began, she couldn't know. Looking now at the creature's outer hide now, she could see that the same was true everywhere else on its body; skin and synthetic components running seamlessly into one another.

The sense of another mind being present that had taken hold of her when she had been near the claw was ten times stronger now; the latent, phantasmal *something* pressed at the outermost edges of her consciousness.

All at once, in response to her ministrations, something shifted inside the wound. The circuit board she had tugged free was yanked back insistently. The blubber and the sinews seemed to roil and bubble, stretching and squirming in contortions no tissue should undergo. Flesh knitted itself together of its own accord, and then having done so, transmuted itself into steel and copper and glass, exchanging organic complexity for mechanical complexity, as though the makeup of its matter on the subatomic level was a plaything to be broken apart and reassembled upon a whim.

Where there had been a gaping wound, there was now a protrusion; a concave glass lens housed in a metal casing, approximating the shape of a human eyeball more than a metre in diameter. A dim blue light flickered on in the centre of the lens, where the iris ought to be.

A camera.

It peered at Jean with what she could have sworn was an expression of curiosity. It wanted to talk; she was sure of it now.

'I can't,' she mouthed at it. She gestured at her helmet, and the anti-Enclave cap beneath it. 'I'm wearing something that blocks us from doing so, and I can't take it off without hurting myself.'

The lens moved. No: it *gestured*. Jean followed its gaze to where it was pointing – the stump of her severed left arm. She realised that the adhesive tape seal she had used to keep it insulated from vacuum had been torn at some point in the fight with the assimilates. And indeed, her suit was working overtime to compensate for the heat leeching out of her body. Between adrenaline and fatigue, she just hadn't noticed.

She thought she understood what the Body was getting at. The effect it generated – what had been the inspiration for Xavier Wong's Enclave Effect – remotely connected two minds and nervous systems. If she was unable to establish such a connection remotely, then she could do so directly. A wired connection, rather than a wireless one, so to speak.

Eight shots left in her maser cannon. 12% oxygen remaining in her suit. A flechette pistol and a low-on-charge combat knife. She couldn't do this creature serious harm with what she had left, and it was pointless to pretend otherwise.

But if she could communicate with it, then perhaps – *perhaps* – she could reason with it.

The Body was the Collective's god; the totem around which it had built its cult. The Collective would listen with rapt attention to anything it had to say, as and when it could talk to it. But if Jean spoke to it first, she could argue on behalf of unassimilated humanity. She could convince it that they were worthy of being allowed to remain as they were, despite all their imperfections.

She had rummaged around in its open wound. She supposed turn-about was fair play. She tore off what remained of the seal over her stump, and gingerly presented it to the Body.

The response was immediate. Tendrils formed on the surface of the Body's hide, and reached out toward her. They wrapped around her stump, and tightened. The sensation wasn't painful, but neither was it pleasant, and Jean forced herself not to cringe away from the intrusion. It extended barbed filaments that pushed into the dead meat of her shoulder. They pushed deeper, wriggling into her torso, toward her heart and spine and lungs and brain, probing for active nerve endings.

And it found them.

***

All at once, Jean was no longer standing on the surface of the Moon. She was no longer in any pain or discomfort. The anxiety and the dread were gone. The mental and physical fatigue were gone; she was as clearheaded as she would have been if she had been coming off eight hours' sleep and a round of stimulants. Neither was she wearing an environment suit. Indeed, she wasn't

424

wearing anything at all, because she had no body. She was a hovering consciousness, perfectly still within a white void.

'Where am I?' she tried to say, but the sound didn't come. There were no lips, no tongue, no lungs to formulate it. The thought extended from her, soundless.

The void responded to her question. It began to differentiate itself, the whiteness subdividing into hundreds, thousands, millions of beings. Entities beyond counting swirled around her. She was at the heart of a cyclone, and every particle that comprised it asked her the same question.

WHY?

The force of that one, unified enquiry made her bodiless self buckle and contract.

'Why what!?' she cried, voicelessly.

WHY? they responded, and the cyclone contracted, enclosing her. Their minds were open to hers, and hers to them. Jean explained her perspective.

The minds expressed surprise, and a measure of disbelief.

Jean begged that they intercede on her behalf. The minds demanded certain terms be met before they did so. Jean protested that the terms were unreasonable. The minds were adamant that they would not accept a lesser standard of proof.

Jean, eventually, accepted. *If that's how it has to be*, she thought.

The bargain was struck, and the wheels were set in motion.

***

Jean was returned to her body. The tendrils detached themselves from her nerves and withdrew from her shoulder, releasing her back into the material world where she was tired and desperate and in pain. She sat down heavily, her back slumped against the Body. Her suit gave her 9% O2 remaining, filling her vision with red alerts.

There were another six assimilates closing on her position, using the same long, bounding, booster-pack-assisted jumps as the two she had killed. She fired a couple of her remaining maser shots at them, mostly for the sport of it, which of course went far wide of their nominal targets.

Then she opened a channel to them. 'Hey Dave,' she said. Her tongue felt thick in her mouth. It took some effort to form the syllables, and even then, they came out sounding mushy and drunk. 'You still there?'

'Hey Jean,' came the reply after a couple of seconds. 'Have you finally come to your senses?'

'Put me through to Vic, will you?'

'You'll be able to talk to her soon enough, Jean.'

She fired a couple more shots at the incoming assimilates, just to make her point clear.

'Jesus, okay, no need to get aggressive,' David said. 'She's been waiting on tenterhooks, give me a second.'

A moment later, Victoria's voice flooded into Jean's cochlear implants. 'Mum! Thank God, thank God, thank fucking God! I'm on my way, okay? The cavalry is coming. Everything's going to be okay.'

'Vic, don't come here.'

'...What do you mean?'

'I've got legions of the Collective bearing down on me, Vic. They're not just going to let me go unmolested, not after what I just did. Any bargain you made with them is null and void, now. And even if, by some miracle, you evacuated me alive, they'll follow me to the ends of the universe to get at what's in my head. I can't let them take me, Vic. I can't let there be any chance of them taking me. You understand what I'm saying, don't you?'

'Mum, what the hell are you talking about? Look, just stay where you are, I'm coming for you right now, I'm almost in lunar orbit...'

'You're a fighter, Vic. I like to think you get that from me. You kicked like a mule in the womb, did I ever tell you that? Anyone who wrongs you, you give them hell. You'll keep giving them hell as long as you draw breath. I have every confidence in you.'

'Mum, Jesus Christ, don't talk like this.'

'I love you, Vic. I'm proud of you, and everything you've grown to be. You're stronger than I could ever dream of being. Giving you breath was the best thing I ever did with my life.'

'Mum, for fuck's sake, NO…!'

'Don't cry for me, Vic. We'll see each other again. I promise.'

Jean severed the transmission.

Her flechette pistol was strapped to the outside of her left thigh. With her one remaining arm, she had to reach awkwardly across her body to draw it. She fumbled with the catch.

The Collective's agents were bearing down on her. They were barely seconds away from being on top of her. Her oxygen reserves were down to 5%.

How many times had she rehearsed this moment in her imagination, since she had been severed from the Enclave? Now that the moment was here – now, indeed, that she had no other choice – she found herself reluctant. But duty called, and she would answer. A purpose had been granted to her, and given purpose, all her fear and doubt was dispelled.

A suited figure descended towards her, the sunlight reflecting from its polarised visor dazzling her, an object which could only be a syringe clutched in its hand.

Quickly, allowing herself no further time to think, Jean Harrison placed her flechette pistol to her right temple, and pulled the trigger. Fragments of glass and bone and grey matter silently spackled the lunar surface, and the secrets they held died with her.

Chapter 26

September 4th, 2327 C.E.

Another conflagration in the far distance; extinguished as quickly as it began. It was only perceptible with the shuttle's sensors magnifying a small square of trans-lunar space, but even so, it was closer and brighter than the last one, minutes before.

Jonah had reeled in shock from Aki's message for perhaps five seconds, before he had hobbled back to James and Alyssa as fast as his leg would carry him. As they had listened to his report, the Collective's reaction had cycled quickly through disbelief, past horror, to resolve.

They had driven north to the landing strip where he had been received the previous year. There, a shuttle had been in the final stages of prep for launch. He realised that they had been waiting to whisk him off to the Moon, the very second he said 'yes.'

While they were on the move, the Collective plied him with real-time updates of the situation as it unfolded. Even as he was explaining the threat to James and Alyssa, the Collective had been positioning telescopes and radio dishes embedded in the geosynchronous ring structure, combing the sky for evidence of Victoria's army. Within minutes, they found it – with the awareness of what they were looking for, the massed cluster of warp signatures a little over an AU distant stood out to their instruments as clearly as the morning. The Collective confirmed Aki's grim claim – something massive was approaching on a course that would intersect with Earth's path at a terrifying velocity.

Jonah had been asked to record a message which would be forwarded to Victoria, and promptly did so. If there was any chance, however slim, that he could talk his granddaughter down from this precipice, then he was obligated to try. Even as he did so, searching for some combination of words that might get through to her, the surer he became that it was a forlorn hope, that he couldn't avert disaster without bloodshed.

Twenty minutes later, her reply confirmed it: 'I hear you, Starman, and I'm sorry. Understand that I don't bear you any resentment. I told you back on TransTerra that I never once stopped loving you. That hasn't changed. But, sadly, you're wrong. It is too late. It's been far past too late, for a very long time.'

Did I drive her to this? Jonah wondered, the idea sitting like a stone in his heart even as he recognised how egotistical it was. Whatever had compelled Victoria to move beyond all sane rules of engagement, to disregard any possibility of a reconciliation or ceasefire, it had to have been festering and suppurating in the Insurgency writ large – otherwise, how could she have bent so many other Archangels to her will? Still, he couldn't help but feel he had been the catalyst – that by leaving her, he had pushed her over some critical, emotional threshold that had thus far held her back.

The Collective was putting a full-scale evacuation into effect. As the shuttle pierced the film of the atmosphere, he saw myriad other vaporous streamers entering space adjacent to his own.

It wouldn't be enough. He had seen enough of the countryside surrounding South Dakota; enough of the Earth under the Collective's control. He understood, from the way the assimilate population was distributed, that even an evacuation under optimal conditions would only admit a few millions at most to the geosynchronous ring in the hours left until the comet's extinction-level impact (and even the ring might not be far enough). And then, there were the supplies of food, water, and oxygen needed to sustain the evacuees.

Jonah's shuttle bypassed the ring, taking the straightest course available for the Moon. He saw fibrous mass drivers extended outward from it toward deep space; hundreds upon hundreds of Scarabs were queuing up to be launched into combat.

He grimaced. He had been too leisurely in giving the Collective his answer. Now time was short, and his moment of reckoning with the Body's passenger had come, whether he liked it or not.

***

The structure on the dark side of the Moon straddled the full width of a crater more than five kilometres across. Bleach white, it sprawled over the landscape like some hybrid of a warehouse complex and a megachurch.

A hangar bay with a three-klick landing strip opened to admit the shuttle. After it closed and the atmosphere equalised, Jonah was greeted inside by David Manderly. He gestured for Jonah to join him in an open-topped personnel carrier. Alyssa and James hung back, their task to deliver Jonah to this place complete. Both immediately slotted into the ranks of assimilates readying themselves to fight or flee.

The hangar was full of frenzied activity. Scarabs received maintenance from assimilate engineers, their hands manipulating their tools as quickly as the human frame would permit. Every unit, upon receiving the green light, was attached to an electromagnetic rail and launched toward the encroaching threat, accelerated many times past the speed of sound.

The personnel carrier bore the pair of them through a tunnel toward the centre of the complex. A pair of double doors closed behind them as they left the hangar, dampening the noise of the mass drivers almost to nothing. The tunnel was the same bright, antiseptic white as the facility's exterior. It curved downward, at first steeply and thereafter more gently, conforming to the slope of the crater where the structure was housed.

'Do you think you can win?' Jonah asked Manderly the question softly. The other man gave him a hard look.

'Do you want us to win?' he replied without answering.

'Mostly, I didn't want it to come to this. Now that it has, though, obviously yes, I want you to win. Victoria's gone insane. However she might feel about the Collective, the idea that she'd resort to destroying *everything*...'

'I'm glad to hear you say that. Please keep it in mind.'

The tunnel was almost flat at this point. The personnel carrier drew up to a second set of double doors, which admitted them to the multiple square-kilometre cavity that formed the main part of the complex.

The sight of the Body's passenger, lying in the middle of the cavernous interior space like the grandest museum exhibit in history, beggared Jonah's sense of proportion. It was larger than the wreck of the *Prospice*. The personnel carrier drove beneath the appendages protruding from the creature's back, and the shadows they cast were like those of the vaults of an incomprehensible alien cathedral.

A small portion of the creature's body was partitioned off from the rest of it – a segment just below the point where the middle appendage on the creature's left side joined with its body was covered by a tent of opaque white fabric. Manderly pulled the personnel carrier over just outside the tent, and gestured for Jonah to follow him inside.

Jonah did so, taking care with his gait under the lunar gravity. What lay within was a patch of the creature's skin, several metres square, the distinction from the rest of its bulk immediately obvious. There was a long strip of what looked like scar tissue, dividing the patch of visible skin vertically, from ground to ceiling. Protruding from the middle of this four-metre-long scar, there was some manner of mechanical appendage, resembling a human eyeball, stalk and all.

This appendage stirred when Jonah entered the tent's enclosed space. He could have sworn its gaze *followed* him.

Manderly was looking at him as well, his gaze no less intent than that of the camera, or whatever it was. 'Do you feel anything?' he asked.

'Besides scrutinised? No, I can't say I do.'

Manderly heaved a sigh. 'This is where she died, you understand? Jean.'

Jonah recoiled. 'What the hell is wrong with you? Why would you tell me that?'

'I'm not trying to be cruel for the sake of it, Captain. It hurts us as well, to remember her. You know, I think every pre-assimilate parent believes their child to be the most special, the most precious, the most unique person in the universe. The birth rate back in 2135 peaked at five-hundred and fifty-thousand babies born a day. That's more than six every second. Maybe not all, but most of those infants' parents looked at them, with complete assurance that their baby was special, among all those billions. It's absurd, really. Solipsism-by-proxy. But you're different, Captain Jonah Harrison. You belong to a rarefied group that can know for a fact that their child really is that special, that unique. Jean thwarted us, you see. She beat us to the punch reaching the Body, and because of what she did, whatever it was, its secrets have been closed to us ever since. Because of her sacrifice, history could have gone one way, and instead it has gone another.'

Jonah heard a note of melancholy in Manderly's voice – something deeper, more personal than the Collective's resentment at being thwarted.

'You loved her, didn't you?'

Manderly sniffed. 'As a pre-assimilate? Yes. Yes, I loved her. As an assimilate, I stand in awe of her: the one who chose not to return. She had every opportunity to. She knew how easy it would have been. But not only did she survive and recover from being severed – she elected to die rather than become a part of the Collective a second time, in order to preserve her vision of what life ought to be. That sheer, stubborn, all-too-human blindness; that frightens us, even as it gives us cause for respect. Her ideals were misguided, but the conviction with which she pursued them is an example worthy of remembrance.

'You asked if we thought we could win, Jonah. Just minutes ago, one of our units breached Victoria's vanguard and self-destructed in the face of the incoming comet. The attack succeeded in breaking it apart.'

For a moment Jonah's heart rose, but Manderly's expression remained grim, even funereal. 'But...?'

'But a large fragment remains on a collision course with Earth. Our best Hail Mary save has failed. We're continuing to launch every Scarab that can be mustered against them, but the tactics Victoria has employed have worked at deflecting them thus far. Barring a miracle, the comet's collision with Earth will soon be a mathematical certainty. We have to assume that, within the next forty-eight hours, over ninety-nine percent of the assimilated human beings currently living will be dead. And Victoria won't be content to stop there. She'll keep killing, and killing, until she's satisfied that every vestige of the Collective has been wiped from the universe.'

Jonah swallowed. 'So, what is it you think I can do about it?'

'About your granddaughter's genocide? Nothing. What we want... what *we* need... from you, is the final revelation of the Body. Bringing you here was some kind of test, set for us for reasons known only to it, and to Jean when she was still alive. The knowledge of how to truly live; the gateway to a better, higher consciousness than even the Collective – it's locked inside, and you're the key, Jonah. Even if most of us die today – even if only a handful survive – if we can just unlock the Body's last secrets, it can be disseminated instantly to agents light-years away. They can start humanity afresh, reproduce and multiply far off in the cosmos on a planet like TransTerra where Victoria will never find them, but better this time. The new human race will be designed according to the Body's gospel, truly free of suffering, truly at peace with itself. The Body's blessing is worth anything to us. Even the loss of Earth itself.'

A low rumble sounded from elsewhere in the complex, accompanied by a tremor that Jonah felt in the soles of his feet. This was followed moments later by the acrid smell of burning plastic.

'She's here,' Manderly said, with a combination of urgency and incredulity, addressed as much to himself as to Jonah. 'A thorn in our side to the bitter end, is it Victoria?' Two more reverberations, harsher and louder than the first, came as though in reply.

'We haven't much time,' Manderly said, turning back toward Jonah. 'Quickly – what's your decision? You've lived amongst us for over a year, now. You must know it by now, surely, that our way is best?'

Jonah chewed the inside of his cheek for a moment, thinking. 'It's true,' he said, slowly. 'You're on to something. You created a society without war, or crime, or poverty. Without unhappiness. But even so...'

Manderly frowned, but Jonah ploughed ahead, regardless. He thought of the old assimilate he'd seen keel over in St. Louis.

'Victoria... I think I understand her at last. I think she's still grieving. For two hundred years, she's done nothing but grieve. But in the world you would build, no-one grieves. And where no-one grieves, no-one loves. No-one lives.'

He raised his head.

'If I understand what you're asking – if, after the past year, I really have come to understand the Collective – then my answer is no. I don't recognise you as the human beings I know. I don't agree with Victoria, and the path of destruction she's taken. I don't want to see you annihilated. But if you're right, and only a handful of people will survive this day, then the legacy I want to throw forward to generations to come, when humanity is rebuilt, doesn't include the Collective.'

As he spoke, Manderly began to shake. He turned away from Jonah, in such a way that his face was obscured. When he turned back, there were tears running down his cheeks from each of his pale blue eyes.

'You mean it?' He asked with the cadence of a chastised child. 'You'd throw your lot in with Victoria's vision of humanity. The one that murders and destroys with abandon?'

Jonah nodded. 'It takes a person able to feel hurt – to feel betrayed – to be capable of such murder and destruction to begin with.'

'I see,' Manderly said. His voice trembled. 'So, our day of reckoning is to be a sad one, after all.' He advanced towards Jonah. From a pouch strapped to his matte-black armour, he withdrew a hypodermic syringe. 'If we must force you to see our perspective, so be it. Please, don't struggle Captain. Accept the inevitable and make this easy, for both our sakes.'

Jonah's gaze followed the syringe clutched in Manderly's right hand, held fast in his grey, cybernetic fingers. In that vial, he knew, was the end of Jonah Harrison. On the other side of it was a being that wore his face, and spoke with his tongue, and referred to itself with his name, but it wasn't him.

Manderly raised his arm, reaching for him.

There's nothing noble about going out this way. You've said your piece; now make it mean something, old man. You're not dead yet, so place some value on your life, goddammit! FIGHT!

Manderly's body, as far as Jonah could see, was cyborg from the collarbones on down. He had to assume that every clothed inch of the man he couldn't see was metal. The hand holding the syringe would be immune to the joint locks or reflexive shocks he could inflict, nor could he materially damage it with his flesh-and-blood physique, however conditioned it might be.

But Manderly's face was flesh and blood too, and it had weathered the ravages of senescence worse than Jonah had. His skin was thin, prone to tearing and bruising. His bones' density would be notably reduced; even if they were reinforced with titanium mesh, his jaw and cheekbones would crumble with enough application of force.

The face. Focus everything on his face.

435

Another reverberation, this one violent enough to cause them both to stumble. Jonah took advantage of the instant of disruption to step inside the reach of Manderly's arms, taking care to keep his centre of gravity low. He wrapped his left arm around Manderly's right, holding it and the syringe its hand clasped away from him. With his right, he hit Manderly in the centre of his forehead with a crisp, sharp elbow strike. The ancient man's head jerked back. His eyes met Jonah with more indignity and surprise than pain.

Jonah struck again, the point of his elbow colliding with the cheekbone. A third strike; this one to the chin. Lucky number three; he felt something give where the blow fell. A spasm passed through Manderly's body, an involuntary reflex from the depths of his brain stem at having his jaw dislocated, overriding the fine motor control he held over his cybernetic limbs. His right arm shuddered where Jonah held it fast. Something clattered softly to the floor.

Jonah, certain he had his foe reeling, wound up for a final, decisive blow that would knock Manderly out when he felt a colossal impact in his right temple. He reeled, his grip on Manderly's right arm slackening just enough for the older man to wrench it free. This was followed by two more crushing blows to his torso. Before he could register the pain of his ribs being shattered, there followed a precise, almost surgical knifehand strike to his larynx. He gasped and choked; his brain deprived of oxygen. He fell to his knees, and from there to the floor, clutching at his throat.

You chose the hard way, Jonah. The text filtered into his vision, his corneal HUD crystal clear even as his eyes watered from the pain. He must have damaged Manderly's jaw too badly for speech. **Don't worry. It'll all be over soon.**

Jonah tried to stand, but his legs wouldn't listen. Instead, he clawed his way across the too-white plastic floor, buying every centimetre he could get from his opponent. His hand encountered something smooth and cylindrical. Still choking, vision blurred, he looked down at what he had found.

It was the syringe.

He grabbed it and raised it so as to smash it on the floor, to buy whatever few short minutes he could. Before he could shatter it, a vice-grip closed on his ankle and pulled him back where he had crawled from, then took hold of his lapel and hauled him rudely to feet that wouldn't support him. One of Manderly's arms closed around his bruised throat, further constricting his already compromised breathing; the other probed for the syringe that he clutched in a desperate death grip. He held on to it as tightly as he'd ever held anything, but not tightly enough. He could feel his grip slackening, being prised apart by Manderly's cold, metal digits.

Just let it go, Jonah. Spare yourself the struggle and let go.

But he wouldn't. Even as his consciousness began to swim in and out, he wouldn't let go.

An explosion blew the tent apart with a deafening roar and a shockwave to match. The pair of them were thrown back like leaves in a hot hurricane wind, Manderly's grip on his neck released. Jonah fell to the floor, spluttering and wheezing for air. The hand that still, somehow, miraculously held the syringe, came into contact with something soft.

Manderly raised himself to a crouch, he having landed three metres away from where Jonah now slumped. He turned to look at him; his face was unrecognisable, swollen and discoloured where Jonah had beaten it. His jaw was hanging at an odd angle. Blood dripped from his injuries, the red standing in a harsh contrast to the room and his skin. But he was still more mobile than Jonah felt at that moment. He stood fully upright, and began advancing on him once more. His eyes were fixed on something just to Jonah's right, alive with fierce, joyous hunger.

Jonah tried to jerk away from his opponent, but he was held fast by something other than injury and fatigue. His right arm refused to budge; the hand holding the syringe felt like it was stuck to something.

A maser blast tore through the tent, enveloping it in fire. It caught Manderly dead on. The ancient man didn't even have time to register surprise before he disintegrated in front of Jonah's eyes, reduced to ionised plasma just as Marcus Lawson had been, what felt now like a lifetime ago.

Jonah saw Victoria stride through the aperture she had burned in the canvas, silhouetted from behind by flame. Her brilliant blue eyes were fixed on the same point Manderly's had been, but her expression was one of dismay, not joy. Jonah turned his head, his vision still swimming, to see what was so fascinating at the end of his right arm. He saw; when he had fallen, thrown by the shockwave, his hand had touched the scar on the creature's hide. As if accepting his flesh as an offering, red and pink tendrils emerged and wrapped themselves around his fingers; his palm; his wrist. They crawled up his forearm. No, he realised, with new barbs of pain cutting through his flickering consciousness; *into* his forearm.

He tried, weakly, to pull away from it, out of visceral repulsion. If this was the holy congress Manderly had been hinting at, then he wanted no part of it. He would not have his body invaded by an alien parasite any more than he would have his mind be. But the more he protested, the more the tendrils squeezed; the more they burrowed into his skin, his sinews, his muscles. He reached across himself, frantic now, adding the strength of his left arm trying to pull himself loose.

'Victoria…!' He choked. He meant to plead with her. *Burn it. Burn me, kill me if you have to, just don't let it take me. Let me end as myself.*

***

He would have said as much, but abruptly, he found the pain in his arm was gone. The smoke was no longer stinging his eyes, its chemical smell no longer prickling in his nose. His head felt quite clear. And, most saliently, he was no longer in the tent at all. He was no longer in the complex.

He was sitting in the dining room of the old farmhouse. Not the museum exhibit the Collective had prepared for his arrival. It was just as he remembered it, from his childhood. The light of mid-afternoon filtered in through the patio doors. The oak table was draped with a lace tablecloth, with places set for three diners; the best china crockery and silver cutlery, and three crystal champagne flutes. The embers of a fire glowed in the adjacent living-room hearth. Above the mantelpiece were displayed two of his mother's proudest landscapes; one of the view of the London Bridge from the shore of the Thames, the other of the Ansel Adams Wilderness. Twin tokens of the home of her birth and her adopted home, she had called them.

The front door opened, admitting a warm, early-autumn breeze. The entrant, calmly and with no excess of haste, wiped off their shoes, hung up their coat, and closed the door behind them. They met Jonah's gaze.

'Hey, Dad,' they said, simply.

Jonah blinked, and stood, sharply.

Was this what was meant by that old cliché? Having your life flash before your eyes? He blinked several more times, but his visitor's face stubbornly failed to dissolve, as a dream or a hallucination might.

He opened his mouth to reply to the greeting, but nothing came. He looked away, looked back, and tried again.

'Hey, Jean.'

Chapter 27

September 4th, 2327 C.E.

'But how...'

'"How can this be?"' Jean finished for him. 'Yeah, that would be my first question too, Starman, if I was in your position. Sit back down, for God's sake, you look like you're standing at attention. We have a lot of catching up to do, so first things first. Let's both have a coffee.'

Jonah did sit back down, heavily. 'They told me you were dead. Your ashes were sitting on that mantelpiece.'

'That mantelpiece? For two hundred years? Wow, that's morbid.'

Jean retrieved a pair of mugs from the dining room cabinet (he was quite sure they hadn't been kept there) and produced a pot of coffee – Jonah couldn't quite see where from, but the aroma of freshly brewed coffee suddenly filled the room. He couldn't take his eyes off her – she hadn't aged a day since the last video message he had seen from her, way back when the *Prospice* had barely completed a fifth of its voyage.

'Am I dreaming?' he asked. 'Is that what this is, some kind of dying hallucination? Or...' He felt oddly embarrassed to bring up the notion that occurred to him at that moment. Jean smiled easily. 'Sorry to disappoint you, Dad. No, this isn't heaven. Although I'm a little flattered that the thought crossed your mind. You're very much still alive.'

'Then what...'

'It's a simulacrum I created ahead of time, to help put your mind at ease when you finally arrived. I put it together from my memories of the times I visited this old place when I was young. I peeked at a few of yours, as well, to round out some of the finer details. I hope you don't mind.'

About a million other questions went through Jonah's mind at that moment, but before he could give voice to any of them, they were interrupted by a pang of alarm. He rose sharply to his feet. 'We don't have time!' he cried. 'In less than an hour...'

Jean ushered him to sit back down with a conciliatory gesture. 'Don't worry about it. Time in here is malleable. An hour outside, a minute, a fraction of a second, even, last as long as we need them to.

'I know all about what Vic's up to. It's odd, you know. I'm disappointed in her that she took this course, but at the same time, I understand why she felt she had to. Honestly, it's my fault. She thinks she failed me, all those years ago, and ever since then, she's been hardening her heart. Steeling herself to do what she feels she couldn't, back then.'

'So, are you still alive?'

Jean smiled again, though this time, he thought the expression was tinged with sadness. She poured them both a coffee. Black, with two stevia sweeteners for him; milk and no sweetener for her. 'I guess you'd have to qualify both "me" and "alive" to answer that,' she said, eventually. 'Bodily speaking, I'm quite dead. There was no other option. If the Collective had reached me again, I would have sold out my past-self and given them Moby's secrets. That wasn't part of the bargain I made, so...' She aimed her index and middle finger at her temple and pantomimed a pistol's recoil. Jonah winced at the gesture.

'But,' she went on, 'Moby's a big guy. There are billions of minds inside him already; he could find room for another one, even one as foreign as mine. It was a pretty trivial matter for him to create a complete copy of my consciousness when we were in contact, and let that copy live on inside him as a guest. I was watching when my other self – my original, flesh-and-blood self – died.' She shivered. 'That wasn't much fun. But I've come to terms with knowing I'm a virtual duplicate. I still *feel* like I'm Jean Harrison. I was created with the original's knowledge and her blessing. I take my coffee the same way she did. I find the same things funny and the same things sad as she did. I take pride in the same memories she did, and I have the same regrets. And I love the same people. That's good enough for me to say that I'm her.'

'Jean... I'm so sorry. For everything.'

There it was. The phrase he had spent almost two centuries rehearsing in his head, the apology that formed a parenthesis around his entire life; and he blurted it out almost without thinking. Here she was, all of a sudden, in front of him. The six-year-old girl who had tearfully asked if his departure on the *Prospice* was because of something she had done. The woman who had been widowed, and never received his message of condolences. His daughter, who had given her life for her species, and whose sacrifice he had never known about. Every test he had failed as a father. Every way he had fallen short as a man and as a decent person. Everything she had deserved from him, and he hadn't provided.

I'm a fool. As though any apology could encompass it all. As though any gesture of contrition could answer for the years and decades he had cheapened with his neglect. The simulacrum they inhabited could dilate time indefinitely; he could spend the rest of eternity admitting to his inadequacy, and it would never rectify it.

'It's OK,' Jean said, lightly.

Jonah almost choked.

'As afterlives go, this isn't a bad one, honestly. I mean, I've missed Mum, and James, and Vic. Especially Vic, if I'm being honest. I've missed getting your messages every few months, I always used to look forward to those. But I haven't been bored, or lonely. When you exist in a dimension of pure thought, and you can create simulacra to your heart's content, there are a lot of ways to amuse yourself, even for two hundred years. And Moby's good company, once you get to know him. Creating a mutual conceptual framework with him was quite a task, but after it was done, he turned out to be an excellent conversationalist.'

Jonah almost laughed out of sheer incredulity. He had imagined this meeting going a thousand different ways. In none of them had it gone like this.

'I have to ask,' he said. '"Moby"?'

'I'll let him try to explain it when you meet him, that should be good for a laugh.'

There came a series of three sharp knocks from the farmhouse's front door. 'Actually,' Jean said, 'that'll be him now.'

***

443

At Jean's ushering, Jonah opened the door. Standing on the front porch was a slender man, wearing a tailored two-piece suit. His features were somewhat androgynous and of ambiguous ethnicity – Jonah would have guessed at some combination of Asian, Caucasian, and Middle-Eastern – with dark hair neatly slicked back, and wide, alert eyes. He reminded Jonah of the Archangels; his locomotion appeared unnatural in a way that was difficult to pin down. Not ungainly, but deliberate and practiced. He seemed to alternate between blinking too often and not often enough.

He peered at Jonah for a moment, the corners of his mouth and the furrow of his brow subtly twitching. The impression was uncanny, and a little sinister, like an AI-generated model of a person cycling through facial expression variants. He finally settled on an expression approximating geniality, and he extended a hand for Jonah to shake, arm stiff and elbow locked.

'Starman,' he said, by way of greeting, 'how-good-it-is-to-make-your-acquaintance-at-last-may-we-please-be-permitted-the-honour-of-entering-your-*home*?' The words tumbled out of the newcomer's mouth in a toneless, staccato rush, save for the last one, 'home,' at which he jumped half an octave. The strangeness of his inflection left Jonah, already reeling from the strangeness of everything else, unable to parse the words he'd spoken. He glanced over his shoulder at Jean, pleading wordlessly for help.

Jean looked bemused. 'Close, Moby,' she said, holding up a hand with the tips of her thumb and forefinger a centimetre apart. 'About ninety-five percent there. Just leave a bit more time between syllables. And you don't need to lean quite so hard on the upspeak when you're asking a question.'

Moby frowned at this. He withdrew his hand, and stared off into space for a couple of seconds, before making eye contact again. 'We ask your forgiveness, Starman.' He was overcompensating slightly, the words coming slowly, each one stressed and precise, but it was much closer now to the rhythm of human speech in English. 'We have practiced for this moment for a long while, but to communicate with semiotics alone remains... difficult, for us.' He extended his hand a second time. 'How good it is to make your acquaintance, at last. May we be permitted the honour of entering your home?'

Jonah glanced at Jean. *Play along,* she mouthed, silently. Hesitantly, he accepted the proffered hand. Moby pumped it once; twice; three times, then released. The ritual apparently having been completed to his satisfaction, he came inside, wiped off his shoes, and removed his suit jacket.

'Call me Jonah, will you?' For some reason, hearing himself addressed by that old nickname, by this entity, whatever he was, made him more uneasy than any other part of this whole, surreal scene. '"Starman" was just something my grandkids called me, long ago.' Moby took a moment to process this, then shrugged, making the gesture with the same stiffness he had used to extend his hand, like a canned animation in an old video game.

'Very well,' he said, 'Jonah, how good it is to make your acquaintance at—'

'*No*, Moby.' Jean chuckled. 'Not necessary.'

Jean was seated at the dining room table; a meal had manifested on the plates set there, and a bottle of champagne chilled between them in an ice bucket, presumably imagined into existence by the same mechanism the coffee pot had been. Jean raised her glass to them, and ushered them both to sit. Jonah took his place opposite his daughter. Moby sat at the head of the table, between the two of them. Upon seeing the dish that Jean had created for them, the corners of his lips flickered, with something that Jonah might have taken for mirth if he turned his head and squinted.

'Fish,' he said, as though the word itself carried a world of significance.

'Poached salmon,' Jean shot back, 'with wild rice and mixed greens, I'll have you know, Moby. I slaved over an imaginary stove for a whole instant to make it, so some appreciation would be nice.'

Moby met Jonah's eye. 'Jean has educated us in our time together, Jonah. We are now familiar enough to know when we are being teased.'

'I promised him I'd let you explain your name,' Jean said.

'Very well,' Moby replied. 'It is our understanding that when your species first encountered us, you referred to us by the designation "Body." We have no preference with regard to our designation, and would have been perfectly content for our congress to be conducted on this basis. However, Jean felt that "Body" was an inadequate name for us; that it was a designation derived from the understanding of us as an astronomical object, and that, being recognised as sentient, we should not be referred to by a generic noun. Hence "Moby," a proper noun of her choosing.

'Jean has familiarised us with the human notions of fiction, metaphor, and allegory. That humans' understanding of the objective universe can be sharpened and clarified by means of reductive, semiotic comparisons is a concept that proved difficult to grasp for us.

'Our understanding of her reasoning is as follows. One: the form of the construct we assumed for interstellar transit loosely resembles a whale, an animal which lives in Earth's oceans. Two: a human living in the Terran Calendar year eighteen fifty-one proposed a counterfactual narrative that involved a whale by the name of Moby-Dick. This narrative, despite being a work of fiction, is a common denominator in the mind of a great many humans. Three: Moby-Dick in this narrative represents, in metaphorical terms, an object of obsession which is frustratingly unobtainable and unknowable. As such, Jean judged that this sequence of correlations made "Moby" an appropriate appellation for us.'

Moby delivered all of this in the monotone of a bored lecturer. Jonah felt like an intruder upon an in-joke, because Jean shook with suppressed laughter.

'Furthermore,' Moby continued, 'she believes your arrival here today adds an additional layer of significance to the name. We understand that there exists another, older fictional narrative in human culture of an individual named Jonah, who survives in the belly of a whale. By virtue of you sharing this name, and by virtue of being "inside" us, in representative terms, the metaphor achieves an additional dimension of applicability. Although, by the standards Jean herself has conferred to us, this seems a gratuitous conflation of two allegories unrelated except for the presence of whales. If your name had been "Ishmael," it would be neater. Perhaps you would consent to be called this, for convenience's sake?'

Jean covered her mouth and laughed all the harder. 'You see what I've had to work with?' she gasped. 'I really do have to take my fun where I can get it.'

Jonah felt himself relaxing. If not for the knowledge that his physical body was presently frozen in time, wounded in the middle of a battle in a burning structure on the Dark Side of the Moon, he could have been perfectly at ease sitting at this table, conversing with the ultimate odd couple.

'I'll stick to "Jonah," please, if it's all the same to you,' he said.

Moby shrugged, the learned gesture an expression of perfect indifference.

'So, it was you, was it? Where all this madness started from?' Jonah said. 'It was you that gave Xavier Wong his inspiration. It was you that led to the creation of the Enclave Effect, and you were the reason that the Collective fought the Insurgency across forty light-years to find me. Why? What was it all for?'

Moby regarded him coolly. Jean sobered and looked at the Body's avatar, where it sat stiffly, its food and drink untouched. 'You should probably start at the beginning, Mob.'

'Indeed,' Moby replied, not taking his unblinking eyes off Jonah. 'Jean has done a great deal to impart to us the virtues of linguistic communication, which we have integrated accordingly. However, we are also aware that it has definite limitations, and in this instance, we feel that direct information transfer would be more apt. Do you consent to this?'

Jonah's brow creased. He wasn't entirely sure what he was being asked to consent to.

'It doesn't hurt,' Jean assured him. 'It's a bit disorienting at first, but it's useful at getting the point across.'

"Fine, OK,' Jonah said. 'How do I...'

His question was disrupted by the sudden disappearance of Moby, Jean, the dining room, and his own body.

***

There was a mid-sequence yellow star in the Scutum-Centaurus arm of the Milky Way, over 50,000 light-years from Earth.

Eleven planets orbited this star, the fourth of which was a gas giant, orbited in turn by seven moons of sufficient mass to hold an oblate spheroid shape. The outermost of these moons was the largest, just greater in mass than Mars. Though the gas giant's orbit lay more than 1.5 AU away from the star, the moon's rotation and orbital path combined in just such a serendipitous way that its surface was evenly warmed by the planet and the star the year round. But for the poles, the water that covered its surface remained almost all liquid.

The massive tidal forces exerted by the gas giant's gravity, in combination with the tectonic forces at work in the deep ocean trenches, turned the moon's seas into a paradise of chemical reactions; abiogenesis there was less a possibility than it was an inevitability. Shoals of trillions upon trillions of single-celled organisms were born near the sea floor; in the churn of geothermal vents, organic proteins were pummelled together into self-replicating configurations by brute force.

Where am I? Jonah thought. *What is this?*

Relax, Jonah. He recognized the reply as having come from Moby, but the words weren't words. They were the concepts that lurked beneath words, which his human cognition forced into shapes that could be represented by Roman characters and laryngeal expulsions.

Pay attention. This is the history of our people.

The organisms rode the vast whorls of the ocean tides up to the surface of the water, where light was abundant and pressure was negligible, multiplying and mutating as they went. Thousands of generations lived and died on that trip up to the surface. The organisms that failed to mutate in accordance with the changes in pressure, light and temperature died, and the ones that adapted thrived, quickly replicating to fill the space absented by their fallen comrades. Over the course of a single trip from the trenches to the surface, the shoals learned to photosynthesise, generating nourishment from the light and warmth of the upper ocean. The tidal churning continued; the newly photosynthetic shoal was dragged back down to the depths. Thousands more generations came and went, selective mutation re-adapting them to the crushing pressure of the ocean floor.

But although the shoal was powerless to alter its cyclical course, its now-redundant breakthrough to photosynthesis was not wasted. It remained in its mitochondrial DNA, and in due course, when it was elevated again to the surface, the adjustment to the surface environment came more easily and quickly. The shoal flourished and grew.

With each turning of the tidal cycle, the shoal became more accustomed to the dynamics of its environment through the processes of selective mutation, each generation iterating on the last. It diversified and spread throughout the moon's oceans, one shoal becoming many shoals, some better suited to the warm waters of the tropics, others to the icy climes of the poles.

Evolution did its work quickly on this moon. Multicellular life emerged within a few short tens of millions of years, and from there came life capable of locomotion, of fighting the tides or riding them. New options and avenues for adaptation opened up. Some of the shoals poked their heads above the surface of the ocean, deploying leaves that kept them buoyant, basking in the carbon dioxide-rich atmosphere and unfiltered sunlight. Others became communities of extremophiles, attaching to the geothermal smokestacks in the deep ocean trenches and learning to nourish themselves in the heat.

One shoal had a more abstract innovation. It developed the ability to communicate with itself; at first, through a simple binary code of excretions into the surrounding water. An organism that reached the end of its individual life-cycle without having reproduced would emit a particular pheromone upon expiry which repulsed its fellows. If there was a corner of the shoal where the surrounding waters were unusually acidic, or where the currents were treacherous, or contained predatory organisms from a rival shoal, or any number of other factors that might contribute to reproductive failure in a certain part of the ocean, the higher concentration of this pheromone acted as a warning to the rest of the shoal: 'beware; stay away.'

The technique was a rousing success. This particular shoal began to move as a unit, avoiding threats and honing in on advantageous waters. With the passage of a few tens of thousands of generations, the technique was refined further, beginning to incorporate more specific warnings. The chemical signifier for 'predator' was distinct from that for 'inanimate hazard,' for instance. Conversely, chemical signifiers for attractive waters were developed, released upon the expiry of an individual with a highly reproductively successful lifespan.

The shoal's growth exponentiated, and it diversified, and soon this form of group communication became fundamental to every shoal in the moon's oceans.

Life on the moon swiftly became more phenotypically varied. Invertebrates arose, some growing to enormous sizes, the moon's gravity permitting for creatures that dwarfed the Earth's blue whales. But these changes were superficial; a shoal's success was less contingent on the size and shape of the

449

organisms that comprised it, than upon the clarity, detail, and speed with which it could communicate with itself. Chemical signals gave way to signals based upon light and electricity. The shoals grew in subtlety and sophistication; soon, they did not only communicate reactive warnings and summons but proactive interpretations of patterns in their environment. Combinations of signals amongst individuals could be used to create plans and strategies.

The shoals, in short, were becoming intelligences – individual organisms functioning as neurons in distributed brains. These minds existed in a state of constant flux, a rolling process of the older generations dying off and being replaced with younger, still-more-advantageously mutated variants.

Shoals were not limited by species; different, mutually incompatible genotypes could commingle and co-operate for mutual advantage, different forms of communication being reconciled and merged in evolutionary hegemony. Indeed, the most successful shoals were the most diverse in their component species, as they had the widest array of options for tailoring their environment to their advantage.

Where intelligence went, technology followed. One larger shoal which hit upon the notion of agriculture enjoyed tremendous success. Algae-analogues would grow in designated, enclosed regions of the ocean, for the orderly and optimal consumption of the larger creatures with whom they shared a shoal. The individual organisms fulfilled the role of living and dying for the sake of the macro-organism.

Eventually, the shoals sought to augment themselves with advantages outside the scope of mere biology. As the shoals grew, so too did their means of bringing their environment to bear. They began to sculpt the ocean bedrock into shelters. They created artificial, rigid platforms of coral extending above the waves. Cities began to rise above the tides, not unlike the offshore arcologies of old Earth. The move to an existence above the eternal tugging of the seas' currents was a paradigm shift that opened up the shoals' potential still further. With access to the atmosphere, there followed fire; from fire, metallurgy; electricity; mechanisation; computation. The organisms comprising the shoals were augmented with robotics and prostheses that quickened their functioning. In time, they achieved the *ne plus ultra* of shoal unification engineering; a loophole in quantum physics that allowed for the remote, instantaneous connection of two nervous systems.

As these things were wont to do, a social revolution accompanied the technological one. As the shoals became more advanced and the moon they occupied became smaller, they themselves became larger and fewer. The rival shoals which might have regarded each other as predators or prey, or as competitors for resources in a more primordial era, found it increasingly pragmatic to abstain from violence in favour of co-operation, which in turn gave way to commingling and eventually, merging. Finally, every one of the moon's shoals was united in a single super-shoal, interpreting and processing stimuli on the network that now encompassed the moon's entire biosphere, from the vents of the ocean trenches from which it had sprung hundreds of millions of years earlier, to the thermals carrying feather-light insectoid creatures all the way up to the tropopause.

A plural, distributed consciousness, engirdling that moon 50,000 light-years away; one so poetically inclined might have called it the animating spirit of the moon itself. But the shoal, in its endlessly malleable immortality, was not content to accept the moon's biosphere as its Omega point. It found philosophical purpose in continuous upheaval and self-redefinition, in ever-greater complexity and scale; above all else, it feared stagnation.

It was fully aware of the cosmos beyond the reaches of its own world, and having conquered its moon, it only became more conscious of how small it really was on a cosmic scale. If the shoal could encompass a world, why not a star system? Why not a galaxy? Why not the universe? Surely, there were wonders out there stranger and more fascinating than any to be found by means of indefinite reproduction and iteration.

And so, the shoal threw itself into the construction of its interstellar ambassadors. With the efforts of quadrillions of organisms coordinated by a single consciousness, in only a few short centuries, their feats of engineering beggared anything the Merantau Program's directors had ever dreamed of. All matter was a plaything in the shoal's hands by now. The means of propulsion across light-years of distance was trivial; manipulating kinetic and thermal energy at the quantum scale, easy.

These interstellar ambassadors were launched in their thousands into deep space. They were designed in accordance with the six-legged morphology of the greatest and most aesthetically splendid of the organisms in their home moon's ocean. In each of these ambassadors was contained a subset of the larger shoal in virtual form. With the advent of quantum computing, the shoal had enlarged itself a thousandfold in digital space, creating servers full of artificial brains adding to the functioning of the shoal as a whole. Where humanity might have found the idea of replacing itself with mechanical doppelgangers repulsive, to the shoal it was exciting, a new avenue of diversity. Just as there had long been organisms that could live in the deepest ocean trenches and those that could live in the sky filling their respective roles in the macro-organism, now there were new components of itself that could survive in vacuum, with no need for rest or nourishment. Ideally suited for the exploration of space, each interstellar ambassador unit contained billions of virtual shoal-proxy organisms.

In their millions of years exploring the reaches of the Milky Way, the ambassadors had encountered many strange and splendorous things, but none had encountered a greater prize than Moby. Many years ago, it had registered peculiarly ordered electromagnetic excitations coming from a main-sequence yellow star in the Orion Spur, not unlike the star of its own home system. Upon closer inspection, they were found to emanate from the third planet in that star's orbit, one occupying the ideal spot for the abiogenesis of carbon-based life.

Eager to follow up on this discovery, Moby had rushed toward the source of these emissions with all haste, and the closer it drew, the more the shoal's curiosity was piqued. The blue planet upon which it had trained its sensors was a cradle of fantastically complex life; the radio emissions a by-product of a technologically advanced society, the likes of which could only have been created by a world-encompassing super-shoal.

This was the first time in millions of years that the shoal had found another like itself, or so it had believed. The heady days of the large-scale mergers were long past, and the thought of another world-spanning mind to commingle with brought back the memory of that time with a giddy thrill. Moby had set itself on a collision course with the Earth. At the time it had been attached to a comet which it was using as a source of propellent – the impact would significantly disrupt Earth's ecosystem, but this, no doubt, would be welcomed by the younger shoal that inhabited it. Moby's shoal had long regarded the impact of meteoroids upon its home moon as a blessing from the heavens –

they would kill off millions of individual organisms, but they churned up the seas and introduced exotic minerals into the primordial soup, catalysing adaptation and transformation. The centuries and millennia in the wake of a healthy comet strike were booms in the shoal's evolutionary economy, periods of especially fecund growth and change.

Any other shoal, it had been sure, would regard the approach of a major comet the same way, and would be delighted to discover that this one contained not only the hoped-for bounty of minerals and organic molecules but a link to a completely foreign shoal from 50,000 light-years distant. Moby's collision with the Earth would be a glorious, ecstatic act of mutual becoming; violent, cosmic insemination.

So it had believed, right up until its approach had been met with a thermonuclear barrage of kinetic harpoons.

The light and the heat of that detonation tore through Jonah's sight, just as the accompanying betrayal and confusion did through his mind.

***

With a jolt that almost tipped over his chair, Jonah found himself back in the farmhouse dining room. Jean and Moby both peered at him, their imaginary meal forgotten, searching for the precise quality of his reaction. For a moment, it was all he could do to gape. Was this what Xavier Wong had received a fleeting taste of? The evolutionary history of an entire alien biome, hundreds of millions of years of accreted experience deposited straight into his brain? There was far more information there than the paltry fistful of neurons he had available could hold. Even as he sat there, the vast depth of space and time his mind had encompassed slipped away from him, as easily as a dream upon waking. The most recent – and most salient – details, however, remained.

'We didn't know,' he said, feeling compelled to apologise on behalf of his species. 'We had no way of knowing.'

'Of course you didn't,' Moby replied. 'No more than we could have. Your kind acted in accordance with its nature, as did ours.' The patterns of his speech seemed to grow more naturalistic from one sentence to the next.

'We've talked about this a lot, these past two hundred years,' Jean said. 'Between Moby and me, we've come up with a range of theories about why consciousness arose so differently on Earth than it did on his home. The consensus at the moment is that it's because the shoal's moon is completely blanketed in water. If there had been natural landmasses for them to crawl out onto, perhaps that would have tipped the balance in favour of consolidated consciousness, rather than distributed consciousness.'

'Consolidated consciousness,' Moby repeated, a slight frown creasing his brow. 'How odd the concept remains to us, even now. For a mind to be localised to an individual organism, with its entire universe confined to a single set of sensory organs. For its *qualia* to be annihilated upon the failure of its metabolism. We find these notions deeply disturbing.'

'There seem to be about seven billion people on Earth right now who would agree with you on that. They revere you as a god,' Jonah replied.

'The so-called "Collective." Yes, we're well aware of them. Our arrival in this solar system was disruptive in ways we had not anticipated. We have discussed with Jean at great length its precise character – the way it appears to have attempted to emulate the makeup of a shoal. Its existence is, in its own right, perverse to us. It is not a truly distributed consciousness, so much as a project to hijack and suppress consolidated consciousnesses by technological means. It is a – what was the analogy Jean used? – a square plug in a round gap.'

'"Square peg in a round hole," Moby,' Jean admonished.

'Is there a material distinction between the two images?'

'He does this on purpose, you know.' Jean winked at him.

'The Collective repulses us on a variety of levels,' Moby continued, ignoring her. 'It values homogeneity over diversity. It seeks to take other minds into itself by means of sequestration, rather than mutual adaptation and transformation. It treats stagnation as though it were virtue. Worst of all, it dogmatically insists upon the correctness of its own existence as both its premise and its conclusion. If it were to receive from us the "gospel" it is so sure would vindicate it, we have no doubt it would reject our real opinion of it as false or heretical. Hence why we have refused to communicate with it, in the time since Jean originally contacted us.'

'You arrived at the same conclusion the free humans did, then? To defy the Collective?' Moby shook his head.

'Not quite. You see, as much as we may find the Collective's aping of the distributed model of consciousness distasteful, in one key regard we feel that it represents an improvement upon the raw consolidated model.'

'Which would be?'

'The elimination of suffering,' Jean finished before Moby could reply. 'A release from the fear of death and pain.'

'Our conversations with Jean have been extensive, Jonah,' Moby said. He leaned forward, propping his elbows on the tabletop and arching his fingers, a gesture he gave the impression of having rehearsed in front of a bedroom mirror. 'Among the topics we have touched upon are human moral philosophy, and the principles at play in your Golden Rule. The idea has a certain elegance to it. And the shoal finds the idea of a mind whose boundaries are as circumscribed as those of a human's – confined to one organism's body, confronted by the certainty that it will die after a few hundred years, at most – distressing. We would not desire such an existence for ourselves. And it seems to us that it would be cruel to allow such existence to continue. The Collective is an imperfect solution, but it is a solution.'

'Our boundaries aren't as circumscribed as you think they are,' Jonah objected. 'We live on through the deeds we do while we're breathing. The things we build, and the stories we tell. The frontiers we push. The other lives we touch. The world we create for our descendants. It's the challenge to make as much of a positive impression on the world as possible that gives purpose and value to our lives. We aren't just sacks of self-replicating proteins. That's what the Collective would take away from us if we let them.'

'Jean has made the same argument before, Jonah,' Moby said. 'We found it unpersuasive then, as now. The fact is, however great an impression you leave in your wake, it will be an imperfect and incomplete representation of your self, your *qualia*, distorted and corrupted across successive generations until it no longer bears any resemblance to your "self". This, it seems to us, is the trap of consolidated consciousness. Your attempts to insure yourself against nonexistence are ultimately futile. The fact that none of your kind willingly leaves the Collective once entering it suggests that they acknowledge this.'

'Is that your judgement then?' Jonah said, coldly. 'That the universe made a mistake when it threw up humans, and we should just relinquish our selves for our own good? That's what you dragged me forty light-years to say?'

'We are not so grandiose as to pass judgement, Jonah. We have spent the past two centuries impartially observing. The Collective is a human creation – something your species concocted to answer the deep pain at the root of consolidated consciousness. Our arrival may have catalysed its development, but it is something you would have arrived at in due course without our help, we're certain. The shoal does not, as a principle, seek to remake other biomes in its own image. We honour diversity above all else. If we are to interfere unilaterally with the path another biome's development takes, we require good reason to do so. *That* is why we dragged you forty light-years.'

Jean grinned. 'This was the best idea I could come up with in a pinch, Starman,' she said. 'Sorry.'

'So...' Jonah was still trying to latch on to their meaning. 'What is it that you want from me? What did I do to be designated the chosen one?'

Jean laughed. 'You're not the chosen one, Dad. Neither am I, for that matter. We're... well, I guess you could call us a case study. The pair of us together.'

Moby inclined his head. 'As Jean says. You argued for an implicit virtue of consolidated consciousness being the impression that individuals make upon one another. Of the means of transcending the boundaries of self by the ways you are reflected in the minds and imaginations of other selves. We insisted we must observe this phenomenon in effect, to be convinced of the power it commands. For this, we needed access to two individuals of pronounced significance to one another.'

'They already had me, obviously,' said Jean. 'But given that the Collective's conquest of Earth was already well underway by that point, the candidates for a second party were limited. Moby was willing to play the long game, and I wasn't going anywhere, so we gave the Collective our ultimatum. Then, we waited. And now, you're here. Cutting it a bit bloody fine, it must be said.'

'Well, I do apologise for my punctuality,' Jonah scoffed. 'What is it that Moby thinks he can do about the Collective? Just wave a magic wand and make it go away? Not that it matters, regardless, because outside there's

456

maybe forty-five minutes before Victoria eradicates everything on the surface of the Earth.'

'One thing at a time, Starman. We have a test to pass, before we get to any of that.'

Jonah sighed. 'What do we need to do?'

***

Jonah had been told, for almost the whole of his life, that he was brave. He didn't know that he had believed it. Brave in the face of existential threats, perhaps. Radiation, micrometeoroids, extremes of heat and cold and acceleration. Hunger, thirst, and fatigue. These things didn't faze him; physical depredations were easy enough to face up to. The only trick was not dwelling on them.

But surrender required a different sort of courage. Allowing himself to be laid bare to another for the charlatan and the failure he was, where no amount of fortitude could guard him.

Within the simulacrum, his mind was an open book, and Moby thumbed through it at leisure.

He was in the *Prospice's* medical bay, more than a hundred years out from Earth, presiding over Robyn's birth from the *in vitro* chamber. He had briefly considered naming her 'Jean,' at the time, before thinking better of it. It would have cast a cloud over every one of their subsequent interactions if he had done so.

He was sitting in his cabin in August of 2146, the lowest point of his captaincy, when every hour had seemed to bring a fresh crisis to morale. He had spent his few spare waking hours in those months at the bottom of a bottle of reconstituted-glucose rum. Vile stuff, but it had taken the edge off the stims which thrust the despondent ship's interior into appalling clarity.

He was reviewing old incoming and outgoing messages exchanged with home, vacillating between time periods at random. Here was one dated April 4th, 2111, when Jean had called to tell him she'd graduated from Scolt Head Island, beaming with pride. He had wondered at the time why she looked so haggard despite sounding so enthusiastic. It was only after he had played the message back that he had noticed the faint but noticeable scar tissue from a recent operation on her arms – a telltale remnant of the procedure used to enhance ORC servicepeople's muscles and bones. He knew from other former ORC personnel that the bones in particular hurt for weeks afterwards, enough to make you lose sleep. Jean hadn't wanted him to worry, so she hadn't mentioned it.

Here was one dated September 29th, 2100, a message from Astrid chastising him. Jean had gotten into a fight at school with a pair of older girls, after being teased about her father having run out on her. Jean had been given two weeks' suspension when she had torn out a fistful of one girl's hair.

The big one – the one he closed out the evening with, before he let the rum carry him off to a short and fitful sleep – was dated August 9th, 2114. Victoria's delivery in the maternity ward of the Royal London Hospital; the moment he had become a grandfather. Jean, exhausted after the eight-hour labour, had held her close to her breast as though she was the only thing in the universe. She was drenched in sweat and draped in a hideous hospital gown. Jonah had never seen anything more beautiful in his life.

The last thing he thought before sleep crept up on him that night was that he was proud of her. But then, he shoved that thought back down. His sleep that night was wracked with nightmares.

Why does it cause you so much pain, Jonah? Moby's query came to him, once again in those words-that-were-not words. He watched from his vantage outside of time as Jonah writhed under the covers in his bunk aboard, implacable as a surgeon, peeling back layer after layer of his mind. *You love your daughter, yes? Why is seeing her happy a source of suffering to you?*

You know why, Jonah thought back at his host, bitterly. *You can feel everything I felt, can't you? All the messy, contradictory, stupid, human feelings that we can't express in words.*

Yes. But the point of the exercise is for you to articulate those feelings, as best you can.

Words. If I'd had any facility with words, I would have been a politician, or a poet, not a Starman.

Perhaps. But we find ourselves with access to a Starman, not a politician or a poet. And it's to the Starman the test is posed.

Jonah searched himself, searched for a way to articulate these parts of himself that he'd never wanted anyone else to see, that he'd kept buried so deep, he'd thought maybe he could make them untrue.

I was proud of her, he thought, at last. *But then, I was ashamed to feel proud. I don't get to feel proud of Jean. I don't get to take credit for the extraordinary person she grew to be.*

The scene changed again, thrusting him forward in time. Moby rifled through his mind according to the shoal's whims, as easily as he had done with the *Prospice's* message logs. The shoal's cross-examination was exhaustive. It wrang out of him every drop of information that pertained to the subject that interested it: Jean. She was the common factor in all the hours and days and years of time they forced him to relive. Jean; Jean; Jean. There was so much of her, he realised. For 230 years, the thought of her had never been far from the surface, sitting like a splinter in his heart. Her existence had been incomprehensible to him, a paradox that he had turned over and over in his head trying to reconcile. How had a woman like her – strong and proud and compassionate, a source of joy and comfort to all those around her – come from him; the fool, the charlatan, the self-absorbed, egotistical coward that he was?

Moby vivisected him. He was made to confide every private fear and doubt, every moment of self-recrimination.

After what felt like hours, or days, or years, there came a perspective shift unlike the others. This memory was distinctly not his. He was in the kitchen of the London townhouse where he had lived when he had been stationed with the RAF, but his point of view was too close to the ground. Angry voices were coming from the adjacent hallway, loud enough to be easily heard through the closed door. 'Go on then! Leave! Get out of my house! What an idiot I was, to ever think I loved you.'

Oh God, no. 'Mum?' His voice was that of a tearful, six-year-old girl. 'Is everything…?' He was interrupted by the reverberation of a door slamming, harder than Jean had ever heard a door slam in her home before. A framed painting fell from the kitchen wall and shattered; she flinched.

Please not this. Moby, please, stop. He was begging, now. His mind felt raw, as raw as flayed skin. Seeing this scene, from this vantage, was like acid being poured on the exposed nerves. *I can't see this. I can't feel this. It's too much to bear.*

You must bear it, Jonah. For the test to be valid.

I can't...

YOU MUST.

Moby didn't stop. He pressed on, the scene shifting again. Now Jean was ten. She was in the playground, where she had been cornered by Eliza and Brianne from Year 7. 'It's not like he's going to *find* anything,' Eliza was saying. 'My dad works in the PNC, and he says the whole thing's just a massive waste of time and money.'

'It is *not* a waste!' Jean shouted back.

'I bet he was just trying to get away from *you*,' Brianne sneered. 'If I had to live with you, I'd want to go to the other side of the galaxy or wherever as well.'

Jean had punched Brianne before consciously deciding to do so. And as for Eliza – her father was an accountant contracted the PNC's Agriculture and Water Reclamation Department. He was a bean counter for farmers. Jean's father was an *explorer*. He spent every day shouldering more responsibility than Eliza's father would bear in a lifetime, and seeing sights Eliza's father never dreamed of in his sad, dreary little existence. How dare he judge a man like Jonah Harrison?

Brianne screamed, clutching her nose, and Eliza dove at Jean in her stead, pulling at her clothes. Jean found a fistful of the girl's hair and yanked as hard as she could. She hadn't meant to pull quite so hard to tear the hair loose, and a piece of scalp with it. Nevertheless, after she was dragged away from the fight kicking and screaming by Mrs. Thurgood, she accepted her suspension with good humour and her head held high.

What is this?

Jean was thirteen, reading up on the requirements for entry into the ORC and the physical training regimen expected of anyone aspiring to perform complex tasks in microgravity. She stumbled upon an article about the historical C-131 Samaritan, colloquially known in its day as the 'vomit comet.' It had risen and plunged almost three kilometres, faster than gravity, again and again, until its passengers grew accustomed to the sensation of zero-g.

Her mind reeled at this knowledge. *This* was what her father lived in, every waking and sleeping minute? And he was able to smile for her in the recordings he sent home, as though he was under no stress at all?

Jean was eighteen, on a clear summer night on the Isle of Skye, one of the few spots left in Britain where light pollution was negligible. She had come here on a fortnight's camping trip with Stephen; the boyfriend to whom she had lost her virginity the previous year, and who she would marry in the years to come. They were celebrating the end of secondary school, and the short window of freedom they would enjoy in each other's company before he left for university, and she for basic training. They were hiking and rock-climbing in the Cuillin Mountains by day, and by night, relaxing next to an open fire, idly sharing their deepest thoughts and admiring the fantastic starfield, with the help of a few light chemical and electronic psychotropics.

'No, *there*,' Jean was saying. She leaned in close to Stephen, aligning her arm with his so he could follow where she was pointing in the sky. 'Just below Cassiopeia, see? The *Prospice* is right around there just now. Give or take a few billion kilometres.'

'He'll know who I am by now, right?'

Jean nodded. 'Your introductory message would have arrived there about a week ago. In a couple of years, we'll know what he thinks of you. You scared?' she teased.

'Terrified,' Stephen replied, taking the question more seriously than it had been intended. 'What if he doesn't approve of me? What kind of wrench would that throw into a three-year relationship?'

Jean gave him a reassuring peck on the cheek. 'Don't worry so much. What's he going to do, turn around?'

Stephen laughed a little.

'And anyway, he's not a dick about stuff like that. He comes across as really stiff and professional in the videos you can find on the 'net, but he's nothing but sweetness and light when he calls home. I think he always felt kind of bad about leaving when I was young, so now he overcompensates by trying to be the best dad he can be. Trust me, he'll be gentle with you.'

I don't understand.

On and on it went like that. In Jean's mind, there lived a Jonah Harrison that Jonah didn't recognise. His doppelganger was a better man than he was; not a betrayer, not a failure, but an aspirational figure, all the more so by virtue of his physical distance. His absence from her life left a sting, yes; but not one so severe that it couldn't be forgiven. He was still someone to strive to emulate. Still someone that made her feel special for being connected to. Someone whose love was meaningful, and worthy of being loved in turn.

***

At last, the deluge of memories ended, and the farmhouse's dining room resolved itself again. When the disorientation of finding himself back in the present moment subsided, Jonah did something that shocked him; he fell apart.

He hadn't cried in his adult life. Not when the *Prospice* had launched. Not when any of his children or grandchildren had been born, or when his friends and crewmates had died. Not when Alyssa had lain on the sickbay bed with her organs exposed to the air, or at Ilsa's last transmission. But now he wept as openly as an infant; in shame, in remorse, and in pathetic gratitude. His eyes screwed shut, he felt a pair of arms embrace him.

'I get it, Dad,' Jean said. She spoke softly, barely breathing the words into his ear. 'For anyone to reckon with their whole life like that, without any of the tools we use to insulate ourselves from it... there's nothing harder you can ask of a person. I was in the same state, after the first time Moby and I interfaced.'

'We believe the phrase you used was: "like going twelve rounds with the world's most opaque talk therapist,"' Moby piped up. 'Though, we understand that "going twelve rounds" refers to boxing, and as to why you would be boxing with a therapist—'

'Moby.' Jean cut him off. 'Time and a place.'

***

Jean held him for he didn't know how long – until the shuddering, wracking sobs subsided, and he was able to resume a modicum of composure.

'We have seen it in action now,' Moby said. The shoal's avatar sat at the head of the table, stroking its chin with affected contemplation, another of its canned animations. 'Metaphor. Allegory. Analogy. Narrative. The imperfect representations by which humans explain their environment to one another are also the means by which they come to understand themselves, and each other. Jean, both you and Jonah occupy the same objective reality. Your experiences overlap, and yet with access to the same facts, you have both created different *truths* from these facts. A consolidated consciousness defines itself not by facts alone, but by their selected emphases and de-emphases. The "self," in a sense, is generated by imperfections in understanding. Jonah's apprehension of his own "self" does not align with yours.'

'This is what I've been telling you for two centuries,' Jean said. 'The "imperfections," as you call them, are what make it possible for us to love and hate. They're what give our lives richness and texture.'

'So you say. And yet your lives are spent desperately attempting to know, and be known by one another. The very imperfections in understanding that give rise to the "self" in the first instance also make it impossible for this to be achieved. Remove the imperfections in communicating with one another, as in the Collective, and you remove the selves you seek to understand. This is a paradox.'

'It is,' Jean agreed. 'And that paradox is tragic and beautiful in equal measure. It's what gives purpose to lives that are short and confined. It's what makes us *strive*. It's a paradox that cannot, and must not, be resolved.'

Moby conferred with himself a moment longer, then sprang to his feet. 'Yes,' he said. Jonah blinked. 'Does this mean…'

'Indeed. You have passed the test, as it were. We have decided that consolidated consciousness does indeed bring something into the universe worthy of being preserved. Life lived with urgency and precariousness – it is a perspective the shoal could do well to accommodate.' He beamed at Jean and Jonah where they sat. 'We believe our peoples could learn a great deal from each other, in time.'

'We didn't get off to a great start,' Jean said, 'but I agree.'

'It's settled then,' Jonah said. 'But we're left with one fairly major issue. How exactly will our people have a chance to communicate with yours, when we're on the brink of extinction?'

Jean and Moby gave each other a conspiratorial look. The expression on Jean's face was almost mischievous. 'We have an idea for that part as well,' she said.

***

Jean accompanied Jonah to the farmhouse door and retrieved her coat from the rack where she had hung it earlier. Beyond the porch, the driveway – really just a pair of ruts worn down over the years by his father's four-by-four – extended twenty metres. Beyond this point, the simulacrum ceased, the ground terminating in a wall of blank white nothing. They walked together down the path to the boundary line.

Jonah had no limp inside the simulacrum. He paused a moment, and stretched his right leg, savouring the feeling of healthy sinew while it lasted.

'You know,' Jean said, 'you could stay longer, if you want. Moby's processing power is absurd – in real terms, it's only been zero-point-eight-nine seconds since you arrived. You could take a while to relax, rather than dive straight back into it.'

'I can't relax knowing something's still undone,' Jonah replied. 'No sense giving myself time to worry about it. And besides, I'm sick of this old place after the past year.'

'Once more into the breach, then?'

'Yes, I think so. Once more into the breach.' He drew a deep breath and exhaled slowly. 'Jean, before we do this, I just wanted to say...'

She hushed him gently. 'Dad, I saw inside your mind, the same as you saw inside mine. There's nothing you can put into words that I don't already understand just fine. The "you" that lives in my mind doesn't match the facts of the matter? Fine. But that doesn't mean that he isn't real, or that he isn't standing here with me now. So, no more apologies, okay? No more regrets.'

Despite everything, Jonah felt a small smile creep across his lips. 'No more regrets,' he agreed.

'We accomplished something great here today, Dad. We've established that humanity is worth saving. All that's left to do now is save it.'

Together, they stepped across the boundary.

Chapter 28

September 4th, 2327 C.E.

The Collective base fell in the face of Victoria's assault like a sandcastle beneath a tsunami. Every combat unit still remaining to the Collective was being launched at her comet, the hive mind's attention bent on preventing its extinction at all costs. The Scarabs she passed by outside ignored her, irrelevant as she was to their primary and only objective. The ones she found inside were in the process of being maintained or configured for space combat with the arrowhead. She slagged all of them with liberal maser fire.

She entered through the open docking bay, simply to save herself the power expenditure it would take to blast her way through the exterior. Once inside the base, she was greeted by a handful of flesh-and-blood assimilates, some armed with handheld masers and antique flechette rifles.

The flechettes ricocheted off her hyperdiamond armour as inconsequentially as foam darts. The maser cannons might have been able to muster enough firepower to give her pause, but she didn't give their wielders the opportunity to find out. Organic reflexes were so slow. Her HUD identified every one of them before they had the chance to take aim, and she reduced them to superheated plasma within seconds.

Some of the suicidal fanatics actually charged her with knives and batons. She took it as an invitation to test out a few of the more macabre configurations of blades and cudgels she had dreamed up for her frame in the past two hundred years. Within minutes, the base was a tableau of fire and blood.

She advanced through the corridors towards the base's centre, burning and butchering as she went. If she didn't find her grandfather there, she would track him down at her leisure; the hangar was sufficiently crippled that he wouldn't be going anywhere without her permission, and the Collective would soon have much bigger things to worry about. When she found him, she was confident she'd know what to do. Reconciliation; or a clean break from the past. She was prepared for either.

One of her maser blasts must have severed a power conduit in the walls, because the base was momentarily plunged into darkness, then seconds later bathed in dim emergency lighting. The antiseptic white of the corridor sloping downward to the centre of the base was stained a sickly, rotten orange by the energy-conserving illumination.

Something skittered to a stop near her feet, thrown from an intersection in the corridor ahead of her; a flat, metallic cylinder ten centimetres across.

Someone on the base had come equipped, at least. She hurled herself back from the detonation in the split second available to her, spreading and beating her wings to propel her away from the device's blast radius.

She was caught by the outermost edge of the EMP's effect. Her frame's functions were disrupted, the electrical signals from her brain intercepted before they could reach the platelets in her armour. She sat frozen on the corridor floor, her gaze involuntarily fixed on the intersection from which the grenade had been thrown.

From behind the corner, an assimilate emerged into view. Although he was clad in an environment suit, and although his face was starting to crease and his hair to thin, Victoria recognised him immediately.

Hello, little brother.

'Hi there, Vic,' James said, as though in response to her unvoiced thought. 'You've caused us an impressive amount of trouble, you know that? The Collective's cause will be set back centuries because of you. In time, you would be consumed by guilt for what you've done today. Let us spare you from that burden.' He drew out a hypodermic syringe and approached her.

No, not like this! Without her will coordinating it, her frame would do nothing to resist the incursion of the Collective parasite. Victoria urged her frame to shake off the effects of the EMP faster.

'It doesn't hurt, Vic, I promise.'

She couldn't focus or move her gaze; it was like being in the suspension gel in the Royal London Hospital all over again. James' body grew until it occupied her whole field of vision. The syringe rose, poised to plunge into the nape of her neck.

'Hold still, sis.'

Come on, you fucking antiquated piece-of-shit machinery! Do the one thing I've ever needed you to do, and move!

Her eyelids flickered. Her prayer was answered.

Victoria stood. She was slow, and shaky, the effects of the EMP taking their time to dissipate, but it was more than she needed to face an organic. Her left hand streaked across her field of view, slapping the syringe out of James' hand hard enough not only to knock it free but also to spin him bodily around. She suspected she had broken his wrist.

Her right hand followed the left, clenched into a diamond-hard fist, and struck James in his left ear. In the throes of pure instinct, she held nothing back. Every bone in her brother's head broke. He impacted the floor with a wet *crunch*, rebounded in the weak lunar gravity, and finally came to rest, sprawled and motionless.

She examined the ruin her wild haymaker had left in its wake. He would live. Barely. Another figure emerged from behind the corner where James had been hiding, this one younger and shorter.

'Bloody hell, coz. You really don't do things by half measures, do you?' Alyssa levelled a maser cannon at her. Under the orange light blanketing the corridor, the scarred side of her face looked positively demonic, even after having a year to heal.

'Out of my way, Lys.'

'I seem to remember you said something when we first met – what was it? Oh yes: "I won't let anything else happen to my family." Nice sentiment, but it hasn't held up to scrutiny very well, has it?'

'No,' Victoria agreed. 'It hasn't. I fell short of the promise I made my cousin the night you erased her and made her into one of you. Everything I've done today, I commend to her memory.'

Alyssa sighed. 'The more things change, the more they stay the same. If there's a hell, Vic, that's where you're going. Maybe not today, maybe not for hundreds of years yet. But eventually.'

Victoria took a step forward, raising her hand toward Alyssa with the palm splayed. Alyssa braced the maser against her shoulder. 'Is that what it's come to, then? You're going to kill me? You'd really sink that low?'

Victoria paused, and after a moment's consideration, lowered her hand. A flicker of surprise passed through the Collective, manifested on Alyssa's face. Her grip on the cannon's trigger slackened, and a second of repose stretched between them.

Alyssa convulsed. Once, and then again, more violently. Her complexion blanched, sweat beading on her brow. Even in one-sixth terrestrial gravity, her arms trembled, trying and failing to hold the maser aloft.

'I don't have to kill you, cousin,' Victoria said. 'You've died already, remember? The night we met.'

Alyssa sank to her knees, and from there to all fours, and finally to a foetal position. She clutched at her ribs, attempting to draw gurgling, rattling breaths that sounded more fluid than air.

'Feel that? Those are your heart and lungs shutting down. For over a year, they've continued functioning thanks to the intervention of billions of molecular platelets, configured to my frame. This body, the one you stole from the Alyssa I knew? It's alive only according to my good graces, and as of this moment, those have run out.'

She approached Alyssa where she lay, and knelt down. She took the girl's head in her hands and pulled it toward her, so their eyes (Alyssa's swimming in and out of consciousness) were inches apart. 'Let the Collective, in its entirety, understand. I've held your fate in my hands for a hundred and ninety-two years. You've been protected by the Insurgency's compassion and Albrecht's spinelessness, but today those protections have reached their limit. And I've had enough of you. I want a universe without *you*.'

She released Alyssa, her eyes now lolling back in their sockets. She was clawing weakly at the floor, mouth locked open, trying futilely to inhale. Victoria proceeded down the corridor without a backward glance. She would recover the platelets she had donated later.

***

Victoria came to the central cavity that made up the core of the base – the enormous, cavernous setting where the Body was housed. It looked at first glance to be strangely deserted; surely the Collective's god warranted more security than had met her? Then, a pair of infrared signatures caught her attention. They were violently writhing against one another in a canvas structure erected against the creature's left-middle limb. She had an idea of who at least one of the struggling figures was, and a notion to break the fight up.

Beneath the floor adjacent to the canvas vestibule, her eyes, tuned to the wavelength of X-rays, found a ventilation shaft. One of the capillaries of the system keeping the base oxygenated – highly pressurised enough for her purposes. She loosed an energy blast toward it, melting through the moulded plastic that comprised the floor in this section of the base in a heartbeat and rupturing the pipe. The blast of decompressed air threw the two figures off their feet, landing metres apart from one another.

Drawing closer, she recognised the distinctive infrared signature of the one on the left. Tall, rake-thin, everything from the collarbones on down a metal alloy. There was no mistaking him – Manderly, the one who had been leading the Collective task force when the FOB had fallen.

He didn't warrant another second of her attention. Her next maser beam burned through the cloth of the vestibule, and exited the other side coloured by Manderly's superheated remains.

Inside, the second of the grappling figures lay against the hide of the alien creature. It was the Starman, right enough, although he had been rendered near-unrecognisable. His face was a ruin, the right side a swollen mass that had almost closed shut on his eye. A livid bruise was taking shape horizontally across his Adam's apple, suggesting a trauma to his throat that was restricting his airways.

He had been struggling. The Collective hadn't assimilated him, after all, even after a year of his having lived in their midst.

It wasn't the sight of her grandfather's brutalised visage that caused her to recoil, though; it was what was happening to his arm, where it lay on the Body's flesh. Ropy, red coils were emerging from it, ensnaring and twisting around his fingers; his wrist; all of his forearm. He blinked up at her, uncomprehending, then followed her gaze.

Incomprehension turned to pitiable distress. He tried to pull his arm loose, but the alien parasite held on all the tighter the more he wrenched at it. He looked back at her, his expression truly wretched; the pleading, trapped look of a cornered animal. A rasp emerged from his ruined throat, a weak, wordless ululation of terror, whose meaning Victoria could infer. *Don't let them take me.* It was the same look that had been frozen on Velasquez' face when she had detonated the EMP at the core of Pisces Station. Then his face slackened, and for a second there was no expression there at all.

Victoria couldn't bear to watch. She extended her left hand toward him, and prepared herself to euthanise the Starman. For the man who had been her source of passion and determination for so many years, it was the least she could do. First him – and then, she promised herself, the Body. It had taken her mother then, and now her grandfather, too. The interloper, the font from which all this madness and evil had sprung – she would burn and burn, until her core was spent, if necessary. She would wipe it from the cosmos, together with all its malevolent handiwork.

Then, the Starman's eyes flickered back to life.

She faltered. The expression that lit up his face now was nothing like it had been in the moments before it had gone slack. Where he had been wretched and dissolute seconds earlier, an old, broken man ready to die, his eyes now blazed. The tendrils wrapped around his arm loosened, and then released him. He rose, falteringly, to his feet. Victoria did not take her aim off him.

'Vvv...' A gurgling, bastardised attempt at vocalisation emerged from his throat. He emitted a couple of racking coughs, doubling over as he did so, then righted himself, the fire in his eyes undiminished by pain.

Victoria, he wrote, starting afresh through his corneal implants. **Thank God you showed up when you did. Any longer, and Manderly would have got me. Quickly – you have to divert the comet from its collision course. We have a way to stop the Collective without any more bloodshed.**

He began to limp towards her, but stopped when the glare of the blue light in her palm's lens intensified. **Do you think I was born yesterday?** Victoria replied. **Do you really think so little of me that you reckon I'd fall for a ploy like this, after everything we've been through these last two centuries?**

Victoria, for God's sake, I'm not assimilated!

Don't humiliate yourself and insult my intelligence while you do it. I literally just saw you attached to the creature that was the original source of the Collective.

Jonah grimaced. **You don't understand,** he insisted. **Moby** – he swiftly deleted the non-sequitur name to replace it with **The Body – was never the source of the Enclave Effect. It just gave the idea to a pack of overzealous human engineers who took the idea and ran with it! The Collective isn't an alien invader; it's a *human* creation, built in response to human needs.**

I've heard this song before, Victoria replied. **It's obscene hearing it parroted by my grandfather's corpse, and I've had enough of it. Die.**

She would have overcome her inhibitions at that moment, and turned the revenant that had been her grandfather to vapour. But her attention was diverted by movement behind him. The Body's skin was twisting and congealing in unnatural ways. A pustule formed on the surface, swelled to perhaps a hundred litres in volume, and then peeled off, flopping to the base's floor in a repulsive act of mitosis.

Victoria raised her other hand to point at this new anomaly. She attended to her right hand's aim; her secondary consciousness to her left. But a part of her was morbidly curious as to what sick spectacle the Collective had to conjure up for her next.

Something pulsated within the egg the Body had laid, as though the sac of grey flesh had a heartbeat. It did so again, and then a third time, each pulse more pronounced than the last. A rupture appeared in the gelatinous mass, and something forced its way out from inside.

It was a hand – a human hand.

A second hand joined the first, and they widened the tear in the sac as though parting a pair of curtains. Arms wrestled their way out from inside, followed by a head and shoulders, and finally an entire person, dripping with the thick, colourless slime that spilled out across the base's floor. Victoria withdrew a couple of steps, uneasy about letting any of the alien muck come into contact with her frame.

The human shape rose to its feet. Despite being drenched from head to toe, the slime plastering its long, thick hair to its neck and obscuring the colour of its skin, Victoria recognised it immediately. There was no mistaking that face – Victoria's primary and secondary consciousnesses had been on an alternating sleep cycle for over a century, one dreaming while the other woke. At any given moment since she had fully transitioned to the Archangel frame, there that face had been in her dreams, smiling before it disintegrated into blood and particles of bone.

'What is this?'

'I did say we'd see each other again, Vic. Well… here I am.'

Her mother looked the same as she had done the day she died, reborn from the Body in the form of a full-grown adult. Victoria was bizarrely, inappropriately conscious of her nudity – of all the things to feel when the world was ending, she concerned herself with a defunct taboo against nakedness? Nothing about these circumstances was remotely appropriate.

Her grandfather was struggling to maintain his balance – he was wavering on his feet, the blows to the head clearly having done real damage. Her mother took her place next to him, helping him keep his feet. Victoria's aim didn't waver.

'I missed you, Vic,' she said, softly. 'It was never my intention to leave you alone in the world, and I'm so sorry. I tried my best back then, but I failed. I played my part in driving everything this far into chaos, and I can understand if you hate me for that. But please, Vic – this has to stop. Even now, the Earth isn't past saving.'

'Don't do that. Don't you dare. Don't you fucking dare.' Despite herself, Victoria felt her voice rising towards a shout. She had thought her anger was spent; exorcised by the violence and destruction she had wrought upon her enemy. But she found it inexorably rebuilding in her chest in a chain reaction, hotter and fiercer than she had ever known until now. Hatred upon unending hatred, enough to quench the sun. 'You use my *mother*? Reanimate her just to use her as a mouthpiece? This is grotesque. Every time I think you can't stoop any lower, you come up with some new offence to human dignity.'

'It's really me, Vic,' her mother's voice replied, unshaken. 'It's true what your grandfather says. The Body and the Collective are separate entities – and now, at last, the Body has thrown its lot in with the humans who oppose the Collective.'

'Shut up. Enough tricks. Enough lies.'

'I was alive inside the Body, ever since that day two centuries ago. I would have reached out to you if I could have, Victoria, and there was nothing I wanted more, but I couldn't have done that without jeopardising the chance we have now.'

'QUIET!' Victoria roared it now, with the full force of the amplification her frame could bring to bear. Her grandfather cringed away from the sound that must have been in excess of a hundred and seventy decibels, but the thing wearing her mother's face, whatever it was, was utterly unfazed.

'I won't be quiet, Vic. Not while I think there's still a chance. You know why? Because that's what you did for me, and it saved me.'

Her mother took a step towards her. The glow in her palm intensified a notch further.

'You remember, don't you? I do. The night in Beijing, after I had been severed. It was you, Vic. You pulled me back from the brink. I was ready to die. Happy to. I thought there was nothing left for me in the world worth the grief. But you reminded me how much there was.'

She advanced another step. She stood now less than three metres from Victoria.

'You haven't killed me yet. That means there must still be some part of you that doubts, Vic.'

Every molecule of her frame was screaming at her to shoot, and be done with this absurd charade. But it was true. Something, some tiny kernel of sentiment that refused to boil away in the furnace of her anger, still held her back from doing what was necessary.

Another step.

'I can't prove myself to you, Vic. There's no demonstration I can offer you that I'm not a Collective agent that you would accept. But I have to believe I can reach you, all the same. Despite everything – despite all the shit and the bad luck life piled up on us both – I'm asking you to trust me.'

Another step. If Victoria leaned forward now, the tips of her fingers might have brushed her mother's face. She was still covered in the slime from the birthing sac. Her whole body was comprised of alien matter whose properties were unknown and unknowable. If it came into contact with her frame, who knew what havoc it could wreak?

And yet, somehow, she still didn't shoot.

'Our species raised itself out of the primordial soup when one monkey extended another a hand, and the other monkey, against all its better judgement, accepted it. Vic, if I can't reach you – if a parent can't reach her child – then we've lost, do you understand that? Destroy them and kill them and burn them to your heart's content, but the moral victory will belong to the Collective, forever.'

Her mother took one last step, bringing her within the reach of Victoria's arm. She embraced her, gently. Victoria, mutely, did nothing to stop her.

She waited for the axe to fall, for her unutterable stupidity in falling for such an obvious trap to be made manifest. The slime being pressed against her frame would infect her, somehow; the creature that looked and spoke like her mother would warp and twist, fingers turning to needles that would stab into her frame, probing for her nervous system like the limbs of a Scarab.

Seconds passed. Nothing happened.

'It's me, hon. It's me.'

'...Mum?' The single syllable escaped her before she could stop it. The nuclear heat of her vengeance escaped with it.

We can unmake the Collective, Victoria, came a message from her grandfather. **The technology that gave rise to it came from the Body, and the Body can reverse it in such a way that will restore individuality without the trauma of severance. But it's all for nothing if there's no-one left to be restored. So please, for God's sake, call off the comet.**

Victoria stood stock still. If it was actually true – if this really was her mother and her grandfather talking with their own voices, then...

No. It can't be true. I've seen it, with my own eyes. They're monsters, alien invaders.

The light in her left palm flickered. *And what if they're not?* Her secondary consciousness, bubbling up again. *All this time, we were so blind. What if an accommodation was always possible? What if we're about to commit the worst war crime imaginable?*

She was her. And she always made too much sense.

Then, what have I done?

'I can't call off the comet,' she said, in a small voice.

'You have to, Vic. Billions are going to die if you don't.'

'No,' she replied, 'you don't understand. I *can't* call off the comet. The engines that were propelling it were wrecked in Hoyt's kamikaze run earlier. It's following its own momentum now. It's out of my control, or anyone else's.'

Can't you just give the order for the Archangels to disperse? Let the Scarabs destroy it.

'That won't work. If I were to give an order that directly contravenes the objective of the whole mission, my comrades will assume that I've been assimilated and ignore it.'

Her grandfather slumped to the floor. **Not like this. After everything, it can't end this way.**

Victoria looked back and forth between her mother and her grandfather. The desperate entreaty in the former's eyes; the dejection and the defeat in the latter's. The greatest mass murder in the history of mankind was impending – the mass murder she had set in motion – and they could do nothing to stop it.

The responsibility lay entirely on her shoulders. It was for her to find a solution – and to pay the price associated with it.

'There is a way,' she said at last. 'I'll stop the comet.'

Her grandfather's head snapped up. **You have an idea?**

'Mum, grandad, thank you. Thank you for everything. I love you both.'

'Vic... oh God.' Her mother pulled away from her, shock in her expression. 'No, there has to be another way. After all this time, I can't ask you to. I could never have asked you to. It's too cruel.'

'You didn't ask me to, Mum. I'm volunteering. If I don't, no one else will.'

Before either of them could protest any further, Victoria turned on her heel and spread her wings. She blasted a hole in the roof of the base, and she soared through it, her QF drive straining to overcome the lunar gravity well.

***

Victoria accelerated towards the heavens as fast as her frame could carry her, pulling over 200 g's. The arrowhead formation swelled in her forward vision, now barely 3 million kilometres above the surface of the Earth. Her HUD showed over three-quarters of her army's names displayed in grey – they had been reduced to barely two hundred, winnowed down by the attrition of the Scarabs.

Still, they had fulfilled their objective admirably. The remaining, larger half of the comet remained on its collision course with Earth. Scarcely ten minutes left until impact. Ten minutes, after a year of travel – less than 0.002% of its total journey. That was the window she had to change its course.

No room, then, for maudlin self-reproach; just action. She had told herself when she had devised this plan that she was doing what was necessary. That ruthless pragmatism had staved off any hesitation then, just as it did now.

An eruption of light unfurled around the arrowhead. A handful more names in her HUD were greyed out. Another Scarab swarm had dashed itself against the arrowhead, with no greater efficacy than all the others before it. Another swarm was approaching behind her, gaining on her thanks to the added boost of the mass drivers they had been launched from. She paid them no mind; she was irrelevant to their objective, and they might actually make matters easier for her.

Is that you, Commander? A transmission from Daniels. **You're early for the scheduled rendezvous. Did everything go OK down there?**

Acknowledged, Lieutenant. Nothing of significance to report. I thought there was a chance of finding the Starman on the dark side and evacuating him, but no such luck.

A hundred and twenty seconds until her course brought her inside the arrowhead. She strained her frame for every ounce of thrust it could give her, trying to buy every extra metre of distance from Earth she could. Her wings gouged a deep furrow into the surrounding space, exerting her core to a dangerous degree. Very soon, it wouldn't matter anymore. The Scarab swarm fell away behind her.

You may want to cool your jets, Commander. You're coming in awfully fast.

This wouldn't do. She couldn't call her Archangels off, but she couldn't leave them with her last words to them being lies. There was nothing she could say to them that would make right what she had done. In all likelihood, she would be remembered by the Insurgency as the one to have led them inexorably down the path of insanity and ruin. Her name would be cursed until the end of time.

Still, she had to try. She racked her brain for the best words she could come up with, all the while aware of the countdown in her HUD. A lifetime measured in centuries, and its legacy would come to be defined by a matter of seconds. It was almost comical.

Taylor, she wrote, now addressing a general channel. **Everyone. I was mistaken. I have failed you as a leader, as a comrade, and as a friend. I accept full moral responsibility, and the consequences that come with it. I have good reason to believe that the Collective will soon disappear without bloodshed. When you receive a transmission to that effect from Earth, be open to it. Don't let yourselves be blinkered by old grudges, as I was.**

There was a few seconds' pause before she received a reply, as the enormity of her message percolated through the remaining Archangels' ranks. **Jesus, Vic,** came the eventual response from Daniels. **Not you, too.** She was cut off from all subsequent transmissions.

Forty-five seconds later, she engaged the arrowhead. The performance she gave was the greatest of her military career, an appropriate crescendo to two centuries of dogfights. In the span of a few hundred milliseconds, she wove her way through the concentrated fire of two hundred opposing Archangel frames without firing a single retaliatory shot of her own. None of their maser blasts so much as nicked her.

A.N. Milne

Vic Viper, indeed.

She encountered the comet at a combined speed of nearly twenty-five million klicks per hour. At a range of less than a kilometre, she dropped her core.

In the few nanoseconds between overriding the magnetic suspension unit isolating the grams of antimatter in her chest, and the resultant flash of light, heat, and radiation, Victoria Harrison realised she wasn't angry anymore.

480

A.N. Milne

Chapter 29

September 4th, 2327 C.E.

Alyssa lay on the floor of the base, dying.

It isn't my first time, she thought. *It should get easier with practice, shouldn't it?* She released the attempt at gallows comedy into the Collective, hoping that its response might bring her a morsel, a gram, a molecule of solace.

It did not.

At the moment Manderly had died, the Collective's last vestiges of hope had evaporated with him. It had undergone one of its convulsive, tidal shifts in mood. No longer was it tuned towards joy, or determination, or even righteous anger. Their best hope of stopping the comet gone, their last recourse at salvaging the Body's secrets foiled, the mass of humanity was now caged together in a state of utter, helpless fear.

Her chest burned like a knife had been left wedged in her breastbone. Her cells screamed for oxygen, but however she struggled, her lungs would not inflate. And the noise in her head would not allow her even the sweet release of unconsciousness.

She lay in a muddy bomb crater in Khe Sanh, her intestines pooling about her. She lay on the plains of the Mercanta Steppe, her midsection pulverised. She begged for mercy, anything, anything to latch onto in this shrieking horror that was the prelude to oblivion. *I don't want to die.* If she could only think it loud enough, she had to believe something, somewhere would answer. *I don't want to die! I DON'T WANT TO DIE!*

All that it elicited was an echo from men and women no less doomed than she. Assimilates born and raised within the Collective knew the terror of mortality for the first time. Infants, their brains not yet fully formed, were pierced by its awful clarity. Communes; cities; continents screamed. Every one of them pleaded for relief that would not, could not come, and the pleas fed and compounded each other. Anguish piled on anguish like layers of sediment, compressing and solidifying, a nightmare with the mass of a planet.

The fear overwhelmed her so utterly, that it took her minutes to realise that her physical pain had begun to abate. The knife in her chest had shrunk. Though ragged and excruciating, air filled her lungs once more.

A message flickered across her view: **Alyssa,** it read, **I don't deserve your forgiveness, so I won't ask for it. But for what little it's worth, keep this to remember me by. Looking back on it, there are two things I did with my life that I take pride in. Rescuing you was the other.**

The Starman is still out there. Keep him safe.

Victoria.

Alyssa felt strength start to trickle back into her limbs. She raised herself, little by little, and propped herself against the wall of the corridor. She could feel a subdermal shifting in her chest, material rearranging itself, scraping against her ribs with a metallic chill. Raising her shirt, she found the silver scar that Victoria had left behind in the *Prospice's* sickbay was shifting. A small volume of the mercurial material accreted at the bottom, then sloughed off, dropping into her lap and solidifying. The mass of platelets, not more than a few grams, resolved itself into a cuboidal shape.

The Starman is still out there. Keep him safe.

The sickly orange light, the screech of alarms, the stench of burned plastic, all seemed distant to her. The Collective, in its entirety, turned its attentions to her. Here it was – something to cling to, after all.

Ignoring the persistent burning sensation, Alyssa raised herself to her feet.

***

Jonah and Jean drove for hours. After crossing the horizon more times than he had thought possible, they finally crossed the boundary dividing the dark side of the Moon from the near side, and the Earth came into view.

Neither Jonah nor Jean, each to the other's surprise, had ever been to the near side of the Moon before. Certainly, they had both grown up fascinated by space travel, and both had pored over countless images taken from the surface of the Moon. Still, it seemed strange to them both how distant the Earth actually was above them. If a casual observer wasn't looking for it, they could quite easily peer up into the blackness of space above the Moon, and not notice the planet which it orbited.

Jonah observed it through the magnification of his corneal implants (really, just the one corneal implant – his right eye had swollen shut to the point of uselessness). It was as he remembered: still a tranquil blue, white and green, encircled at the equator by a gossamer-faint ring in geosynchronous orbit. He was unsure whether this new incarnation of Jean had corneal implants in the same sense that he did, but she seemed capable of at least the same feats of perception he was, because upon seeing it, she let out a noise somewhere between a sob and a gasp of relief.

Victoria had successfully averted the comet's impact. By extension: Victoria was dead.

This time, it was Jean's turn to weep. Jonah offered her his shoulder, as she had offered him hers in the simulacrum.

The escape from the Collective base had been trivial. Victoria's massacre had cleared the way back to the hangar thoroughly enough that it had been simple to purloin weapons and environment suits from the dead assimilates. Jonah had needed his daughter's help to pull on his suit; the pain of his shattered ribs had been severe enough that it was causing him to swim in and out of consciousness. The suit provided him a dire bill of health once he had secured it in place. He had done the needful and scrolled through the manifold warnings being projected onto his HUD, and given it the order to flood his system with enough stims and painkillers to keep him alert and upright. Then they had retrieved the rover they were driving now from the wreckage, and picked their way through the rubble, out onto the Lunar surface. Taking a page out of Victoria's book, they had blasted their way out through the base's wall.

The Collective was in disarray from the Insurgency's assault in orbit, but they would be looking for them again soon. Manderly had seen Jonah come into contact with the Body before he had been killed, and the hive mind's priorities would shift back toward him when the Earth's safety had been confirmed. All the forces remaining to it would be combing the Moon's surface for him with tireless and monomaniacal intent. Their run of good luck in eluding it wouldn't last. It didn't have to.

You're certain this will work? His throat was still too bruised to speak.

'Bit late to be asking that now, isn't it?' Jean fired back. 'But yes, as sure as I can reasonably be of anything that hasn't been tested in physical space. Moby thinks in deep time – he plans a long way ahead, for every possible contingency. He's been running simulations for over a century, on the off-chance he came down on the side of consolidated consciousness. With my help, naturally.'

They parked the rover at the top of a crater rim, the view of the Earth above them unobstructed. They released the hatch in unison, and stepped out onto the surface of the Near Side.

This is it, then.

'The moment of truth.'

Will I get to see you again? It feels wrong, meeting you here, only for it to be over so soon.

'This body wasn't built to last, Dad. Moby isn't in the business of wholesale resurrections; that would be its own set of problems. But you can always find me in the simulacrum, if you get lonely.'

That sounds like a hell of a way to spend the rest of eternity.

'It has its upsides. I get to see the ways the human race will grow and change. The next few thousand years will be amazing, Dad. There are marvels out there in the universe beyond your wildest dreams. Even the shoal has barely scratched the surface. They're sitting there just waiting for people like you to find them.'

More lives lived with urgency and precariousness.

'It'll be hard. There'll be more dead ends, and heartbreak, and failures. And we'll never be satisfied with our lot. Every bar we clear, every summit we attain, there'll be another, higher one waiting for the next generation. But the moments of triumph, when we cross those thresholds, will be worth it a hundred times over. Humanity will surpass even the shoals, I'm sure of it. I'm a bit jealous. I wish I could be a part of it. But I can bear witness, and that's a privilege in its own right.'

Ever the optimist. I'm sure you don't get that from me.

'On the contrary. Why do you think I spent so much of my life looking toward the stars?'

Touché.

They stood a moment longer.

I thought for so long about how to say I'm sorry. Saying 'goodbye,' somehow, is even harder.

'It is,' Jean admitted. 'But however hard, it's better for being said.'

They embraced once more, and for the last time.

Goodbye, Jean.

'Goodbye, Dad.'

Jean strode away from the rover, removing her suit helmet as she went. Whatever strange material comprised her resurrected form, it was unperturbed by vacuum. She had worn it only as a concession to Jonah in the first place, so that they could communicate by means other than text. She stopped perhaps a hundred metres away from the rover. Jonah didn't follow her – nominally because he had been warned the process would be dangerous to him if he was too close, but in truth, he was past caring about any further harm done to his body. Rather, it was out of respect for the moment's air of ritual. This was his daughter's hour – she was to be the bridge between one moment in history and the next, the conduit for forces greater than any one person's life. For him to stand next to her felt like it would have been a failure of propriety, a lack of respect for the solemnity the occasion demanded.

Jean removed the rest of her suit, and stood unclothed on the surface of the Moon, her back to Jonah, her face turned upward toward the Earth, perfectly still. For a moment, nothing happened. Then, her skin began to glow.

Dimly at first, then brighter, as though lit from within by a kindling fire. The veins and capillaries beneath her skin were outlined by the light, giving the uncanny impression of a medical diagram. The light changed colour as it intensified – red at first, then orange, then yellow, and finally a blinding white, the white that preceded the state change of heating steel. Brighter and brighter she burned, every cell in her resurrected flesh incandescent with light. Impossibly brighter – so bright that Jonah had to shield his eyes with one hand, even with the tinting of his helmet's visor and his corneal implants contracted to pinpricks.

Finally, the light she contained crossed its critical threshold, and could no longer be contained. Jean's resurrected body detonated, and in doing so, flooded Earth's orbit with the Body's final revelation.

Jean's radiance took just over a second to reach Earth's atmosphere, where it was refracted and reflected all around its circumference. In the span of that near-instant, the Collective ceased to exist.

***

During what had been known as the Engagement in Jean's time – the moment of the kinetic torpedoes' impact, at 2.21 am, GMT, October 21st, 2135 – Moby had been unprepared for what it would find on Earth. The radiation it had emitted then, which had caused the psychic rupture across the world, had been a kind of involuntary convulsion, a scattering of random fragments of information.

Now though, thanks to Jean, Moby had had the better part of two hundred years' familiarity with humans. Their psychology and their culture, but also the physical makeup of their brains.

The limitation of the Collective, Moby and Jean had concluded, was that it was always 'on.' This was the small and yet critical way Xavier Wong had misunderstood when he had tried to reverse-engineer distributed consciousness. Within the shoal, the remote, quantum-level connections between separate, sub-sentient brains and nervous systems that together formed distributed consciousness were as natural as breathing. Individual organisms shared information and sensory data with the larger shoal *when there was something pertinent to share*. By comparison, Moby had found Jean's characterisation of the Collective absurd and risible. A shoal where every member organism was inundated with the sensory information of every other, at all times? It was analogous to a race of eunuchs being granted reproductive organs, and then going on to spend every moment of every day engaged in a species-wide orgy.

So, between them, they had devised a countermeasure to the Enclave Effect. Not a way of undoing it, or permanently shutting it off. Jean had been adamant that that was not an acceptable solution. It would destroy the human race, she had insisted, no less certainly than Victoria's comet would have. Having barely survived the pain of severance herself, and having witnessed the bloodbath resulting from Secretary Koo's operations in the 36 Enclaves on December 9th, 2135, she knew full well the chaos that would unleash.

Instead, the Second Engagement – Jean's saturation of Earth's orbit in tuned particles, much as Moby had done two centuries earlier – contained a very specific piece of information directed at every human brain. The effect that Jean's radiance introduced to the entangled hive-mind was similar to that of a line of code changing the entire function of a piece of software. The structure of the Collective was immutably altered by the addition of one simple function – the presence of an 'off switch.'

The billions of minds connected by the subcutaneous devices implanted at the nape of the neck would find themselves abruptly severed from one another, as Jean had been when she had regained consciousness in that Beijing motel room. But, when they desperately tried to spread their minds out the way Jean had done then, they would be answered. The deafening, horrifying silence that precipitated suicidal despair and madness among ex-assimilates would not be all-consuming and irrevocable, the way it had seemed then.

At that moment, the assimilates Jonah had lived with in the farmhouse for the past year – Nora, Jane, Barry and Tim – who had been born assimilated, would be experiencing, for the first time in their lives, silence inside their skulls where they had never known anything but the presence of other minds. They would be having a taste of what it was like to perceive their environment on their own terms, and articulate it in their own words.

When he had heard this plan in the simulacrum, Jonah had raised the objection – what would there be to stop the Collective from reverting to the 'always-on' model it had been using for two centuries now?

The answer Jean had given him was simple – nothing. Nothing, except for the better angels of human nature. The same aspects that drove people to climb mountains and cross oceans. The human experience was forever looking for new corners to grow into. Perhaps being a part of the hive mind was as natural as breathing to the human race, now – *but then,* she had added with a smirk, *not being able to breathe didn't stop us from colonising space, did it?*

The existence of the technology to remotely connect minds couldn't be walked back, any more than could the discovery of fire or electricity. There would always be those who relied on them excessively, and whose ability to live without them would atrophy. But then there were the iconoclasts – those who would wean themselves off the hive mind and reacquaint themselves with private thoughts and emotions. They would gain a new appreciation of connection by voluntarily experiencing its lack. The 'self,' the concept that the Collective had trampled for two centuries, would re-enter mankind's vernacular.

Jean commended every molecule of her resurrected body to the solar wind to give humanity back the choice between self and non-self. The rest was up to the people in whom she placed such indefatigable faith.

***

Jonah contemplated this as he sat in the driver's seat of the stolen rover. He wondered at the acts of devotion his daughter and his granddaughter had respectively committed – to have given themselves to the world.

His own time wouldn't be long. The beating he had taken from Manderly had been more severe than he had realised, between the stims and the painkillers and the urgent adrenaline high of the flight from the Collective base. One of his lungs had collapsed, and he had heavy internal bleeding. Breathing was difficult, and he was increasingly lightheaded. His life would be measured in hours now. Maybe minutes.

Before he had left the simulacrum, Moby had given him the option of leaving behind a copy of himself, as Jean had. He had declined. Jean – her virtual ghost, at least – seemed positive about remaining there indefinitely, but for him, he wanted none of that gilded prison. He had lived long enough, and he was spent. His role, such as it was, was at its close, and he was ready for the curtain to descend.

Text flickered across the HUD in his one good eye, but he found it hard to focus on. He found it hard to focus on anything, except the nagging doubt that remained at the back of his mind.

Was this victory, then? This was what he had chosen, after all. He had fought for this: the right to die free, and as himself. To own his life and his failures – not to accept the easy self-negation the Collective offered, but to depart the mortal coil proudly. To declare to the universe, *I am Jonah Harrison, and I am not ashamed of the way I used the time I was given.*

Was it true? Could he really face nonexistence without shame? Was he worthy of the gift Jean had given the world? The uncertainty was the worst part. If he had someone here with him, someone to share his deepest fears with now at the end, maybe they could reassure him that he had been a good person. That might make his passage easier.

But then, there would always be something missing. He was the oldest man in the universe – he should know that better than anyone. There would always be that nagging suspicion that, with just a little more time, there was something he might have completed or achieved, some wrong he might have righted. If that insistent itch wasn't there, then you were never fully alive in the first place.

The text in his eye was coming faster now, or maybe it just seemed that way because he kept dipping in and out of consciousness. Eventually, he simply wouldn't jerk awake. If that was all dying really was – simply not waking up – that didn't seem unreasonably cruel, in the grand scheme of things. Nothing to go to insane lengths to escape.

The periods of waking were becoming less frequent and less lucid. During one of them, he thought perhaps he saw the rover's cockpit being prised open from without, and blurry figures clambering inside with him. He was grateful for the company, but even so, their presence felt hazy and distant.

Still, it would have been nice if I could have said…

***

When Jonah woke up, the date on his HUD read September 8th. The first thing he felt was surprise at finding himself alive. The second thing he felt was a great deal of discomfort in his torso and his head.

He was still under lunar gravity. The sensation of weight was the same, but it was a great struggle to raise his limbs from where they lay beneath thick bedsheets. He could just about turn his head, but doing so caused him considerable nausea, so he resigned himself for the time being to contemplating the featureless ceiling of whatever room this was.

'Aha! Welcome back, Captain. Glad you could join us.' The voice had an accent Jonah felt like he recognised, but couldn't place.

'Who...' Jonah began, or tried to, but all that emerged was a harsh rasp and a livid streak of pain across his Adam's apple.

'Easy there, sir, baby steps. Don't try to talk, it'll be a few weeks before your throat has healed enough for that. Are you okay to use your corneal implants?'

Jonah tried. **O tginj sp.** Even his eyeballs lacked dexterity. He tried again, more slowly. **I think so.**

Good. You know, it's lucky we found you when we did. A few minutes more, and you would have been past the point of brain death. Not even the platelets you've got holding your internal organs together would have been any help after that. Even as it was, you were an edge case. Alyssa was beside herself, you know, you shouldn't make your granddaughter worry like that.

Jonah read the words as they scrolled across his HUD, but he couldn't make any sense of them. **What's going on?**

Sorry Captain, of course, you're disoriented. You've been out of it for a while. Give me a second, I'll explain.

Someone outside his field of view adjusted the bed where he lay, propping it up to a reclined sitting position. Jonah was given a view of a room not dissimilar to the *Prospice's* sickbay. On his left-hand side stood Aki, apparently the one who had been administering to him. On his right side, sure enough, sat Alyssa.

'How's this for a role reversal?' she said with a wink.

Lys? I thought you were... He wasn't quite sure how to finish that. Dead? Assimilated? A part of the hive-mind the Insurgency had sworn to destroy, despite now being in their company as though it was the most natural thing in the world?

After Vic destroyed the comet, we had no idea what the hell had just happened, Aki wrote. **We thought we had the operation in the bag, when all of a sudden, we're stranded right on Earth's doorstep, 200 of us, with no option for retreat and surrounded on all sides by extremely pissed-off**

Collective forces. Naturally, we thought we were finished. For want of any better ideas, we scattered, tried to shake the Scarabs as best we could in the hope that even one of us might get back to Taurus station alive. But then...

'The Body's final revelation happened,' Alyssa finished for him.

Right, the crazy light show on the near side of the Moon. I was over 0.1 of an AU away when it happened, but even I saw it. It lit up the electromagnetic spectrum like... well, like something really bright on some really weird wavelengths.

'There was a message, together with the on/off switch,' Alyssa continued for him. 'The Body – you called it Moby? *Really?* – it let us know everything it showed you, everything it talked about with you and Aunt Jean. Nobody could believe it at first, that this could be the answer we'd been looking for the last two centuries. That all this time, we'd had it wrong. I understand now though, why it had to happen the way it did. If we'd just been *told*, we never would have accepted it. It was a great upheaval that created the Collective. It had to take another great upheaval to move past it.

'The Collective isn't *gone*, exactly, but it's different now. More nuanced. Things are crazy groundside. Billions of people have woken up to the possibilities of being individuals that they've either forgotten or never known before. It's scary for most of them, but not the way that severance is scary. Exciting-scary, not mortal-dread-and-despair scary, 'cause we still have the safety net of each other's minds if we need it. People are experimenting with separate units of linked individuals, like groups of three or four, or limited to a single commune. Some people, the really brave ones, have gone full-regression, and are trying out complete severance. The mental topography is changing by the hour. It'll be decades before it comes to any kind of equilibrium, if it ever does. But it's safe to say, we've woken up to the value of the "self" again. The mission to eradicate it is finished.'

So that happened, Aki appended, and minutes later, the Insurgency gets a hail from Earth, requesting a ceasefire. Most of us were suspicious, but Victoria's last message suggested that something like this would happen. Lieutenant Daniels was acting Commander after Victoria... well. He took a leap of faith and answered the Collective's hail. From what we know now, it seems we almost made a big mistake.

493

'A very big mistake,' Alyssa corrected.

About the biggest mistake that has ever been made in all of history, yes.

So... Jonah's head hurt enough just from being awake; being made aware of the sudden and seismic shift in the circumstances of the human race wasn't helping. **It's over?**

Alyssa and Aki glanced at each other. 'These are early days,' Alyssa said. 'Human emotions being the messy things they are, there are those on the ground who still see the Insurgency as terrorists who came within a hair's breadth of destroying the world. And it'll be a long time before word reaches Albrecht and the other Archangels. But for the moment? Yes. Yes, the war is over.'

***

After Jonah had thanked Aki for the debriefing, the Sami Archangel made himself scarce. They were, he learned, aboard a transport ship that had been grounded next to the ruins of the base Victoria had gutted. It was serving as a field hospital for the handful of wounded assimilates who had been left alive. The Archangels were donating what platelets and expertise they could spare to help with the recovery. James was convalescing in a room just down the corridor from Jonah, recovering from the near-fatal blow to the head Victoria had inflicted.

Alyssa and Jonah were left alone in each other's company. The silence between them stretched uncomfortably, but she made no move to leave.

Lys, Jonah wrote eventually, **maybe this is a personal question, but are you connected to anyone else right now?**

'No, it's just us here. I'm one of the ones going full severance.'

How do you feel about that?

She didn't reply straight away. She chewed the inside of her cheek, not making eye contact with him. 'It hurts like hell,' she said, finally, her tone perfectly flat. 'Every time I close my eyes, I see that clearing, back on TransTerra. The flames in the rain. I can hear my mum and my dad. Everyone was screaming, and I don't know which voices were theirs. God, it hurts so much. And all I can think is how easy it would be to just slip back into the multitude and lose myself again to make it go away, and that makes it hurt more.'

She met his gaze, and he could see her eyes were shining. 'But then I think, it should hurt, you know?'

Lys, you don't have to...

She shook her head. 'Not in the sense of "I think I deserve to suffer." I just miss them. And that's good, isn't it? Because if I didn't miss them, it would be like I was pretending they were never real. They don't deserve that.'

After everything that had happened, she was still the Alyssa he knew. The girl who always wanted to be brave.

Jonah ignored the spike of pain that went through his temple and the accompanying wave of nausea, and pushed himself to a sitting position. She stood, looking alarmed, but he gestured for her to sit back down. **Lys,** he wrote, **just because you're not connected, it doesn't mean you're alone.**

She smiled, and it was full of sadness and warmth. A pair of tears spilled down her cheeks.

'Thank you, grandad.' She sat quietly for a moment, then she stood again. 'I told Aki I would help him with his rounds. I'll visit again soon, okay?' Before she left, she fished a small, cuboidal object out of her trouser pocket, and pressed it into Jonah's hand. 'She left me something, before the end. A keepsake. I think it should be you who has it.'

Jonah raised the small object to look at it. It was a personal SSD drive; his implants automatically synced to it. The drive's storage capacity, good for several terabytes of information, contained only a single, 30-minute audio file, entitled 'Words that Stay Unspoken.'

The composition had been completed. Its final notes were sweet.

THE END

Glossary

A glossary of unique terms and concepts that might not be familiar to a wide audience:

1. **Starman**: An explorer or astronaut, specifically used to refer to Jonah Harrison, a central character in the story.

2. **The Body/Moby**: Initially known as "The Body" due to its perception as an astronomical object, it is later named "Moby," a sentient entity whose form resembles a whale and which plays a central role in the story's climax, influencing the conflict involving the Collective.

3. **The Collective**: A hive-mind entity or group consciousness, significantly altered by the end of the story.

4. **Assimilates**: Individuals who have been integrated into the Collective, losing their individuality and becoming entirely transparent to one another in thoughts and sensations.

5. **Scarabs**: A type of unit, likely a form of technology, used by the Collective, equipped with weapons and capable of intricate maneuvering and formation tactics in combat situations.

6. **The Insurgency**: A group opposing the Collective, which the main characters are associated with.

7. **ORC (Orbital Reconnaissance Corps)**: An organisation formed in response to threats in space, evolving into a significant entity in space exploration and scientific advancement, particularly in particle physics and technological innovations.

8. **The Prospice**: Initially a spacecraft with a long history of service in deep space, it eventually becomes a significant location, repurposed into the center of a settlement on a planet after its retirement from active duty.

9. **Platelets**: A term referring to specialised molecular components used in various technological and medical applications within the narrative, including emergency medical procedures and communication functions.

10. **Archangels**: Members of the Insurgency, characterised by their ability to drop silently and rapidly into conflict zones, physically resembling decorated soldiers but with wings, and capable of burning targets to cinders in a microsecond.

11. **Full Regression**: A process or decision by characters to disconnect from the Collective and live as individuals.

12. **Severance**: The process or experience of disconnecting from the Collective, with significant psychological impact.

13. **Masers:** A futuristic weapon technology used in space combat. It is employed both as handheld weapons and as part of larger combat systems, indicating its versatility and importance in the story's warfare context. The term "maser" in a real-world context refers to "Microwave Amplification by Stimulated Emission of Radiation," which is a device similar to a laser but operating at microwave frequencies. However, in the novel, it seems to be used more as a futuristic weapon technology.

14. **Wasp:** An agile type of space combat unit or vehicle.

15. **Enclave Effect:** A delicate and significant influence, related to a collective consciousness, impacting individuals' perceptions, emotions, experiences, and potentially even their actions and thoughts.

16. **Delta-V:** In astrodynamics and aerospace, refers to the change in velocity needed to perform a maneuver or reach a destination.

17. **Vernier Engines:** Small rocket engines used for fine control and adjustments of a spacecraft's orientation or trajectory.

18. **Warp Signature:** This term is associated with space travel technology in the story's universe. It specifically refers to the detectable trace or characteristic of a warp drive used by the Scarab transport, a scout unit. This suggests that "warp signature" is a way to identify or track spacecraft employing warp drive technology.

19. **TransTerra:** An exoplanet with two moons discovered in the 2070s with an oxygen-rich atmosphere that showed potential for supporting carbon-based life, featuring a 22-hour day and a unique Steppe landscape.

20. **The Merantau Program:** Considered the costliest scientific expedition launched in response to photographs taken by trans-Neptunian telescope arrays in the 2070s.The project's aim was to confirm the hypothesis of carbon-based life.

21. **Pilgrim's Progress:** The sole settlement on TransTerra, situated in the midst of its unique landscape. It plays a central role in the story.

WHAT IS OTHERWORLDS INC?

We are at the helm of a vibrant indie creative studio and publishing house, a venture we embarked upon in 2017. Our core mission is to craft groundbreaking stories that resonate in the realms of high fantasy, science fiction, and cosmic horror. We're not just storytellers; we're universe creators, committed to the art of weaving narratives that stir the soul and challenge the imagination.

Our team, a close-knit crew of 13, is comprised of passionate artists, writers, programmers, and dreamers, each dedicated to exploring the boundless 'what ifs' and unseen vistas of creativity. At Otherworlds Inc, we are currently channeling our talents into a variety of comic book titles and an exciting mobile game project, while also navigating through a strategic company restructure to enhance our creative output and reach.

WORLDS TO EXPLORE

- Glacias
- Lunora 》》》》
- Draggo
- Sanctuary
- White Scar
- Tales of Yesterday

GETTING STARTED GUIDE FOR OTHERWORLDS INC. COMMUNITY

Hello and a warm welcome to all the new members of our Otherworlds Inc. family! This guide is your starting point to navigate and thrive in our vibrant community. As the CEO of Otherworlds Inc., I'm thrilled to introduce you to our cosmos of boundless narratives and creative exchanges.

Dive into Our *Stories:*

Glacias:

- **Story:** Follow Juka, an orphan raised by a dragon, on his quest to build a city where humans and dragons coexist peacefully. But dark forces and dragon hunters threaten his dream.
- **Join the Adventure:** Discuss theories, share fan art, and explore this world in our discord channel - #Glacias-story-discussion.

Genre:

01.

High Fantasy

02.

Dragons

03.

Adventure

Dive into Our *Stories*:

World Location: Caligo

Lunora:

- **Story: A tale of time, love, and curses spanning generations. Experience a world where myths are warnings, and a group of heroes embarks on a quest to reveal a generational lie.**
- **Engage with the Saga: Share your interpretations and artwork in our discord channel - #Lunora-epic-journey.**

Genre:

01.

Epic Fantasy

02.

Science Fiction

03.

Shonen

OTHERWORLDSINC.COM

Dive into Our *Stories:*

World Location: Draggo Planet

Draggo Sanctuary:

- **Game in Development:** Help a baby dragon restore life in an incremental game filled wit exploration and discovery.
- **Be Part of the Creation:** Give feedback and ideas directly to our game developers in **#Draggo-Sanctuary-Dev-Chat.**

Genre:

01.	02.	03.
Science Fiction	Dystopian	Platformer Video Game

The Author

My full name is Andrew Neil Milne. I was born in Arbroath, Scotland, on December 3rd, 1990, where I was raised by my parents together with my younger sister.I was, and am, bookish. Growing up, I was obsessed with the bleak intensity, the thorny moral dilemmas, and the interstellar scope of K.A. Applegate's 'Animorphs' books. From those, I graduated to authors like Frank Herbert; Dan Simmons; Ursula K. Le Guin; Alfred Bester; Samuel R. Delaney; Peter F. Hamilton; James S.A. Corey.

I graduated from the University of Dundee in 2012 with a first-class M.A. in English and Politics. I found it easy and natural to string sentences together while writing essays, and I always had it in my head that I would write a novel one day (I made my first, unfinished attempt when I was 10).

It wasn't until 2015, though, that I really took it upon myself to try writing fiction in earnest, in the spirit of 'if not now, when?' I wanted to pay forward the influence of the authors who inspired me growing up, and create heady, twisty, epic sci-fi stories that younger readers might get lost in for days and weeks.Now, in 2024, I present my best effort to do so.

By day, I work as a Business Development Manager for a small consultancy; otherwise, when I'm not writing, I'm an avid hiker, always seeking out new long-distance routes all over the world. I'm a fan of prog metal, JRPGs, and 1970s kung-fu films. I write a lot about movies on Letterboxd - find me here: https://letterboxd.com/Thrash/

I am not, by the way, in any way related to or affiliated with the estate of Alan Alexander ('A.A.') Milne, (1882 - 1956), the author of the 'Winnie-the-Pooh' series of children's books. If that's who you were looking for, and Google led you here by mistake... hang around anyway! Maybe I've written something you'd be interested in. Stranger things have happened.

My Social Media Links:

Twitter | X: @anmilneauthor

Instagram: @anmilneauthor

Facebook: @A.N. Milne, Author

DON'T FORGET TO ALSO REQUEST A COPY AT YOUR LOCAL LIBRARY!

9 781960 067036